Rebel Hearts Anthology

Kat Martin   C.K. Crigger   Sharon Sala
Jenna Hendricks   Kit Morgan
Kathleen O'Neal Gear

WOLFPACK
PUBLISHING
— EST 2013 —

Rebel Hearts Anthology
Paperback Edition
Copyright © 2022 The Individual Authors:
Kat Martin; C.K. Crigger; Sharon Sala; Jenna Hendricks; Kit Morgan; Kathleen
O'Neal Gear

Wolfpack Publishing
9850 S. Maryland Parkway, Suite A-5 #323
Las Vegas, Nevada 89183

wolfpackpublishing.com

Paperback ISBN 978-1-63977-304-6
eBook ISBN 978-1-63977-306-0
LCCN 2022945011

Rebel Hearts Anthology

Outlaw Ghost

Kat Martin

Chapter One

Sweet Springs, Texas

A HARSH WIND PULLED AT THE BRANCHES OUTSIDE THE WINDOW. The howl of a coyote echoed mournfully from the hills overlooking the property at the edge of town. Beneath the old-fashioned quilt on the antique iron bed, Callie Sutton listened to a different sound, this one coming from inside the old Victorian house.

It was an eerie sound, disturbing, and strangely human. As if someone walked through the silent rooms then climbed the stairs. As if someone opened the door and came into her room. As if he stood at the foot of her bed.

Since the door was firmly closed and locked, it was impossible, yet the feeling of being watched would not go away.

The tempo of her heart increased, and her nerves stretched taut as Callie searched the darkness but found no one there. She told herself it was all in her mind, nothing more than the normal creaks and groans of a house this old. The Victorian home she had inherited from a distant aunt had been empty and in disrepair for more than thirty years.

But the moment she had seen the charming turret in front and wrap-around porch, the lovely built-in bookcases, molded ceilings, and ornate woodwork, she had fallen in love with the place.

The renovations she'd had done before she moved in were mostly finished, the kitchen and baths remodeled, the hardwood floors refinished, the fireplace repaired and a fire crackling in the hearth in the evenings.

The work that remained was mostly superficial and of course she had a ton of decorating to do. Callie was looking forward to that. Or at least she had been until the ghostly sounds in the house at night continued to grow more pronounced.

Awake now, Callie stared up at the ceiling, her ears straining for any indication of a threat, but the house had fallen silent. Eventually, her heartbeat returned to normal and her body relaxed.

She yawned, sleepy from a long day at the clinic and putting up wallpaper in the kitchen when she got home after work.

As a veterinary technician, she had been hired by the county vet, Dr. Reynolds, who was badly in need of help. Callie worked mostly with small animals, while Doc Reynolds specialized in large animals, a necessity in a ranching community like the tiny Texas town of Sweet Springs.

Since the clinic at the end of Main Street was always busy, Callie would be facing another hectic day tomorrow. She needed to get some sleep. She yawned again and her eyes drifted closed as an odd sense of peace stole over her. It had happened before and perhaps that was the reason she wasn't more afraid.

She didn't believe in ghosts. On the other hand, if there were such a thing, this one seemed strangely protective. A smile touched her lips as she drifted deeper into sleep and Callie started to dream.

He was tall, in snug, dark pants, a full-sleeved white linen shirt, and tall black boots. He wore a black flat-brimmed hat, and a gun belt hung from his lean hips, the pistol strapped to a muscled thigh. She tried to see his face beneath the brim of the hat but caught just the hint of a hard jaw covered by several days' growth of dark beard.

He stood at the foot of the bed as if he watched over her. He looked like an outlaw, she thought in some corner of her mind, a gunslinger right out of the Wild West. She should have been frightened but she wasn't afraid. Instead she felt safe, protected.

She settled into an even deeper sleep and didn't wake up until morning, the dream no more than a hazy memory.

Callie showered and dressed in jeans and a lightweight sweater just warm enough for the end-of-October weather, then headed downstairs for coffee and toast before she drove to work.

She loved her newly remodeled country kitchen. She'd almost had the servant's stairs removed but they were part of the original structure, so she had left them. Turned out they were handy and added a certain charm. She'd found an antique oak table and topped it with pretty yellow placemats that matched the walls, making the big kitchen feel cozy.

Callie glanced at the table, an uneasy feeling creeping through her. At the sight of the single red rose laying on top, her insides tightened. Someone had been inside the house!

Her hands shook as she pulled the phone out of her pocket and dialed 9-1-1. Dear God, was the intruder still somewhere inside? Her gaze shot to the back door, saw that the lock had been pried open, and a chill rolled down her spine.

She thought of the eerie sounds in the house last night and how she had felt safe and protected.

Clearly, she wasn't as safe as she thought.

Chapter Two

"SWEET SPRINGS SHERIFF'S OFFICE," A WOMAN'S VOICE answered. "Millie speaking, what's your emergency?"

"Someone broke into my house last night. They left a rose on my kitchen table while I was asleep upstairs."

"A rose, huh? Old boyfriend, maybe?" Clearly a town the size of Sweet Springs didn't have a lot of crime.

"I don't have any old boyfriends," Callie said. "I just moved here. I-I'm afraid he might still be in the house."

Millie's voice sobered. "What's your address?"

Callie gave her the property address on Pecan Lane. "It's the old Victorian at the edge of town."

"Stay on the line. I'm calling Sheriff Trask. He isn't that far away."

Callie's stomach churned for the entire five minutes that passed before she heard the crunch of gravel and the engine of a vehicle pulling up in front. Through the dining room window, she saw a white extended cab pickup, the word SHERIFF in big blue letters on the door.

The sheriff got out, a tall man in dark brown uniform pants and a light beige short-sleeved shirt, a badge pinned to the front. He wore a beige cowboy hat and a pistol holstered on the belt at his waist.

"He's here," Callie said to Millie with relief. The call ended and she hurried to the front door to let him in.

"Callie Sutton?" the sheriff asked, looking down at her from beneath the brim of his hat. He had the bluest eyes Callie had ever seen.

"That's me. Please come in."

"Sheriff Brendan Trask. Let me take a look around then we'll talk."

"Thank you. I don't think he's still here, but I don't know for sure."

He nodded and started moving silently through the house. She noticed he unsnapped the flap on his holster, and the chill returned.

Callie was five foot three, the sheriff at least a foot taller. He was swarthy and with his strong jaw and incredible blue eyes, he was handsome. A pair of powerful biceps stretched the sleeves of his uniform shirt. His shoulders were wide, his waist and hips narrow.

If he wasn't married, he was probably the most eligible bachelor in Sweet Springs County.

He returned a few minutes later. "Nobody here. Looks like he came in through the back door."

"I guess I should have bought a better lock."

"Rob Solomon over at the hardware store can sell you something reliable. He can install it for you, too."

"Okay, thanks."

"Millie mentioned the rose. You found it on the kitchen table?"

"Yes. I haven't touched anything." She glanced toward the kitchen. "I suppose it could be kids or someone's idea of a joke. If it is, it isn't funny."

"Breaking and entering is never a joke, Ms. Sutton."

They walked together into the kitchen and he took a second look around, focusing his attention on the rose. "You didn't hear anything?"

How to answer. She heard the same noises she'd been hearing every night, the sound of a man's boots on the stairs and someone walking into her bedroom. But she couldn't tell the sheriff there might be a ghost in the house.

It was ridiculous. She didn't even believe in ghosts.

"I didn't hear anything that sounded like a door being forced open or anyone moving around in the kitchen. *Just someone upstairs in my room*. But she didn't think a ghost could force open a door or carry a rose into the kitchen.

"I want to dust the door for prints. I'll be right back." The sheriff disappeared outside and returned with what she assumed was a fingerprint kit.

He set his hat aside as he dusted the door and the table, and she admired his thick, slightly too long, dark-brown hair. He bagged the rose as evidence and asked her a few more questions, then she walked him to the door.

"Be sure and take care of that lock," he said.

"I'll call Rob Solomon right away."

He nodded as he glanced around the living room. "You did a nice job restoring the place. Looks like it must have more than a hundred years ago, only better."

She smiled at the compliment. "Thank you." Not many people had been over for a visit since she'd moved in, just her best friend, Lanni Bridges, who'd come down from San Antonio, and one of the girls who worked part-time for Dr. Reynolds.

The sheriff pulled open the front door. "Like you said, it's probably just kids, but you don't want to take any chances." Those amazing blue eyes fixed on her face. "I'll give you my cell phone number. I don't live far away. If you hear something, call me."

She punched his number into her phone. As the sheriff put his hat back on and settled the brim low across his forehead, Callie felt a warm tug in the pit of her stomach.

She blinked in surprise. She hadn't felt the least attraction to a man since she and Adam had split up almost a year ago.

"I'll keep you posted on what I find out," Sheriff Trask said.

Callie watched him walk away and tried not to think he looked nearly as good from the back as the front. She hadn't noticed a wedding ring, but that didn't mean he wasn't married or seriously involved with someone. A man like that had his choice of women.

Not that it really mattered. She was too busy getting settled at the clinic to think about a man.

Well, other than the ghost upstairs.

Chapter Three

AFTER A HARD DAY AT THE ANIMAL CLINIC THAT INCLUDED A battle with a wily Siamese cat named Hugo armed with the sharpest claws Callie had ever seen, she prayed for an uneventful evening. Besides working late to help the doctor sew up a car-chasing dog hit by a pickup, she had worried about her intruder all day.

The house was quiet when she got home, no sign of anything out of place. She zapped a frozen lasagna dinner in the newly installed microwave, ate, and went straight up to bed. She drifted off more easily than she had expected and settled into a deep slumber.

She wasn't sure when she started to dream, only that the tall outlaw cowboy was back in her room and this time he was in her bed.

He was leaning over her, kissing the side of her neck, his big hands lightly caressing her breasts through her thin white nylon nightgown. She moaned as he trailed kisses along her throat and over her cheek, and soft male lips settled on her mouth.

Warmth spread through her, slid into her core. *It's a dream*, she told herself as a memory of last night's dream returned. *Why not enjoy it?*

Parting her lips, she opened to invite her dream lover in,

and the kiss turned hot and deep. A hard chest pressed against her breasts and big calloused hands roamed over her body.

It had been so long since anyone had touched her that way, so long since she had actually felt this kind of desire.

The dream shifted a little and he was naked, his body hard and muscled over hers. She could feel his heavy arousal nestled between her legs—for a dream, it was incredibly real.

She allowed the fantasy to continue, her body responding to the skillful touches of the outlaw's hands and the saturating pleasure of his mouth moving hotly over hers.

When a noise downstairs penetrated her senses, threatening to disturb the dream, irritation trickled through her. Damn, she didn't want the dream to end. With a sigh of resignation, Callie stirred awake and opened her eyes, expecting to be looking at the ceiling above the bed.

Instead, she stared into the bluest eyes she had ever seen.

Callie screamed.

Chapter Four

IN AN INSTANT, THE MAN WAS GONE, VANISHED LIKE THE ghostly vision he had been.

Her heart was racing, her body still flushed with heat. Callie tried to tell herself the face of the outlaw she had seen was just part of the dream, that she hadn't awoken and seen a blue-eyed man in bed with her who looked almost exactly like the handsome county sheriff.

It was the *almost* that was the problem. The outlaw had a scar along the bottom of his jaw that the sheriff did not have.

The noise came again, pulling her back from the fantasy, the sound of glass shattering downstairs—someone breaking the window in the kitchen. Fresh fear assailed her. The ghost was gone but what about the man who had broken into her house last night?

She grabbed her phone off the nightstand and hit the sheriff's contact number.

"Trask," he said, his voice crystal clear, as if he'd instantly come awake.

"Sheriff, it's…it's Callie Sutton. He's…he's in the house. He broke out a window. Oh, God…he's…coming up the stairs."

"On my way. Lock yourself in the bathroom, Callie. Stay

there till I tell you to come out. I'll keep the line open, but the call may drop. I'll be there as fast as I can."

She heard fabric rustling as Trask pulled on his clothes. Callie grabbed her white terry robe and hurriedly shrugged it on.

As she turned toward the bathroom, she heard sounds outside the bedroom door. A struggle, some kind of fight going on, a foul curse, then the heavy thud of something crashing down the stairs.

Oh, dear God. "Sheriff? Sheriff Trask are you there?"

But as he had warned, the call had dropped and the line was dead. *He's on his way,* she reminded herself. *All I have to do is survive until he gets here.*

Her gaze shot to the bedroom door. Rob Solomon had installed a new lock on the kitchen door downstairs, but the lock on the bedroom door was old and hadn't been replaced. She should barricade herself in the bathroom as Sheriff Trask had told her, but the lock was no better in there and she didn't like the idea of being trapped inside.

Callie listened. The only sound was the fierce beating of her heart. Instead of the usual creaks and groans, the house was eerily silent. Too silent, she thought, a shiver running over her skin.

Headlights flashed into the bedroom. She hurried to the window and saw Sheriff Trask's pickup pull up in front of the house. *Thank you, God.*

Her cell phone rang. She answered with unsteady hands.

"Callie, are you all right?"

"I think he's gone. Just in case, I'll come down the back stairs and let you in through the kitchen."

"Be careful," Trask said.

Callie grabbed the flashlight she kept beside the bed, unlocked the bedroom door, and peered into the hall. Seeing nothing, she quietly headed for the servants' stairs leading down to the kitchen. As she passed the round oak table, she shined a light on top and there it was—another long-stemmed red rose.

Fear quickened her footsteps. She unlocked the newly

installed deadbolt, the sheriff strode into the kitchen, and relief poured through her.

"Stay here." His gun was in his hand as he made his way out of the kitchen and began to search the house.

She couldn't help noticing the lack of a scar beneath his hard jaw.

Chapter Five

BRENDAN MOVED SILENTLY THOUGH THE HOUSE, QUIETLY checking each room. *First floor clear.* He headed for the staircase, shined his light in that direction, and stopped cold in his tracks.

Death had an aura about it. The bald, muscular man sprawled on the stairs with his mouth gaping open, sightless eyes staring up at the ceiling, reeked of it.

Brendan knelt to check for a pulse, but there was really no need. He stepped back and took a moment to study the scene. From the angle of the man's neck and the way the body had landed, it didn't look like the guy could have accidentally fallen down the stairs.

Brendan's gaze shot to the landing at the top. If it wasn't an accident, who had killed him? Was the perp still in the house? Brendan made a room-by-room search but found no sign of an intruder. He returned to the crime scene and phoned the coroner, a local physician named Elias Halpern, rousing him from sleep.

Brendan looked back at the dead man on the stairs. The guy was big and strong. Had the pretty little brunette in the kitchen somehow managed to overpower him? It didn't seem likely. Even if by some miracle she had killed him, he was trespassing in her house. The lady would have been justified, at least as far as Brendan was concerned. Still, she could be in for a lot of trouble and legal expense.

Brendan thought about her as he returned to the kitchen. He had run a check on her after the first call she'd made. Callie Marie Sutton was twenty-seven, just five years younger than he was, originally from San Antonio. With her big brown eyes, long, dark-brown curls, and dynamite figure, he hadn't been able to get her out of his mind since the first time he had seen her.

He and Deb Younger were no longer dating. If Callie gave any indication she was interested, Brendan planned to ask her out.

He just hoped like hell she wasn't a killer.

Chapter Six

AWAITING THE SHERIFF'S RETURN, WHICH SEEMED TO TAKE forever, Callie tightened the sash on her robe and wished she'd had time to put on some clothes. Finally, Trask walked back into the kitchen, his features grim.

His glance strayed to the table, and he noticed the long-stemmed red rose.

"It was him," she said, her pulse hammering again.

"Looks like." He fixed her with a stare. "But you don't need to worry about him anymore."

"You caught him?"

"Your admirer is lying at the bottom of the staircase. He's dead."

Callie gripped the back of a kitchen chair. "He...he fell down the stairs?"

"No, Callie. He was pushed."

THE CORONER ARRIVED, a local physical who said his name was Elias Halpern. While Dr. Halpern examined the body, Callie sat in the kitchen drinking coffee, doing her best not to think of the dead man in the other room and answer the sheriff's questions.

"So you heard noises on the stairs but you didn't go outside your bedroom to see what was going on?"

"I told you, I was waiting for you to get here." She frowned. "In a roundabout way, that's the third time you've asked me the same question. You don't think *I'm* the one who pushed that man down the stairs?"

Before Sheriff Trask had time to answer, Dr. Halpern walked in, an older man with thinning gray hair and glasses. "It wasn't Ms. Sutton," he said. "Bruising on the neck indicates a big man's hands, someone strong and extremely fit. The struggle didn't last long, then one good shove and it was over. This little gal ain't big enough nor strong enough to do the job."

Trask looked relieved. "Looks like you're in the clear, Ms. Sutton."

"I wasn't really worried since I knew I didn't kill him."

Trask's sexy mouth edged up and she felt a slide of heat. It was crazy considering the circumstances.

His smile faded. "This is a crime scene. Is there somewhere you can stay for a day, maybe two?"

"I just moved here. I don't know many people. The Westerner Motel will have to do."

He nodded. "Pack what you need, and I'll follow you over there. Use the back stairs so you don't disturb anything."

"All right. So…who do you think killed him?"

"We'll know more in a couple of days."

Callie hoped so. But as she climbed the backstairs to her room, a strange thought occurred. Was it possible for a ghost to kill?

While the sheriff spent the next few days searching for a killer, Callie went to work searching the past for the man she thought of as her protector.

Chapter Seven

AFTER THE MURDER—AS THE CORONER HAD LABELED IT—HER boss at the clinic, Dr. Reynolds, had insisted she take the next day off. Callie used the time to begin her search, starting at the local library.

She wanted to know the history of the house, who built it, who had lived there, and who might have had a reason to stay in the house long after he was dead.

It was insane. No way was the man in her dreams a ghost. On the other hand, the intimate kiss they'd shared in her bedroom seemed far more real than any dream.

Fortunately, the task she had set for herself proved easier than she had imagined. The old Victorian was a landmark in the community. Barb Dawson, the local librarian, a silver-haired lady in her seventies, knew all about it.

"I love history," Barb said. "It's one of the reasons I wanted to be a librarian. Since my family has lived in the county for three generations, I know all about Sweet Springs."

"My aunt, Mary Sutton, owned the house before she died and left it to me. Can you tell me who owned it before my aunt?"

Barb walked over to a big leather-bound book, set it on

the library table, and opened it. She shoved her half glasses up on her nose.

She ran a finger down the list of names. "Otto Lansing. Now I remember. Lansing built the house in the eighteen sixties as an anniversary gift. He and his wife lived there a few years then sold the place to the Trask family. They were some of Sweet Springs's original settlers."

Callie's head came up. "Sheriff Trask's family?"

"That's right. He's a descendent, named after a great-great-grandfather. The first Brendan Trask lived here with his wife, Priscilla, before they moved out to the ranch. Ranch stayed in the family. Land belongs to the sheriff now, though he doesn't do much ranching these days."

Callie's mind was spinning, running through possibilities, all of which connected the blue-eyed outlaw in her dreams to the equally blue-eyed Sweet Springs sheriff.

"The Trasks were very successful ranchers," Barb continued. "When they moved out of the house, they rented the place instead of selling it. Years later, when Priscilla began to have medical problems, they moved back in. She was in her eighties by then. She died peacefully in her sleep, and her husband sold the house. He died a few months later. A real love story, it was. Kind of a romantic legend."

"You wouldn't have any sort of photo of the original Brendan Trask?"

"The library doesn't but the sheriff has all kinds of family memorabilia."

And since Trask had called to say he needed to speak to her in regard to the case, she would have a chance to ask him about it.

Barb returned her attention to the book and went down the list of owners through the years, using county clerk records, but Callie had the information she needed, at least for now.

"The house is more than a hundred fifty years old," Callie said, approaching the subject carefully. "Anybody ever say anything about ghosts?"

Barb shook her head. "Nope, not that I ever heard. Kids used to make up stuff to try to scare each other, but none of the owners ever said anything like that. At least nothing that was ever passed down."

Callie wasn't sure if that was good news or bad. "Thanks, Barb. You've been a great help."

"No problem. Always fun to talk history."

From the library, Callie drove to the sheriff's office on Main Street at the opposite end of town. With its false front brick buildings and slant parking in front of the stores, Sweet Springs had an appealing, old-fashioned charm. Or at least Callie thought so.

The sheriff's white pickup sat in front of the office when Callie walked in, ringing the bell over the door.

"May I help you?" a large woman behind the counter asked. MILLIE, read the sign on her desk.

"I'm looking for Sheriff Trask. I talked to you the other night. Thanks for your help, by the way."

"You must be Callie Sutton. I'm glad you're okay. Welcome to Sweet Springs."

Callie looked up as the sheriff walked out of his office. He smiled when he saw her, and she felt a little kick. There was something about a man in uniform, or so it was said. Plus this man was just flat-out hot.

"I'm glad you stopped by, Callie," he said. "I was on my way out to get something to eat. You got time to join me?"

"I'm off today. I could use something myself."

The sheriff seemed pleased. She figured he probably just wanted to discuss the case, but she couldn't help hoping it was more.

At the Sweet Springs Café, they sat down in a red vinyl booth across from each other and both ordered burgers and fries.

"So how is the case coming along?" Callie asked as the waitress brought their food. "Do you have any leads?"

Trask swallowed the bite of burger he had taken and set the rest back down on his plate. "On the killer? No. No

DNA, no fingerprints. Nothing left at the crime scene. The guy did a spectacular job of cleaning up. Must have been a pro."

Or he wasn't really a guy, or at least not the living, breathing kind.

"We ID'd the man who broke into your house. His name's Raymond Whitley. He's wanted for serial rape."

The french fry she had just picked up dropped from her suddenly nerveless fingers. "Oh my God."

"Whitley's signature was a single red rose. He broke into his victim's home and left a rose while she was sleeping. Then he returned on a different night to attack her. He was brutal, liked to inflict pain. Four women that we know of— all ended up in the hospital."

Callie swallowed, no longer hungry.

"His last victim was in a small town outside Shreveport, Louisiana. No reason to think he'd show up here. You're a very lucky woman, Callie."

"Yes...yes, I am." But maybe it wasn't luck. Maybe someone had saved her. Someone who looked a lot like Sheriff Trask. "I was wondering...I've been researching the history of the house. Barb Dawson told me it once belonged to your family. Would you happen to have any information on the Trask family who lived there?"

The sheriff smiled, a flash of white against his swarthy skin. "I've got a ton of old stuff out at the ranch. I'm not a great cook, but I'm a kick-ass barbeque griller. I could fix you dinner and show you what I've got."

"No wife or kids?"

"Nope. Never found the right woman."

She toyed with another fry. "Barb told me about Brendan and Priscilla. I guess you're waiting for that kind of romance."

The look in those intense blue eyes softened on her face. "Yeah, I guess I am."

Callie couldn't tear her gaze away. "I'd love to come out for supper," she said softly.

Trask's eyes remained on her face. "How about tonight?"

"What time?"

"Gets dark early. I could pick you up around six. It's not that far to the ranch house."

Chapter Eight

BRENDAN WAS RIGHT. IT WASN'T THAT FAR. THE ORIGINAL ranch house was gone, he told her as they drove along the two-lane road. She couldn't see much through the darkness, but she knew the terrain was rugged in places, lots of trees and the river not far away. The house had been built by his parents, Brendan said, who had wanted to be closer to town. He'd moved back in a few years ago, when his dad and mom retired to Florida, a long-time dream.

He pulled up to a two-story brick house with upstairs dormer windows and a long, covered porch out front. "Welcome to my humble abode." Brendan went around and helped her down from his truck then walked her to the door.

"I haven't changed much since I moved in," he said as they stepped into the entry. "I'll get around to it eventually."

Callie glanced at the comfortable living room furniture, the antique buffet, and the handmade doilies. "I like it. It has a very warm feeling."

"It's homey, I guess."

"Nothing wrong with that."

They went into the kitchen and Brendan poured her a glass of white wine. He grabbed a beer for himself then started making supper.

As eager as she was to see the information Brendan

might have on his family, she decided to relax and enjoy herself. She was out with a gorgeous man, and she hadn't done anything but work since she had moved to Sweet Springs.

She smiled as she watched him work. Brendan was a serious griller. While Callie made a salad and put a couple of potatoes in to bake, the sheriff used his big stainless-steel barbeque to perfectly cook two medium-rare steaks.

It was a delicious meal and Brendan was a good conversationalist, asking questions about her job and telling stories about his work as county sheriff.

From the moment she had met him, she'd felt a deep pull of attraction, not just because of his good looks and hard muscled body, but because he was smart, and she felt that she could trust him.

The attraction seemed to be mutual, reflected in those amazing blue eyes. There was heat there, plenty of it. Like the blue tip of a flame.

When the meal was over, she helped him clear the dishes, then he led her into the living room where an overstuffed burgundy sofa and chairs sat in front of a mantled brick fireplace. Photos dominated the wall above an antique mahogany buffet.

"You wanted to know about my family. I've got old letters, photo albums, all kinds of stuff. The photos are my favorite."

Callie walked over for a closer look, an odd sensation prickling her skin. "Some of these pictures are really old."

He nodded. "The daguerreotypes date back to the eighteen sixties."

She studied the early tintypes. Two in particular caught her eye, a man and a woman in oval mahogany frames facing each other. Her pulse quickened. "It's them, isn't it? Those two photos. Brendan and Priscilla."

He nodded. "Silla, he called her. He would have been in his late thirties, early forties at the time the picture was made." He turned toward her. "There're a lot of photos up there. How did you know which ones they were?"

She toyed with a pretty lace doily on the sideboard. "If I tell you, you'll think I'm crazy." She gazed up at him. "I don't want that to happen. I really like you, Brendan."

He smiled. God, she loved the way he smiled, like it was always close, ready to surface at the first opportunity.

"I really like you, too, Callie." One of his big hands settled at her waist and he drew her closer, until they were touching full length. He framed her face between his palm and Callie closed her eyes as he tipped her head back and settled his mouth over hers. Softly at first, then deeper, their lips melding, fitting perfectly together.

A little whimper escaped at the rush of heat that burned through her and her arms slid up around his neck. She could feel the muscles moving beneath his shirt as Brendan deepened the kiss, which went on and on, long, hot, and hungry, thoroughly arousing.

The ghostly Trask had nothing on the living, breathing version standing right in front of her. When the kiss finally ended, Callie swayed toward him, and Brendan steadied her.

He ran a finger along her cheek. "I had a feeling it was going to be like that."

Callie looked up at him. "So did I." But then she'd had a sneak preview.

Brendan's gaze returned to the pictures on the wall and Callie's gaze followed. "You thought it was the outlaw Trask because he looks like me?" he asked.

Outlaw. Shock rolled through her. "Your great-great-grandfather was an outlaw?"

"For a while he was. He was pardoned. Something about helping catch a bunch of smugglers down in Natchez. They wrote a book about him, one of those pulp fiction Westerns that made him more of a hero than he probably was. It's called *Natchez Flame.*"

"I'd love to read it sometime."

Brendan studied the photos, including one taken with the couple and their kids years later. "You know, you look a lot like Priscilla."

She'd noticed that, too. "I've done some family genealogy. I don't think we're related, but looking at her picture, I can certainly see the resemblance. It's uncanny how much I look like her." She studied the face of the woman with big dark eyes and thick dark hair. Same chin, same nose, same mouth. "Maybe that explains it."

"Explains what?"

She turned and looked up at him, into those amazing blue eyes. "The reason he came back to the house. Maybe he thinks I'm Silla."

"Wait a minute—"

"I know, I know. But he's been coming into my bedroom at night. At first I thought I was dreaming, but one night… one night he kissed me and I opened my eyes and I saw him. He was dressed like an outlaw or a gunslinger. He looked just like you, Brendan, except for the scar below his jaw."

"Whoa. You think the ghost of my great-great-grandfather is in your house?"

She managed to nod. "He's young, though. Somewhere around your age."

"Sorry. I don't believe in ghosts."

"Neither do I. At least I never did. You know what's even crazier? I think he protected me the night Raymond Whitley broke into the house to rape me. I think Brendan killed him."

Chapter Nine

SHE HADN'T SEEN BRENDAN FOR THE LAST THREE DAYS. SHE'D said she had seen a ghost. He thought she was crazy. No way would he ever call her again. It bothered her more than it should have, considering how little time they'd spent together.

It was probably that amazing kiss. She couldn't remember a kiss affecting her so strongly, turning her knees to jelly and setting her body on fire. She'd wanted to tear off his clothes and drag him into the bedroom. She'd wanted to make love with him all night long and start again in the morning.

It wasn't like her. She hadn't thought about sex for nearly a year, not since she had ended things with Adam. Now Brendan was gone and there was no way he was coming back. It made her heart hurt a little.

She was working at the clinic when her cell phone rang. She had just finished stitching up a little white schnauzer that had cut its paw on a barbed wire fence.

"I'll finish up," Dr. Reynolds said. He was mid-forties, a little too thin, and a really nice guy. "Go ahead and take the call."

Callie hurried over and picked up the phone. "This is Callie."

"It's Brendan. Have you got a minute?"

Her stomach clenched. For him, she had all the time in the world. "I'm not busy at the moment." She walked into the back room for a little privacy, the phone pressed against her ear.

"I can't stop thinking about you, Callie. I really want to see you."

A warm feeling spread through her. She'd begun to accept that she wouldn't be seeing him again. "I'd like that, too."

"Good. That's great. Has the…ahh…ghost been back?"

Her fingers tightened around the phone. She didn't want to talk about ghosts. She didn't want to ruin things again. "No, not since…not since the night of the murder."

"I'm glad to hear it," he said firmly. Something in his voice, impossible as it seemed, sounded a lot like jealousy.

"I know someone who…ahh…thinks she can help," he said. "Any chance the two of us could come over tonight?"

He wanted to see her. He wanted to help her. He wanted to come over to the house. The warm feelings expanded. "Tonight would work."

"Say eight o'clock?"

"All right. I'll see you then." She ended the call but still held onto the phone. Brendan was coming over. She glanced at the clock. It was almost six. If nothing last-minute came up, she could go home and figure out what to wear. She wanted to look good for him.

She just hoped all this talk about ghosts wasn't going to send him running again.

Chapter Ten

Brendan stood on her doorstep at exactly eight o'clock. "Miss Aggie, this is Callie Sutton. Callie, I'd like you to meet Agatha Hennessey. Everyone calls her Miss Aggie."

Callie smiled. "It's nice to meet you, Miss Aggie."

"Miss Aggie's from over in Jasper County." His gaze went to the woman beside him. She was huge. Not tall, but square, built like a box. She must have weighed three hundred pounds. "Miss Aggie is a seer. My mom used to visit her for...ahh...advice."

Callie inwardly smiled. The sheriff must have had an interesting family.

"I appreciate your trying to help, Miss Aggie. Please come in." Callie stepped back to welcome her guests into the house. "Why don't we sit in the parlor? There's coffee and chocolate chip cookies. Not homemade, unfortunately, but the bakery in town is always good."

They all took seats, Brendan next to Callie on the sofa, Miss Aggie in an overstuffed chair. Callie filled her aunt's pretty porcelain cups with coffee and passed them around, and Miss Aggie helped herself to cookies. At least five of them vanished in her direction.

"I told Miss Aggie a little of what's been going on," Brendan said. "She knows the story. Hell, everyone in Sweet

Springs County knows the story of Brendan and Priscilla. It's kind of the Old West version of Romeo and Juliet except with a happy ending."

"Or mostly happy," Miss Aggie said. "They had a long, happy life, but the end wasn't so good for Brendan. A problem came up at the ranch. While he was gone, Priscilla took a turn for the worst. She died while he was away. As the story goes, he never forgave himself. He died a few months after she did."

Callie set her cup and saucer down on the coffee table. "I know it sounds crazy, but I think he might still be here."

Miss Aggie smiled. "To someone like me, it doesn't sound crazy at all." She finished the last of her cookie and heaved her big bulk up from the chair. "I'm going to take a walk. I'll be back." She didn't say more, just lumbered off down the hall.

Callie's gaze went to Brendan. "I didn't think I'd hear from you again."

A faint smile touched his lips. "Because of the ghost?"

"Most guys wouldn't want anything to do with a woman who thinks she lives in a house with a ghost."

"You don't seem like the kind of person who goes around making up stories. Plus, there's the dead man on the stairs and no prints, no DNA, nothing. In this day and age, that's not easy to do."

"That's sort of what I was thinking."

"Miss Aggie's been a friend of the family for years. I went to see her to ask her opinion. She said she wanted to see for herself."

Callie hadn't seen the woman go upstairs, but she watched her making her way carefully back down. She looked different somehow, calmer, an oddly vacant expression on her face.

"Have you got any candles?" she asked.

"Of course. In case the power goes off. I'll get them." Callie returned with an assortment of candles. She set two of them on the coffee table and one on the oak sideboard against the wall. Brendan pulled a box of wooden matches out of his jeans and lit them. It gave the living room a soft, eerie glow.

"Be patient," Miss Aggie said. "He's here. I could feel him."

Callie's heart began to pound. Brendan flashed her a glance but made no comment. He reached over and caught her hand, steadying her.

They sat in silence for half an hour, by the antique mantel clock. It was strangely peaceful, until the candle flames started to flicker, and Callie felt the sensation of a big hand sliding beneath her hair, settling possessively around the nape of her neck.

It wasn't Brendan, whose hand still held hers. Callie made a little sound in her throat that drew his attention. His expression changed as he watched the dark curls move though no one else was touching her.

"I know you're here, Brendan," Miss Aggie said. "And I know why you came. But the lady in the house isn't Priscilla. She looks like your Silla, but her name is Callie. Your Priscilla has gone on to the other side. She's waiting for you there. She misses you terribly. She's been waiting a very long time."

The candle on the sideboard flickered and went out.

"It's true," Miss Aggie said. "She was gone when you came home, but you can find her again. You don't have to live without her. You just have to look for the light. Do you see it, Brendan?"

A loud whooshing sound filled the room, stirring the draperies.

"Callie belongs to the Brendan of this time. He'll take care of her. He'll protect her."

In the candlelight, Brendan's features looked hard. He glanced at Miss Aggie, who nodded. "Callie's mine," he said. "She belongs to me. She's mine to protect. I give you my solemn pledge that I will."

Callie's heart was beating. Brendan sounded like he meant every word.

"Go on now," Miss Aggie said. "Move toward the light.

Go and find your Priscilla. She's waiting. She loves you. Just the way you love her."

The house began to shake, rattling the windows, jiggling the antique stemware in the glass curio case. A sudden burst of light lit the room, so bright Callie had to close her eyes.

Brendan's hand tightened around hers. "Jesus," he said.

A roaring began, rising to a crescendo. The bright light flashed again and something whooshed past them. A fierce crack sounded, then a long heavy roll, like lightning followed by thunder.

Silence fell. The old house slowly settled. Brendan drew Callie into his arms, and she felt a tremor run through his hard body.

"It's over," Miss Aggie said. "He won't be back." She smiled. "He's found her again after all these years."

Callie turned her face into Brendan's chest and started to cry.

Epilogue

IT WAS THE BIGGEST SOCIAL EVENT IN SWEET SPRINGS THAT
year. The wedding of Sheriff Brendan Trask to the town's
new resident, Callie Sutton. Those that couldn't make it to
the ceremony in the little white church showed up for the
party out at the ranch. Bets were made how long it would
take before the first little Trask was born.

Not long, Callie figured, considered how much practice
they got. She grinned.

The ghost of the outlaw Brendan Trask had never reap-
peared. Callie firmly believed he was happy with his
beloved Priscilla on the other side.

The search for the man who had killed the Red Rose
rapist eventually came to an end. Brendan let the case fade
away on its own accord. Though he never mentioned it
again, like Callie, he believed the outlaw Trask had saved
Callie that night.

All was well in the little town of Sweet Springs.

Callie believed, at last, all was well on the other side, too.

Author's Note

I hope you enjoyed *Outlaw Ghost*. If you're curious about the outlaw Brendan Trask, check out *Natchez Flame*, one of my first Historical Western Romance Novels. I hope you enjoy it! Till next time, all best wishes and happy reading!

    – Kat

Heart's Great Temptation

C.K. Crigger

Heart's Great Temptation

HE'D BEEN WATCHING THE WOMAN FOR THE LAST FOUR DAYS, unable to decide if he admired her pluck and wished her well, or if he hoped she'd fail and move on. One thing certain, her presence made his mission more difficult.

Boone Tingley whispered to his horse Mister and reined him around, heading back into the woods where he'd spotted another maverick. He doubted the woman had noticed him or his horse standing still at the very edge of the thick timber. Mister being a grulla of the mouse-gray variety, his coloring made him difficult to spot at a distance. And Boone wasn't a whole lot more visible. Dressed in faded denims and a worn gray shirt, he also blended into the background. A gray hat covered his head and shaded his face.

A once-handsome face scarred from beatings and bleached from spending the last three years in Walla Walla State Prison.

Returning to a camp consisting of a tarp pegged down over a brush shelter, a fire kept small in a rock-rimmed pit, and a picket line for Mister, he lay back on his bedroll and pondered.

What was the woman doing here? Aside, that is, from trying to plow a straight furrow in what had once been a large kitchen garden. With a dray horse he recognized from years ago, gone skinny with age and most certainly turned loose to die. The place should've been empty. Abandoned and allowed to return to the wild.

Boone meant to pay a visit there as soon as she went off somewhere and he got the chance. The woman must leave the place sometimes, he figured, although she hadn't in the days he'd been watching. But women liked to visit other women, didn't they? Needed to socialize? Or at least, get to town and shop? He'd been keeping an eye out and waiting for her to saddle the old horse and ride off. If she didn't soon, he'd have to give in and go while she was there. Best though if she never knew he was around.

Boone wished he knew her name. And how she'd come to live in his old home. He reckoned it had something to do with the only visitor he'd had during the years of his incarceration. The time six months ago when Sheriff Riker came to see him.

Eyes drifting shut, Boone let those memories, ones he generally never let surface, roam free. Had there been a clue as to what happened in that visit? He hadn't thought so at the time. He'd thought...what?

———

"VISITOR FOR YOU." The guard, a man the convicts called Bully—for obvious reasons—grinned through the cell bars at him with a show of stained, yellow teeth.

Boone, who'd been reading a newspaper someone had left in the common room, looked up. "Something funny about that?"

The grin dropped away, leaving Bully with a sneer on his face. "Well, it ain't like you've got a lot of friends coming to mix and mingle, is it?"

The truth, as Boone had to admit. He didn't, which suited him fine. "People don't socialize in prison," he said, cold as could be. "Who is it?"

"Put your hands through the bars so's I can cuff you."

Bully waved the metal bracelets overhead. "You'll find out when we get to the visitor's room."

The visitor's room? That made him think it must be some official, although Boone had no idea what the purpose could be. He'd been tried and convicted and was serving his time. His life was in ruins. What else did they want from him?

"Hurry up." Bully thumped along the bars with his baton. Boone had never seen the guard without his club in hand, eager to whup on some unsuspecting prisoner. "I ain't got all day. Neither, I 'spect, does the feller waiting on you."

Boone, who'd been seated on the edge of his bunk, got up. "What if I don't want to see anybody?" And he didn't yet, then. Six months of solitude—except for Bully and a few others just like him—had failed to wear him down. Six more months on his three-year term and he'd be free.

"Don't matter what you want. Get over here."

No matter how it chafed him, Boone eventually had to give in. Had to let Bully lock on the cuffs and parade him through the corridors to the visitor area. The guard made sure to push, prod, and provoke him into a snarling response until they arrived at the destination with Boone sporting a new bruise on his cheekbone and another on his forearm.

Bully was grinning again as he chained Boone via a leg shackle to a staple in the concrete floor. Treating the convicts like wild animals always seemed to give him a thrill. Their ultimate insult, his ultimate pleasure.

"Here you be, Sheriff," Bully said to the man waiting in the room. "He didn't want to see you. I had to persuade him."

"I see." The man watched the shackling procedure quietly, though his hands clenched. "No," he said, "I don't suppose he did want to see me."

The voice shifted Boone's attention to the visitor, only now recognizing who it was as Bully got out of his way. "Sheriff Riker. He didn't tell me it was you." Anger boiled up in him like steam boiling from a kettle.

"Would it have made any difference?"

"No."

They waited until Bully left the room, both of them knowing the guard would stay close and try to hear what was said. They outwaited Bully, until finally, a fellow guard called him away.

Now, lying on his bedroll in camp, Boone remembered how they stared at each other, he and the sheriff, until Riker cleared his throat and said, "How are they treating you?"

Boone snorted and touched the new bruise on his face. "It's prison, how do you think?" He made no effort to hide his bitterness. "What do you want?"

The sheriff threw up his hands. "What makes you think I want anything? Or what if I just want to help you? I'm aware what happened wasn't all your fault, Boone. I figure Louis was there in the background egging you on. And your dad…he didn't—"

Boone didn't bother to deny Riker's words. He'd been tried and convicted. What was the point now? "No," he cut in on the sheriff's stammer. "He didn't. I repeat. What do you want?"

"Nothing," Riker said again, although Boone knew the denial for a lie. "I just figured to give you one last chance, is all. You know, due to Louis running out on you."

Boone didn't know why he bothered, but he had to try. "Louis didn't run out on me. We were never together. Anyhow, last chance at what?"

"Huh." Riker stared at him. "Sometimes I almost believe you're as innocent as you make out. Nevertheless, with your pa dead, your old place is going up for sale for back taxes. Whether it's sold to the highest bidder or abandoned, it ain't yours anymore. If you got anything to say, or a way to save it, now's the time."

Boone had known the ranch would be lost. He looked Riker in the eye. "I've got nothing to say."

Sighing, the sheriff stood up. "So be it then. Over and done, but I tried." He walked to the door, then turned. "Oh, by the way. About the grave up on the knoll—"

"What about it?"

"There's been some talk of digging into it, just to see what might be in there besides your dad's body."

"Are you asking permission? I can't stop you, you know. I wasn't there for the burying."

The sheriff shook his head. "Yeah, well, there's been talk of folks seeing your brother at a distance. Louis alive, I mean. No ghost."

"Stepbrother," Boone corrected automatically, then shrugged, though his heart gave a sudden bound. "Why would you think he's a ghost? He ain't dead, as far as I know."

"That ain't what your pa said." Riker had watched him, as if looking for a lie.

Boone shrugged. "Yeah? Well, go ahead and dig, then." Nonchalant. Like it didn't matter. Inside, he'd about froze solid. A final indignity. Blast his old man, the hussy he'd married, and her thieving son.

And now? Blinking his eyes open, Boone sat up and tossed another small piece of wood on his fire. Time to find out if anybody had excavated that grave.

———

HEART BEAVER'S late husband had been a miserable excuse of a man. Unclean and ignorant, among other things, one being that he was downright mean. And no good when it came to practical decisions. She could attest to that, and it wasn't anything to make her proud. In plain fact, nothing about him had ever made her proud. She hadn't shed a single tear when he never made it home from the saloon one night. Seems he'd gotten drunk, abused his horse so it bucked him off in the middle of the river, and he drowned. Too late for her to salvage a thing, of course, since it happened after he'd spent every last penny her grandparents left her on this godforsaken, run-down excuse of a ranch. If she wasn't mistaken—and didn't believe she was—he'd taken up thieving now and again, as well.

Her guardians had certainly done her no favors, forcing

her into a marriage when she'd been only sixteen. A secret sin lurked somewhere in the transaction, but she supposed she'd never know what. Probably didn't matter anymore. Ten years she'd spent with him. Ten long years of trying to remain invisible.

She'd only learned he actually owned the old Tingley ranch a month after his death, when she'd received a letter from a lawyer. She'd thought they'd just been squatting here. The place had been abandoned a couple years previously and why Beaver bought it remained a mystery. Not only had he never spent much time there, but he never lifted a finger to improve the place. Apparently, he simply roamed the land like he was looking for something to pop out at him. Or so she'd been told.

The ranch was hers, they said. Having no place else to go, she'd stayed. At least it was a roof over her head. An imperfect roof until she patched it, crawling around on the rafters after a rain so she'd know where to place the shingles.

It wasn't much of an existence.

These days, when her needs grew desperate, she trudged from home to town, collected a few items she could hand carry, and then trudged back again.

She rarely made this trek because she had only enough money to eke out the food she could hunt or grow. Her meager earnings depended on what people would pay her for hauling the occasional load of wood or helping sickly Mrs. Stevens, who lived five miles north, with her heavy chores. The old workhorse she'd found wandering lost in the woods one day helped immensely. She always made sure he got lots of rest after he'd put in a day of service.

Folks in town had taken to calling the place "Beaver's Lodge" due to the way she made do with bits and pieces and other folks' leftovers. Kind of like the way beavers built their dams out of this and that. Her thriftiness and name had turned into a standing joke. Except to Heart. But it was what she had to deal with.

On this particular spring day, dreading the necessity, but with the garden harrowed and in need of seeds, she started off late in the morning to pay the town a visit. Worse yet, a queasy feeling of being watched had grown on her, making the trail seem downright dangerous. The sun blazed down during her walk. By the time she finished her business and started her return, though the queasy feeling faded, it was hot enough to nearly cook her. In winter, she'd found, snow tried to bury her. Sometimes rain threatened to drown—

Heart, she interrupted herself, *shut up. You're being melodramatic.*

She shifted her parcel to her other hand as she walked. The parcel contained a pound of stew meat and some withered carrots Mr. Swanson, the middle-aged widower who ran the store, had included in an effort to flirt with her. That's when the heavy chuffing sound of an animal forcing a way through the bushes alongside the winding wagon road came to her.

An obvious sound, this time. Almost a relief after her earlier fright.

Heart stopped in her tracks and turned, her eyes widening. Daisy Burch, one of the few people to speak to her, had passed on a warning, saying a mangy mama black bear seen in the vicinity had become a real nuisance.

"Be watchful, Mrs. Beaver," Daisy had said. "I know it's easy to daydream when you walk to pass the time, but keep your eyes open. That bear is dangerous."

Wondering how Daisy knew about her daydreams, Heart forced a smile and tried not to show the warning did indeed scare her. "Yes, ma'am." She saluted Daisy; a smart touch. "I will. Keep my eyes open, I mean. Thank you."

Not for the first time, Heart wished for a horse. Not one like the old fellow she'd found loose in the woods. A fast horse. One to carry her away from all her troubles. There was a saying: "If wishes were horses, beggars would ride."

She guessed she wasn't a beggar because no horse was forthcoming.

So she kited up her skirt and began running.

On her weekly jaunts to town, depending on what she carried, Heart often ran along this stretch of road. She liked to run, and it saved time. Plus, with the care of the run-down excuse of a house, the cooking and cleaning, and the garden she grew to ensure there'd be something for her to eat—even if it was onions cooked in bacon grease—she had to maintain her stamina. This helped.

She ran now with her head high, knees lifting and arms pumping, breathing easy and sure she could outrun any bear. The creature, she figured, would soon lose interest in chasing her.

Until, instead of leaving the chuffing sound behind, it grew louder. She fancied she could smell the beast, rank as a rotting corpse. Remembering she was still carrying the pound of raw beef, she resolved that if worst came to worst, she could always throw the meat to the bear.

But she didn't want to.

A quick glance backward nearly gave her a seizure. The mama bear, far from losing interest, was going flat-out and gaining.

With a gasp that set her to coughing and disturbed the previously even pace, Heart compounded her efforts. Going so fast the rush of wind brought tears to her eyes, she didn't see the two black cubs cavorting in the middle of the road until she was right on them.

A startled leap in the air took her over the top of one, clipping it with her foot. It squealed like she'd half killed it, the second cub joining in the complaint. Both took off galloping straight down the road in front of her. Regaining her balance, she struggled to stay on her feet. Behind her, the sow roared.

Heart, thoroughly frightened, threw the package of stew meat at the bear, sacrificing her supper. Spotting a branching deer trail, she shot off to the left, down a steep slope toward the river. If those cubs wanted to play in the road, let them. They could have it.

She rattled through a tough cluster of bushes, stones rolling, sliding, and skidding. Panting now, Heart risked a look over her shoulder—and promptly tripped over a boulder. She landed face down in dirt mixed with smaller rocks, pine cones, dropped needles and was that…yes. Deer scat, the trail being liberally sprinkled with the pellets.

For a moment, she simply lay still, waiting for the pain to ebb. Which it did, mostly, after a while. Muffling a good many imprecations, she pushed herself up on scraped palms. Her knees stung and she tasted blood from a smashed lip.

In the distance, she heard the bear snuffling and calling to her babies. Up ahead, one cub answered. The bears were moving on.

Shaken and angry, Heart glared at the offending stone. Her squint turned into a wide-eyed, questioning stare, then a closer examination. Reaching out, she managed to tumble the boulder a few inches to the side. "What in the world is this doing here?" she whispered.

This was a much-stained canvas bag, as she could plainly see. Though still half buried under the large granite stone, she saw the words Exchange National Bank of Spokane printed on the bag's side in what had originally been deep blue ink. Over time, the color had leached to a watery imprint. Sitting back, aches and pains forgotten—along with the bears—she pondered.

Someone, she concluded after a while, had deliberately dug a hole beneath the stone and placed the bag there. *A bank bag.* Her heart beat faster. Something fishy was going on and she intended to find out what. Scrambling to find something to dig with, she found part of a broken tree branch and used it to poke under the stone.

Sweating again, she finally pulled the bag free and sat staring down at it. It had taken more effort than she'd expected. A part of her mind noted the soil had been undisturbed for quite some time. A second part realized the bag was heavy and clinked when moved. And then a third thought struck. *It's on my land. Finders keepers.*

But did that really make it hers?

A final part of Heart's attention was wholly involved in untying the knots holding the opening closed and discovering the contents. She hoped it wasn't somebody's head. Or hand. Or something equally as grisly.

Silly, she thought. Of course it wasn't. The bag wasn't the proper shape. Anyway, a head wouldn't clink.

Even so, when the knots came free, she looked carefully all around. Nothing threatening leaped out at her. The woods were quiet, the sound of birds and insects and the susurration of the trees all as they should be. Nobody watching. And no sign of the bear—a relief.

Finally satisfied, she poked her hand, the bloody palm making a fresh stain on the canvas, into the bag. She clenched her fingers around a couple of loose objects and drew them out.

Choked.

"A horse, a horse," she cried, forgetting any need for quiet. "My kingdom for a horse."

Although, when she thought about it later, if she'd had a horse, she never would've found *this.*

Heart's euphoria didn't last all the way home, as it happened. Her spritely march turned into dragging footsteps. The Exchange National Bank of Spokane bag, already plenty weighty, grew heavier and heavier. Twenty-dollar gold pieces are not as light as they look. And doubts—call them second thoughts even weightier than the gold—dragged at her.

Who did the money belong to? The bank? A private citizen? Who had hidden it under the boulder? Had it been her husband? He hadn't been beyond committing theft.

She had no idea, but Heart expected whoever had hidden the bag—if alive—would come looking for it. Then what would she do?

A memory surfaced. Hadn't she heard the property she now owned had once belonged to a thief? Was this money the proceeds of a crime? Any way you looked at it, it didn't belong to her. Not really. But what if no one ever came looking for it? What if... A different thought jolted her. Is this why Beaver had bought the place? Was it his?

Impossible.

Heart wanted justification for taking it. For spending it. After all, she needed the money as badly as anyone.

Maybe there would be a finder's fee. A single one of those coins would be a godsend to her. If she took only one, perhaps it wouldn't be missed when she turned the money over to the sheriff tomorrow. Or if not tomorrow, then soon. What was his name again? She couldn't remember.

If she turned it over.

Unable to still a mind that spun first one way and then another, Heart didn't sleep that night. Possibly because, or so she tried to tell herself, after tossing the makings for her supper to the bear, she went to bed hungry. The egg her only hen had laid that day did little to fill the yawning hole in her belly.

BOONE AWAKENED in the morning filled with impatience crawling over him like flies on a pile of horse manure. Today was his fifth day back, and so far, he hadn't learned a thing. Not about Louis, the money, or even the ranch, except for the presence of a strange woman living there. He'd finally convinced himself there was no need for this self-imposed secrecy. He could ride over and confront her. He'd served his time. He was free to go where he wanted.

If only what Sheriff Riker had said all those months ago didn't keep resonating in his mind. The part about some folks thinking they'd seen Louis. Louis in the flesh, that is. Not a ghost. If Louis had stayed around, there had to be a reason.

Boone lifted the saddle onto his horse, yanking the cinch tight with enough force Mister turned his head and gave him a reproachful look.

"Sorry." Boone gave his horse a pat on the neck. "Didn't mean to hurt you. But I've been thinking. Louis isn't a ghost because he isn't dead. Or if he is, someone other than me killed him. He's bilked enough men—and women—out of their life savings, I can't be the only one with a grudge. In any case, the authorities know I can't have done him in. Being in the hoosegow is a pretty respectable alibi."

Mister shook his head up and down as if agreeing—unless he was telling Boone to hurry up.

Banking the fire in its shallow pit, he dumped the last few dregs of coffee over the coals, counting on the embers to soon fizzle out. Time he made a move, the first being to discover who the woman living in the old house—his old house—was. He'd check on his father's grave, too, and he'd do it whether she liked it or not.

Boone hadn't spent every minute of these last five days watching the woman or lying around in his camp. His first day here he'd had a run-in with a cow perturbed over him getting between her and a calf. The cow, he'd noticed, bore no brand. Neither did the calf. He had a notion she'd been part of his fledgling herd three years ago. One escaped from whoever rounded up the rest of them. She'd been hiding out in the woods ever since, becoming ever wilder and procreating every year. In his eyes, that made her and her progeny his. What's more, if one cow escaped, likely there were more.

With this thought in mind, he'd scoured the woods and when he rode up to the ranch buildings later in the morning, he pushed seven cows, four with calves, ahead of him. Mister did most of the work, him being as good of a cattle horse as Boone had ever ridden.

Cattle not being a silent bunch, a certain amount of noise and dust heralded their approach. Enough so the woman came flying out of the house at the commotion. Flapping her apron at the cattle and yelling her head off with a colorful choice of words, Boone's first startled thought was that she might have a loose cog in her brain.

Mister most certainly thought so considering the way he had to work to keep the cattle in a bunch.

Irritation frazzled Boone's temper. Shouldn't she be glad to see these critters? As poor as she seemed to be, they spelled wealth. Well, maybe not wealth, but an asset. Or at least they would as soon as she knew he was giving them to her. And he'd tell her the second she stopped scaring the little herd into a stampede.

"Quit waving that infernal rag, woman," he roared over the thud of hooves and the mooing of eleven bovines.

"You stop crowding those cows into my garden, you nitwit," she yelled at the very same time.

Neither appeared to hear the other.

Until he got close enough to rip the apron out of her hands and glare down into a pair of the prettiest brown eyes he'd ever seen. Yes, pretty, even if they were snapping with anger and glaring right back.

"Those cows are not in your garden," he gritted. "And they won't be if you'll stop screeching and flopping that rag around. You're scaring them."

"Screeching? Rag? I'll have you know..." She stopped abruptly and gazed at the cloth in her hand like she'd never seen it before. She took a few deep breaths, her chest—clearly unfettered by corset or stays—heaving as she forced herself calm. "Who are you and what are you doing with these cattle?"

Her question was quiet and if Boone had to judge, it was in his thoughts she was about half scared of him. Maybe even three-quarters. Granted, he hadn't shaved in a while. Nor had clean clothes or a bath, but he hadn't exactly been rolling in the dirt, either, and he'd washed his face and hands a couple times every day in the little stream flowing past his camp. He didn't think he looked too awful bad. Not scary bad, anyhow.

Since she toned down the animosity and spoke in a normal tone of voice when asking a pertinent question, he stepped out of the saddle, leaving Mister to keep the cattle bunched while he talked.

"Are you the owner of this ranch?" he asked, though it hurt to say those words. "If so, these critters belong to you. I found them wandering in the woods and figured to gather them up."

He frowned a little and saw her trembling. Barely notice-able, but there. Plus, as he looked more closely at her down-turned face, he saw she had a swollen, split lip and barely scabbed-over scrapes on her face and hands. What the holy dickens? Looked like she'd been in a fist fight.

"They belong to me?" She blinked. "First I've heard of it."

"Well, they do."

Worried now, he scanned a barn which had acquired a lean during the last few years. The corrals were empty but for the ancient workhorse. She was alone here as far as he could tell. But wounded somehow.

"How'd you get hurt, ma'am? Did somebody—"

She faced him at the question, touching her swollen lip with a careful forefinger. "No. Nobody—unless you count a bear. A bear chased me through the woods and I fell getting away from it. It had cubs," she added after a second.

"But you got away."

"I did."

Warily, they eyed one another.

Boone didn't know what to think, standing there. His brain had gone numb of a sudden, his thoughts all jumbled together. First, irritation because the woman hadn't greeted his gift with whoops of joy. Far from it. Anger made the mix as well, due to the way the property had practically disinte-grated into ruins in only three years. Evidently she, or whoever had taken over here, hadn't lifted a finger to keep the place up. Then the fear he sensed in her, easy for a parolee to see, but with it the notion it might not be his fault after all. And finally, the one thing setting him all awhirl. He felt drawn to her, and he didn't like it.

Could it be he just needed the companionship of a woman? Three years is a long time for a man full of juice, and this was the first young woman he'd been close to in the time he'd been free.

Turned out once he got through the scowls, the yelling, and a dress even shabbier than his old shirt, he liked the way she looked. Especially those eyes so dark they were almost black. Striking at any time but put together with Nordic blonde hair and a nice shape, she knocked him for a loop.

Looks, he reminded himself, aren't everything. Not even half.

Boone came to his senses when she poked a forefinger into his chest. Not hard. Just forceful enough to gain his attention.

"Mister, are you having a fit or something?" she was asking. "Should I slap your face? Douse you with water?"

"What? No." A flush of embarrassment swept through him. Even Mister must've felt it as the horse tromped up behind him and nosed him hard between the shoulder blades. The shove brought Boone to his senses—and closer to the woman.

"I'm gonna pen these cattle for you," he said. "Looks like the corral will hold 'em."

"You're sure they're mine?" She still seemed doubtful. "I don't want anybody coming around accusing me of cattle rustling."

"Yes, ma'am, I'm sure they're yours." He answered her in order. "No, ma'am, they ain't stolen. They're unbranded mavericks and belong to whoever finds them. Which I did. Now I'm giving them to you."

Her mouth kind of twisted, enough to make her touch the swelling again so he knew it must hurt.

"Why?" she demanded.

He had an answer all ready, thought up on the way over. "Keeps 'em from running through my camp and tearing up my stuff." And worked as a bribe for him to stay and see if Louis had been here.

"Your camp?"

"Yes, ma'am. I've been camping in the woods."

She eyed him with a funny mixture of suspicion and... was it relief? Why?

Although, according to the look on her face she remained doubtful, she started walking toward the corral gate where the old horse hung his head over the top rail and watched the action. She had, Boone noticed, a bit of a limp, like maybe her knees were banged up as badly as her hands and face.

"Use this one," she was saying, pushing past Mister, who still held the cattle in a tight bunch. "It's in the best condition. I've fixed it up a little."

The little she mentioned didn't impress him, consisting as it did of tying the rails to the posts with bits of rope. Good enough for the tired gelding in the corral, but probably not adequate for the cattle. A relief. It gave him an excuse to stay around—if she would agree.

He followed her over and helped open the gate, leaving Mister to chase the little herd on through where they milled around the work horse.

"Well," she said when the gate closed up again, "at least they stayed out of the garden." She turned to pat Mister on his neck. "This is a smart horse you have. He doesn't even need you to tell him what to do. What's his name?"

Boone made no attempt to fight back his grin, even though he heard the implication that his horse was smarter than the master. She may have been right. "Mister," he said. "His name is Mister."

She nodded. "Good name." Squinting into the sun, she stared up at him. "What's yours?"

———

HEART HAD BEEN in the kitchen part of the house, attempting to affix a wide board to the wall next to the kitchen stove. The stove itself stood like a desert island with nothing surrounding it. No mistake, she was happy she had a real cookstove with an oven. She figured the only reason it was still in the house was because cast iron stoves are heavy and hard to move.

Besides, the reputation of this place may have kept thieves away. Perhaps they were afraid of Louis Tingley's ghost.

If he was a ghost.

The gold she'd found made her doubtful. Ghosts had no use for gold.

The drill bit she'd been turning finally broke through the

wall, the last hole ready for bracket pegs. Now she could mount the board and she'd have a real counter as a landing place for cooking utensils. She just prayed she'd gotten the thing level.

The sense of accomplishment had her rock back on her heels and admire her own work, which is when she became aware of some kind of ruckus headed her way.

No. Not her way. Her garden's way. The garden she had just planted after so many hours of laborious work and stingy spending while she saved enough money to buy the seeds. Looking out the open door, she spotted a cloud of dust and a mixed bunch of cows and calves running into the yard.

"What the..." Snatching up the first thing within her grasp, Heart rushed outside, hollering at the top of her lungs and waving whatever she'd grabbed over her head like a semaphore spelling out danger.

The cattle, taking fright, shifted into a swooping turn, evading the man on the handsome and hardworking dun horse. She saw his mouth moving, an indistinguishable roar issuing forth.

Not to be bested, a pithy retort of her own crossed over his.

They came to an impasse. He saying one thing, she another, until it sank into her brain he meant these cows belonged to her. Why, she didn't know, but apparently, he thought she should be grateful. What was she supposed to do with several cows and one, two, three, no—four calves, for goodness' sake? She was no cowman. Cattlewoman. Rancher.

Besides, she had a sackful of twenty-dollar gold pieces, which she hadn't even counted as yet. She had no need of cattle.

But, Heart decided, eyeing the man and trying to decide if she could believe a single one of the words he said to her, he didn't strike her as dangerous, exactly. Just a bit odd. Even when he went off into some kind of trance and she thought she might have to take drastic action. In fact, he looked almost as down at the heels as she. The nerve of the man, calling her apron a rag. Which it was, although she didn't appreciate attention being called to the fact. But he had a good horse and, patting the animal on the neck, she told him so.

And then they got to names. Mister, the horse.

"And yours?" she demanded.

He hesitated. "Boone Tingley," he said.

Tingley. A name she'd heard before. One that sent a shiver down her spine and made her, if she'd only known it, turn pale as a snow drop. The reported ghost's brother.

"Oh." The single soft word slipped out. A giveaway acknowledging his notorious name. "You're him. You owned this…" She waved a hand, taking in the run-down homestead. It hadn't always been in this condition, she was sure. There were still touches about the place to show it had seen better days. Until he had gone to prison, probably. An outlaw, according to what she'd been told. A thief and maybe a killer. *Why is he here?*

Her insides quivering like custard, she took a breath and rushed into speech. "I'm sorry you find me such a pathetic caretaker. Believe me, I'd do better if I could. I—" Heart floundered to a stop, unable to think of an acceptable excuse.

It occurred to her the cows he'd just brought to her had probably belonged to him at one time. The mama cows, anyway. The next question to strike her concerned why he was being so generous. From the look of him, he needed the proceeds from selling the cattle as badly as she.

Why was he here? She had the answer. Because of those twenty-dollar gold pieces, of course. He knew they were here and wanted them.

And she had them.

The panic dashing through her was as paralyzing as ice water, until it occurred to her Boone Tingley couldn't possibly know she had found the money. If he had, he wouldn't have shown up chasing cows into her yard and declaring they were hers. If he was as bad as he'd been painted, he'd probably just shoot her and take the money.

Or, if he didn't ordinarily kill his victims, torture her until she told him where she'd hidden the loot—it wouldn't take long—and be done with it.

Did it count as robbery to take something from the person who stole it in the first place?

Steadying herself, she took a calming breath and took a hard look at him. *Show no fear,* she told herself. A tactic she didn't recall ever working on Beaver, her late husband. He'd been prone to knock her around at first resistance. Worse if she defied him.

"Mr. Tingley," she began pleasantly enough, although the hard swallow afterward worried her. Beaver had always known he had her cowed when she did that. She tried again. "I do appreciate you thinking I could use these cattle, sir, but really, I have no way to care for them. I think you'd be better off driving them into town and selling them to Mr. Berenger. He's the butcher."

He had very dark blue eyes pretty enough to belong to a girl, she noticed, and when he cocked back his dusty gray hat, revealed thick, wavy brown hair in need of cutting. A few years ago he might had been called handsome, but now his face looked hard. Scarred, worn, and overly pale. He was thin, too, as if victuals had sometimes been scarce. Well, she knew all about that.

Heart had heard Boone Tingley had been in his mid-twenties when the conviction sent him to prison. He appeared older.

But then, the wry thought struck her, she likely did, too. Hadn't life with Beaver been incarceration of a sort?

Tingley had said something she'd entirely missed as her thoughts spun in widening circles. The way he cocked his head as if waiting for an answer drew her attention.

"I beg your pardon?" she said.

Those blue eyes narrowed. "It ain't such a strange idea," he was saying, as if he believed she knew what he'd just proposed. "Another while and these calves will be ready to wean. Then you can take half and I'll take half. Sound fair?"

Heart felt like a fool. "Another while? How...what...?"

There had to be a catch. And just how long was a "while" anyway?

His gaze drifted around the yard. "I'll take care of the animals. Looks like a few things could stand some fixing up. I can mend some fence. Replace a few boards. Fix the hinges on the house door. Make the place a bit safer for you. Maybe even help out in the garden. Guess I know a weed from a bean. I ain't got any place else to go and looks like you need the help."

Oh my goodness, it was like a dream to think of having help with this place. Of hanging another board shelf by the stove. One where she could set the bread—when she had bread—to rise. Of repairing the steps into the house. Of fixing the hole in the barn floor, where she was afraid to stable the poor old horse she'd named Bucephalus.

"Again, in exchange for...?" Heart felt a flush coloring her cheeks. Indelicate, the thought that crossed her mind. "What would I be doing?"

"Nothing out of the ordinary." He put on a show of surprise. Something she couldn't decide was real or not, most likely because of the flush as deep as her own painting his face. "The same things you always do, I expect. Just carry on. I'll stay out of your way. You won't hardly ever see me. If anybody comes for a visit, I'll fade away and nobody'll even know I'm around."

At this, she gave him *such* a look. "Are you out of jail for good?" she asked, suspicion in every word.

"Yes, ma'am. I served my time. I'm no threat to you."

He seemed so sincere. She probably would've believed him if she hadn't found a whole bagful of money hidden under a rock. And nobody, rich or not so rich, put a whole lot of money under a boulder sitting in the middle of a deer trail instead of in a bank vault. When the subject of money came up, people were ready to say anything, do anything to protect it. This man, she couldn't forget, had served time in prison for theft. And for the possible killing of his step-brother—if his brother was even dead.

The question remained. Should she do as he proposed?

Let him stay around and keep her eye on him? Or say no and fully expect him to keep hiding out in the woods as he had been?

If it had been him.

Of her druthers, Heart decided, she'd rather have him where she could keep an eye on him than sneaking around watching her when she least expected it.

Beaver'd had a pistol, she remembered. He hadn't taken it with him the day he drowned, so she'd dig it out of the trunk where she kept it, load it full of ammunition and keep the thing out of sight, but handy.

"All right." Her reply came rapidly. "It's a bargain. We'll see how it goes. If either of us wants to renege in the next week, we'll call it off, no harm done."

He held out his hand. "Shake on it?"

His grip was firm, but not brutal. Maybe he held on a little too long. Long enough, at least, to say, "Done. Now, ma'am, do you think you could tell me your name?" His eyes were dancing, his face completely sober.

Heart knew he was laughing at her. She jerked her hand away. "Heart. My name is Heart Beaver," she said, and recognized his immediate reaction as distaste. Her dead husband's reputation at work.

"Mrs. *Roger* Beaver?"

Unable to prevent it, Heart's head hung low. "Yes." Then, a second later. "He's dead, you know."

"No, I didn't. Nobody told me. Can't say as I'm surprised. Who done it?"

She made a funny little huffing sound. "Nobody. According to the sheriff, he got drunk, fell off his horse, and drowned."

"Huh," he said, like he didn't quite believe her. And for the first time, probably due to her relief in having her husband gone, she wondered, too. Nobody had questioned the manner of his death when they found his body. But what if somebody—

"I'll settle into the barn," Tingley was saying, drawing her attention back to him. "If that's all right with you."

"Of course, Mr. Tingley." She made a strangely helpless gesture. "Let me know if you need anything. Supper will be at six o'clock. You'll need to fend for yourself at noon."

A faint smile crossed his face. "Yes, ma'am. Thank you, Mrs. Beaver."

The name, coming from his mouth, put her in a quick tizzy. "Don't call me that."

"Call you what?"

"Beaver. I hate that name. Call me Heart." Embarrassment flooded her the moment the words emerged. She'd let him see too much. What in the world had gotten into her?

"Heart." Boone Tingley spoke as if he hadn't heard the rest. "Now, that's a pretty name."

———

I'M IN. Boone's idea of rounding up those mavericks had worked a treat, even if the situation turned a little dicey there for a bit. But he could plainly see she lived in the utmost poverty. A chance for something to improve her lot had won her over.

Heart Beaver. He hadn't been lying. Heart was a pretty name. Beaver, though. That kind of threw him for a loop. Roger Beaver had been one of Louis's cohorts. Worse even than Louis himself when it came to downright mean and sneaky.

He gave a soft snort as he led Mister toward the barn. How much did Heart Beaver know about her husband's goings-on? Was she part of the gang that had framed him and got him put in prison? Hard telling—for now.

A warning came floating after him. "There's a hole in the barn floor, Mr. Tingley. Don't you or your horse step through it."

He waved over his shoulder. Apparently, she wasn't ready to see him dead. Yet, anyway.

Boone spent the afternoon fixing the barn floor, which looked to him to have been deliberately cut, then roughed up to appear natural. Proof, if he'd needed it, that Beaver had been looking for the loot missing from the bank robbery. What other reason would the man have had to claim the place and bring his wife here? Beaver hadn't attempted to ranch, that much was certain. Didn't seem as if he'd found the money, though. Not if this run-down outfit proved anything, except that Beaver hadn't cared a whit about his wife.

Heart said as much that first night, when Boone appeared at the house door and smelled the fragrance of baked beans and fresh-baked bread. Plain food, but enough of it. Well-cooked, too, something he'd been missing for years.

"Your husband had plenty of money, before he died?" he'd asked.

Her swollen lip had curled. "Sometimes. Not lately. And he spent every cent as quick as he got it."

He recognized from knowing Louis the come and go cycle regarding the possession of money. Steal some, spend it, then go steal some more. But nothing here showed the amount missing.

Thanking her for supper, he went out to the barn and spread his bedroll on a spot fairly clean of mouse droppings and dust. Tomorrow, ran his last thoughts of the night, he'd fix up a corner where he'd be more comfortable. How was he to know she'd used nearly all her meager supply of food to give him a real supper?

———

HEART STOOD in the dark little nook that served as a pantry and felt along the single shelf in case she'd missed anything.

Nope. Empty as a hay loft in May.

Last night Boone Tingley had complimented the beans and bread, making her feel almost happy, just for a moment. He was an attractive man, she thought. So different from Beaver. Boone talked to her as if...as if...well, she didn't really know. Maybe as if she could talk back?

Sighing, she turned to the flour bin and scooped every

last puff into the bread bowl. It would have to do. But this was it. She had a decision to make. During the afternoon she simmered, mixed, kneaded, chopped and baked, and put one last respectable rabbit stew on the table with pride. Only after Boone left, did she put her head down and bawl for all of five minutes.

"Oh, what a tangled web..." she moaned, and sat up to dry her eyes. After a while, she heated water, washed dishes, and generally tidied the room. Then, slipping outside, she sat on the back steps and watched in the dark until the lantern Boone had lit in the barn went dark.

Crickets chirped, the cows in the corral stirred and murmured, and off in the distance, an owl hooted as it hunted for its supper. A breeze blew clouds scudding across a starlit sky. In the hills north, where the river ran between steep rocky banks, coyotes cried like crazed, grieving women.

Heart shuddered, disliking that particular noise.

Now.

Carefully, making certain her movements were silent, she pulled aside two of the eight-inch boards that provided a skirt to stop skunks, raccoons, and various other critters from taking up residence under the steps. Reaching through, she dragged out the old pillowcase hidden there. One she'd deliberately dirtied to disguise its color. She replaced the boards, then, careful to prevent any noise, she took the pillowcase inside, to the bedroom where she slept on a thin mattress laid on the floor. She had no bedstead. Beaver had had one, but she hadn't ever been able to sleep in the same bed where he had slept. It remained unused in the other bedroom.

Lighting a candle, she set it on the floor and opened first the pillowcase, then the drawstring on the Exchange National Bank of Spokane bag. Sighing, she began making stacks of twenty-dollar gold pieces until she counted out ten thousand dollars. Well, plus another five coins.

The amount left her breathless. A little lightheaded.

She'd been aware the bag was heavy. Getting it home

from where she'd found it had been genuine labor. No easy task, on foot and lugging it in her arms. But this! Over ten thousand dollars. A fortune.

Quickly, before she changed her mind, she put the gold back—all but one single coin. Finder's fee, she reminded herself. She was entitled to that. She just wouldn't mention it to the sheriff when she saw him tomorrow.

Pausing at the door to listen, she restored the dirty pillowcase to its hiding place under the steps. Sleep did not come easy.

————

IN THE MORNING, she fed Boone her hen's two eggs and the leftover bread. Leaving him to work on the corral, she slipped away unseen and made her way to town. This time she took the canvas pack Beaver had used on his so-called hunting trips—although he never came home with game—to carry her purchases home on her back. She intended to stock up with as much as she could carry. And she'd buy another chicken, too. Or more, if possible, so both she and Boone could have an egg for breakfast. Plans whirled through her head, so many and so fast the walk ended before she was ready.

Daisy Burch, whom she passed at the drug store on her way to the sheriff's office after her shopping spree, didn't bother hiding her surprise at seeing her back in town so soon. "You don't usually make more than one visit to town a week, Heart. You don't mind if I call you Heart, do you?" She went on without waiting for a reply. "I worried all the rest of the day, after I told you about the bear. You know, walking home all by your lonesome. You don't even carry a gun to protect yourself. But I guess you didn't meet up with it after all. Thank goodness!"

"Yes, thank goodness," Heart agreed weakly, barely preventing herself from recounting how Daisy's warning had played out. Mention of events along the deer trail to anybody except the sheriff didn't seem like a good idea. Particularly to someone as chatty as Daisy.

Daisy, being the curious sort, squinted nearsightedly at Heart's face. "At least, those marks don't look like bear scratches. What did happen?"

Heart shrugged. "Nothing much. I stumbled over a loose rock and fell on my face, is all."

"Oh. Well, where are you off to now?" Frowning a little, Daisy pressed on. "I was thinking maybe you'd like to join me at the drug store. We can have a soda. Mr. Avery just added a...a...thing," she faltered, "that makes bubbles. I've been wanting to try one."

Heart loved the idea, but decided to decline. She hadn't the money to pay for luxuries like sodas. Not even with the remains of the twenty-dollar gold piece residing in her pocket. Hard telling how long it would have to last. But what she had left was too dangerous to flaunt. Word might get around.

So, hemming and hawing while putting Daisy off, she spotted the sheriff hurrying out of his office and swinging into the saddle of a bay horse waiting at the hitch rack. A man, his clothing dusty, armpits dark with sweat, followed him out, mouth moving and arms waving. As she watched, the sheriff checked his scabbard to make certain of his rifle and, spurring the horse into a lope, rode away.

Daisy followed her gaze. "Hmm." Her gaze narrowed. "I wonder what set a fire under Sheriff Riker. He doesn't generally like it when people ride their horses too fast and there he is, doing the same thing he preaches against."

"He's headed out of town," Heart said. In plain fact, he'd headed in the direction of the Beaver ranch, and, as far as Heart knew, she was the only resident out that way for several miles.

Her pulse thudded. Did he know about the money? Or about Boone Tingley holed up at her ranch?

She turned to Daisy. "Thank you, Mrs. Burch, for the soda invitation. Maybe another time. I need to get home."

Daisy's mouth turned down. "Oh, please do say you'll join me."

"I'm sorry. I wish I could but...but it'll soon be chore time. I can't be late."

The other woman stared at her. "But you don't have any animals, do you, Mrs. Beaver? I heard—"

Heart interrupted. "I guess you heard wrong. I have some cattle and a horse and...and some chickens." Or at least she'd have chickens when, on the way home, she picked up the two new hens Mrs. Emerson said she'd box up for her.

"Thank you," she repeated, and strode off, walking fast.

She was halfway home, carrying a box containing a complaining red hen in each hand, when she recalled she reverted to being Mrs. Beaver when she turned down Daisy's invitation. Used to being lonely and ignored over this last year as a widow, she still felt a pang of regret.

A pang nothing like the one when she met Sheriff Riker as he rode back toward town. Only this time the pang was fear, not remorse. They met in almost the exact same spot where she'd met the bear family only three days ago. Thinking she'd better start taking a shortcut around this particular bend, Heart stopped when Sheriff Riker turned his horse to block the road.

"Mrs. Beaver." His weather-beaten face was set in stern lines. His mustache, curled upward on the ends like a genuine British dandy, was stiff with wax. "I've been looking for you. Went to your house, but I see you've been to town." He surveyed her burdens. "That's quite a load you're carrying. Must've cost a pretty penny."

"Just about all I have left. I hope it'll keep me until the garden produces." Heart couldn't help herself. She started shaking, first in her hands, then her knees. "You wanted to see me? Whatever for?" She didn't mention she'd seen him ride out of town.

He held up a finger. "Where'd you get those cows and calves I seen in your corral, Mrs. Beaver?"

Heart sucked in a breath. "Found them in the woods. No

brands. I believe cattle without brands are called mavericks, and since they were on my land, I gathered them up and shooed them on home. Didn't want them getting in my garden, you know. I expect they were strays missed by whoever stole the rest of the cattle three years ago. You know, when...when the previous owner..."

"I know what you mean." One bushy eyebrow raised as he ignored her comment about the other cattle being stolen. "Drove them by yourself, did you?"

"Why, yes. I didn't steal them from anyone. I need the money they'll bring." She allowed herself to appear surprised, and angry, he even asked. "But I doubt you rode out here to ask why I've been rounding up cattle."

More the point, why hadn't she said anything about Boone Tingley? Easy answer. *I don't know why.*

"I didn't, you're right about that," Riker said. "First thing is, I came to tell you Boone Tingley has been released from prison. Never know but what he'll show up around here, especially since I got an eyewitness says he's seen Louis Tingley nearby. Seen him in the flesh."

"Not his ghost?" The corner of her mouth quirked upward.

Riker's horse swiveled, wanting to go, but the sheriff held him back. He scowled at her remark. "Not according to the witness. And he's the reliable sort. Second thing is—"

"What?"

"I dug into that grave on the knoll about your place."

Her stomach gave a twist. "And?"

"Well, it isn't Louis Tingley buried there. It Boone's pa."

Heart swallowed. "No love lost between those two, the Tingleys, I guess."

"No." Riker studied her a long moment. "You're sitting on land both of them claimed once upon a time. And your husband came into ownership by a back door. Might not be the best place to be. Best if you came into town and stayed a while. But of the two, Boone is the better man. You see him, you come tell me. You see Louis, you run."

"I don't know what he looks like."

His eyes narrowed. "Boone or Louis?"

Heart cursed her wayward tongue. "Neither one. But sheriff, this is my land now. I don't intend to run from either."

"Do as I tell you. Don't matter which you see, you come tell me." He glared. "You hear?"

"I do hear you." Who could help it?

Message delivered, he rode on, and Heart continued her walk. Evidently Boone had done as he promised—faded from the visitor's sight.

————

BOONE, being far from a fool, had gotten a good deal wiser during his years in Walla Walla State Prison. As soon as he got up in the morning, he rolled his bedding into a tidy bundle and stuffed it in an empty feed barrel, along with his few other accoutrements. A downright search and they'd be found, but a quick glance would miss them. He also saddled Mister, ready to ride off at a moment's notice.

A moment was about all he had, too, when he spotted the sheriff riding toward the house from the main road. He wouldn't have had that long if he hadn't been up on the barn roof searching out the most fragile shingles in need of replacement. Mrs. Beaver—Heart—had worked on the house roof, but not the barn. The sun glancing off Riker's silver star gave a couple minutes of warning. Scrambling down from the roof, he led Mister into the woods mere seconds before Riker rode up to the house and stopped.

Holding Mister's nose to keep him still and quiet, they'd stood and waited, listening.

The sheriff had sat looking around for a full minute, possibly waiting for an invitation—or at least a greeting—before he dismounted, went up to the house and knocked, then, after a wait, set his ear to the door. A moment later, he boldly entered the house. Nervy of him, considering Boone hadn't seen Mrs. Beaver leave. As far as he knew she was inside staying silent in order to avoid the lawman.

He watched, puzzled, Mrs. Beaver being nowhere to be seen or heard. Boone cocked his head. Riker hadn't even called out to ask if anyone was at home.

Several minutes later, Riker exited the house, closing the door behind him. True to Boone's expectations, he walked over to the corral and surveyed the cattle, then went on into the barn. He was gone long enough to have had a good look around, but when he came out, he was carrying a shovel, whereupon he rode up to the knoll and dug around. Soon, shaking his head as if disappointed, he came back down and replaced the shovel.

Boone's mouth curled, glad Mrs. Beaver—Heart—hadn't been in the house, and therefore missed Riker's visit. If asked, she'd almost certainly reveal that he was here, and he didn't want the sheriff to know. Not yet. Not until he'd seen Louis and settled things between them.

Which, he figured, was going to end with one of them dead. He didn't intend for it to be him.

Meanwhile, where had Mrs. Beaver gotten to? *Why didn't she tell me...* Boone put a foot on the thought, metaphorically speaking. She didn't owe him any explanations and he knew it.

But he'd let himself get a little worked up by the time he spotted her trudging up to the house like someone ready to collapse. And no wonder. She was loaded down like a pack mule, including a box in each hand that, according to the complaining clucks, held a chicken. He'd already seen she had only one hen, which meant she'd gone without an egg this morning. The pack on her back bulged with items and looked heavy. Her pale hair straggled over sweaty cheeks, and even the thick braid dangling down her back looked limp. Her dark, dark eyes, on the other hand, flashed with some kind of hot emotion.

Leaving off measuring wire for a new gate latch, he took a careful look around before hurrying over to relieve her of the chickens. She must be strong, he thought, seeing those chickens were plenty weighty. Her strength surprised him because of how fragile she appeared.

Still, her arms shook with the strain.

"How far did you have to carry these birds?" he asked.

"Three miles. All the way from town." She sounded scratchy, as if her mouth were dry.

He held one up, peering through a crack in the lid. The hen's bright beady eyes glared back, looking angry. "Where do you want me to put them? With the other one?"

"No. The woman I got them from said to keep them separate for a while, otherwise these new ones might peck the other one to death."

"They do that?"

She nodded. "So I'm told."

"Ain't that something." Setting the chickens in the shade of the porch, Boone moved behind her. "Wiggle on out of them straps. I'll take the pack. Holy smokes, woman, this is too heavy for you to carry. You need a horse!"

Her sudden smile took him off guard. "You're not telling me anything I don't know, Mr. Tingley. But the poor old creature in the corral is no saddle horse."

Boone glanced over at the workhorse standing hipshot in his favorite spot by the watering trough and grinned. "No, ma'am. That he isn't. Ole Lightning never was much for carrying anybody on his back. Made him itch."

He said the part about itching at the same time as she said, "Makes him itch." Then added, "Lightning?" Her laughter pealed. "Lightning!"

It was the first time he'd seen her so much as smile. But even hearing the old horse's name didn't make her laugh as much as when one the chickens started flapping its wings inside the box, which made the container, complete with screeching bird, go rolling across the porch.

Boone and Heart, both startled, jumped to right the carton. Boone got to it first, but as he did, the porch board under his foot gave way. Stumbling with a boot yanked half off, he thumped down on his behind and gave voice to a yelp that sounded like a howling hound.

Heart's eyes opened wide. "Are you hurt?"

Boone staggered to his feet, reached behind him and, making an odd, jerky motion, looked down at what he held.

Heart looked, too. Then covered her mouth with both hands. Her shoulders shook, only not with fatigue this time.

Oh, no. Not by a long shot. This time she was laughing. With him. At him. But mostly at the sight of a long, sharp splinter with a bloody tip he'd plucked from his rear.

"Sorry," she said, choking up. "It's not funny, really. I'm sure it hurts." She laughed more. "But the look on your face! You did look...er...surprised."

Boone rubbed his offended body part. "Huh. Says you. Surprised ain't what you'd be saying if it was your behind got poked."

Her laughter froze. "Yes. You're right."

She sounded, Boone discovered, as if she were afraid. Of him? Did she think he'd slap her around because she laughed? Well, yeah. He could see she thought exactly that. No shock when he considered it. Although he'd never met the man, Roger Beaver had a reputation when it came to people weaker than him.

He set the box with its squawking chicken upright. "Nah. Go ahead and laugh, but I think this biddy needs to go into solitary confinement." He chuckled a little to show he wasn't serious about the whole thing, relieved when the tension that had frozen her laughter eased. It didn't all disappear, though, for which he was sorry. She'd been pretty with her mouth curving up in laughter.

"There's a screen in the chicken house," she said, barely above a whisper. "I'll put it between them for a couple days. Let them see and get used to each other."

"Need help?"

Her eyes rounded, as if astonished he would offer. "No, thank you. I can do it."

If she could plow a field, which he'd seen her do, he figured setting up the chicken coop was no real test. Nodding, he said, "Then it looks like I'd better fix this porch before somebody breaks their neck."

"Yes." But she didn't move, and neither did he. "I met

Sheriff Riker on the way home," she finally said. "He said he'd been here. Did you talk to him?"

Alarm shot through him. "No. Truth of the matter is, when I saw him coming, I took Mister and we stood off in the timber where he couldn't see us."

"Why don't you want him to see you? You served your time—didn't you?"

"I did. I don't mind talking to him, but not here. My whereabouts is none of his business. I'd just as soon he didn't know you and me have met. Unless…did you tell him?"

She shook her head.

Boone's teeth gritted together. "Good. It ain't fair to have your name mixin' it up with me and him and—"

"Louis, your brother?"

"He's not my brother. He's the offspring of my father's second wife."

Heart frowned. "But his last name is the same as yours."

"No, it's not. He uses it." This was a conversation Boone had no wish to continue. "It ain't something he's entitled to. But Louis has always been good at taking what don't belong to him."

Heart, aware of showing Boone Tingley the very thing she never wanted anyone to know of her former life, was unable to prevent the unease that swept through her. But he didn't smirk, or sneer, or laugh. What he did, to her complete astonishment, was help her get beyond the awkwardness. But, as he carried the heavy packsack into the house and she went to fix the screen in the chicken coop, she couldn't help wondering if he simply put on a show.

Beaver used to do that once he vented his rage. Until the next time something she did put him crossways.

She made plans as she got the chickens all straightened out. Come nighttime, she'd bar the doors and keep the pistol under her pillow. For a while, anyway, until she was sure—

Sure of what? she asked herself. Sure he didn't have nefarious designs on her? *Nefarious designs! Hah. Laughable.* She'd read those words in a book one time and they caught her fancy. But plain old Heart Beaver (and how she hated the name) wouldn't be of interest to any man. Beaver had made sure she knew as much, every day. Let her know she was stupid, freakish with her dark eyes and almost white hair, and unworthy of any man. It made sense the only reason Boone stayed on here, aside from the fact he used to own the place—and possibly still should—was because he knew about the money. Oh, not that she'd found it. Only that it was here, somewhere.

Ignoring an attempt by one of the new chickens to peck her, she lifted the creature out of the box and set it free within the enclosure. Another thought came to plague her.

Was it the money Boone sought? Or his brother—not brother?

Boone had set her pack on the table, a clumsy affair that had been missing a leg since Beaver shoved her into it and broke the already dilapidated old thing. She'd mended the leg, more or less, by splinting it with a broken tree limb. The table wobbled now, but at least it was a place to eat.

Speaking of eating, Heart took pride in loading the supplies on the almost empty pantry shelves and beginning supper. A treat. Beef, and safe this time from the bear.

A pattern emerged over the next few days. The seeds Heart had planted sprouted from the soil in short order. So did weeds, which she hacked with the hoe Boone sharpened for her. She made a couple more trips to town and, a little at a time, added to her supplies. By now the pilfered double eagle was nearly spent.

As for Boone—well, Boone lay low, staring off at the hills, the nearby woods, even traipsing down to the river that lay a scant quarter mile from the house. Otherwise, he spent hours fixing items in need of repair around the buildings. Sometimes he asked for her help, and they talked. As if they were a man and a woman who liked each other.

Once, just once, when they'd been placing a heavy four-by-four beam under the sagging corner of the barn, they'd come together, faces touching. Her lips had parted, wanting to seek his. Wanting to feel his mouth on hers. Blood had pulsed through her veins. Heavy. Hot. He'd turned to face her, eager, knowing, wanting the same. And—

The beam slipped, tearing them apart at that first butterfly touch.

"Not now," he'd whispered. "Not yet."

She hadn't known what he meant by that. She only knew regret. And embarrassment because of the regret.

He didn't say anything to her, but she knew he was watching and waiting for Louis to show himself. She suspected he was using her as bait, expecting Louis to make contact with her although he never said why.

Neither of them ever mentioned the money. Boone, perhaps because he didn't figure she knew anything about it, and Heart because she wanted to keep it that way.

As for Sheriff Riker, he didn't show himself at the house, but she thought he might be nearby. Boone took to making his rounds of the area on Mister, once in the morning and again at night. He didn't say anything to Heart. She imagined he looked for the money every time he went riding. It crossed her mind to wonder how he managed to avoid the sheriff.

Or if he did.

Then, one day as rain clouds blew in from the north, the sheriff dropped by yet again. He sat his horse, looking over the repairs Boone had made to the corral and its occupants of cows and calves. Then there was the neatly swept porch, the door solid in a frame sporting real hinges. His gaze settled first on the house roof, then the barn, both bearing shingles of a different color than the old sun-faded ones.

He pointed up at the house's roof. "You do that, Mrs. Beaver?" His frown seemed suspicious.

"Of course. Why not?" Heart, who'd come outside to greet him, pushed errant strands of pale hair behind her ear and presented her most innocent face. "I'm able to wield a hammer as well as anyone. Better," she added, "than Beaver used to do."

"I don't doubt but what you do." Riker's eyes shifted to the corral where the cattle, fatter than they'd been when foraging through the woods, nosed the ground looking for graze.

Boone turned them into the meadow every evening just before dark. Mister kept them in line and got them back in the corral with little effort. A treat to watch the horse work, or so Heart thought, until she noticed the sheriff studying the ground.

"These tracks," he said. "You got a horse I don't know about? Besides that worn-out old plug?" He meant Lightning, standing hipshot with his eyes half closed, a wisp of grass hanging from his lips.

Before she could question her wisdom in answering him at all, she said, her surprise clear. "Is it any business of yours?"

He had the grace to turn red. Could be he took that to mean she was having some of those *nefarious activities*.

Hah, she thought. Let him. Heart didn't mind. Even if she were, what she did was none of the sheriff's business. Nor anyone else's, come to think of it. Besides, although she sometimes saw Boone watching her, he hadn't tried to touch her. Not since that one day.

And how she felt about the lack was hard to explain, even to herself. Excitement still shook her when she let herself think of it. She'd wanted his touch. Still did.

"Only if you got somebody here who shouldn't be," Riker said, confusing her for a moment. "With your husband dead, it's my job to keep you safe, Mrs. Beaver. You and every other citizen of this county."

Coolly, she gazed up at him where he sat his horse. "A sudden decision?" She looked him in the eye. "Strange, the way you've been coming around here the past couple weeks. You hadn't shown any concern before. What is the difference between now and the whole of last year?"

Heart hoped the sheriff wouldn't have an apoplectic fit.

The way his face colored and he started blowing like a winded horse, she had to wonder. Her chin lifted. Nevertheless, she had every right to ask.

After a minute—maybe less—he dismounted. "We need to have a little talk," he said as she stepped back. "Maybe you'd be so kind as to fetch me a drink of water first?"

What else could she do. "Of course." She hesitated. "Come in. I don't have much in the way of furniture but there is a stool."

As a matter of fact, there were two. One for each as Heart took a tin mug from her shelf and dipped water into it. She put the mug in front of the sheriff, who perched awkwardly on one of the stools and chugged the water.

She sat, too, hands folded demurely in her lap in front of her, waiting for him to speak. When she remained quiet, the sheriff was forced to open the conversation.

Riker thumped the mug onto the table. "Boone Tingley been around?"

"Is there any reason he should—or should not be?" Heart countered.

"He is a convict, you know. A dangerous man."

"I was told he served his time and is free. Is this true?" She knew it was.

"Yes." Agreement seemed drawn from him. "But—"

"Has he done something he shouldn't?"

Riker huffed. "Not that I know of."

"Well then."

"Well then?"

She shrugged. "I'm told it's a free country."

The sheriff switched direction. "Any sign of Louis Tingley?"

Heart shook her head and started to rise. "I wouldn't know him if I saw him. He never, that I know of, came around when Beaver was alive. Now, if that is all—"

Riker waved her back. "You've taken against me, Mrs. Beaver. I don't know why. But there is one more thing you should know."

Blood pulsed in Heart's veins. Something bad, she'd be bound. "Which is?"

"Last year, when your husband drowned." He hesitated. "It wasn't an accident, like I told you then. Like I thought it was. It was murder."

"Murder?" A question, barely audible. "You're just now telling me?"

"Didn't want to worry you."

Heart twitched. *Liar.* "Why would anybody murder him? Who did it?"

"I don't know. I'm investigating." His eyes were cold.

"Are you?" She cleared her throat and shook her head. "Then why are you looking at Boone Tingley? He was in prison."

"True enough, he was." He had more to say, a lot more, and although she heard him and absorbed his words, it all seemed distant and far away. Silent, head down, she pondered. But she wasn't shocked, even if the sheriff thought she was. Actually, all this time, she'd suspected as much. Beaver had been a man to make enemies.

Sheriff Riker rose. "The evidence don't mean Tingley's innocent. Boone might know something about your man's murder. Him and his brother might be in cahoots."

"Cahoots? Over Beaver? Why?"

"No need for you to know. But you best beware, Mrs. Beaver. Neither of those men are safe."

Heart didn't see Sheriff Riker as providing any sort of safety either. Not to her. She didn't trust him any further than she trusted the Tingley men, not even Boone as much as she wanted to. Why? Because, as Heart noted, neither said a word about any missing money. And that, she felt sure, was the only reason Boone was interested in staying around. The same with Louis. And why the sheriff was, too.

"Ho, mama cow. Get back to the family." Boone nudged Mister after the recalcitrant cow, pushing through a cluster of bushes and glad of an old pair of chaps he'd found wadded up in a corner of the barn. He and the horse were gathering the cattle to herd into the corral for the night. He reined Mister to a stop fast enough to set the horse on his haunches.

"What's this?" On a hunch, he called out, "Louis? You here?"

No answer.

He'd been expecting something like this. *This* being the remains of a small fire, the smell of smoke recent enough to linger under the pines. The tracks of a single horse showed where it had stood for some time after the rain stopped.

His blood turned cold.

The tracks, Boone figured, could've belonged to anybody's horse. The design of rocks surrounding the fire were what convinced him his stepbrother Louis was making himself known. The arrangement of rocks was a twin to the one Boone had used around his own campfire. It could only have been learned from Howard Tingley. *Pa.* Louis had depended on Boone to find it. He probably sat higher on the hill, watching him and Heart, and figuring to give Boone a case of the nerves. He had before, years ago. If so, he was mistaken this time. Boone was not the same man who'd entered prison three years ago. The wait was over.

And Louis, he vowed, was going to be disappointed.

But for now, as if he hadn't noticed anything wrong, Boone put Mister back to working the cattle as he tried to pinpoint the most logical area for Louis to take cover.

He'd fixed on a clearing on the hill facing the house when he spotted movement. "Got you," he muttered, a plan already forming to confront Louis. Move in on him unexpected-like and get the truth out of him. Louis liked to brag. What happened then depended on Louis and which one of them walked away alive. If either did.

He'd have to move soon, he reckoned. Louis would've seen Riker's visit with Mrs. Beaver. *With Heart.* Boone had taken to calling her Heart in his head. She disliked the name

Beaver, and with what she'd let drop regarding her husband, so did he. The man and his name.

Boone did, however, like Heart. Something about her attracted him like a bee to honey. And there'd been times he'd seen her looking at him, her dark eyes big and soft, when he'd done something, said something, to please her.

He liked to please her. He'd like to please her more. Boone often found himself wishing he'd kissed her that day under the beam. Her lips full and pillowy, those dark eyes showing she wanted his kiss. But he hadn't, well, a touch only. The time wasn't right. Not until—or if—he settled with Louis.

Riker was bound to find out Boone had been staying here pretty much all along. Could be he and Heart should just come right out with it. They weren't doing anything wrong. Not in anybody's eyes.

When the cattle were penned, he'd talk to her. See what Riker'd said to her—if she'd talk to him. And warn her about Louis's proximity.

———

ON FINE NIGHTS, Heart and Boone had taken to sitting on the porch steps. Heart liked the outdoors, looking away from the poverty of a run-down old house, to where she could pretend worries over her next meal didn't exist.

Boone liked the freedom. The elbow room. Where he finally felt he could breathe. Until his release from prison, he hadn't quite realized how the stench, the noise, and the brutality had suffocated him. Nor how his pent-up anger at being convicted of Louis's crimes had changed him.

On this particular night, they watched the stars from the porch. Boone talked some about prison, about Bully, the guard, about Louis—and he worked in mention of Sheriff Riker.

Heart talked a little about Beaver. Not much. As anyone could see, speaking of her guardian—a cousin of her mother and his wife—who'd pawned her and her inheritance to

Beaver to settle the cousin's gambling debt, caused a great deal of pain.

If she'd only known, Boone had been able to see every bit of that pain and rage reflected in the dark depths of her eyes.

Just as she could read in the hardened lines of Boone's face how he'd suffered the degradation of prison.

But first he told the story of Louis Bedecker and how he'd stolen Boone's birthright.

"His mother—Louis's mother," he began. Crickets chirped from under the newly repaired porch steps, loud in the soft night air. He leaned back with his elbows on the stair above him and stared upward at the stars. "She entranced my father. My mother had only been dead six months when he met Eva May Bedecker. It took her no time at all to marry him and bring her son into our house. Didn't take Louis, being a handsome boy with a wide smile, any longer to become his favorite. Pa told me once it was hard for him to look at me. I reminded him too much of my mother. Could be it made him feel guilty."

Heart gave a muffled gasp and reached out to take his hand.

"The little ba...brat could do anything," Boone went on after a moment. He wrapped his fingers around hers. "Steal from other boys. Rustle cattle. Play fast and loose with the girls. Got one in trouble when he was sixteen and she fourteen. All Eva May had to do was weep crocodile tears, give my pa a long passionate kiss, and Louis's 'missteps' would be paid off or forgiven." He paused. "Or the blame put on me. He...they were good at that."

Boone looked down at her. "He's done the same blamed thing right up until this day and getting away with it. But it ends here. Sheriff Riker knows different—finally. Says he does, anyway." He shrugged. "Unless he thinks I'll confess to whatever Louis's latest crimes might be."

"You don't know?"

"No." He drew in a breath. "But I know he's here and he must have a reason. So you, Heart, had better watch out. The good Lord only knows what he's up to. I'd hate to see you taken in by him, too."

She smiled a little. "I'm forewarned. Believe me, Boone, I've heard enough about him to know he's a lot like Beaver was." Her voice hardened. "And there's nothing I loathe more than men like him."

Boone sighed a little. "Unless his passionate kisses work like his ma's did."

Heart tilted her head toward him. "He'd never get that close."

"Would any man?" Boone couldn't believe he'd said that.

And then she said, "I don't know. I guess any other man would have to try and we'd see."

So Boone, being any other man, tried it. And they saw.

————————

HEART HAD BEEN STANDING over the stove with her back turned to the door, sprinkling cubes of beef with salt as they splattered and browned in bacon fat. The first she knew of having company was when he said, "Time you and me was introduced, I believe."

Startled out of her wits, the battered tin salt shaker flew upward, scattering the contents across the floor.

Spilled salt. The thought shot through her mind. *Bad luck.*

She knew who he was the second she spun and saw him. Or at least she made an accurate assumption. He terrified her on sight. Not because he was ugly or rough looking, but because he was handsome in a smarmy kind of way—and smooth. After everything she'd heard about him, it just made sense. And because, being something of an expert, she glimpsed pure meanness beneath his smiling exterior.

Louis Tingley didn't look a thing like Boone. But of course, why would he? Boone had said he was no relation. Just someone who'd stolen the Tingley name.

Heart bent, picked up the shaker and, taking a pinch between her fingers, tossed the salt over her left shoulder. She may have followed instruction on how to blind the devil and prevent evil, but she was very much afraid it was too late.

"Did you knock?" Her voice was enough to put frost on the windows. *Where, oh where, is my doggone pistol when I need it?*

"Sorry." He smirked. "Old habit. I'm not accustomed to knocking before entering my own house."

"Except it's not your house and, I'm given to understand, never was. Now it's mine."

His eyebrows lifted. "Is it? So what are going to do about it?" It sounded like a dare, one she didn't take up.

"Go away," she said. "You're not welcome here."

"What? Roger always said I had a standing invitation. Are you saying different?"

She said nothing and he sniggered. "I didn't think so. Sit down, woman. We'll wait for Boone. I see him coming in every evening for supper. You and me together'll give him a nice surprise."

Surprise, maybe, but Heart knew it wouldn't be anywhere near nice.

Heart sat, but only after she put water in with the meat and onions and got the stew to simmering. He watched her, going so far as to confiscate her paring knife when she was done. He sat trimming his fingernails with the knife, dulling the blade.

An hour passed. Two. Darkness filled the room, and he lit the lamp.

"From a distance I thought you was an old woman," Louis said. He'd become impatient, walking around the room, pawing in boxes, going through the pantry, even looking through the ragbag where she'd been saving up scraps in order to braid a rug. Although, since the clothes she wore had to do for a very long time, the rug-making was still in the distant future.

Or maybe, she thought, never. She didn't like the way he looked at her. As if he were judging a horse before buying.

When she neglected to reply, he came to stand in front of her. "Your hair. It looked white from where I was, up on the hill. But it ain't. You ain't old, after all. Sure do look strange with them dark eyes, though. Bet men would pay a good price to have a piece of you. You know anything about that?"

Fury rose up in her. She said nothing.

He laughed. "Got a nice body on you. I heard you was stupid. Nobody told me you was a looker."

He reached out to touch her and Heart lunged backward so far, so fast, she almost fell off the stool.

He laughed harder. And that's when they heard the knock on the door.

Louis lifted a rather large pistol from the holster dragging at his hip and licked his lips. "Finally," he said. "Tell him to come in."

Heart froze for a moment, seeing the gun. Her mouth opened, thoroughly frightened by now and ready to obey, only to discover her voice had a mind of its own. "Go away," she yelled instead. "Run!"

Louis's fist slamming into the side of her face knocked her to the floor. "Stupid..." The name he called her was one she'd never heard before. Her vision blurred and her tailbone, jarred from the harsh landing, sent a stab of pain up her spine.

Louis's tantrum lasted plenty long enough to allow Boone to charge inside with his gun drawn. Although he didn't fire, his expression showed he wanted to. "Drop the gun, Louis, and step away from Mrs. Beaver."

Dumbly, Heart looked up at him, although he didn't spare her a glance. But then, how could he?

Louis ignored the demand to drop his gun, though he did take a step away from her. The step took him closer to Boone.

"Where is it?" Louis roared. "Where is my money?"

"How should I know?" Boone roared right back. "I've been in prison for the last three years. Where you should've been, not me."

"You must have it. They said you had it."

"Who said?"

"Jerry. Rog. Well, Jerry wouldn't say so I killed him right off. But Rog said so. He swore." Louis blustered as he admitted to murder.

Heart gaped at him. "Rog?" she quavered. "You mean my husband, Roger Beaver?"

"Yeah, yeah." Louis whirled on her. "He had it, didn't he? If Boone don't then Rog must've, after all. And he told you where it is, didn't he?" Lunging toward her, his voice rose higher. "Didn't he?"

She scrambled backward, shoe heels propelling her on the floor. "No," she said. "I didn't...I don't know anything about any money. We were poor. Always poor."

He eyed her as if she were an idiot. "Well, of course. We couldn't spend it right away. People would've noticed. Then he turned on me. Wouldn't tell me where it was when I needed my share."

Boone stepped toward his stepbrother, pistol trained at Louis's chest. To Heart, he looked as if he were fighting himself not to pull the trigger. She shifted her attention back to Louis, slowly rising to her feet when she thought he wouldn't knock her down again.

"So you killed him, too, didn't you?" She put the table between them, fragile protection though it might be. "Drowned him when he was drunk. The sheriff said—" Breaking off, she glanced at Boone. "My husband was often drunk." Better not to bring Riker into it.

Louis, looking a bit rueful, nodded. "Lost my temper. He was dead before I realized."

"Well," she said. "Isn't that too bad." Limping, she edged around the table to stand behind Boone, making certain to stay out of his way should he have to defend himself. What did he intend to do with his stepbrother? Seemed to her they were at an impasse, or as if Boone was waiting for—

The idea no more than touched her mind than the door slammed open yet again, one of the recently repaired hinges giving way. Sheriff Riker, with a deputy at his shoulder, shoved his way inside.

Finally.

"Louis Bedecker..." Riker announced and got no further as Louis raised his gun and without hesitation, fanned the hammer, firing at the sheriff, again at the deputy, another time just any old place his pistol happened to point. One being her. Another being Boone.

Really, Heart took it for granted when the sheriff, prepared for the action, shot Louis down like a mad dog, right then and there. She let out a little screech; Boone jerked as a final bullet from Louis's pistol grazed his arm. The sheriff and his deputy both shouted curses. Then it was over. The men moved to look down at Louis's body.

"Dead?" the deputy asked, untouched by Louis's spray of bullets.

"Looks as if," Riker said. He prodded Louis's body with the toe of his boot. "It don't much matter. Louis was a bad, bad man. We heard him confess to the robbery, plus two murders, but doggone it, he didn't know where the money is either. After all this time, I reckon nobody does."

Heart, with blood rising hot in her cheeks, believed it was a good thing Riker wasn't looking at her just then. She was glad to rush to Boone, crying something, she didn't even know what, and fling herself into his arms.

Boone, having holstered his unfired gun, gathered her close in the crook of one arm. "You all right, Heart? I'm sorry we didn't get here sooner." His concerned gaze took her in. "You're gonna have a bruise. And a black eye."

She nodded, reluctant to admit it wouldn't be the first time a violent man had given her a black eye. But maybe, this once, worth it, to have Boone hold her as if he cared.

————

EARLIER, when Riker stopped him just short of the ranch yard, Boone had been tempted to ignore the sheriff's motion to stop. He felt a need to see Heart. Make sure she was safe. Riker made that difficult, dismounting and taking hold of Mister's bit.

"Gonna have us a little confab," he said. "This is where we both gotta hold to the plan."

Riker was one tough lawman. Boone stepped down to stand beside him.

"Buck," the sheriff motioned his deputy forward, "you run those cows on into the pen. Stay out of sight from the house."

The deputy nodded, leaving Riker and Boone to it.

"Louis is already inside the house," Riker said. "He's been there a while."

"In the house? You didn't try to stop him?" Angry now, Boone made a motion as if to storm the building.

Riker held him back. "Not so fast. Haven't heard any gun shots or screaming so I figure Mrs. Beaver is all right. We need to handle this like we talked about."

"I've had enough talk." Boone's rage unfurled inside him. Louis up to tricks and Riker hadn't stopped him? "I don't want Mrs. Beaver getting hurt. She ain't done anything to deserve it."

Riker stared at him, maybe questioning his motive. "I don't want to see her hurt either. But be careful what you say, or he might just shoot you." The sheriff's face wore a worried expression. Even his mustache seemed to droop. "Course, he might just on general principals. Make sure you leave the door open enough for me and Buck to hear what he's got to say. Draw him out. He has to confess, and we need to witness what he says."

Boone nodded and moved restlessly. "Yessir. I know. I've been waiting three years for this." Even, he admitted to himself, if the process hadn't quite kept to the original plan. Especially regarding Heart. He hadn't planned on caring for her.

Riker shook his head. "I know you have. We get him on this, it'll wipe your slate clean." He aimed a piercing glare at Boone. "You toe the mark. You've waited this long. You bust in there and start shooting, I might have to throw you back in jail."

Not for the first time, a measure of doubt rose in Boone. He knew Riker would follow up on his threat. But it wasn't so easy to make a prison sentence disappear from the books. Or from people's memories. He wasn't any too sure Riker had that kind of clout. Best he could hope for was the possibility it would remove any doubts Heart—and the townsfolk—had about him. Any fear she might harbor. That was most important to him.

So that's how he happened to stand between Louis Bedecker, aka Louis Tingley, and view the death of his nemesis as though from a distance.

Until he happened to glance at Heart. And he took a wild guess where the money she'd used to buy food had come from.

HEART WATCHED, her vision blurring. Her hearing faded in and out, leaving her to wonder if the jar to her backside had addled something in her head. Right up until common sense told her the roar of gunshots in a closed room was the cause. Or was it something else?

Riker and his deputy's every action took ages to accomplish. She thought they'd never get done sifting through Louis's pockets—and finding nothing—then waiting until the deputy backtracked him and found his camp and horse, and brought everything to the sheriff to catalog.

Like some sort of mechanical doll, she set the stew to the cool part of the stove so it wouldn't scorch, all the while closing herself off from the sight and smell of death.

It could've been Boone, lying still on the floor, his blood spreading, his face frozen in death.

If I had just given the money to Riker in the first place, this wouldn't have happened.

If I had given the money to Louis when he demanded it, this wouldn't have happened.

Boone could've been killed.

Riker and his deputy could've been killed. Even me.

My fault. All my fault.

And still she couldn't bring herself to confess she'd found the money.

The thoughts ran through her mind over and over. Boone wouldn't even let her bandage his arm when she tried.

"It's nothing much," he said.

She longed to touch him. Why wouldn't he let her?

At last, Riker and the deputy loaded the body onto his horse, and they trailed off toward town.

"I'll be around, Tingley. Don't go anywhere," the sheriff told Boone, who nodded. And to Heart, he said, "Sorry for all this, Mrs. Beaver. But it's over now."

Was it?

The bag of coins weighed at her. She wanted the money. The money wasn't hers. Heart's conscience wavered back and forth.

And the way Boone looked at her with a question in his eyes. It felt as if he was waiting for her to do...well, something. But what? He couldn't know she'd found the money. The cause of all his trouble. The cause of two...no, three...deaths.

Could he?

Heart used every rag from her ragbag to mop the blood and other matter from the floor. When she'd done the best clean-up job possible, Boone took the bundle of rags from her. "I'll take these out and bury them."

She looked up at him, wondering at his cool regard. Hadn't she seen something more there, earlier? Had he put on an act until they'd taken care of Louis?

"Thank you," she said. "Boone, you should let me—"

"I'm fine." He hurried out with the bundled rags before she could even finish her sentence.

While he was gone, she set out spoons and bowls and set the pot of stew on the table. Pretending all was well is what she was doing. Fooling herself. Trying, anyway. She wasn't sure he'd be back.

It was full dark now, and she went out onto the back steps to savor the fresher air of the outdoors while stubbornly, she waited for Boone to return. Out to where the

Exchange National Bank of Spokane bag sat hidden behind the steps. Then, like the need to scratch an itch, an overwhelming urge made her remove the boards and grab hold of the bag, dragging it out and dropping it with a thump and a clatter. Sitting again, her head bowed into her hands.

"It's dirty money, Heart." Boone's voice came out of the dark. "You don't want it. It'll be too heavy for your conscience to bear. Weigh you down until you can't rise up again."

Heart froze, her eyes squeezing shut. "I know," she said after a while. Her heartbeat heavy and sad in her chest. He'd despise her now. And she'd deserve his disgust. But he'd come back.

He stepped into the light spilling from the open door and sat on the steps beside her.

"I was hungry," she said, "the day I found it." The story of the bear, of scant rations, of just plain being so poor she couldn't even feed the old workhorse a proper bait of oats poured out. "I didn't spend it, you know. Except for the one double eagle. And I've got some of that left." Unable to look at him, she stared down at the bank bag laying at her feet, hands twisting in her lap. "I'll pay it back, soon as I can."

"There'll probably be a reward," Boone said gravely. "That'll help some. Until we get on our feet with this place. These cows and calves I rounded up. They're a start."

Heart didn't consciously hear the part about cows and calves. She was stuck on *we* and *our*.

"On *our* feet?" Was that her voice, all quavery and almost inaudible?

He reached for her restless hands, stilling them with his own, calloused and a little rough. "You and me, we could do this together."

A huge sigh shook her whole frame. "This place. It should belong to you. They took it from you. They took everything from you."

"They did. Can't go back, though. What's done is done." So he said, but anger still showed through.

Heart made as if to rise. "It should be yours," she

repeated. "I'll take the money to Riker tomorrow and then I'll leave." Just thinking about putting things right eased her. But why then, didn't she feel better.

"And go where?" He pulled her back down beside him and put his arm around her.

Heart's mind went blank. She had nowhere else. There must be something she could do, though. She'd figure it out. As soon has he moved his arm, warm and heavy, from around her shoulders.

But Boone tilted her head up with a forefinger under her chin and looked into her eyes. His mouth came down on hers, first soft, then firm, then...then as if he wanted more. And after a breathless while, he came up for air long enough to whisper something about her being a regular reformed outlaw and that he had a question for her.

"What?" Heart could barely breathe.

He whispered again, his mouth right up against her ear.

"Yes." She shivered with delight. "Oh, yes." Joy flooded over her. They'd figure out the rest later. Right after another of those kisses.

Irish Kelly and the Heartbreak Kid

Sharon Sala

I dedicate this story to Bobby, the cowboy who loved me.

Chapter One

Southwest Texas: 1890

IRISH KELLY STOOD SIX FEET FOUR, WITHOUT HIS BOOTS. AT thirty years of age, he was broad in the shoulders, whip thin, and poker-faced, with a voice so deep that when he yelled, his ranch hands felt the echo in their chests.

Zephyr Bloom, his widowed aunt, was the only mother he'd ever known. Together, they ran the Shamrock Ranch outside of Delphi, Texas, and it was said that Irish came by his demeanor honestly. Even at the age of seventy-three, Zee Bloom was still a law unto herself.

They raised cattle and kept a big string of horses for the ranch. Longhorns were Irish's passion. Zee's passion was horses, and she had a weakness for flash—for horses prettier than the people who owned them. And the day she bought the big Dun, her eye for flash became Irish Kelly's Waterloo.

———

IT WAS MID-JUNE, which meant miserable heat, and dry as a drunk's mouth thirsting for a shot. The sun had already bored a hole through the day, bringing a lazy wind with it when Irish and Zee went down to the corral. The powder-dry dirt stirring restlessly beneath their feet was as loose as the fancy women in the Delphi Saloon.

They'd gone down to see the Dun.

At this point, the horse had been on the ranch for more than five weeks now, and was magnificent in every way. All it needed was to be broke to ride, but it turned out, that had become easier said than done.

Irish had tried to ride him first, and afterward, couldn't stand up straight for a week.

Billy Riley tried next, and was still on crutches.

Jake Ambrose's left arm was in a sling.

Liam Brownley was still walking with a limp.

After five straight weeks of broken bones and egos, the score was four to zero—in favor of the Dun. The Dun was mean as a snake, and so averse to human presence that no one could even get close to him now.

Zee was upset.

Irish was frustrated beyond words.

Five weeks, three hands out for the count, and they were right back where they'd started on the day the horse was delivered—at the corral, staring in silence at the Dun.

The Dun was motionless, covered in sweat and dust, and staring back. Its ears were laid back, head up, nostrils flared. They'd challenged him, and the challenge had been met.

Zee glanced up at her nephew, then back at the horse. She couldn't read either of them. But after her confession last night, he was almost as angry as the Dun. For a man who prided himself in never failing to deliver, finding out she'd sent for some hotshot bronc buster named Hank Doyle, had been an insult to his manhood.

He'd argued.

She'd shrugged.

And the resentment was still on his face.

The harshness of ranch life had yet to chip away at the stubborn jut of her nephew's chin, or the classic cut to his features. He was a fine man who needed someone to make him laugh. Someone to love. Someone to be his backup when she was gone.

Her face reflected every hot day of her life in this land. All the months without rain. She was old and it showed, and today she was as frustrated with the Dun as she was with her nephew, who'd already proven he was as unbreakable as that horse.

Her last try at finding him a wife ended the year he turned twenty. She'd been so sure the tall, leggy blonde who'd come with her father to buy a new horse, was 'the one', but she'd been wrong, and he'd never let her forget it.

———

HER NAME WAS PENELOPE—PRETTY, witty, with a tendency to giggle. She was a shameless flirt with a slight overbite, but it was obvious from the start that Irish wasn't sold. After two hours of enduring their presence, he quietly told Zee that the woman didn't have the sense God gave a goose.

Zee still held out hope when Irish took Penelope and her father out riding, trying first one horse, and then another, trying to decide which one she wanted.

When she finally announced her choice of horse on the basis that its mane and forelock were the same color as her hair, and that the mane was long enough to braid, Irish handed them over to Zee to finalize the sale, but not before giving Zee 'that look'.

That night at supper, Irish laid down the law.

"Aunt Zee, I honor and cherish the ground you walk on, but don't ever do this to me again. I would rather die in my bed alone, than be tied to a self-centered vamp with a brain the size of a walnut. I love you like the mother I don't remember, and I would lay down my life for you without thought, but not for that. I'll pick out my own woman, or do without."

That was the night Zee saw the man he had become.

It didn't mean she'd given up hoping, but in that moment, she gave up interfering.

———

AND NOW HERE THEY WERE.

Stymied by a horse as hardheaded as the man who owned him, and on this morning, they'd come to the corral together, because Zee wanted to tell the horse what was about to happen.

Irish thought it ridiculous of Zee's need to inform a horse of anything, but he didn't laugh. Zephyr Bloom had her quirks. Instead, he steadied her as she climbed to the top rail of the corral.

The Dun's head came up as he snorted disapproval.

Zee raised her voice.

"You, sir, need to know your previous behavior is unacceptable. You also need to know that someone's coming to teach you manners, since you seem to be unable to do that on your own. You should also know, that as the grown male you are, you are entirely too old to be acting like this."

Irish grinned. He'd gotten the same speech on his sixteenth birthday. It was the first and last time he'd been drunk.

The Dun snorted again.

"You heard me," Zee said, then reached behind her. "Help me down, Irish."

When he grabbed her by the waist, he gave her a spin before putting her down.

She laughed aloud.

Irish was still grinning when he looked up to see a faint plume of dust rising over the hill. At first, he thought it was just another dust devil, but the longer he looked, the larger the plume grew.

"Someone's coming, Aunt Zee."

She turned to look. "It'll be Hank Doyle."

He arched an eyebrow. "And you can tell that by the shape of the dust?"

When Zee ignored him, he kept watching the dust trail, rising higher into the air.

THROUGH NO CHOICES of her own, Hannah Doyle was a nomad.

A single woman of twenty-three years, an old maid by territory standards, and for the last six years, considered a wild and shameful woman to be roaming the territory on her own. She'd had no family other than her grandfather, Peter Doyle. And after his sudden and unexpected death, it became painfully apparent what life had to offer a young girl alone. She could sleep with men for money, or marry one, and she'd rebelled on both choices, simply because she had yet to find a man she could trust. So, she rejected that life and its rules, and chose to live by her own.

She packed away Hannah and her dresses, put on her grandpa's pants and became Hank. Then she began earning her living from the skill she'd been born with, and took off across the territory, breaking horses to ride, while living in her grandfather's *vardo*, the only home she'd ever known.

The *vardo* was a small, but ornately decorated Romany wagon, pulled by a large, cantankerous mule by the name of Lefty. It housed a tiny cast iron stove, with a stovepipe that went up through the roof, a bed at the far end of the wagon with a mattress stuffed with sweet grass and goose down, and a pile of ancient quilts for covers on the long winter nights.

A tiny cupboard hung on one wall, and below it, a small table with a tin basin and a pewter ewer for bathing. The storage area below the bed was for clothes and valuables, and her rifle was—at all times—either on the floor by her bed at night, or beside her on the wagon seat during the day.

A big yellow dog named Pup was Hannah's companion by day and her sleeping buddy at night. She hunted for rabbits with Pup at her heels, and when she had coin, purchased dry beans and hardtack, and now and then, a bag of salt and a bag of ground coffee as she'd pass through a town.

She'd been breaking a string of horses for a rancher south of Austin for more than two months and was at the end of the job, when she received a telegram requesting her presence at the Shamrock Ranch, south of Delphi. Two days later, she was on the road. It took five days to get to Delphi, and upon her arrival, she sent a telegram to the ranch, confirming her arrival. Then she spent her first day in Delphi while the farrier reshod Lefty, and she restocked her supplies.

She left town the next morning before daybreak, with directions to drive nine miles south, following the road out of town. It would take her to the headquarters of the Shamrock Ranch.

The sun came up on her left as she traveled, and kept moving ever upward across the sky, turning up the heat as it went. She'd traveled on better roads, and she'd traveled on worse, and she left Lefty to walk at his own pace. Her best guess was that she'd arrive at the ranch by midmorning.

Pup ran alongside for a while, chasing a jackrabbit without catching it, then finally caught up with the wagon and barked for a ride. Hannah pulled up long enough for the dog to jump on, and then flicked the reins on Lefty's rump, and they were back on the move.

It wasn't until she began seeing massive numbers of cattle in the distance and barbed wire fencing along the road that she realized she was already on the ranch. A short distance later, she came over a hill and saw the ranch house below.

The white-washed, two-story house with a wraparound porch shimmered behind the heat waves like a mirage, rising above the rolling landscape like an oasis in the sage and scrub brush. There was a multitude of outbuildings and corrals, and as she drew nearer, saw two people in the distance, and a horse in a nearby corral.

Pup sat up a little straighter and whined, an indication that he'd seen them, too.

"I know. I see them," Hannah said. "You will be good. Hear me?"

Pup whined again, then nosed the side of her cheek.

She laughed. "Yes, you're still my best boy."

THE ONLY HANDS still on the ranch during the day were Billy, Liam, and Jake, the three who'd been injured. Then Bud, the ranch cook, and his wife, Mina, who was the housekeeper and cook at the big house. The rest of the men, nearly two dozen of them, were out with the cattle.

Liam Brownley had gone to the windmill to get a bucket of water for the bunkhouse when he saw the rising dust. Visitors were few and far between, and he was curious. Once the bucket was full, he limped back to the bunkhouse to spread the news. Moments later, the Dun's victims exited the building, hobbling toward the corral to see who it was.

———

IRISH SAW the colorful caravan as it topped the rise, and frowned.

"Your bronc buster's wagon is being pulled by a mule."

Zee glared. "For heaven's sake, Irish, if you can't behave, go back to the house."

He grinned, but the grin didn't last long. What he first thought was a man with long hair, turned into a woman in the seat, with a dog beside her.

"You read the dust wrong, Aunt Zee. That's a woman."

Zee didn't say a word. She already knew Hank Doyle was a woman. It was part of the plan.

Irish watched as the woman pulled the mule to a halt, tied off the reins, then climbed down from the seat. As she did, she whacked her hat against her leg to knock off the dust, and then tossed it on the wagon seat.

Irish was momentarily transfixed by the wild mane of black curly hair, the fragility of her features, and her thin, slender build, and when she spoke, he heard Ireland in her voice.

"Mrs. Bloom, I presume?"

Zee nodded. "Yes, I'm Zee."

"Pleased to meet you. I'm Hank Doyle."

Irish was in shock, but his aunt's obvious lack of surprise was suspicious. She'd known all along!

Zee stepped forward, offering her hand. "Welcome to Shamrock Ranch, Hank. Please call me Zee, and this is my nephew, Irish Kelly. We own this ranch together, but he's the one who runs it."

Hank shook Zee's hand, but only nodded at Irish. She'd already read the rejection on his face.

"You're a woman!" he said. She laughed, and the sound rolled through him.

"I already knew that," Hank said. "Tell me something I don't know, like... where's the horse you want broke?"

He pointed toward the corral, and then caught himself.

"Miss...uh...Miss Hank, I can't let you go in there. He'll kill you."

"Just Hank," she said, but she was looking at the horse. "A dun. What a beauty," she said, and walked toward the corral, ignoring the injured ranch hands lingering nearby.

As Zee and Irish followed, the men gathered behind Zee like a bunch of baby ducks following their mama. They didn't want to miss out on whatever was about to happen. Then just as Hank reached the corral, Irish caught up with her and pulled her back.

"I cannot let you do this. I will not be responsible for your death."

Hank shrugged off his hand. "If you only knew how often I've heard that," she muttered, and before he could stop her, she'd gone over the fence.

The moment the Dun saw her, his head came up. He snorted, tossed his head, and began stomping his front feet as she walked closer.

Then she suddenly stopped and whistled softly between her teeth.

The Dun stilled, and when she began to speak in a whisper so soft no one could hear what she was saying, the horse's ears came up, and then there was a long moment of silence between the woman and the horse before she whistled again, this time like a quail.

The horse nickered.

Zee grinned. "Fey! She's fey, I tell you."

Irish didn't believe what he was seeing. Not only had the horse not charged her like he'd done everyone else, but he'd actually responded to her in a nonthreatening way.

All of a sudden, Hank turned and walked back to the fence.

"How long has this horse been standing in the sun?" she asked.

"As long as he dang well pleases," Irish said.

Hank frowned. "Where's his water? He's had no hay."

Irish's big voice rose above her indignation.

"His water is in the trough there, and his feed is inside his open stall, right where he left it. He's out here at his own free will, and can go back inside at will, as well. Do not walk up to my ranch and start accusing me of anything...Hank."

"I am not accusing you. The horse did."

Irish blinked.

Zee gasped.

"I don't—" It was the last thing out of Irish's mouth before she interrupted.

"There is a long piece of rawhide tied up in the horse's mane. I think he was a warhorse. Probably Caddo. Sometimes, when a great warrior dies, his warhorse is turned loose, and its name no longer spoken. It is their way of honoring the horse that sacrificed its freedom to the warrior. Also, the horse said the water in the trough is not fresh."

Zee shivered. Hank Doyle had 'talked' to the horse. *Lord a'mercy!*

"Then if he's been ridden, what's up with this attitude," Irish challenged.

Hank looked at the man as if he'd just lost his mind.

"I said Caddo warhorse, and you men tried to ride him with an iron bit in his mouth and a saddle on his back, didn't you?"

Irish blinked.

"Exactly," Hank said. "He's only been ridden bareback, and I doubt ever had anything but a war bridle in his mouth.

From his attitude, I'd say he's been running with the wild bunch for a long time now." She paused, her eyes losing focus. "He was lost without his warrior, and now he's lost without his herd."

Irish heard the sadness in her voice. He didn't understand that it came from the horse, and not her. He didn't know her story, but he guessed it wasn't a good one, or she wouldn't be out here in this land on her own. Then, before he could begin to feel sorry for her, she turned on the three ranch hands.

"You with the spurs and crutches. You made him bleed. You with your arm in a sling, you tore his mouth with the bridle. You with the limp, you smell bad to him. This is why he is the way he is now. Not only did he lose his freedom again, but when you hurt him, you became the enemy."

Billy Riley frowned. "I don't take orders from no gypsy, and I dang sure—"

Hank came up over the corral like a spider, climbing so fast that she was on the other side before they knew it was happening. When she began shouting and waving her arms at them in furious abandon, they backed up in shock and said nothing more.

Satisfied that she'd made her point, Hank took a breath and gave Irish a look.

"Am I hired?"

He wouldn't admit he'd known nothing about her arrival until last night. "I thought I'd hired a man," he muttered.

"No, you just bought a horse unseen. What you did was hire Hank Doyle, and here she is. It's not my fault you assumed I was male."

"Yes, you're hired," Zee said.

"Then I need to water my dog and my mule and get them settled. Is it okay if I set up camp back there under that stand of trees?"

"Absolutely," Zee said.

Hank left them standing, and when she got to her wagon, she gave her mule a tap on the shoulder and clicked her tongue a couple of times, then took hold of the mule's harness and led it to their new campsite.

Once she was out of earshot, Liam sidled up to the boss and lowered his voice.

"What in tarnation did she just say to us?"

Irish shoved his hands in his pockets. "Likely cussed us all in about three different languages. Put fresh water in the trough, and toss some hay in the stall while that devil is still out in the corral."

"Yes sir," Liam said, and limped off in haste, passing Zee, who was headed to the house, laughing beneath her breath.

Irish took off his hat, and ran his fingers through his hair in frustration. He didn't know what to make of the woman or the Dun, but he knew none of this was his fault.

Aunt Zee had been the one to buy that dang horse, and the one who'd hired a bronc buster, sight unseen. If he didn't know better, he'd think she'd done it all on purpose, just to throw a single woman at him one last time.

Chapter Two

HANK UNHARNESSED LEFTY FROM THE WAGON AND TIED HIM UP beneath the trees, leaving the rope long enough for the mule to graze on the grass beneath, then watered both of her animals before grabbing a length of rope and going back to the corral. Once there, she crawled up onto the top rail and sat down, tossed part of the rope into the corral and tied the other end to the fence.

The Dun was watching.

Hank whistled a perfect quail call several times, and when the horse finally calmed down and walked to the water trough, she began to sing. It was an Irish lullaby.

She was still on the fence when the cowboys who'd been out with the herd came riding in for the evening. Seeing a woman on site was one thing. Seeing her singing to the devil in the corral was another, and they continued to cast curious looks at the woman as they stalled their horses.

When Billy Riley hobbled out to spread the news that the boss had hired her to break the Dun, all of them laughed, except for the foreman, Jim Brody.

"Ain't nothing funny about that woman. I know who she is, and if anyone can make a workhorse out of that devil, it'll be her. I seen her up in the Kansas Territory about five years back, working horses. That's Hank Doyle, the Heartbreak Kid."

All of a sudden, Jim had their full attention.

"How'd she come by that name?" Billy muttered.

Jim shrugged. "She don't just break horses. They say she's a heartbreaker too. Men try to get friendly with her, and she cuts them off with a look before the words leave their mouths."

"Don't make no sense her dressin' like a man, and doin' a man's job," Billy said.

At that point, Irish walked up behind them. The sharp tone in his voice was all it took to shut them up.

"Maybe she doesn't like the choices left to single women out here. Mind your business, and don't mess with her. Understood?"

They all ducked their heads. "Yes, Boss," they echoed.

"Good. Everything go okay today, Jim?" Irish asked.

"Yes, sir. Just fine."

"Good. Bud's got grub ready. See you in the morning."

They quickly finished what they were doing and headed for the cookshack, but Irish stayed, hidden within the shadows of the stable, listening to a song he hadn't heard since his childhood, being sung to a horse. And it was apparent the horse liked it. He'd never seen the Dun so docile, nor had he ever been this confused about a woman.

He didn't know how to take her. What to say without giving insult? Or how to make peace with their first meeting? And then he remembered the cookshack and needed to tell her she was free to eat with the men. He started toward the corral, only to realize it was empty, and both the Dun and Hank Doyle were nowhere in sight.

Just as he was about to head to her camp, she came walking out of the stables, dragging a rope. She looked as startled as he felt.

"Uh… I stabled the Dun. See you in the morning."

"You stabled…?" Then he stopped and started over. "He let you lead him in?"

"No. He followed me in."

Irish was dumbfounded. "How did you get him to do that?"

"It's all part of the process," she said. "Horses are like most males. They don't want to be told what to do, so you have to make them think it's all their idea."

Irish took the rebuke without comment. "There's grub down at the bunkhouse."

Hank paused. "Are your men already there?"

"Not likely. They're probably still at the bunkhouse, washing up."

"Umm, okay," she said.

"Are you afraid of them?" he asked, then realized by the look on her face that she didn't like the question.

"Afraid is the wrong word. I'm careful, Mr. Kelly. That's all."

Irish frowned. "Irish, please, and I'll walk you down and introduce you to Bud. He's been feedin' hands on the ranch for over twenty years. While you're working for me, you get the run of the place like the rest."

The thought of eating something besides cold beans and hardtack was too good to ignore.

"I'll get my tinware. Wouldn't want to use a plate and leave someone without one," she said, and took off at a lope.

She reminded Irish of a young colt—long, nimble legs, a little skinny, not yet filled out, then he caught himself. It wasn't polite to notice women's legs. Still, he could hardly ignore them, considering she was wearing men's pants.

So, he waited, and when she came loping back bareheaded, carrying her plate and cup, he noticed she had taken time to wash the dust off her hands and face. That's when he saw the true color of her eyes—so blue it was like looking at sky.

"It's this way," Irish said, and started off.

"This is kind of you," Hank said, as Irish led the way to the food, although she could have probably found it by simply following her nose.

"I have my moments," he said.

She looked up to see if he was joking, but she couldn't tell, and ignored him the rest of the way.

BUD MILLER WAS a man somewhat past his prime. Mostly bald, not very tall, one leg shorter than the other. The apron he was wearing came near to dragging the ground, and he was standing at the cookstove when he heard footsteps, and turned around. The surprise on his face was evident. He'd been expecting cowboys. Not the boss and some woman in pants.

"Boss?"

"Hey Bud, this is Hank Doyle. Zee hired her to work the Dun. She's welcome at the table for as long as she's here, okay?"

Bud's bushy eyebrows rose as he nodded.

"Sure thing, Boss. Grab a plate, girly."

"I brought my own," Hank said. "And no offense to your kindness, but I'll take my food back to my campsite to eat. I don't want to put a hitch in the men's routine."

"Suit yourself," Bud said. "Hold your plate out and I'll fill 'er up."

Bud ladled out a heaping serving of beans, cut a chunk of meat from the hunk of beef roasting over the fire, put a prune hand pie on the side, and added a couple of soda biscuits.

"For soppin'," he said, then filled up her cup with hot coffee.

"I thank you," Hank said, and walked off with both hands full.

Bud glanced at the boss as she walked out the door.

"I never saw a woman wearing men's pants," he muttered.

"She's already got the Dun all but eating out of her hand," Irish muttered. "So, as far as I'm concerned, she can wear anything she pleases."

The old man's eyes widened.

"You ain't serious?" he said.

"Dead serious," Irish said, and that was only the half of it.

Things were serious, and getting more so. Hank Doyle was intriguing. He'd give her that. But, a woman he couldn't read might turn out to be as dangerous as the horse he couldn't ride. However, this was concern for another day. Right now, Mina and Aunt Zee were waiting on him for supper, and neither of them liked to be kept waiting.

———

THE GRANDFATHER CLOCK in the downstairs hallway struck midnight. Zephyr Bloom had been in bed for hours, and had yet to close her eyes.

Her nephew was upset with her, and she hated when that happened. He was already irked with her for buying that Dun, and now she'd gone and hired a woman to break it.

The West was a man's world. Zee had long since accepted that, although she'd never given up her autonomy, and she admired any woman who did the same. Hank Doyle was as uncommon as they came. She'd not only managed to survive in this country, but she'd taken a skill she'd been born with, and made herself indispensable while doing it. Zee sighed. If only Irish could see past Hank Doyle's wall, to the woman behind it.

She rolled over again and turned her pillow before settling, trying to find a cool spot. Even though her windows were up to catch the breeze, the curtains were hanging limp. The night air was stifling. *If only it would rain. Something. Anything to break this miserable heat.*

She took a deep breath, and as she did, got a faint whiff of wood smoke, and then heard the mournful plaint of a coyote on the ridge beyond. So tired of being tired, Zee finally closed her eyes and dreamed of the time before. When she was still in Ireland, and rain was as predictable as her mother's smile, and the world was forever green.

IRISH WAS SUFFERING from a similar malaise in his bedroom down the hall. His windows were all open, and he was lying abed, mentally identifying the night sounds as they drifted into his room. Like the coyotes yipping, and a dog barking an answer. A horse nickered. A mule brayed. He knew what was his, and what belonged to Hank Doyle. Nothing to worry about. Then he thought of her, and wondered if she ever felt safe? Part of him wished he'd never met her, because he knew he was never going to forget her, even after she was gone.

———

ONCE INSIDE HER LITTLE WAGON, Hank gave way to Hannah. After eating all she could of the fine meal she'd been given, she fed the scraps to Pup, used up the last of her water to clean her eating utensils, and took Pup with her as she walked back down to the windmill with her empty bucket.

Happy to be at her side, the yellow dog danced ahead of her in the moonlight, tongue hanging, tail wagging, as it sniffed the night air.

But as far as Hannah was concerned, the air was too still and too thick to breathe. The half-moon hung low in a sky full of stars, without a cloud in sight. There were no lights shining through curtains, or from an open window anywhere.

As she walked, she heard the near-silent flapping of wings as the resident barn owl sailed over her head, and moments later, coyotes began to yip up on the ridge to the west.

Once she reached the windmill, she pumped her bucket full of water and began walking back, with Pup beside her. As she passed the big house, she thought of Irish Kelly. He was a handsome man, by her standards, a rich man. She felt his disregard as keenly as if it had been a knife cutting into her skin, and was immediately angry with herself for caring what that man thought about her—what any man thought. If she was to survive in this land, she couldn't afford to be weak. She couldn't afford heartbreak, and thrust the thought of him aside.

Once she was back at her wagon, she gave Pup a pat on the head.

"Stay," she said, then went up the steps and locked the door behind her. After stripping out of her clothes, she filled the washbasin, then vigorously brushed the dust from her hair before tying it up with a piece of rawhide to keep it off her neck. Normally in this heat, she would have made camp by water and gone in for a swim. But that wasn't possible here, so she settled for her washrag and the basin, and began washing herself from head to toe.

By the time she'd finished, her skin was already dry. The thought occurred that it would be cooler to sleep without clothes, but that would have left her vulnerable, and in this land, that couldn't happen.

So, she dug out a clean shirt and another pair of pants and put them on, then took her lantern to the bed and shook out all the covers, just to make sure she wasn't about to bed down with a scorpion, or a snake.

Once she was satisfied of her well-being, she opened the door to let Pup in, then locked it again. She checked her rifle to make sure it was loaded, checked her cartridge belt to make sure it was loaded as well, then put the rifle on the floor by her bed and lay down.

She'd made a point of parking the wagon so that the little window would be open to the south to catch the breeze. It was too small for a man to crawl through, and Pup would alert her if anyone was poking about outside, so she felt safe enough to leave it open while she slept. Lefty would take care of any prowling coyotes, and Pup would take care of her. It was as safe as she knew how to be.

Once in bed, she relaxed. It felt good to be off her feet, and tomorrow would be a long day. She thought once of Zee, asleep in her fine house, and of Irish Kelly and the flash in his eyes when he looked at her. She had yet to figure out if the flash was a challenge, or distrust. Either way, she didn't need the hassle. She closed her eyes and slept without dreaming.

————

PUP WOKE HER BEFORE SUNRISE, and since she was already dressed, she sat up and reached for her shoes, shaking them to make sure they were free of scorpions before she put them on, then finger-combed her hair.

She ate hardtack and jerky, washed it all down with water, tied Lefty up in a new spot for grazing, put Pup on guard at her wagon, and headed for the stable.

And for the next four days, this would be her routine.

Random glimpses of the boss, curious glances from the men, and just her and the Dun, trying to come to terms with each other, until on the fifth night, when the cowboys rode in from the range.

Hank heard them talking as they were stabling their horses. Something about tracks near the herd, and whispers of rustlers. Her skin crawled. Danger in this land was always a given, and it appeared she might have just made camp in the middle of it.

————

JIM BRODY CAME in with the men, and when they went to the stable, he went straight to the big house and knocked.

Irish had been working on the books, posting expenditures, and making notes of the debts left to pay when he next rode to town. Keeping books was something Zee had always done, but as she grew older, she insisted he must know all of the ins and outs of it, for the time when she was gone. He didn't like to think about living without her, and he didn't like keeping books, so when the knock came at the door, he got up to open it, glad for the interruption.

"Jim! Come in," Irish said.

"No, sir. I'm too dusty. Could I have a word?"

"Sure. Take a seat and I'll join you," Irish said, then poured a shot of whiskey and carried it out to Jim, before sitting down beside him.

"Thanks, Boss," Jim said, and downed the shot in one gulp. "That hits the spot."

"So, what's up?" Irish asked.

"Me and the boys have been seeing tracks on the ridge above where we've been bedding the herd. The tracks are shod, and the last time I was in Delphi, I heard tell the Dawson Gang was in the area and suspected of rustling cattle. We're just now seeing tracks close to the herd, but there's no way to know if they've been working farther out. Since them boys got hurt on the Dun, we've been short a few hands, and haven't been riding fence like usual."

Irish frowned. "I don't like the sound of this. Tomorrow, when you ride out, I'll ride with you. I want to see these tracks for myself. Maybe trail them a ways, to see where they go."

"Yes, Boss," Jim said. "I'll have your horse saddled."

"Thanks. Now get some food and rest. Tomorrow may be a whole other kind of day."

Irish picked up their shot glasses as Jim headed for the stable, and went back inside. Keeping books on the ranch was a pain, but rustlers meant big trouble, and he was about to trade one for the other.

He thought of Hank Doyle as he was sitting down to eat with his aunt, and wondered what would happen if he ever asked her to join them. On one hand, he knew Aunt Zee would be delighted to know he was interested in a woman—in any woman, but until Hank Doyle knew it, too, he wasn't telling anyone else.

———

Irish was awake and dressed before Zee's rooster crowed. He'd already told his aunt last night about his plan for today, so he didn't bother waking her to let her know he was leaving. He took the stairs down as quietly as a man his size could manage, grabbed his rifle and saddlebags as Mina came in to start the fire to make Zee's breakfast.

"Mornin', Mr. Irish," Mina said.

"Morning, Mina. I'll be riding out with the boys today." The screen door slammed behind him as he headed to the cookshack.

His arrival dampened the ranch hands' rowdy meal. He sat down and ate beans and soda biscuits with them, washing it all down with coffee hot enough to scald the feathers off a fryin' hen, and left strict orders for the three injured men left behind.

"Billy, Liam, Jake...you three are on guard here today," Irish said. "I expect you to look after the women, and don't give Bud or Hank Doyle any grief. Muck out the stalls and pump up some fresh water into the horse tank, and put some in the trough in the corral, too, understand?"

"Yes, Boss," Liam said, and the other two nodded, watching in silence as Irish and the hands went to saddle up.

Sunrise was less than an hour away as they entered the stable. The men headed down the open aisle to the stalls where their horses were bedded, and began saddling up. Then, one by one, as they began leading them out, they realized Hank Doyle was already in the corral with the Dun.

The men stopped to stare, Irish with them, mesmerized by the silhouettes of horse and woman, standing face to face and less than five feet apart, with no sound or motion between them.

Irish took a deep breath, letting the wave of emotion move through him without comment.

"Dang it, Boss, if I warn't seein' this with my own eyes, I wouldn't a' believed it," Jim whispered.

Irish had seen the intensity in her gaze. He knew what it had done to him, and wondered if the Dun was as hypnotized as he'd been.

———

HANNAH KNEW when Irish Kelly walked out of the big house, because she'd heard the door slam. She wasn't bothered about the hot breakfast she was missing, because she didn't want the distraction. Today, and every day she was here, was for the Dun.

She had stopped at the tack room to get a saddle blanket, then went into the Dun's stall.

The horse lifted its head at her approach, and softly nickered.

She stood without entering, letting the horse make the first move, and held out her hand.

When the Dun caught a whiff of what she was holding, he took a step forward and mashed his nose against her fist.

A simple little handful of salt.

She opened her fingers and whistled once, soft and low.

Moments later, the velvety touch of the horse's mouth was in her palm as it began to nibble up the treat. When the salt was gone, Hank turned and walked away, dragging the saddle blanket as she went, leaving the horse to follow her out.

She circled the corral without stopping, dragging the blanket and humming beneath her breath, listening to the clop of the horse's hooves as it followed behind her. She didn't know how close it was behind her, until she felt a tug on the blanket and realized the Dun had it in his mouth. Instead of stopping, she just walked a little faster and pulled it out from between its teeth.

She knew when the men entered the stable to get their mounts, but just kept walking, until finally she walked out into the middle of the corral, then turned and stopped.

Startled, the Dun also stopped, and there they stood, as one minute passed into another, and another, and that's what the men saw when they came out of the stalls, leading their horses.

Hank heard them ride off, and then glanced at the sky. Dawn was on the horizon. She moved to the side of the corral, threw the blanket over the railing, then grabbed an empty water bucket and headed for the windmill. She could already tell the day was going to be another hot one, so working the horse now before midday was the plan.

She was at the hand pump, filling the bucket when she heard footsteps behind her.

It was Liam, bareheaded, and still limping.

"Mornin', ma'am. I can get that for you."

"Thanks, but I've got it," Hank said, without looking up.

Liam nodded, wiping his hands nervously on the front of his shirt as Hank Doyle picked up the bucket and walked away. He was staring and he knew it, but seeing a woman in men's pants was a revelation in more ways than one. She was shapely, for certain, but she was real scary too. He didn't have any experience with a woman who talked back, and after the dressing down she'd given them the day she'd arrived, he didn't want another dose.

Hank knew he was watching her. She could feel it. She didn't even consider trusting him, but she'd already put the fear of God in all of them, and guessed Irish Kelly had done the same, or the man wouldn't have come to offer his help.

By the time she got back to the corral, the Dun had the saddle blanket in his teeth and was shaking it. She came through the stable with the water and dumped it into the water trough at the end of the corral. As she did, the horse dropped the blanket and came to the trough.

She waited until the horse's nose was in the water before she dared stroke the side of its neck, and when she felt muscles tense, she backed up and went to retrieve the blanket and shook out the dust, but she was pleased her trick had worked. The Dun had tasted and smelled the blanket, and the next time she used it, it would smell like the horse, and it would no longer be viewed as a threat.

She threw the blanket back over the top rail and picked up the rope. The Dun was watching, and now that she had his attention, she began making a big show of looping the rope on one of the posts before going back to her wagon. He could chew and yank on the rope all day, or drag it around the corral to his heart's content. But it would no longer be a threat.

Having figured out the horse had once been used to carrying riders, she knew it was only a matter of time before he caved. A few years back she'd acquired an Indian war bridle, just for its curiosity. But now, she was wondering if the Dun would accept it.

Pup came out from under the wagon, wagging his tail in greeting as she approached. Hank dropped to her knees to give the dog a big hug.

"Pup, you are my good boy!" she said, then hurried up the steps into her wagon.

The bridle was hanging from a peg on the wall. She took it down, fingering the feather still attached at the ring where the reins were tied, as she went out the door. She put Pup back on guard, then headed back to the corral.

As soon as Irish and his men reached the herd, he checked in with the ones who'd been there all night and got an 'all calm' report. At that point the hands began their day, checking for any late-birth newborns, and looking for signs of predator kills, while Jim took Irish up to the ridge to where they'd seen the tracks. To Irish's dismay, there were fresh tracks from at least a dozen riders.

"The boys said they didn't see anything last night, but this doesn't look good," Jim said.

"How long has it been since we had anyone riding fence?" Irish asked.

Jim shrugged. "Three, maybe four days."

"You go on back to the herd," Irish said. "I'm gonna follow these tracks for a bit, just to see where they're coming from. If there's fence cut, then I'd lay odds they've been picking off the strays to suit themselves for some time."

"I don't think that's a good idea, you goin' off by yourself, Boss. What if you ride up on them camped somewhere?"

"If they've got cattle with my brand on them, they're the ones who'll need to worry."

Jim Brody was concerned, but the boss was the boss, and he'd been on the ranch long enough to know Irish Kelly could take care of himself.

Chapter Three

IRISH WAS A GOOD TWO HOURS ON THE TRAIL HE'D BEEN
following, riding through brush and sage, down into draws,
following a trail of cattle and shod horses up an out of an
arroyo, always on the alert with Jim Brody's warnings
uppermost in his mind. He was alone and trailing rustlers—
a dangerous situation to be in.

Then just as he rode out of a gulley, he flushed a covey of
quail. The whoosh of fluttering of wings as the birds flew up,
startled both him and his horse, and if anyone ahead of him
had been watching their back trail, the birds would have
alerted them to his presence.

He immediately dismounted, and led his horse off the
trail, tied it to some bushes, then grabbed his field glasses
and rifle, and crept up the rise on foot, using the waist-high
brush for cover. Just before he topped it, he went belly down
and crawled the rest of the way up.

The vista below was picturesque. Longhorns grazing and
three men on horseback riding herd. The size of the herd
was shocking. At best guess, close to five hundred. And one
quick look through the glasses revealed Shamrock brands.
Anger swelled. The cattle were his!

But Irish was uneasy. He'd seen tracks of at least a dozen
riders, and all he could see were these three. So where were

the other nine? Were they riding ahead, or had they gone back for more cattle?

He began scanning the area closer, sweeping the field glasses from one side of the valley to the next, looking for signs of a camp. Finally, on a third sweep through, what he'd first thought was dust, became a thin wispy spiral of smoke rising from a campfire a couple of hundred yards behind the herd.

"There you are," Irish muttered, and began inching backward until he could stand upright, then ran back to his horse and began circling the area, until he had eyes on the camp.

Some of the men were sleeping, likely the ones who were making night raids, resting up for another sweep through his herd. A couple looked like they were repairing gear. At that point, he began counting heads, looking for guards, and checking the layout of the camp.

They'd strung a rope between some trees and had their mounts tied to it like a hitching post. One man was stirring a pot of something over an open fire, and another one was sitting on a rock, skinning a rabbit.

Even though the wide brim of Irish's hat was keeping the sun off his face, his clothes were sweat-stained, covered in dust and dried bits of the brush. He had two choices. Go back for help, or do something now, and he chose now.

"My land. My cattle, and they're going home with me," he muttered, and urged his horse forward.

All he had to do was get in front of the herd.

The cattle would do the rest.

BOWLEG DAWSON WAS A LIAR, a thief, and a heartless killer. He'd shot settlers in the back, and took their women for sport, leaving their broken bodies in the dirt for the vultures and the wolves to claim. There were wanted posters all over the territories with Bowleg's name and bounty on them. Every time he ran across one, he tore it down and took it with him as a souvenir. His daddy used to tell him he wouldn't amount to nothin', but Bowleg considered the posters proof the sorry bastard had been wrong. He was worth cash money, which was more than his old man could have ever claimed.

For the past two years, Bowleg and his gang had been all over the territories creating their own version of murder and mayhem. But for the last six months, they'd been in the Texas brush country, picking off strays from the big ranchers, while staying as far away from the ranch headquarters as they could get. When they got a big enough herd together, they'd head for the San Antonio stockyards with fake bills of sale to explain the random brands of the cattle they'd driven in.

He and his gang had scouted out the Shamrock Ranch for days, getting the lay of the land and a feel for their routine. He knew the number of men who rode herd on the cattle during the day, and that some rode the fence lines almost daily, while others were left on guard at night.

He knew who Irish Kelly was, and knew of his reputation for being hard-nosed, but he also knew Zephyr Bloom, the old woman who'd raised him, was his weak spot.

The gang had already made two sweeps through the Shamrock cattle, and last night they'd gone in for a third round, taking as many as they could cut, without spooking the main herd, then drove them back into the valley to their camp.

This morning, Bowleg was at the campsite, complacent with their accomplishments and eating rabbit stew when he crunched down on a bit of bone. He cursed from the pain and spit it out, and was reaching for his coffee cup when he heard three gunshots in rapid succession, followed by a loud, blood-curdling scream.

He dropped his stew and drew his gun in a crouch, trying to decide which direction the shots had come from, when all of a sudden, the ground beneath his feet began to shake, and the cattle began to bawl like they were being butchered. His blood ran cold!

Stampede!

"Get up! Get up!" he began shouting to his men, and started running toward the horses, but it was already too late.

The horses were rearing and pulling against the rope to which they'd been tied, and one by one, they began to break free and run.

Bowleg was in a panic. He looked over his shoulder at the moving mass of hooves and horns coming at them, and started running.

IRISH CAME RIDING out of the brush toward the grazing herd, firing shots over the longhorns, and screaming like a wild man. The herd reacted like the prey animals they were, turned tail from the noise and the gunfire, and began moving like a tidal wave in the opposite direction, their horns clacking like rim fire, bawling their retreat.

The three men riding herd were immediately trapped within the stampede and swept away with the herd's momentum, doing all they could to stay in the saddle, knowing their fate if they did not.

The cattle ran through the camp, the campfire, and through the rustlers running for their lives, stomping saddles, bridles, and blankets where the men had been sleeping, destroying everything in their path.

Irish kept riding, and firing until his pistol was empty, then grabbed the reins with both hands and leaned forward. If there was anyone left standing when the stampede passed, he wasn't giving them a target to shoot at. He was taking the herd home, and he never looked back.

THE HERD RAN for miles before finally slowing down to an exhausted walk. Not long after, they caught the scent of water, and kept moving forward, with Irish in the dust behind them.

Jim Brody saw the dust cloud long before he saw the cattle, and then when he did, he gave a shout-out to his men and pointed north. After that, it was a simple matter of getting out of the way.

It seemed like forever before the last longhorn finally crossed Cougar Creek to join the herd, and the ranch hands still didn't know where the cattle had come from until they saw the brand, and then the boss riding out of the dust, like a ghost on horseback. His hat was pulled low over his head. His bandanna pulled up over the lower half of his face.

"Lord, lord," Jim mumbled, and rode back toward the creek just as Irish rode into it.

Irish dismounted and dropped the reins to let his horse drink, hung his hat on the saddle horn and reached for his canteen. But instead of taking a drink, he poured what was left of the water all over his face, and kept pouring until he'd washed enough dust from his eyes to be able to see.

Jim came off his horse in haste, and waded into the creek with his canteen, and handed it to Irish.

"Too dang many beeves to drink behind," Jim said.

"Thanks," Irish said, then lifted it to his lips and took a drink, and then another, and didn't stop until Jim grabbed his wrist. "Take a breath, Boss."

Irish took one more drink before handing it back.

"What happened?" Jim asked.

Irish's voice was raspy from all the dust he'd swallowed. "Found the rustlers. Brought my cattle home."

Jim's eyes widened. "What happened to them? Where are they?"

Irish shrugged. "When I turned the herd, they stampeded. The rustlers on foot might have been in the way. Stealing cattle is a dangerous business."

Then he reached for the reins dangling in the water, and led his horse out of the creek, remounted, and rode back to the herd.

The ranch hands were stunned when they started seeing cattle coming up from the creek in droves, and moving into the herd like kinfolk coming home to visit. It took them a few moments to spot the Shamrock brand and realized what was happening, but they didn't know what to think until they saw the boss, and the trail-weary appearance of both him and his horse.

Stump Miller had been riding for the Shamrock brand for nearly six years, and he'd learned a long time ago that Irish Kelly wasn't a man to fool with. But bringing back this many head of longhorns on his own was a feat to remember. All he could figure was Boss either found a whole bunch of strays, or gave out a dose of payback.

The men could only surmise it had been a wild ride, and from the look on his face, most thought it best not to ask for details. But when Irish began waving them all in, and one by one, twenty-plus cowboys rode up and gathered around him, they soon found out.

"Do you have provisions to make cold camp tonight?" Irish asked.

"Most of us do," Jim said. "If some don't, we'll share."

Irish shifted wearily in the saddle. "Okay. So, here's what you need to know. I trailed more than a dozen riders for nearly two hours. Found most of them bedded down in a valley, with a few riding herd on cattle stolen from the Shamrock."

The men were visibly angry, and experiencing embarrassment and guilt that had happened on their watch and Irish saw it.

"It's nobody's fault. It's what happens where thieves abide," Irish said. "Tomorrow, some of you will be riding fence, looking for holes where they've cut the wire. Once they've been located, we'll be fixin' that fence. But in the meantime, we'll need to keep a closer watch on the herd. Jim says who stays, and who comes in for the night, but whoever comes back out tomorrow, they'll be bringing the wagon, and fence fixings with them, understood?"

The men nodded, and then one of them asked.

"Hey Boss. Do we need to worry about the rustlers makin' another raid tonight?"

Irish's face was void of expression. "Doubt it. They made

the stupid mistake of bedding down behind the herd. I have no idea what happened to them when I turned the herd and headed them home, but it got a little rowdy. If any of them are still alive, they're on foot."

————————

HANK MADE GOOD PROGRESS TODAY. She had the war bridle on the Dun, and the saddle blanket on his back as she walked him around the corral, and every so often, she'd stop, climb up on the fence, then sit with the reins still in her hands, and every time she went to get down, she'd lean forward just enough for the Dun to feel her weight on his back as she slid off.

The first time she did it, the Dun shied, but then she clicked her tongue and whistled to get his attention, and he stopped, and she did it over and over throughout the morning and then every day after, until he took it as a matter of course.

Finally, she slipped the bridle from his lower jaw, hung it on a fence post, and took herself and her rifle back to the wagon to check on Pup and Lefty.

Pup was asleep in the shade beneath the wagon, and Lefty was scratching his backside on tree bark when she walked up.

The mule brayed.

Pup opened one eye, thumped the dirt with his tail, but didn't get up.

Hank gave Lefty's head a good scratch between his ears, then got her little washtub and scrub board from the wagon, filled the tub with water, and took what was left of her bar of lye soap, and began scrubbing her dirty clothes.

She was staring into the tub, completely focused on getting a stain out of her shirt when everything faded around her, and she saw Irish with a gun in his hand and riding behind a stampede, and then she saw nothing but dust as the vision faded.

In that moment, her heart thudded so hard against her

ribs it hurt to breathe. She didn't know what was happening, but she knew Irish Kelly was in danger. And then a chill ran through her.

What if he got hurt? What if he died? Her heart began to ache, like she'd just been kicked in the chest. *Stop it, Hannah! This is just another job. He's the man you're working for, and when you're through you'll be gone, and he'll forget you exist. He didn't intend to hire a woman. You mean nothing to him.*

But that didn't help how she was feeling. Something terrible was happening. She shouldn't feel like this, but she did. He was starting to mean something to her, and if he died, then that dream was gone.

Troubled in her soul, she finished scrubbing the clothes, put them in clean water to rinse them, then wrung them out, and draped them on the wagon wheels to dry.

When she walked back to the corral, Zee Bloom was there, looking at the horse.

"Oh, there you are," Zee said. "Have you given up on him for the day?"

"No, ma'am. We had a good morning. I just gave him a time out." Then she climbed over the railing and whistled at the horse.

The horse nickered back and walked to her. Hank put the saddle blanket back on the Dun's back, and slipped the war bridle between his teeth again, letting the reins fall down from the ring below his lower jaw.

"Oh my! You have made progress!" Zee said. "What kind of bridle is that?"

"It's called a war bridle. It's Indian. The Dun remembers it," Hank said.

Zee was fascinated by the young woman.

"How did you learn to do what you do?" Zee asked.

Hank shrugged. "Just picked it up along the way, I guess."

"Do you really talk to them? The horses, I mean," Zee asked.

Hank wasn't about to talk about her 'knowing' or anything to do with it.

"It's just communication. Like watching people's expressions and knowing when they're angry or happy, even though they said nothing to you. People learn to communicate with each other as they grow up, and animals are the same, but in their own language." Hank smiled at Zee.

When she did, Zee stifled a gasp. When Hank Doyle let down her guard, she was stunning, and then she realized the girl was talking, and made herself focus.

"They communicate with each other, just like we do. But what they hear coming out of our mouths is just noise. They can only react to how we sound and what we do. If we're angry or demanding, that's what they feel. If we hurt them, they won't forget. Horses are prey. All animals who do not eat meat, are prey to those who do. That's why horses exist in herds—for protection. So, when someone separates them from safety, which is what happens when a wild horse is caught, their first instinct is escape, and to get back to their family. Then when man gets hold of them and starts demanding the horse bend to his will, it's both frightening, usually painful, and an intrusion into the world they know."

Zee's eyes welled. "I never once thought of an animal having those thoughts. I don't think I'll ever look at a horse the same way again."

Hank shrugged. "I'm not saying it's wrong to train animals to help us, but when we do that, we should be decent enough to care for them. An animal who bonds to its master will work harder for them than one who works by force and fear. That's all I mean."

Zee sighed. In all of her seventy-odd years of life, she'd never met anyone like Hank Doyle. "You, young lady, are a very special person."

A gust of wind blew through, stirring up the dust and tugging at Zee's old cowboy hat. She pulled it down a little tighter on her head and then noticed Hank's hat, hanging down the back of her neck, with the cords caught beneath her chin and her long dark hair blowing every which way. The girl wasn't fighting the wind...or the horse. She'd just taken her space within, without ceding to either.

"You're fey, aren't you, girl? And don't take that the wrong way. I was born and raised in Ireland. I knew people like you there."

Hank frowned. She wasn't about to answer that. The last thing she wanted was for someone to start calling her a witch. She looked away, and as she did, saw Irish again. This time he was covered in dust, and standing in a creek with water up to his knees. She went weak with relief.

Thank the lord, he's still alive.

"I should get back to work, ma'am," Hank said, and when she tugged on the reins, the Dun followed.

Zee frowned. Hank Doyle wasn't giving anything away. Frustrated, she dusted off her hands and headed back to the house.

But Hank was still bothered by the vision she'd had of Irish Kelly. She was looking into the west when she felt the Dun's nose against her neck and smiled to herself. *So, you aren't such a tough guy, after all, are you?*

She slowly turned, leaned her cheek against the horse's neck, and closed her eyes, absorbing his scent just as he had mastered hers, then began to whisper.

"I would see farther if you would let me ride you. I could go faster than my own legs would carry me. I would feel the wind in my face and in my hair. You would give me some of your magic, and I would love you for the beauty you are."

The horse stilled, ears twitching at the sound of her voice.

Communication was happening, and Hank Doyle was winning over another heart. That it was a horse and not a man was something of a tragedy, but she'd already accepted her worth and would not settle for less.

———

It was late in the day when she finally took the Dun to the horse trough to drink, then led him back to his stall and hand-fed him the loose hay Liam had left in the stall. She brushed him down until he was standing with his eyes closed, his head down, lulled by her voice and her touch.

Satisfied the Dun was settled, she fastened the door to his stall and headed toward the windmill with her empty bucket. When the bucket was full, she headed back.

Her belly growled from the scent of meat roasting in the cookshack. It had been a long time since her hardtack and beans this morning, and as soon as she took water back to her wagon, she was going back for supper. Then she heard the sound of hoofbeats behind her. She turned to the west and saw a big man riding in on horseback, silhouetted against a setting sun

As he rode closer, she realized it was Irish.

Her heart was pounding.

Was he real, or was this just another vision?

———

IRISH BREATHED a quiet sigh of relief when he saw the ranch house. There'd been a time today when he wasn't sure he'd live to see home again.

He started down the trail toward the ranch, and as was his way, began checking everything in sight. Smoke rising from the cookshack was a sure sign of supper in progress. Chickens had been put up for the night, which meant Aunt Zee had done her chores. The Dun wasn't in the corral, so Hank must be done for the day.

But as he rode closer, he saw her filling a bucket at the pump. His heart leaped. A random chance to say hello was always a delight. He saw the slump in her shoulders right before she picked up the bucket and started back across the yard, and thought she looked as tired as he felt. Then she suddenly turned toward him and nearly dropped the bucket.

Thinking she might be ill, he dismounted quickly and ran to her. But before he could say a word, she grabbed the front of his shirt. Her eyes were wide with shock.

"You're real!"

For a moment, it felt like he'd been branded. He couldn't

move. Couldn't think, and when she turned him loose, he reeled like he'd just been punched.

"Why did you just say that?"

Hank's gaze moved past his face to the sky over his shoulder, blankly staring into the gathering dusk.

"Because I've seen you twice today. Once riding behind stampeding longhorns, waving a gun over your head before you faded into the dust. And again, standing in a creek with your horse beside you, just before you disappeared again. When I saw you now, I just...I thought maybe...maybe you were another vision."

Irish paled, and took a sudden step back. "How did you know that?"

She frowned, instantly hurt, and on the defensive that he did not understand her.

"I saw it. The first time, I thought you would die. I was afraid all day until I saw you in the creek, and then I knew you had not. Then I saw you coming out of the setting sun, and for just a moment, I thought you were a ghost."

"Who are you? What are you?"

He saw the flash in her eyes, and heard the anger in her voice, but it was too late to take back what he'd said.

"I am a woman. Have you never met one before? I am not a lily-white female who flirts to get what she wants. Lilies are fragile. They die in this land. I am not fragile. I did not die, even though I've tried that dress on before. You want to know *what* I am? I'm like that horse you want broke to ride. He won't ever let me on him, unless he wants to. And when he does, he will do it out of love, not because I broke his will. I will not explain myself. I will not excuse myself. Either take me as I am, or shut your mouth."

She picked up the bucket, then paused, and this time looked him straight in the face. "They didn't all die. It's still not over."

Irish forgot to breathe. He could only stand and watch as she walked away, mesmerized by the sway of her body, the long, steady stride in her walk, and all that black curly hair hanging down her back.

In that moment, a heat washed through him. He wanted his hands in that hair and her beneath him and with him, for the rest of his life, but he was in doubt of that ever happening. She was beautiful, and the strongest woman he'd ever met, and she scared the bejesus out of him.

Chapter Four

After Irish's set-to with Hank Doyle, it had taken all of the energy he had left in him just to stable his horse before calling it a day. His heels were dragging as he finally made it to the house and walked in the back door. He hung his hat on a set of elk antlers mounted on the wall before entering the kitchen. It was hot outside, but even hotter in here.

Mina had a beef stew warming on the back of the stove, a pan of cornbread in the warmer, and what looked like a dried apple pie cooling in the pie safe.

She looked up from her chair in the corner as he walked in.

"Evenin', Mr. Irish. Miss Zee's in the library. She had me draw you up a bath. Don't dawdle. Supper's waitin'."

"Yes, ma'am," Irish said, and kept on walking.

Zee heard his footsteps in the hall and called out.

"Irish, come talk to me a moment."

He sighed. She was gonna give him what-for because of how he looked, but he obeyed.

"Evenin', Aunt Zee. Have you had a good day?"

She took one look at him and then blinked. "Better than you've had, I would say. What happened?"

"Rustlers. I tracked them. Found them, and about five hundred head of our beeves."

She frowned. "Alone? You did this on your own?"

He nodded.

Her heart skipped a beat just thinking of her world without him in it.

"Joseph Michael Kelly! What possessed you to do such a thing? Are you okay? Do we need to send for the sheriff?"

He hadn't heard her call him that in a good ten years, but it was a sign of how he'd upset her.

"I'm fine, Aunt Zee. Just tired and dirty. No need for the sheriff. I dealt with it."

Zee's frown deepened. Now Zee was imagining a gunfight. "What did you do?"

"Circled their camp, started a stampede, and brought my cattle home."

She paled. "And the rustlers?"

He shrugged. "Cattle don't have brakes. They ran over everything in their path. I don't know what happened to them, but I reckon they were running, or getting run over. Either way, the cattle are back with the herd. Tomorrow, we ride fence and fix the gaps. Mina said supper's ready, but I gotta clean up first. All I can taste is dirt."

Zee didn't ask another question, or say another word. But the set of her nephew's shoulders as he walked out of the room, said it all. He was as used up as a man could be and still be walking.

————

BOWLEG DAWSON LOOKED like he'd been in a fight with a bobcat. He was scratched and bleeding, had bruises upon bruises, and was alive only because the horse in front of him stumbled as they were running. When the horse went down, Bowleg leaped on its back, grabbed the mane with both hands, and gave it a kick in the ribs. The horse was back on its feet in a heartbeat and running for its life, with Bowleg clamped to its back like a tick on a dog.

The horse's instinct for survival is what saved him.

Long after the stampede passed, Bowleg turned the horse

back to the valley where they'd made camp. He needed a saddle and a bridle, and whatever else he could salvage to get him to a place to regroup. He didn't know what happened to his men, but he saw the man who started the stampede when he rode right past him. He knew him, and he was going to make him pay. Bowleg had a reputation to uphold, and no side-winding Irishman was going to take that down.

———

HANK WENT to sleep that night with Pup at the foot of her bed, thankful for the slight stir of air coming through her little window. Her set-to with the boss had bothered her enough that she didn't go back to the cookshack for her supper and was surprised when Bud sent Liam with a plate of food for her.

Still reeling from the slap-down the woman had given them days earlier, Liam ducked his head when he brought it.

"Bud sent this," he mumbled.

Hank took the plate with both hands, as if she was receiving crown jewels, and then smiled.

"Thank you, Liam, and tell Bud I appreciate it. It looks good."

It was the smile. Liam's heart skipped a beat. He nodded, then stumbled over his own feet as he turned and walked away.

After Hank ate, she folded up the clothes she'd put out to dry, then went outside to feed Pup, and stayed to get some fresh air.

The full moon put out plenty of light to see by, and she felt bad for neglecting Lefty for the job at hand. So, she buckled on her holster, made sure her pistol was loaded, and took the old mule for a walk, heading away from the ranch to the hill beyond, with Pup at her heels.

———

REFRESHED FROM A BATH AND A MEAL, Irish left his aunt sitting in the parlor, reading by lamplight, and walked out onto the front porch. The air was stirring. Good for sleeping, but the moon was big and bright in the sky, which meant the herd would be jumpy tonight. He stepped off the porch and out into the yard, glancing first toward the bunkhouse, then at all of the other outbuildings.

He heard a horse nicker from its stall, and another answer, and wondered what they had to talk about, then thought of Hank Doyle. Before her, he would never have given rise to the notion that horses were having a conversation. He sighed. A lot of things were different with him since her arrival.

The barn owl swooped past him in the dark, and as he turned to look, caught movement up the road and shifted his gaze. It took exactly two seconds for him to realize it was her, on foot, walking the mule, with her dog at her side.

He was still bothered about upsetting her, but he'd been so shocked by what she'd said. He hadn't meant for her to take the questions as an attack—that he was questioning her word, or her reliability. But she had, and knowing he'd hurt her was laying heavy on his heart. Now that he'd seen her, he decided this was as good a time as any to apologize, and started walking up the road, past the stable, past the corral, all the way to where she'd parked her wagon, and then stopped. Watching. Waiting.

When he saw the dog suddenly disappear then heard her laugh, a sadness washed over him. He'd only made her angry. He'd give anything to have made her laugh—like that —with him.

———————

A NIGHT BIRD called from somewhere out in the brush, and Hank whistled the same call back, smiling to herself as it answered.

Pup whined, which meant he smelled something he wanted to chase.

"Go on," Hank said. "But no skunks. No coyotes. Understood?"

Pup leaped like he'd been shot from a cannon, and disappeared into the brush.

She laughed, unaware that the sound had carried all the way back to the man behind her. Lefty kept plodding along without complaint, until he suddenly went sideways. The only thing that mule gave way to were snakes, which put Hank immediately on guard. She didn't like rattlers either and glanced down to make sure it had slithered on past. Once they reached the rise, she gave a slight tug on the rope.

"Whoa, boy. It's too dark for losing sight of home," and turned the mule around and started back.

She could hear Pup still thrashing about in the brush and guessed he was chasing a rabbit.

"Pup! We're going home now. Either catch it, or let it be," she said, and kept walking.

She was more than halfway back when someone stepped out of the shadows into the road below. Her hand went straight to the pistol in her holster before she recognized the height of him, and the breadth of those shoulders.

Irish!

Breath caught like she'd been gut-punched, but she never broke stride, and he was still there when she paused at the trees and tied Lefty back up for the night.

"Are you lost?" she asked, as she approached the wagon.

"No, ma'am. I always pay my debts, and I owe you an apology. I'm sorry if I hurt your feelings. It was never my intent."

"I'm fine," Hank said. "I've had worse said to me for less reason."

Irish winced. "Maybe so, but I don't want my name on that list." Then he took a deep breath. "They say confession is good for the soul, and I have something to confess. I can count on one hand, the number of times I've *ever* had more than one conversation with the same woman, so I'm no good at communicating what I'm thinking and feeling. Except for Aunt Zee, you're the only one who's taken me to task and made me sorry. I don't want you to hate me. I am sorry if I offended you. Will you forgive me?"

Hank was in shock. Never in her life had a man apologized to her for anything, not even her grandpa. Her throat swelled with an emotion she wasn't prepared for, and was grateful it was dark, because she was blinking back tears.

"Apology accepted, but don't feel bad. No one understands me, and I tend to rub everyone the wrong way. I can't explain what I know how to do, and I can't explain how the visions happen. I was in shock that you were really there, or I would never have touched you... or said what I said."

He shook his head. "I think you're special, in a way few people are. Never apologize for it. One day, I hope you trust me enough to share your true name with me."

She was silent, weighing the wisdom of what she was about to do, and then spoke.

"My name is Hannah."

Irish held out his hand. "Joseph Michael Kelly. Pleased to meet you."

Hank clasped her fingers around it. "Likewise, Boss. I trust we're keeping this between ourselves?"

"Absolutely," Irish said. "And actually, I didn't hire you. Aunt Zee did. And that blasted Dun is her horse, too, so I'm not really your boss."

Hank blinked. "Then what do I call you?"

He shrugged. "An admirer? But Irish will do. Sleep well, Hannah Doyle." And then he turned and walked away, leaving her in the middle of the road, with the sound of Pup's footsteps running up behind her.

———

HANK WAS grateful for the stirring air and fell asleep with the slight breeze blowing on her face. Pup was snoring at the foot of her bed, and her rifle was on the floor beside her. She was dreaming of a waterfall, and standing naked beneath it, washing herself clean when the dream shifted, and suddenly she was sitting at a campfire, staring across the flames into the dark. In the dream, an old man walked out of the shadows, and she knew him. It was her grandfather. His image was wavering, and just as he was beginning to disappear, she heard his voice in her ear.

Beware the scar-faced man who rides the roan.

Hank woke abruptly, her heart pounding. She grabbed her rifle and ran out of the wagon, her heart pounding from the adrenaline rush of the dream.

Dawn was already breaking.

Lefty saw her and brayed.

Pup was at her heels.

It was time to start the day.

———

IRISH WOKE before daylight with one thing on his mind. Hannah Doyle had given him a gift last night. Her trust. And he would go to his grave before he'd break it. Now all he needed was her love.

He smelled coffee brewing as he began to get dressed. Mina was in the house, and he needed to talk to Zee. By the time he got downstairs, she was in the kitchen with Mina, having coffee.

"Mornin', Aunt Zee. Mornin', Mina."

"Morning, Mr. Irish," Mina said.

Zee put down her cup as she gave Irish the once-over. "Good morning, darling. No lingering aftereffects from yesterday?"

"No, ma'am. But I have to go into Delphi to talk to the sheriff about it. He needs to be made aware of what happened, so others can be on the lookout."

Zee frowned. "Sit down and eat some breakfast before you go."

Irish sat, and Mina put a plate of fried eggs and biscuits in front of him, and poured him a cup of coffee. As he began to eat, Zee began to question him.

"I thought those rustlers got caught in the stampede."

Irish shrugged. "So did I, but Hank said otherwise."

Zee's eyes widened. "What do you mean? What did she say?"

He took a quick sip of coffee. "That it wasn't over… whatever that means."

Zee's eyes narrowed. "Then it means exactly that. If some of them survived, they may not be the kind to go scurrying with their tails between their legs. We'll have to be on alert."

"I'm aware of that. I already have the men on double shifts until we get fences mended and the herd moved. If you need anything ordered from Delphi, now's the time to speak up. I'm not taking the wagon unless you do." Then he finished off his last few bites and chased it with the last of his coffee.

Zee glanced at Mina. "Do we need anything? Flour? Beans? Coffee?"

Mina shook her head.

"Nothing here then," Zee said. "But I have a request. If they still have some of that Cashmere Bouquet bar soap from back East, I would love some. If they don't, just bring me some of that white bar soap, and the soft bar soap we use for laundry."

"Yes, ma'am, and I won't need a wagon for that," Irish said. "As soon as I talk to Jim, I'll be heading out."

"You be careful," Zee said.

Irish got up from the table, then leaned over and kissed her cheek. "Always, and you two be good," he added, and gave them both a wink.

Their giggles followed him out the door.

A short while later, Irish was in the saddle. As he rode up to the corral, he stopped and called out to Hank.

"I'm riding into Delphi. Need anything?"

Hank paused, and then walked over. "No, sir. I stocked up right before I came out here."

Irish frowned. "Not sir, Irish. Remember? Be careful. See you later," he said, then rode off up the road at a lope.

Hank sighed. The man did sit a horse in fine fashion, and it didn't hurt that he was fine-looking, too.

The Dun snorted.

She turned around, her hands on her hips, and laughed. "What? Are you jealous now? God forbid I'd pay attention to anyone but you."

Then she bridled him up, threw the saddle blanket on his back, and walked him to the fence before climbing up to the top rail. There she sat, toying with the idea of mounting him. She knew he remembered his rider. And he'd long since accepted her handling him. Now was as good a time as any.

She leaned forward as she'd been doing for days now, putting her weight across his back before sliding down to the ground, only this time, she slid her leg over his back and slipped on.

The Dun's ears twitched.

She could feel his muscles bunching between her legs.

"Good boy," she said softly. She whistled her quail call, rubbed the side of his neck, then grasped the reins a little firmer and turned him away from the railing. He began to walk, following her commands, backing up, turning, then riding him at a walk, before moving him into a lope.

It was glorious. He rode like a dream.

She didn't know Zee was watching from her bedroom on the second floor, and clapping her hands with delight for what she was witnessing. In Zee's mind, it would be no time before she could ride that beauty herself. It took her a few moments to realize Hank Doyle was on the Dun without a saddle or a regular bridle, and at that point, realized they were still a distance away from success. But it was a start, and that was farther than they'd been before her arrival.

Unaware she had a spectator, Hank was in her element as she rode, wishing she trusted the horse enough to take him out of the corral and give him his head. Instead, she finally rode him to the water trough, and dismounted. Without hesitation, she slipped the bridle from his mouth, took the blanket off his back and put it back in the tack room, then stabled the Dun and wiped him down. Since he'd accepted that far smoother than she'd expected, she decided she would give him another workout later and went back to her wagon to get the plate and cup Liam brought from the cookshack and headed down to see Bud. She was hungry, and hoping for leftovers.

Bud was scrubbing down the tables and benches when she walked in.

"Hey Bud, thank you for the food last night."

He grinned. "Aw, that's alright, girly. Have you et yet?"

"No. I was hoping there might be a cold biscuit or two laying around."

"I can do better than that," he said. "Sit yourself."

Hank sat and ate cold biscuits and beans, with red-eye gravy for soppin', and washed it all down with cold camp coffee.

"Thank you, Bud. I'm gonna miss all your good cooking when my job here is over," she said, and walked out.

Bud was beaming. Nobody bragged on his food. They just ate it. But the girly was nice, and she was kind. He'd happily feed her any time of the day.

––––––––––––

IT WAS MIDMORNING when Irish rode into Delphi.

As territory towns go, it wasn't much, but it was enough. There were people on the clapboard sidewalk, and riders and wagons in the street with no rhyme or reason to the order of traffic, other than to stay out of each other's way. A couple of kids and a dog were playing in the street, and a drunk was sleeping it off beneath a bench outside of the Delphi Saloon.

Irish rode straight to the sheriff's office, then braced himself as he went in. Thanks to the row of cells at the back of the room, it always smelled like vomit, urine, booze, and stale coffee, and the man with the badge sitting behind the desk didn't smell much better.

When Irish walked in, Omar Ledbetter looked up.

"Morning, Irish! Haven't seen you for a while. What's up?"

Irish nodded. "Morning, Sheriff. We had an incident out

at the ranch. Thought I better let you know," then he proceeded to explain what had happened.

By the time Irish had finished, Ledbetter was frowning, bothered by the news. The last thing he wanted was an all-out war between rustlers and ranchers.

"You're not the first to mention rustlers to me, but you are the first I know of to have had contact with them, and lived to tell it. We have reason to believe it's the Dawson Gang. Did you get a good look at any of them? Dawson has a big nose and a long scar on the right side of his face, and he's so bowlegged he walks on the sides of his boots."

"No, I only saw them through my field glasses, and I couldn't say if any of them lived through the stampede, although it's possible. I set out to get my cattle back, and I did. Whatever happened to them in the process was their problem."

Ledbetter nodded. "Bad business... rustling, but the Dawson Gang is worse. They aren't picky about what they go after, and aren't known for leaving witnesses."

"So, I've heard," Irish said. "If I hear of anything further, I'll let you know."

Ledbetter walked Irish out the door. "Gonna be another hot one. Give Miss Zee my regards."

"I'll do that," Irish said, got back on his horse and rode down the street to the Ellis Dry Goods.

The aroma of the dry goods store was just as eclectic as the jail, but less offensive. The shelves had small packets of premeasured coffee and salt, a few cans of peaches and tomatoes, as well as bags of beans stacked beside boxes of ammunition and, to Irish's relief, the fancy-wrapped bars of soap. Aunt Zee was going to be pleased.

Gert Ellis, the owner's wife, clerked at the store. She slapped her hands on the counter as Irish approached. All business and no smile.

"Morning, Irish. What can I do for you?" she asked.

"Aunt Zee's wanting some bars of that Cashmere Bouquet bar soap, and some laundry soap too," and even as he was saying it, he was thinking of Hannah. He didn't know if it was proper to give a lady soap. He didn't want to offend her by having her think she needed a bath. And, while she'd given up her femininity for a livelihood, she surely still thought and felt like a woman.

"How many bars do you want?" Gert asked.

"I'd say three bars of the fancy soap, and three bars of the laundry soap outa do it." Gert grabbed them off the shelf and set them on the counter. But before she could get them wrapped up, Irish took up a single bar of each soap and set them aside. "Wrap these separate," he said.

Gert nodded without comment, took the coins he laid on the counter, and dropped them in the till.

"Give my regards to Miss Zee," Gert said.

"Yes, ma'am," Irish said, and exited the store. He put the packages in his saddlebag, eyed the saloon across the street, then untied his horse and let him drink from the water trough beneath the hitching post, trading the notion of a shot of whiskey for a drink from his canteen, then mounted up and rode out of town.

High noon had come and gone when Irish topped the rise above the ranch. He saw Hannah on the Dun, galloping around the arena like they'd been doing it all their lives, and felt like he'd been gut-punched. He didn't want this to be happening, because once she got the horse broke to ride, she'd be gone. His only saving grace was that she was riding the horse bareback, and until it was broke to bridle and saddle, it wouldn't work for Aunt Zee.

He headed down the hill with a heavy heart, and stopped at her wagon.

Pup came out from under it, eyeing the man without moving. Pup was hesitant about his welcome, but had already associated him with Hank, which didn't make Irish the enemy.

"Good boy," Irish said. "I'm leaving your girl a little present. Take care of it, and her for me, will you?"

Then he put the little package of soaps on the top step of the wagon, and got back on his horse. As he rode past the corral, he tipped his hat to her.

Hank smiled, and raised her arm in greeting.

After stabling his horse, he headed for the house.

Zee was all smiles when she met him at the door.

"Brought your soaps," he said, and handed her the package.

"Thank you, darling, but did you see? Hank is riding the Dun."

He nodded, and turned away.

Zee frowned. "What's wrong?"

"When she finishes what she came to do, she'll be gone," he muttered.

"So? You didn't want her here. I'd think you'd be happy," she said.

He sighed. "I don't want her to go," and walked out of the room.

Zee blinked, then blinked again, and then she smiled.

Praise the Lord, I never thought I'd live to see this day.

————

HANK FOUND the package that evening as she returned to the wagon. She recognized it as having come from the dry goods store in Delphi, because they'd wrapped her purchases the same way, so she sat down on the top step, with Pup between her knees. She gave him a quick hug, and then moved him aside.

"Pup! Sit!" she said, pointing at the ground.

Pup sat, tongue lolling out the side of his mouth, grinning for all he was worth. She was still smiling at his goofy expression when she untied the string and unwrapped the gift.

The laundry soap was a thoughtful surprise, but the fancy soap took her breath away. It wasn't just a gift. It was a girly gift. Her first present ever, and before she knew it, tears were welling.

"Oh my, oh my," she whispered, as she got up and went inside.

She sat down on her bed and began smoothing out the

paper they'd been wrapped in then folded it into a neat square, tucking the string within the folds before putting it in a drawer. She put the laundry soap in a cupboard, but she kept back the fancy soap and inhaled the aroma. Cashmere Bouquet. Even the name sounded exotic. It smelled like flowers and everything fresh and clean. Like a woman should smell.

Tears rolled. The bar of soap represented a world and a life she'd never known. She knew who it was from, but she didn't know what it meant. Was this just more of his apology, or something more.

She was scared of her feelings. If she read too much into this, he would break her heart. If she pretended it meant nothing, she could, unintentionally, hurt him. She'd spent her whole life keeping men at bay, and now that she'd found one who might actually matter to her, she was terribly afraid she wasn't enough.

But that night, when she stripped to wash up, she used the fancy soap. It felt like velvet on her face, and when she lay down to sleep, she could still smell it on her skin. She'd never slept with a man, but tonight, she was sleeping with something a man had given her, and that was a first.

Chapter Five

THREE MORE DAYS PASSED, AND EVERY DAY WHEN SHE CAME back to the wagon, there was a gift lying on her step. Once it was a handful of wildflowers wrapped in a handkerchief. The second time it was a little basket with three fresh eggs put just inside her door. A treat she hadn't had in ages. And the last time, it was a length of pink ribbon tied to the doorknob.

She was gathering the gifts to her like the treasures they were, but waiting for the day when Irish would put one in her hand. After he'd started leaving gifts, he'd kept his distance, as if he was afraid to ask something of her for fear of being turned down. She didn't know how to communicate her appreciation and feelings without making a fool of herself, so she did nothing but cast shy glances when she thought he wasn't looking.

The next day when she woke up, it was with a feeling of dread, and didn't know why. She needed to say something, do something, at least send him a signal of her feelings, and so she tied the pink ribbon into her hair, and went to the corral.

She was already working the Dun, trying to get him to accept a saddle, when the ranch hands came into the stable to get their horses. She knew today was branding day, and that they'd be working cattle less than a mile from the main house. She guessed Irish would ride out with them. When she saw him come into the stable, then walk past all the stalls to the gate between the stable and the corral, she led the Dun to the gate to greet him.

"Morning," Hank said.

"You make it a good one," Irish said, and when he saw the pink ribbon in her hair, the delight on his face said it all.

She ducked her head, and then took a deep breath. She couldn't believe she was afraid of the sound of two simple words, but they had to be said.

"Thank you." Once they'd been said, the rest of her joy spilled out. "I am sadly lacking in social graces, but nobody has ever given me a gift before. You have showered me with treasures, to the point I am overwhelmed. I don't quite know how to act, or what to say, but you have to know how dear they are to me, and how much you...uh...what I think of... that you are..." She rolled her eyes. "Obviously, I am hopeless."

Irish reached across the gate and cupped her face in both hands.

Breath caught in the back of her throat. It was the same scary feeling she always had when she first met a new horse, thinking, *could it hurt her?*

"You are exactly how you are meant to be, and you have stolen my heart," he said softly, then leaned down and kissed her.

The world tilted beneath Hannah's feet. She dropped the reins she was holding, and had it not been for the gate between them, she would have been in his arms.

When he turned her loose, the blaze in his eyes seared straight to her soul.

"The men are waiting on me. Will you talk with me tonight?"

Too stunned to speak, she could only nod.

"Until tonight," he said, and left her standing.

One of the men had Irish's horse saddled and waiting, and he mounted in one leap, then they were gone.

Only then did Hank realize she'd dropped the reins, and that the Dun had pulled the ribbon out of her hair. Her whole body was humming with an energy she'd never known. She was both excited and anxious for tonight, but right now, she still had this horse to deal with.

"You are a menace," she muttered, as she snatched the ribbon out of his mouth and tied it back in her hair. She grabbed the reins and led him to a saddle horse by the horse trough, with the saddle hanging on it. "The ribbon is mine, and that is yours." She swept her hand into the air in a dramatic gesture, knowing the horse was watching and listening to the sounds of her voice. "This is your life now. You think you are in charge but you're not. I am, and last night, they told me your name. *Taysha*. Friend. It means the same in both languages. So, Taysha, today you will stand still for me and learn something new."

Then she tied the reins to the corral and swung the saddle onto his back. She'd set it on his back numerous times before, but she'd never fastened the girth.

The Dun's ears flicked as he felt the weight. His nostrils flared as he recognized his own scent on the leather. He was listening to her voice, to the little bird calls, and the gentleness of her touch as she stroked his neck and brushed a horsefly from his rump.

Hank exhaled slowly, then reached beneath his belly, and before the Dun knew what was happening, she had the girth tight beneath his belly and fastened down. She tugged slightly on the saddle horn, checking for any give, untied the reins, and pulled them over his head. She was in the saddle before he knew what was happening.

"*Taysha...Taysha*, we ride now."

And with one gentle nudge, the horse began to trot, and then moved to a lope, and around and around they went until she and the horse were one. Her heart was pounding as she rode to the end of the corral, leaned down and opened the gate, and then rode the Dun out of the pen.

Zee was coming from the chicken house with a basket of fresh eggs when she saw Hank and the horse come flying around the stable. The girl was laughing, and the horse was pure beauty in motion. Zee gasped at the sight, and then lifted her arm in a wave of victory as they rode past.

"Lord, lord," Zee muttered, as she watched them go. "I am past the age of mounting a horse like that. It will never be mine. He has given his heart to her."

———

THE MEN WERE SEPARATING calves from their mothers and running them into the pen where they would be branded. Branding irons were already heating in the fire, and lassos were flying. One rider was heading, the other heeling. Once the calf was on its side, the branding iron went down, searing through hair and into the flesh. The noise of mad mama cows and bawling calves was deafening, and the stench of burning hair and flesh, a stink not soon forgotten. As soon as the brand was done, the ropes came off, and the calf was released back into the herd, and the process repeated.

The herd was milling, and riders were on the alert, doing all they could to keep them calm. Irish was working the gate, letting out the branded calves, when he saw movement on the ridge. For a moment, he didn't believe what he was seeing, but there was no mistaking the Dun, or its rider. Hannah and the horse were flying.

She'd done it! She was in the saddle.

She'd broken the Dun to ride.

He lifted his hat to his foreman, then pointed.

Jim Brody turned to look, and then took off his hat as a salute to the rider.

One by one, the men became aware and stopped to look, mesmerized by the sight. That a woman had accomplished something none of them had been able to do was remarkable to all. Even those who'd been most skeptic of her presence were now believers. For a horseman, what they were witnessing was a sight to see. And in that moment, as Irish watched her riding out of sight, he knew his world would never be complete without her in it.

———

WHEN BOWLEG DAWSON made it back to the camp after the stampede that first day, he'd found two of his men afoot and alive. The next day, three of their horses came back to camp, and they immediately headed north out of Texas to the Cimarron Strip in the Oklahoma Territory. They needed to lay low, get well, and let the search for them calm down. The strip was wild and lawless, with plenty of guns for hire. It was hard riding all the way, but Bowleg was focused on one thing and one thing only. Payback.

By the time they reached the panhandle, they began hitting every saloon on the trail for the whiskey and women, and gathering himself a new gang along the way. But as he did, the story of his put-down rode with him.

How Mr. Bigshot Kelly recovered his own stolen cattle from the Dawson Gang, and that he'd done it without firing a single shot at the rustlers. How he'd stampeded his own cattle into their camp and rode over them without looking back. What was left of the Dawson Gang had become a laughingstock, and Bowleg was determined to make Irish Kelly pay.

With every passing day, Bowleg's rage at Kelly grew, until he hit the breaking point. He fired up his new gang as to what riches lay waiting and headed south again, back into Texas. They kept riding and raiding as they went, until they were back in the brush country of Southwest Texas, heading straight to the Shamrock Ranch. But this time, they weren't cutting fences and sneaking in the back door. They were coming in the front door, uninvited.

———

ON THE MORNING of branding day on the Shamrock Ranch, the Dawson Gang was ten miles outside of Delphi, and riding at a lope. In Bowleg's mind, he was already celebrating. He'd sleep good tonight knowing he'd taken down the mighty Irishman. It should up the bounty on Bowleg's head at least a thousand, and put fear in all who heard his name. And it would be Bowleg who put a bullet in Zephyr Bloom's head. Kelly would live out the rest of his life knowing he'd let down the only person who mattered to him.

AT THE SAME time Bowleg Dawson was riding south toward the Shamrock, Hannah was riding in from the west. She'd just topped the rise looking down onto the ranch, and pulled up the Dun. The horse was drenched in sweat, and so was she, but never had she felt so alive, or so at peace.

From where she was sitting, she could see Bud outside at the woodpile, and Mina hanging clothes on the clothesline behind the big house. Zee's chickens were under bushes, hunkering down in the shade, and fluffing their feathers in the dirt.

Billy Riley was finally off his crutches and limping his way back to the cookshack, carrying two buckets of water. She was thinking to herself what a beautiful sight it was to see, when the sight began to fade, and all of a sudden, she was seeing strangers on horseback riding toward the ranch with their guns drawn, shooting at everything in sight, and the man leading the gang was riding a roan.

Her heart thudded so hard against her chest she lost her breath!

The man from her grandfather's warning!

Even as the vision was fading, she knew outlaws were already riding to the Shamrock. She didn't know how far away they were, but she had to warn the others. They had to be ready for them, or they wouldn't survive the onslaught.

She tightened her hold on the reins, and gave the Dun a quick kick. He leaped forward and came down the rise on the run.

When Billy Riley saw her coming, he frowned. Something was wrong. He set the buckets inside the cookshack, and then shouted out the back door at Bud, and pointed.

Bud turned, and when he saw her riding in like that, dropped the ax and started toward the cookshack yelling at Mina, who was outside the big house, as he went.

Mina heard Bud shout and turned to look. She dropped the wet laundry back into the basket and went running toward the house, calling Zee's name.

Zee came out onto the front porch, and when she saw Hank coming back on the run, her stomach knotted. Hank Doyle was no longer laughing, and she was riding like the devil was on her tail.

HANK PULLED the Dun up to a sliding stop right in front of Zee, as the others came running.

"What's wrong, girl?" Zee asked. "Is it Irish? Has something happened at the branding?"

"Zephyr Bloom, do trust me?" Hank cried.

"Yes, of course, but what's..."

Hannah shook her head. "Please. Hear me out! I can see things before they happen. Irish knows it. But he's not here to give the orders to act. There's a gang of outlaws riding toward the Shamrock. I saw them in my mind, shooting at everything in sight as they stormed the ranch. They came to kill you, Zee. To hurt Irish. And they're gonna burn this place down before they leave. We don't have much time. Will you trust me?"

"I knew you were fey," Zee muttered. "What do we do?"

"We need three men in the stables, armed and hidden out of sight. You, Bud, and Mina get in the big house and gather all the weapons you have with you. Bud and I will stay on the ground floor. You and Mina take the second floor. The minute they ride past the stables, we'll all open fire. Shooting at them from the back and from the front. They'll be trapped in between. Irish and the hands aren't far away. If we're lucky, they'll hear the gunfire. If they don't, then it will be up to us to save the ranch. I'm going to get Pup and bring Lefty to the stables. If I don't, they'll shoot them as they ride in."

"Good lord!" Bud muttered. "Who are these men?"

Hannah shook her head. "I'm not sure. But it has to do with the rustlers from before. That's all I know."

"That's bad," Bud said. "The sheriff told Irish the rustlers were part of Bowleg Dawson's gang. If this happens, we're in big trouble. Okay, girly, we're in. It ain't gonna hurt nothin' if you're wrong. But it'll mean everything if you're right. Billy, you and Liam take the stables. Jake, you climb like a monkey. Are you up to climbing the windmill? I know you're a good shot, and that platform would be a real good place to pick off any of them trying to take cover."

"Yes sir," Jake said.

"Then go! All of you," Bud said. "Grab your weapons and all the ammunition you have then get in place and stay put. We don't know when they'll get here, but I believe Hank. And I don't want nothin' to happen to my Mina, or Miss Zee."

"I'll be right back," Hank said, and took off to the stable. She unsaddled the Dun, scooped water out of the trough and put him in his stall and locked him down, then took off running toward her wagon.

Pup saw her coming and jumped up to greet her, then sensed her anxiety and growled as she ran into the wagon. She buckled on her holster and gun, grabbed her rifle, shouldered both cartridge belts and jumped out of the wagon, running for Lefty. Pup was at her heels as she untied Lefty's rope.

"With me," she told Pup, and began leading her mule toward the stables on the run.

Lefty sensed something was wrong, and kicked and brayed, but when she gave the rope a hard yank, he took off behind her at a trot. Seconds later, she was leading him into the stable when Billy came out of a stall.

"I've got him, Hank. You get in the house," he said.

Hank then turned to her dog. "Pup. With Lefty. Stay. Guard!"

To Billy's surprise, the dog followed the mule to the stall, and when he shut the mule in, the dog sat down in front of the door like a soldier on guard as Hank disappeared inside the house.

The windows were up, as they would be on a hot day like today. The curtains were hanging limp in front of them, hiding where Bud was standing.

"Is everyone in place?" Hank asked.

Bud's eyes widened at the firepower Hank had with her.

"Yes, ma'am. Mina and Zee are at the upstairs windows facing the road. They have pistols and boxes of bullets. Jake's on the windmill. Billy and Liam are in the stable. We got the front."

"They came for Zee, but they'll kill us all. We can't let them get in," Hank said.

Bud nodded.

Hank moved into position at the window on the other side of the front door, laid out the cartridge belts, checked to make sure her pistol and rifle were loaded, then knelt to wait.

"Is that a Winchester 73?" Bud asked.

Hank nodded.

"Have you ever shot at a man before?" Bud asked.

"Yes."

"Did you kill him?" Bud asked.

"No, but I don't have a problem killing snakes if the need arises," Hank said, as she shifted her position at the window. Then her eyes narrowed at the dust cloud on the horizon. "Riders coming," she said.

Bud's gut knotted. "Dang it, girly. I was sure hopin' you were wrong."

Hank looked out the window toward the windmill. It appeared Jake had already spotted the dust cloud and was lying flat, his rifle at the ready. Her heart was pounding and there was a rivulet of sweat running down the middle of her back. She had a death grip on her rifle, and a fixed stare on the road. When the first of the riders appeared, she felt like crying, wondering if she would live to tell Irish Kelly she loved him.

"Here they come," Bud said, as the rest of them topped the rise and came riding toward the ranch in wild abandon.

———

Bowleg Dawson let out a whoop when he saw the ranch and gave his horse a swift kick, urging it into an all-out run. His men followed, their guns drawn, riding at breakneck speed toward the idyllic scene below.

They rode past Hank's wagon, then as they passed the corral, began shooting toward the house. Bowleg was in the lead as they passed the stable, and was already picturing himself riding his horse into the house and shooting the old woman where she stood, when all hell rained down upon them.

Gunfire came from everywhere, dropping his men like flies. Rifles were firing behind him and in front of him and from somewhere above them. They'd been ambushed again, but there was nowhere to run. All of a sudden, his horse went down, and he fell with it before scrambling to his feet. All he could think was to finish what he'd started, and began running toward the house, firing into the windows as he went.

———

Mina took out the last man on horseback. Zee shot one trying to crawl out of sight. Bud saw the leader's horse go down, and then the man was up and running toward the house.

Hank's rifle was empty and she was frantically reloading her pistol, when a bullet grazed Bud's head and he went down.

"Bud!" Hank screamed, but he didn't move, and she could see the scar on the face of the man coming up the steps. She had to stop him before he got in the house or Zee and Mina were done for.

She jumped up and ran toward the stairs, and spun just as the door flew inward.

There was a single moment of shock when Bowleg saw the woman, and the woman saw him, and then they fired.

Bowleg took the bullet between his eyes without fanfare and dropped where he stood.

Hank spun from the impact of the bullet in her shoulder, and fell backward onto the stairs, still clutching her pistol.

The ensuing silence was almost as frightening as the barrage of gunfire had been. There were dead men all over the place, and their horses running wild. Billy and Liam came out of the stable, while Jake began climbing down from the windmill.

Mina and Zee were still upstairs afraid to move, until they saw their boys coming out of the stable, and knew it was over. But the silence downstairs was frightening. Bud should have been calling out for Mina, and Hank's silence was ominous.

The women came out of the rooms they'd been in, just as the ranch hands ran in the front door, leaping over the dead man in the doorway.

"Oh man...Bud's down," Liam said.

Then Billy pointed. "So's Hank."

At that moment, Mina and Zee appeared at the top of the stairs. They saw Hank lying in a pool of blood on the stairs below, and Bud on the floor by the front window.

Mina screamed and ran down to Bud, but he was already coming around and moaning.

"He's alive!" she cried.

Zee dropped to her knees beside Hank and began a frantic search for a pulse. Relief surged when she found one, then pulled back her shirt to find the wound. There was an entrance wound, but no exit. She jumped to her feet just as Jake appeared in the doorway.

"Jake! Saddle up and go get Irish and the boys. Liam, ride to town and get the sheriff and the doctor out here.

Mina, bring water and bandages, and hurry. Hank's got a bullet in her shoulder and we've got to stop the bleeding on the both of them."

"What about me?" Billy asked.

Zee was so angry she was shaking, and she'd lost every vestige of ladylike manners as she handed him her pistol.

"You go back outside, and make damn sure they're dead."

"Yes, ma'am," he said, and the first body he checked was the one he stepped over coming in. "Pretty sure this one's done for. He's got a bullet between the eyes."

Zee's eyes welled as she read the scene. "Hank was standing between him and us when he came in the door. She put herself in harm's way to keep me and Mina safe. I can't have her death on my conscience. Irish would never forgive me."

Billy took off out the door as Jake rode west and Liam rode north.

———

THEY'D JUST PUT a brand to the last calf and let him out, when Jim shouted at Irish from the other side of the lot.

"Boss. Rider comin' in fast."

Irish recognized Jake, but he'd left Jake at the ranch. His heart stopped. Something must be wrong. And then Jake's horse slid to a stop right in front of him.

"Boss! Come quick. The Dawson Gang hit the ranch. We had one heck of a shootout, but the gang is all dead. Bowleg Dawson is lyin' dead on your threshold. Hank put a bullet between his eyes. She's down, and so's Bud, but they were both alive when I left. Miss Zee sent me to get you, and sent Liam to Delphi for the doctor and the sheriff."

Irish could barely form thought. "How did—?"

Jake took a deep breath. "Hank came riding in like the devil was behind her. Said she had a vision. Said she saw them comin', and Miss Zee believed her. It's a good thing or we'd all be dead. There were ten of them, Boss, and they rode in shooting. You gotta come. There's dead men ever'where."

Irish spun on one heel and began shouting at the men. Minutes later, they'd doused the branding fire, and the men were riding out behind Irish, leaving two men behind to load up the supply wagon and get it back to the ranch.

When Irish and his men topped the western rise and saw the carnage laid out before them, they could hardly take it in. They rode down in haste, but then had to dismount and walk their horses to the stables to keep from running over bodies.

Irish handed the reins of his horse off to Jim, as he ran to the house.

Billy Riley was in a chair on the front porch with a rifle across his lap and a pistol in his hand. He looked dazed.

"They're all inside, Boss."

Irish stepped over the man in the doorway and kept walking. He saw blood on the floor beneath the window to his right, and Bud reclining on a sofa with his head bandaged, and a shot glass half full of whiskey in his hand.

"We fought 'em off, Boss," Bud said.

"I will owe you forever," Irish said. "Where are the others?"

"Upstairs."

Irish turned, saw the blood dripping down the stairs, and ran up. He heard voices coming from the spare bedroom, but wasn't prepared for what he saw when he walked in.

Hannah was unconscious, bare from the waist up but covered with a sheet, except for her shoulder. He saw the makeshift bandage, and with every breath she took, the continuous spread of seeping blood. He felt the world going out from under him.

"No, please God, no."

Zee turned. "She's holding steady, Son. There's a bullet still in her, but the doctor's on his way."

Irish pulled up a chair beside her bed and sat down.

"There's nothing you can do," Zee said.

Irish's voice was shaking. There were tears in his eyes, but his jaw was set, and he wasn't moving.

"Yes, there is, and I'm doing it... making sure she never goes through another day of life on her own."

An hour later, he was still at her side when the doctor arrived and hurried inside and up the stairs. He shed his coat and opened his bag, then poured whiskey over his hands before he got to work, asking questions as he went. Irish could only listen in quiet horror as Zee and Mina related every aspect of the raid. They kept saying how Hannah had saved them with her warning, and then killed the outlaw who'd come for Zee.

And all the while, Hannah was motionless, still breathing, still bleeding, while the doctor continued to probe for the bullet lodged in her chest.

———

SHERIFF LEDBETTER AND A DEPUTY ARRIVED, followed by a man driving the dead wagon from the funeral parlor.

Ledbetter walked through the bodies to get to the house, and saw Bud reclining on the sofa with a bloody bandage on his head.

"Where's the doc?" Ledbetter asked.

Bud pointed up. "Tending to the girly."

"Did you see who shot you?" Ledbetter asked.

"Hard to say. Bullets were flying," Bud said.

"Did you shoot him?" Ledbetter asked, pointing to Dawson.

"No. I was already unconscious. I didn't see him come in. Our girly, Hank Doyle, shot him, and he shot her. She was the better shot. He got her in the shoulder. Her shot went right between his eyes."

Ledbetter frowned. "Hank Doyle? The bronc buster? Where's Kelly?"

"Upstairs with Doc and the women."

"Tell Kelly we'll get the bodies carted off. And tell Hank Doyle she's due the bounty on Dawson's head."

"Yes, sir. I'll do that," Bud said, and downed the rest of his whiskey and closed his eyes.

———

PAIN HAD PUT HANNAH UNDER, and pain woke her up just as the doctor hovering above her found the bullet, and clamped down on it with tiny forceps.

She cried aloud, moaning beneath her breath as he pulled it out. Then she felt a hand on her brow and opened her eyes. It was Irish.

"I'm here, Hannah, I'm here. You are so brave. Take it easy. The doc just pulled a bullet out of your shoulder."

She grabbed his hand, clenching her jaw and moaning beneath her breath as the doctor poured a decent amount of whiskey into the wound.

"Sweet merciful God, that hurts," she cried, as tears rolled down her face.

"I'm sorry. I'm so sorry, darlin'," Irish said.

Her eyelids fluttered, and then she squeezed his hand again and said one word.

"Bud?"

"He's okay. Just a graze. I'm so proud of you, Hannah."

"I thought I would die before I could tell you..."

She sighed, and passed out again.

"She's okay," Zee said. "The sheriff's here. I'll be here with her while the doctor finishes."

Irish gave Zee a look, then walked out of the room.

Zee knew what it meant. Don't let her die while I'm gone. She would do everything in her power to help the girl heal. Hank Doyle deserved happiness, more than anyone she'd ever known, and she knew Irish would give her that, and more.

———

WITH ALL THE hands back on the ranch, it didn't take long to get the bodies loaded up into the dead wagon and headed back to Delphi, with Ledbetter and his deputy riding along beside it.

Zee and Mina were downstairs scrubbing blood off of the floors. Bud was stretched out on the sofa, and Irish was back upstairs at Hannah's bedside.

Every time she came to, he was there to give her a drink, to put a fresh compress on her forehead for the fever that had risen. She wanted to tell him something, but couldn't stay awake long enough to get it said.

For the next four days, Irish rarely left her side, except for when the women came to bathe her, and tend her needs. At night, he slept on a pallet beside her bed, with Pup at his heels, and when she began waking long enough to eat, he fed her, falling more and more in love.

Bud's head wound was healing, and he was back to cooking for the men, but with Mina's help making all the hand pies, and baking the bread.

———

THE DAY HANNAH's fever broke was a celebration.

And the next day, she was finally strong enough to sit up and feed herself, with Irish and Pup watching her every bite. Finally, she put down her bowl and spoon and pushed it aside.

"Had enough?" Irish asked.

"Of food? Yes. I have a question. Is Lefty okay?"

"Yes, ma'am. I turned him out to pasture with our other horses. He fit in just fine."

Hannah sighed. "Thank you. Pup and Lefty are all the family I have, and I don't want Lefty to feel abandoned, and thank you for letting Pup in my room."

He leaned forward, his elbows on his knees, and fixed his gaze upon her face.

"You're welcome for everything. Now I need to say something to you. I saw you ride the Dun. It was the most beautiful thing I'd ever seen."

Hannah smiled. "He has a name. Taysha. It means friend."

Irish didn't ask how she knew that. He knew better now.

"When I kissed you..." he sighed. "That feels like a lifetime ago. Anyway, when that happened, I promised you a talk. Can I talk to you now?"

Hank's eyes widened, and she went still. "I'm scared."

"I'm scared too," he said. "I'm afraid to say I love you and hear you turn me down."

Hank's eyes welled with tears. "You love me? Truly?"

Irish reached for her hand. "Truly. When I wasn't looking, you stole my heart. Is there any chance for me that you feel the same?"

Hank threaded her fingers through his and felt the strength of him flowing into her. It was so vivid she looked down, expecting to see the reality of it happening, but it was just them, holding hands.

"I dream of you, Joseph Michael. I dream of belonging here with you and Zee. Of never again having to move from place to place. Of never having to be afraid and alone. You didn't steal my heart. You bought it with a bar of soap and never knew it. I've had that scent on my skin from the first day you gave it to me, but you were under my skin from the day we met."

Irish went weak with relief as he cupped his hands upon her face.

"Will you marry me, Hannah Doyle? Will you be my wife?"

"Yes, and thank you for the offer," she said, and fell into his arms, crying and laughing from the joy.

Pup began barking.

Zee came running, and when they gave her the news, she wept tears of delight.

———

THE WEDDING WAS the talk of the territory.

Irish Kelly and the Heartbreak Kid.

Getting married on the Shamrock Ranch where they first met.

And her wedding gift, besides the ring on her finger, was the big Dun, the horse that brought them together.

Some said Hannah Doyle had the gift of sight.

Some whispered that she won Irish Kelly's heart with a spell of magic.

The most eligible bachelor in the territory, falling for the woman who would not be tamed.

And some said it was just the hand of fate dealing from a fresh deck.

A strong-willed man who yielded to nothing, falling for a woman who yielded to no man.

The Reluctant Train Robber

Jenna Hendricks

Chapter One

"I SWEAR, IF YOU HARM EVEN ONE SINGLE HAIR ON MY daughter's head, I will hunt you down and destroy you myself!" Trent couldn't believe what he was looking at.

Not five minutes ago a rude customer shoved past him, then he heard a ringing in his coat pocket. Never could Trent have imagined something out of a thriller movie would be happening to him. No—scratch that—a horror movie.

And now? He was looking into the phone that had been secretly placed inside his jacket pocket.

The image that came up when he realized the phone in his pocket was ringing chilled him to the bone. At first, he thought it was a sick joke. But when the caller initiated a video call, with proof of life, he knew they had his little girl.

"Daddy?" The little girl with tears streaming down her face caused him to drop the shopping basket he held. Trent didn't even realize what he'd done until someone yelled at him to clean up the milk that was pooling at his feet.

"Baby? Are you alright?" Of course, she wasn't alright. Some unnamed and masked kidnappers had her in their clutches. But what did he say to his twelve-year-old girl? Could he promise to save her?

A man with a black ski mask yanked the phone from Cecilia's clutches. Was it a good thing he kept his face a secret? That meant he did intend to release Trent's little girl, right? Then a bone-chilling thought entered his mind. "What did you do to her mother?"

A harsh chuckle came over the phone. "You know, it really is too easy to grab a kid off the street when they're walking home from school. I don't know why public school districts did away with the buses." The man *tsk tsked* and shook his head, as though the lack of school buses was Trent's fault, or something.

Trent looked at his wrist. It was already past four in the afternoon. Which meant that they must have abducted Cecilia almost two hours ago. They couldn't be too far from the Phoenix suburb where Candace and her new husband lived with Cecilia. If they didn't mess with his ex-wife, then maybe he could get her to call in the local police and they could find her.

So many people these days had cameras on their houses that pointed to the street. And cars, some of them even had cameras now. Maybe someone in the area recorded Cecilia's abduction and they could get her back before dinner.

"I see those wheels turning, Trent. There is no way you are going to find us. And if we even think cops are closing in, your little girl here won't see another day." The man pulled the phone closer to his face and growled. "But do exactly as I say, and you will get your baby girl back unharmed very soon."

"What do you want?" It was all Trent could do to keep from yelling into his phone. He did his very best to calm himself and clear his mind. If he could think of a way for Cecilia to get out of this, he would. But getting emotional and angry wouldn't help her. Not now. The anger could come later, when he had his daughter back safe and sound.

"First, I need you to leave the grocery store and go home. Our conversation is best had with no one else around." The man hung up the phone without another word.

Did that mean Trent had time to call the cops? The bad guys in the movies always said no cops. But when the victims failed to report the crime, then it never turned out well for them. Trent may have been an Army veteran, but he wasn't trained in rescuing kidnap victims. He didn't even have a job that would help him fight. At least, not in this situation. No, his job had been something that would only help him if he had one of the kidnappers to interrogate. Didn't matter that he'd never tortured or interrogated anyone in real life. His training had included ways to get information out of someone, but he'd only done it in a classroom setting.

He bit his lip and looked around to see if that man who bumped into him earlier was anywhere nearby. That guy had to know what was going on, didn't he? Maybe he was even one of the kidnappers.

Trent almost jumped when the new phone began ringing again. He hesitantly answered while he scanned the faces around him. "Yes?"

"I told you to head home. No stops along the way, no phone calls. I'll know if you deviate from my instructions." The man hung up again.

Trent started toward his truck, leaving the shopping basket on the floor and ignoring the stares and glares from those around him. He figured there were eyes on him from someone working with the kidnapper, so he'd wait until he got into his truck and then call Candace to see what she knew.

Only once he was in his truck and on the road did he realize that his phone was gone. "Great, they picked my pocket when they dropped the new phone into my jacket." Trent hit the steering wheel with his hand while he sat at the red light waiting impatiently to get home. The sooner he got home, the sooner he could get more information.

He had no clue what they could want from him. If it was money, they were out of luck. He didn't have anything of value. The divorce cleaned him out. One would think that if the wife cheated and remarried, she'd get nothing in the divorce. But somehow, his ex found a way to squeeze blood from this turnip.

If they were after money, they would have had better

luck with Candace and her new husband. While they weren't rich, they did have a lot more money than Trent did. This kidnapping was making no sense to Trent whatsoever. What could he have that they wanted?

Then it dawned on him. "Oh, crap on a cracker."

Chapter Two

"I KNOW, I'M REALLY EXCITED FOR THIS WEEK, TOO. LET ME TELL you." Dakota Spencer rolled her eyes and shook her head. She loved her job, but sometimes a person just needed a break. And this next week was going to be wonderful. She had every day planned out like the Army planner she was. Well, Army Reserve logistics specialist, to be exact.

While Dakota was what some people called a "weekend warrior," she also worked for the Grand Canyon Express as an HR supervisor. She didn't actually supervise people, she just managed paperwork and employee files. But to her, it could be a rewarding job. Just not as rewarding as her weekends in the field with her Army platoon.

The railroad she worked for just finished laying off a dozen linesmen. She hated layoffs. That was the worst part of her job, but at least she still had a job. It seemed the railroad was always shrinking. While she didn't work for one of the big lines that delivered cargo, she did think that her job would be relatively secure. Who didn't enjoy a pleasure ride on the rails? Especially when those rails ended up in a place as beautiful as the Grand Canyon? But recent inflation and loss of jobs all over the world, also meant that people weren't traveling for pleasure like they once did. Her company had cut back on the trips they offered, so that meant they also needed to cut employees.

"How long has it been since we've all gotten together?" Darla, Dakota's older sister, asked.

Dakota thought for a moment. While she did have vacation, she rarely took it. Since she was gone one weekend a month and two weeks every summer, she didn't think she should take a real vacation. She felt guilty even taking a three-day weekend. But this time, she knew she needed to get away and recharge. "I think the last time we were all together was about five years ago."

"That's right. It was when mom graduated with her master's degree. Now, that was a party." Darla laughed and then reminisced about the party.

"The last time I saw your kids was last Christmas when you came to visit for a weekend. I bet I don't even recognize any of them now." A slow smile spread across Dakota's face as she remembered how shy Matty was. Matilda, or Matty as everyone called her, was already running circles around her mother when she was only two and a half. Now that she was three, would the pretty little girl be running marathons?

"You better recognize them all. I send you enough pictures on a weekly basis that you should have every freckle on their faces memorized." Darla huffed and then laughed. They spent another fifteen minutes going over their itinerary for the trip that would start the next day.

To say that either woman was excited would be an understatement. They had rooms at the Edge of the Rim Hotel and Resort. It was the only 4-star hotel on the rim with views of the canyon from the rooms, as well as an outdoor dining venue that looked out over the vast expanse of the canyon.

Even though it was early October, Darla and Steven had agreed to take the kids out of school for a week to enjoy this opportunity to see one of the best natural wonders of the West. Dakota always wondered why the Grand Canyon wasn't one of the official seven wonders of the world. Maybe because it was a natural wonder, and not a man-made one?

Either way, she had put it on her list of the seven best places in the world to visit when she was only eight years old and her family had spent a Christmas there.

"You know, one of these years we really should do Christmas up big at the canyon, like when we were little kids. Remember that?" Dakota went on to wax poetic about their time there, especially the snowcapped ragged edges of the canyon.

"When Matty is a little bit older, we can talk about it. Right now, I doubt she'd understand how Santa could find us if we didn't wake up in our own home on December twenty-fifth."

Dakota remembered what it was like to believe in the magic of Christmas, and she wished she still did. "Okay, one day. And soon, we will do that. But for now, let's make sure we have packed enough layers for October in the canyon. I hear it can snow as early as Halloween. And the nights can get down into the fifties this time of year."

"Or, maybe you can meet a man who will keep you warm?" Darla giggled.

Dakota had hoped that her sister would stop with all the not-so-subtle comments about meeting a man. Any time they got together, she'd ask when Dakota would be getting married and having kids. Darla's kids wanted cousins to play with before they got too old.

"You know that I'm not interested in meeting a man right now. Work is my focus. It has to be." Not to mention that her heart still hadn't healed from the wound a certain man who shall remain nameless inflicted back in college. Dakota had sworn off men so she could finish her degree. Then it just became easy to stay away from the lying and cheating pigs when she started her new job.

Okay, okay, so maybe not all men were lying and cheating pigs, it was just the ones she tended to choose.

Darla must have gotten the hint because she went on to tell a quick story about Matty and how she had a boyfriend in Sunday school.

When they hung up, Dakota could feel the smile on her

face from ear to ear. She needed this break from the company as well as time with her family. She had purchased her ticket to ride the Grand Canyon Express at the local ticket booth, instead of claiming the free ride she was able to get. Mostly so no one on the train knew she was from HR. The last thing she needed was for something to come up needing a corporate person to handle.

No, she'd go incognito and get treated just like everyone else.

The next morning Dakota was up and getting ready before her alarm had even considered sounding off. The idea of sleeping in didn't even register in her mind, even though it was a Saturday. At least not yet. Not only was she too excited to sleep any more, but her internal clock didn't understand vacation time. It better get the memo, and soon. She had hoped to sleep in at least one or two mornings while on vacation.

When she realized how early she was, Dakota decided to head out to the local coffee shop that she rarely allowed herself to visit. Now that she was on vacation, she'd spend the six dollars for the peppermint mocha and another five dollars for the breakfast sandwich. It was vacation. What better time to splurge on empty calories?

Besides, if she knew her family, she'd burn off more than what that breakfast put on in no time flat. The itinerary did call for daily hikes and a donkey ride to the bottom of the canyon. That ride alone would probably burn off three days of coffee shop breakfast. She grinned and happily placed her order when it was her turn.

For the first time in who knew how long, Dakota Spencer relaxed and sipped her coffee while eating her breakfast. She had at least thirty minutes to enjoy the peace and quiet and fantasize about the upcoming journey. .

Even though she worked for the Grand Canyon Express, Dakota rarely rode the train, or any other mode of transportation to the canyon. She never had time to stop and smell the monkeyflowers. But this trip would be different.

Dakota pulled out the small book on Grand Canyon flora

and fauna and leafed through it once again as she took her time. Plants such as the toadflax penstemon and Palmer lupine caught her attention. Too bad most of the flowers she wanted to see were no longer in bloom. Although, the hoary tansyaster should still be in bloom this late in the year... maybe she could take a few clippings home with her to add to her desert landscaped yard.

Something inside screamed at her to look up. But when she did, all she saw was a few railway employees. Not that she knew them personally, but their uniforms made it almost impossible to miss who they worked for. Two men in the dark blue with red trimmed collars ignored her and saun-tered over to pick up what must have been a phoned in order of coffee and pastries.

The round patch on their chests signified that they were train workers, which also reminded Dakota it was time to get a move on. Not that she needed to see the pre-show entertainment, but it was kinda fun to see the bad guys get hauled away to the hoosegow before the train departed.

She shook her head thinking about fake train robberies and cattle rustling. Not that those things didn't happen, they were just from a bygone era. One which she was very glad not to live in. Watching the show from the bleachers was so much more enjoyable than experiencing a real-life train robbery.

One of the things that drew Dakota to this job, was the history of the train. A hundred years ago it wasn't uncommon for the average traveler to experience a robbery, or see cattle being hustled away from one of the ranches the train steamed past.

Thankfully, today was very different. Trains no longer carried large loads of cash or gold from one banking location to another. Armored cars were used when money, in any of its varied forms, moved locations. Along with a host of armed guards.

No, the only thing the Grand Canyon Express trans-ported was people, food, and the occasional tchotchkes and trinkets that were sold in the Grand Canyon. While she had ridden a train that staged robberies in the past, this particular one didn't have any such plans. Which she was very glad for. In fact, she chose this particular departure because it was the only one on Saturdays that *didn't* have a train robbery. The ride would be almost two and a half hours and she brought a book she'd been meaning to read for ages, but never had the time for.

In fact, she had three books on her e-reader that she hoped to read this week. It was a vacation, after all. Sure, she'd do the hiking, swimming, donkey riding, and all the normal stuff one did when visiting the Grand Canyon. But, she'd also have downtime each day to sit out in what was left of the sun and read.

Well, that was if a freak snowstorm didn't come through and force her inside. Then, she'd be by the fireplace reading, drinking hot cocoa instead of a fruity summer drink. Still, she'd get her reading time in.

It was too bad that fate had other plans for her trip. Or was it a good thing fate had other plans? Only time would tell.

Chapter Three

NOTHING WAS GOING THE WAY TRENT PLANNED. NOT ONLY DID he not get a chance to call his ex, or anyone else for that matter, but he was being forced to do something he swore he would never do—help a kidnapper get his way. It was all fine and good for the American government to say they didn't negotiate with kidnappers, especially when it was adults they abducted. But when it was one's own daughter?

Somehow, they had this planned out extraordinarily well. When Trent arrived home, there was another masked man already waiting in his living room. While he couldn't be sure, he thought it was a different person from the one who bumped into him at the grocery store, as well as different from the one he spoke to on the phone. This man was short and stocky, while the man from the phone was tall and thin. The man in the grocery store seemed average and rather easy to forget.

Trent had to stop himself from throttling the man standing in his living room just staring at him. On any other day, he would have thought the intruder was your ordinary house thief. But on this day? He knew it was just one more person in this cockamamie scheme. One he still didn't understand. "What?"

The door closed on its own behind Trent who stood in

the doorway glaring at the man wearing all black, along with a black ski mask. It was too cliché to be real. If he hadn't spoken to his daughter, he would have thought he was being punk'd. But this wasn't a reality TV show trying to pull one over on him. This was real.

"I'm here to make sure you follow the rules." The man had a deep voice, but it wasn't indistinct from any he'd heard in the area. Which meant he was most likely a local, or from somewhere else in the Southwest.

Trent crossed his arms over his chest. "And what rules would those be?" No one had said anything to him besides the order to not call the police. It was all so sketchy at this point; he wouldn't even know if he was breaking a rule. Other than the police one.

The man took an intimidating step toward Trent and there was just enough opening in the eye slits to see him narrowing his dull, brown eyes. "To keep your trap shut and do exactly as you're told."

Anger boiled up within Trent and his arms flew out of their own volition. "Other than go home with no groceries, and don't call the cops, I haven't been told one daggone thing yet. What is going on? Where is my daughter and why do you have her?"

Without even realizing it, Trent had taken two steps closer to the man who was considerably shorter than himself. He knew from past experiences that anyone else would have been intimidated by his move. But not this guy.

In fact, the intruder took two steps of his own closer. Then his beefy finger came up to stab him in the chest. Trent noticed that the man was holding a small plastic toy. He wasn't sure, but it looked like something his daughter might have received from a happy meal.

Trent grabbed the man's hand and brought it closer to his face. "Where'd you get this toy?" On closer inspection, it was one of those colorful plastic toys that resembled a dog character from a cartoon his daughter hadn't watched in years—Dog Patrol, or something like that.

The man pulled his hand back. "That's mine. Don't

touch my stuff." The glare coming from the little man should have frightened him, but it didn't. Not after realizing that this man played with kid's toys. Somehow, that knowledge took the scary away and replaced it with a sense of uncertainty. Either this man was a little slow, or he just hadn't grown up yet. *Who still played with toys designed for kids under eight?*

"Fine. Give me back my daughter." The words came out as more of a growl than a request.

The short chuckle that emanated from the kidnapper's chest sent Trent back a few steps. One second the guy was growling at him and the next he was laughing. What was wrong with the man? Now that he thought about it, it might not be a man, but a boy. With the mask covering so much of his face, it was hard to tell the age of the male figure standing before him.

But the moment words came out of the masked man's mouth again, Trent knew it was a man, and not a boy. The deep tenor of his voice was a dead giveaway. As well as the confident way he stood up to Trent. "Your daughter is safe, as long as you follow our orders."

"What in tarnation do you even want from me? Is it money?" Trent flew his arms all around him. "Look around, I've not got much of anything worthy of kidnapping a kid for. I'm strapped for cash all the time. If not for my job, I might go days without a decent meal." His job afforded him a hot meal once a day when he was on the clock, and that was usually the best meal he ate all day.

"We know all about your financial problems." The stranger smirked. "You really should have accepted the bribe a few months back. Then your daughter would never have been kidnapped. So, if you think about it, it's all your fault your darling little girl is in danger right now."

Trent couldn't believe his ears. This man was sick. His temper was about to flare again, when he heard a voice inside his head tell him to calm down. He knew from all his experiences and training that cooler heads always prevailed. He took a few calming breaths and then sat down on his well-worn La-Z-Boy recliner. "Alright, why don't you tell me what you want from me."

Once the man gave him his orders, he didn't leave as Trent thought he might. Instead, the man stayed with him all night and ensured that he couldn't get online or make any phone calls before leaving for work in the morning.

And then just before leaving for work, he received a picture of his daughter holding up the morning paper. She looked frightened, but unharmed. At least, he couldn't see anything wrong in the photo.

Before Trent walked out the door, he looked back at the man still standing in his living room. Chug had been the only name the stranger gave him the night before. "Can I have my cell phone back now?"

He shook his head. "You'll get it back along with your daughter once this is all over. Do as you're told and neither of you will be harmed. Oh, and if you're thinking about telling a coworker, don't. We have eyes and ears everywhere. You never know who is a part of our team." An evil grin accompanied his final words.

The entire drive to work Trent couldn't get those words, and that look, out of his mind. Once he arrived at the station, he looked around at everyone he knew and wondered who had accepted their bribe, and who, like him, was being forced to assist. He'd likely never know. And that thought rankled him. It wasn't like they were his fellow soldiers on the field of battle, where their lives depended on each other. These were the people he'd worked with daily, for years.

He'd never once thought he couldn't rely on them to have his back on the train. However, with the recent cutbacks and the economy the way it was, maybe someone felt they had no other way out? Surely, none of them had anything to do with his daughter's kidnapping. Who in their right mind would be part of abducting a child?

Wasn't humanity, in general, hardwired to protect kids? It seemed every year there was more and more evil in this world and Trent couldn't understand why.

Every part of him wanted to scream at the top of his

lungs what was going on, but then he saw the picture of his little girl holding that morning's newspaper in her hands. Tears were on her cheeks and her eyes were red, probably from crying all night long. He could read the fear on her face and it gutted him.

No, he'd do as they said. But the moment he got his little girl back, he'd turn over every single rock to find anyone and everyone who had any part in this. It didn't matter who was involved, he'd find them and make sure they paid for what they'd done.

Now, he had to put his soldier cap on and follow orders to ensure his little girl survived the day.

Chapter Four

DAKOTA FOUND HER SEAT ONCE SHE ENTERED THE CAR TOWARD the end. She'd booked herself one of the more expensive tickets in the observation dome. There really wasn't a bad seat in the entire train. However, the seats in the observation domes afforded a little bit of a different view. One that tended to show a little more of the beauty and majesty of the Arizona skyline.

After walking up the small set of steps, she took her seat and looked out the window at the hustle and bustle of the people on the platform. For the first time in a week, she sat back and sighed with relief. She had finally gotten away from the stress of her job and would soon be headed toward her family and the fun they always had together.

While she waited for the train to depart, she leaned her head back and closed her eyes. People watching was always fun, but a wave of exhaustion filled her, and she could barely keep her eyes open. Her last easy thought was how much could a little catnap hurt?

"Boo!" a voice exclaimed, causing Dakota to jump in her seat and put a hand on her chest.

"What?" Dakota blinked back the fuzz of her tiny catnap and looked around. A few people smiled and looked away. The train was still in the station, so she hadn't been sleeping for very long. "Darla? What are you doing here?"

"Surprise, little sister. I'm riding with you all the way to the Grand Canyon." Darla took the seat next to Dakota and turned to look straight in the shocked face of her sister.

Dakota's mouth opened and closed like a fish gasping for air. When she finally got her jumbled thoughts in order, she asked, "Where's your family?"

Darla waved a hand in front of her face. "They're probably already at the hotel checking in. I decided to surprise you and get in some quality sister time. It's been ages since it was just you and me."

"Wow. Don't get me wrong, I'm very excited to see you, but can your husband handle all three kids on his own? I know Matty is quite the handful. Elizabeth and William are too young to be of much help." Unsure if her sister was teasing, or telling the truth, Dakota couldn't help but look past her just in case the kids were standing there.

Darla shook her head. "Nope. They aren't here. It's like I said, they are probably already up at the canyon. But don't worry. We hired a nanny, and she's terrific."

One of Dakota's brows arched. "A nanny? And you left your husband alone with her at a hotel? Are you sure that's wise?" All Dakota could think of was how so many men with zero intentions of straying did when presented with a young, beautiful woman who was good at taking care of his kids.

The laughter that bubbled out of Darla had Dakota wondering if her sister was alright.

"Don't even go there. I know what you're thinking. Trust me, this nanny is nothing like what you read about in your romance novels. She's more like Mrs. Doubtfire." Darla put a finger to her chin. "Scratch that. Steven swears she's Mrs. Miracle."

"Really?" Dakota loved that book series by Debbie Macomber and even watched the movies every Christmas. "And how do the kids like her?"

"They love her. Just you wait and see."

"When did you hire her?" Dakota knew that money was tight with her sister and brother-in-law. Not because he made too little, but because they were saving for a rainy day.

"Steven got his promotion to junior partner two years earlier than we planned. That's part of what this week is about, celebrating his new role with the firm, as well as talking about our plans with the family." Darla bounced in her seat as though she were the three-year-old who still needed a nanny to watch over her.

"Congratulations. That's fantastic! But why didn't you tell me sooner? When did it happen?" A few more questions popped out of Dakota's mouth before she realized she wasn't letting her sister speak.

Darla laughed. "Whoa, slow down. Give me a chance to answer one question before you move on to the next. And before you start up again, we decided to wait until the entire family was together to tell everyone. Besides," her smiled faded and Darla bit her lower lip. "You haven't exactly had much time to chat lately. What with all the pink slips you had to deliver."

Hands in the air, Dakota shook her head. "I know, I know. And I'm so sorry for that. I've left work behind and am here one hundred percent. This week is going to be all about the family, not my job and the stress of the layoffs."

"Well, I would rather wait until we're all together to give you the details, but I've decided to start up my DIY channel on YouTube." Darla clapped her hands in front of her face and waited for her sister to react.

Pure joy and excitement filled Dakota at those words. "Oh, Darla. I'm so excited for you. I know this has been your dream for ages. Do you think you'll really have the time to do this?"

Over the years Darla had made some beautiful pieces of furniture as well as handcrafted items. In fact, most of the gifts she and her husband gave to the family every Christmas was something that Darla had created. "But, the kids. Aren't they too loud for you to film your videos?"

Darla nodded. "They have been, yes. But since Mrs.

Miracle joined us, they've been so good and quiet when I needed to film."

"Mrs. Miracle?" Dakota's brows furrowed.

Darla put a hand over her mouth. "Sorry about that. Steven and I joked a few times about her name. Her name is actually Mrs. Myrtle. Anyway, when I need to film, I head to the office we renovated recently and Mrs. Myrtle takes the kids outside to play. It's been working and I have already put together enough crafts to attend a craft fair next month and so far, I have about a month's worth of videos for YouTube. When we get home, I'm going to get started posting."

It was obvious that Darla had put a lot of energy and thought into this. Dakota almost felt slighted that her sister had said nothing about it until now. But then a noise interrupted her thoughts and she turned her head.

"I'm doing exactly as you said, keeping people away from the rear car." The male voice was familiar, but Dakota couldn't put a name to it. Not yet, at least.

"You're bringing attention to that rear car with your antics. You had better knock it off if you want your daughter to make it out of this without injury." The growled response sent shivers up Dakota's spine. That voice didn't sound familiar, but it did set off alarm bells. Was the man really threatening the life of someone's kid?

"Dakota?" A hand waved in front of her face. "Dakota, did you hear me?"

Dakota put up her hand and shushed her sister. When she noticed the questioning eyes, she pointed to her ear then down below them. The area below the observation dome Dakota and her sister were in was a lounge. It didn't open until the train was moving. For now, it was just a walkway used mostly by staff. This was the last passenger car, so no passengers would have need to be in there, at least not until the train got underway.

In a whisper so low, Dakota wasn't sure her sister was even speaking to her, Darla said, "I can't hear a thing."

Dakota looked around and realized that she was sitting

next to an air vent. She lowered her head closer to the vent and picked up more of the conversation. Then she pointed to the vent and her sister nodded her understanding.

"I'm doing exactly as you said. No one should be back here to begin with, not even staff yet. So it should be no surprise to anyone when I turn them away." The voice was sounding more and more familiar.

Dakota almost had the man's name in her head when the other voice said it.

"Trent, I swear, if you say one thing to anyone, and I mean one thing that gets anyone to even give that last car a second glace, I'm going to kill your daughter slowly in front of your eyes and then torture you until you finally give out."

Dakota almost yelped. Instead, she put a hand over her mouth and jumped up in her seat.

"What? What did you hear?" Darla's whispered request sounded so loud in Dakota's head, that she almost cried.

"Shh." Dakota looked around to make sure no one was paying them any attention. Then the whistle blew and the sound of the engine picked up before the entire train lurched forward. After that, Dakota couldn't hear anything else being said below stairs.

"Darla, I'm going to ask you to do something for me and I need for you to do it without question. Can you do that?" Dakota worried that her sister would be in danger, but if she didn't do anything at all, the entire train might be in danger.

Without a peep, Darla nodded her understanding.

Dakota leaned toward her sister and in a low voice told her what to do.

Chapter Five

TRENT RAN A SHAKY HAND DOWN HIS FACE AS HE WATCHED Max walk away. The man seemed to be in charge of the entire operation. He also seemed to be the one who was with Cecilia the one time he actually got to speak with her. Since then, he'd only received a couple of pictures proving she was still alright. Well, alright might not be the right term, but she was still in one piece.

He couldn't think about the alternatives. Trent had to think that she was being taken care of and everything would work out. But what about Candace? Since Trent couldn't call her, he wondered what she knew, or didn't know. Had the kidnappers contacted her? If so, what did they tell her?

And if Max was the one who took Cecilia, who was caring for his twelve-year-old daughter now?

He shook the thoughts out of his head. The last thing Trent needed was to go down that rabbit hole. He had to focus on the present and his mission. While he was going to do whatever it took to ensure his daughter made it out of this alive, he also needed to think about the safety of the passengers on this train. He was the conductor. And as such, every single soul aboard this train was his responsibility.

There had to be a way to inform the authorities without tipping his hand to the kidnappers. He knew what they wanted and even though Trent would most likely end up in prison for it, he'd help them get it.

However, he did not agree with their plan. It was ludicrous and would most likely backfire on them. It was obvious to Trent that someone else on the inside had given Max and his crew details about the shipment, but they were outdated. Did their insider know the information was outdated? Or did he just not know about the upgrades that had been installed only last week?

Either way, this might be his only way to notify someone without it coming back on him. With the train leaving the station, he'd have to bide his time and wait for the right moment to make his move. Hopefully, no one caught on to what he was up to.

For now, he had to keep people away from the last car. And if at all possible, he needed to keep crew and passengers out of this lounge.

But first, he had to walk through the cars and say hello to the passengers and make sure his staff were on time with their duties. Trent ran a well-oiled crew. Even with the recent layoffs, he knew his job was secure. For the moment anyway.

So, with all of that in mind, he stepped out of the lounge and ran right into the last person he expected to see on his train.

"Oomph." The pretty auburn-haired passenger blinked and then backed up a step. "Trent? I'm sorry, I didn't see you."

"Dakota Spencer. Are you alright?" Trent looked the woman up and down to make sure that he hadn't hurt her. The last thing he wanted to do was upset, or hurt, one of the HR supervisors. Especially this one.

While Trent wouldn't call her an enemy, he knew she wasn't his biggest fan. In fact, he'd heard that she had short-listed him for the recent layoffs, but her boss crossed his name off the list.

"I'm fine. Are you in a hurry to get somewhere?" Dakota looked around before settling her gaze back on him.

"Actually, yes. Sorry for bumping into you. I was going through the checklist of what still needs to be done. And I didn't expect anyone trying to enter the lounge. It's usually not open yet." Trent scratched his chin and rubbed up against a few short stubbles that would be hard to hide from the rule-following HR person. Either he needed a new razor, or he just wasn't paying attention to his morning routine. Most likely the latter.

"Oh, right. I wasn't actually coming to the lounge. I was just hoping to get in a walk and stretch my legs before settling down with a good book for the journey." She smiled, but it seemed forced somehow.

Trent reached behind him and closed the door to the lounge. "Actually, I think this lounge might need to be closed for the duration of this trip. I'll put in a work order when we arrive at the Grand Canyon."

"Oh?" A neatly groomed brow arched above one eye and Dakota seemed to be waiting for a reason behind the closure.

Trent hadn't expected to need to give a reason for closing the lounge. At least not yet. Shoot, he'd only just decided to close it when he ran into Dakota. He'd have to come up with something that needed to be fixed that also couldn't be done during the journey. "Ah, yes. If you will excuse me, I need to make my way through the passenger cars and greet the passengers. I'll be sure to send in the work request when I get to the engineering car."

"Is there anything I can do to help?" Dakota asked.

The woman wouldn't leave him alone. If he wasn't careful, Max would think that Trent was already spilling the beans. The hairs on the back of his neck stood at attention as though someone was watching him. He looked around and spotted another member of Max's team.

The young man was called Magnet. The guy looked to be college-aged and if he hadn't been with Max, Trent probably wouldn't have even noticed him. The guy was average in every way—height, build, looks. Was this the man that bumped into Trent at the grocery store? If so, that made three members of the kidnapping team that Trent could identify.

A throat cleared and brought his attention back to the woman in front of him. "Trent? Is everything alright?"

"Hm? Oh. Yes. Sorry. Where are my manners. I was thinking about what message I needed to send when I got to the engineering car. Dakota, if you'll excuse me, I really must get back to work. There's a lot to do right now." He gave her a nod and half a smile, hoping she would get the hint and leave him alone.

Dakota moved to the side and motioned for him to move along. "Of course. I'm sorry to have gotten in your way. I'll just get in my walk and head back upstairs to my e-book."

"Enjoy the ride." As Trent walked toward the next passenger car, he noticed Magnet eyeing Dakota. He hoped that the woman would be safe. She may not be his favorite person in the world, but he certainly didn't wish her any harm.

Chapter Six

Dakota watched Trent walk away. At one time, she had thought he was a handsome man. Not that she was ever interested in dating anyone. Just that he had caught her eye, once or twice. Now? She was glad that she'd never done anything about it.

This was exactly why she was done with men—none of them could ever be trusted.

She'd noticed the only other person near them, and how Trent had recognized him. The stranger was at least ten years her junior. He was average looking with blond hair. And when she looked closer, she noticed his blue eyes but thought that he'd be handsome if his eyes weren't so close together. Dakota had read somewhere a long time ago that when eyes were set too close, it meant the person could have a tendency toward criminal behavior.

Dakota had scoffed at the idea that a person's eye placement would mean they could be psychotic, or criminal. But now? The way he looked at Trent, then her, sent chills down her spine. The man had blue eyes, but they were tiny and dark—almost like a black dot at the center of the blue iris. She had to stop herself from rubbing her hands along her arms.

Once Trent exited the small antechamber they were in,

she was alone with the man. Well, almost alone. At the top of the steps she had come down from were four or five other passengers. The train wasn't fully booked that day, and neither was the observation car she was riding in. So, while she wasn't truly alone with the man, she did *feel* as though she was.

The first thing Dakota wanted to do was run back up to safety, but that might look strange to the man. She'd noticed the way he looked at Trent and how Trent had recognized him. Was he the one Trent had been arguing with? She couldn't be sure, so she remembered her manners and gave him a slight nod and a tiny smile as she made her way to the exit. She had to begin her walk like she had told Trent she was doing.

If the man had been polite, he would have moved back a few steps, so as to stay out of her personal space. Apparently, he wasn't. Instead, he blocked her path. "Well, hello." The smile that followed his words was hollow.

"Hi." While Dakota was doing her best to be polite, her skin prickled at the audacity of the man to block her path.

"What's your name?" The man put his arm up over the door and looked her up and down.

Her polite smile turned upside down and she felt her disdain for the creep coming through. "Excuse me." She looked at his arm, indicating she expected him to move it.

He chuckled. "Where are my manners." He took his arm down and put his hand over his chest. "I'm Magnet. And seeing how we are on this train together, I just thought it might be nice to get know one another a little bit better."

Dakota rolled her eyes. "Magnet? Not interested. So if you'll excuse me I have somewhere I need to be."

If he hadn't of backed off, she considered pushing him to the side. Her mother would have a cow if she knew what Dakota was thinking. Even when a man was being a jerk, a lady never acted rude, or shoved a man. Well, unless he was threatening her. Then her momma would completely approve the use of force to get the man away from her.

Thankfully, it didn't go that far. Magnet moved back and

pursed his lips. Under his breath he said, "Manners." As though she was the one who needed a lesson in good manners.

Internally, she scoffed at his attitude, but she said nothing as she exited the train car and moved to the next one as quickly as she could. At least that car had a decent number of travelers. Even if the rude man, Magnet, as he called himself, followed her, there would be plenty of people around to help her feel somewhat safe.

Magnet had distracted her long enough that Trent was already at the other end of the car and preparing to exit. While Dakota wanted to hurry and catch up to the conductor, she knew that she had to play it cool. She sensed that someone was watching her from behind, most likely Magnet. The last thing she needed was to cause a problem for Trent.

But she did need to find out what was going on with the conductor. Part of her wanted to call the line sheriff. They never knew when one would be on the train, but there was always one close by. If she called him, and he wasn't already onboard, he could catch up to the train and board it while it was in motion. There were a few spots where the train slowed due to the terrain and the sheriff could get on board then. Or at least, that was what she remembered from her new hire onboarding class a few years ago.

Either way, she needed to find a way to contact the sheriff. The safety of the passengers was her number one priority. Maybe he could even find a way to check on Trent's kid?

Dakota took her time weaving through the kids scampering about *oohing* and *aahing* as they watched the desert scenery go by and give way to a high desert view with green trees on either side of the railway. As part of her own ruse, she stopped once to look out the window as they passed a copse of particularly tall evergreen trees with what looked to be an eagle soaring above. "Huh, that's a rare view."

"Lady? Is that an eagle or a contour? My dad said we might see some California contours on this ride." A young boy looked from her to the bird outside.

Dakota had to hold back her giggle at the way the little boy said "condor." She leaned down so she was on the same level as the little boy. "You know, I'm not really sure. Maybe your dad will know?"

The boy looked down at his feet. "He's not here. He's at work."

Remorse flooded Dakota's system as she had been trying to get away from the kid so she could do her own thing. But the face on the little angel standing next to her was enough to melt even the Grinch's heart. "Why don't we ask one of the people who work on this train? I bet they'll know."

This wasn't a move to get away from the kid, it really was to get an answer. Since Dakota didn't ride the rails much, she had no clue how to tell the difference in the birds that could be seen on this route. When she stood up, she noticed a service attendant looking out the window and motioning, most likely to the bird they were looking at.

"Let's go see what he is talking about." Dakota pointed to the man in a Grand Canyon Express uniform and the little boy took her hand and walked with her. As they walked only a few steps, she wondered where the kid's mom was. Or who he was here with.

When they joined the attendant, who must have also doubled as the train's ornithologist, she got her answer. The boy grabbed the leg of a tall woman and smiled.

"Timmy, do you see it? It's a real California condor!" The woman must have been Timmy's mom. They both grinned from ear to ear and pointed to the rare bird flying over the trees.

Dakota watched, too, as it flew in a circle then disappeared over a ridge. Other than the fact that it was a rare bird, she wasn't sure why people were so excited over it. The black bird looked more like a vulture than anything cool.

She turned her back to the small group that had gathered by the railway employee who was giving out interesting facts about the condor. "As of Christmas 2021 there were only one hundred and eleven condors in the wild here in Arizona. California has only one hundred and eighty-three wild condors..." As Dakota left the train car, she heard the man mentioning a third protected site in Mexico, but she had heard enough about the rare birds. She had her own rare expedition to begin, if only she could lose the tail she'd picked up.

She felt, rather than saw, that Magnet was following her. A small voice inside her head said he wasn't following her, but Trent. If that was the case, then she could stop and look out the window at the scenery and he should pass her by. But if she did that, then she might miss out on a chance to see what Trent was up to.

Decisions, decisions.

The moment she entered the next car, her decision was made for her.

Dakota almost turned around when she gazed into the face of the man speaking to Trent, but she knew she couldn't. Instinctively, she knew this was the ringmaster. He had the stance of someone who would never take orders from anyone, or allow someone to disobey his orders.

The man was very tall; he had to be at least six and a half feet tall. It was difficult to judge height from the distance she was at. The two men were having an intense discussion at one end of the train, while Dakota was at the other. The man had thick blond hair, but she wouldn't call him handsome, although rugged was a good description. He had that tough look to him, as though he'd grown up on the streets and wouldn't be someone to mess with. But at the same time, he had the look of someone who grew up without much food. He was pretty skinny for someone who gave off such a tough-man vibe.

"Whatcha looking at?" an unwanted voice said from directly behind Dakota.

She almost jumped. "What?" Dakota turned and glared at Magnet. "Look, I don't know what you're up to, but I'm not interested. I'm taken. So back off." While Dakota hadn't had a boyfriend in quite some time, she'd used that excuse more than once. Usually, it worked.

His eyes sparked. "Oh, really? Would that someone happen to be named Trent?"

Dakota's brows narrowed and she glared at Magnet. "No, it wouldn't. Now stop following me or I'll have to report you to the conductor." The moment the words were out of her mouth, she realized her mistake.

Magnet laughed. "Yeah, like he's going to do anything about it. But fine, if you aren't interested, I'm not either." He moved past her and headed toward the two men Dakota had been watching.

When they both looked her way, she realized that Magnet told them she was there and watching them. The three of them moved to the next compartment, leaving Dakota wondering if she should continue her walk, or head back to get her phone. It might be better to just use her own phone to make the call.

Simple won out and she turned to head back to get her purse. Leaving it behind wasn't really smart anyway. Although, it was rare people snooped inside someone else's luggage on a train. There was an unwritten code that people on trains and planes left other passengers' stuff alone. Especially when they were stored inside a compartment above, or below, someone else's seat.

Once she was back in the observation deck, she grabbed her purse from beneath her seat and checked that everything was still there. It was just as she expected. Then she looked around at the people in her section and realized that they were all too engrossed in looking out the windows to have even noticed she left, or returned.

Dakota wanted privacy. And the only place on a train with any modicum of that was in the latrine, or an empty lounge. Making a phone call from a cramped water closet wasn't something she wanted to do. While technically she shouldn't go into the closed lounge, she was a corporate employee of the railway. And with all of the attendants down in the other section at the moment, she'd probably have no issue with getting inside.

What she didn't count on was the fact that Trent must

have radioed for someone to close the lounge. There was a sign on the locked door apologizing for any inconvenience, but this particular lounge was closed due to a leaky faucet. She tried the handle anyways and was frustrated when it wouldn't budge.

"Can't you read the sign?" Trent's agitated voice startled her.

Dakota turned around, telling herself she needed to pay better attention to her surroundings when she was trying to snoop. He was the second man so far on this trip who has snuck up behind her. She held her cell phone up. "I'm looking for a private place to make a phone call."

He pursed his lips. "What is so important that it can't wait until we arrive at the Grand Canyon Station?"

Dakota hesitated for a moment, not sure if she should confess what she knew, or lie. Deceit wasn't something she abided. But, would this be one of those situations where it was better to lie and ask forgiveness later? She bit her lower lip and looked around to make sure no one else was close enough to hear what she was about to say.

Once she was satisfied they were alone, or as alone as two people on a train can be, she heaved a heavy sigh. "I heard you." She pointed to the locked lounge behind her.

Trent narrowed his eyes. "Heard me?"

"Yup." Dakota nodded. "When you were speaking with Magnet just before the train left the station. I don't know what all is going on, but I do know that your little girl is in trouble. And you're being forced to do something you don't want to do."

With a heavy sigh, Trent closed his eyes and shook his head. "You need to forget everything you heard. Just go back to your seat and read your book, or nap. Everything is going to be just fine."

"No, it isn't. If those guys are up to something on this train, then the safety of the passengers, and the crew, are all on your shoulders. And you've been compromised. You know as well as I do that your decisions can't be trusted right now." Dakota was going to say more but thought better of it. What she wanted to say was that *he* couldn't be trusted. But he probably understood that as well.

Trent looked back over his shoulder and stiffened. "Look, you have to go back upstairs, and now. These men are very dangerous. Please know that I'm doing all I can to keep everyone safe. If you just mind your own business, all will be fine."

Dakota looked past him and realized why his demeanor changed. Both men were coming toward them. "I'll go, but we need to talk. When it's safe." She turned and headed back up the stairs to her seat.

Chapter Seven

THIS WOMAN WAS GOING TO GET HIM INTO HOT WATER. TRENT was going to have to find a way to keep her distracted. He watched Magnet as the two men entered the car and he wondered for a moment if he could use the guy to distract Dakota.

"What's going on with that woman?" Max pointed to the observation deck where Dakota had gone.

Not sure what to say, Trent took a moment to think. Thankfully, Magnet stepped in.

"I think she was complaining about me." The man looked at Max's scowling face and then down to his shoes.

"Were you harassing someone while on a job? How many times must I tell you to leave the women alone when we're working?" Max slapped the back of Magnet's head and the man almost toppled forward from the force of it.

"Sorry, I'll keep away. I just thought—"

Max interrupted before Magnet could say anymore. "That was your first mistake. Never think on a job. Just do exactly what I say. I told you to keep an eye on Trent here," he pointed to the conductor who stood silently watching, "and stay out of the way."

Trent noted that these two must have worked many jobs together. The younger man seemed to know his place with

Max. Once Max had finished making the young man cower, he turned his ire on Trent. "Who is that woman?"

"No one. Just a passenger." The sooner they forgot about Dakota, the better. "Look, I've got the lounge closed. Can I get back to my real job?" Changing the topic was the only thing Trent could think of to keep Dakota safe. If they stopped thinking about the woman, maybe they would leave her alone.

Max turned his attention toward the locked compartment. "Good. Now keep it that way until it's time we make our move." He looked up the steps to the observation deck. "How many people are up there?"

"Not many. Maybe six?" Trent knew that one passenger had moved forward to one of the lounges closer to the engineer, but he didn't think anyone else had left. "I can go look if you like."

"No. Is there any way to get them out of there? Or keep them up there? They just need to stay out of our way until it's done." Max rubbed his chin.

"They have one of the best views on this trip. The only time passengers up there move is to use the services." Trent knew that some would need to use the bathroom in the next car, since the lounge was closed. And they might want to head to the snack car for drinks. But other than that, they should stay put for most of the trip.

"Good, good. Let's keep them up there as long as possible. Does that cowboy with the guitar ever go up there and entertain?" Max had commented earlier on the entertainment. He had scoffed at the cowboy singing old campfire songs, but Trent knew that the passengers always enjoyed the entertainment.

"As a matter of fact, he does on the last thirty minutes of the trip."

Max didn't say anything, he just nodded before turning to head out.

Trent watched the two men leave him alone in the car. While he didn't know the entire plan, he did know that there were more than three of them on this train. Max said as much earlier, when he was warning him to do his job.

They were already thirty minutes into a two-hour-and-twenty-minute ride. He didn't have much time to come up with a solution that would save his daughter, while also protecting the train's passengers and crew. Then an idea hit him so hard he gasped. Why he hadn't thought of it sooner had his mind spinning. Maybe Dakota could help him, after all.

With a plan already forming, Trent looked through the small window on the door leading to the other train car. Max and Magnet were nowhere in sight. "Good." He turned and headed up the stairs to check on the passengers he had yet to look in on.

The moment Trent's eyes landed on Dakota, he realized she was waiting for him. She looked behind him and when she didn't see anyone following him, she released a breath and sagged in her seat. "Ma'am. How is your trip so far?" He had to play the part of conductor when in front of other passengers.

A look of confusion passed through her eyes, but then she sat up straight and smiled. "Good, actually. Well, except for the fact that the lounge below is closed."

"Yes, I'm sorry for that. But there are services in the next car, and then two cars down is a bar with a large assortment of drinks and snacks. If you need anything." He spoke loud enough that he hoped the other passengers heard his speech. He didn't want to have to tell each and every person up there the same thing.

Before he could say anything else, one of the other passengers walked up to him. "Will the lounge below be closed for the entire trip?"

"Yes, it will. I'm sorry for the inconvenience." The conductor manual had stated that short and sweet was the best way to diffuse any situation. Not that this man seemed upset, but one never knew.

"Okay, thanks." The man smiled and then turned to head back to his group.

"Well, that was easy," Dakota said under her breath.

In a whisper of his own, Trent asked if he could borrow her cell phone.

"What?" Dakota furrowed her brow and stared at Trent.

"Follow me." Trent led her downstairs. He moved them both out of the way of the portal in the door separating the two trains.

"What's going on, Trent?" Dakota demanded.

He rubbed a hand over his face. "I'm sorry, I really can't tell you, but my daughter is in danger, and I need to call my ex to see what she knows. I'm being monitored. Can I use your phone?"

"So I did hear correctly." Dakota put a hand over her mouth and stared at Trent.

"Dakota, quickly." Trent looked around to see if anyone was watching.

She startled back to the conversation and pulled her cell phone out of her back pocket. "Here. You can keep it if it will help."

"Thanks. It might be best if you go back upstairs and stay there. Oh, and stay as far away from those two men as you can." Trent nodded and pointed to where the two black hats had gone. The idea that Trent would now be considered a black hat, or criminal, didn't escape his notice. He probably should have warned Dakota to stay away from him too.

But he just couldn't.

Even though they'd never been friends, he had always thought her a beautiful woman. And until recently, she seemed friendly enough. His only issue with her had been when he heard that she had submitted his name for termination. However, just now, the way she looked at him had him wondering if she was beginning to see him differently.

Chapter Eight

DAKOTA HATED WALKING AWAY FROM TRENT. NOT WHEN SHE knew he needed help. It was very evident that he was being forced to do whatever he was going to do. Those men were keeping an eye on him, and he couldn't even call his ex-wife to see how their daughter was doing? Dakota wondered if it was time for her to call in her own reinforcements.

Instead, she hovered around the top of the stairs hoping to hear the conversation. At least Trent's side of it. Maybe if she could find out what was going on, she could help him. Dakota knew that most men had a tough time accepting help from a woman. But what he didn't know was that she had resources. Resources it sounded like she might have to call up.

It was a good thing she'd packed her satellite phone. With spotty cell reception up at the canyon, she had brought it at the last minute. Normally, she only used it when out on maneuvers with her Army Reserve unit. Now she was glad she listened to her instincts to bring it.

Dakota listened hard in an effort to pick up on what Trent was saying, but with the noise of the train she had a tough time. All she could pick up was little bits here and there. None of it made sense, though. It sounded like Trent didn't even get to talk to her for very long. Which made no sense. If their daughter was missing, then his ex would want to talk to him. Wouldn't she?

———

"CANDACE, it's me. Do you know what's going on?" Trent rushed his words and then realized she might not be able to talk. Like him, she could have someone monitoring her.

"Not really." The unfriendly reply set the hairs on the back of Trent's neck on edge.

"Listen, if you're not safe to talk, then tell me you aren't interested in a time-share and hang up. But if you can talk, then tell me what you do know." He prayed she was safe.

"I really wish you telemarketers would take my number off your lists. I'm not interested in a time-share." Then Candace hung up.

That settled it, they were all in danger. If there were others on this train working with Max, Trent didn't doubt that there were. And if someone was watching Candace, and another person watching Cecilia, then this was much larger than Trent realized. Could he even trust Dakota?

At this point, he couldn't trust a single person.

He started to pace back and forth in the small space. Trent needed a plan. There was no question he'd help them pull off their scheme, but at what cost? Was he willing to put the entire train and all of its passengers at risk?

Before he could formulate a plan, Dakota walked back down the stairs.

"Trent, I don't know exactly what is going on, but I can help. If you let me." Dakota's green eyes looked directly at him.

He had never noticed how beautiful, and deep, her emerald eyes were. In that very moment, he almost believed she could help him. But he couldn't take a chance that she was in on it all.

If she was, then Max would know at any moment that Trent had called his ex-wife and had someone else's phone. He knew he should give her the device back, but he couldn't. He needed it to be able to contact the outside, should anything go awry.

And if Dakota wasn't in league with Max, then he'd have at least one surprise on his side. Although, whoever was watching Candace might call Max and let him know what just happened. Depending on the level of security, they might have her phone tapped. Or been sitting right next to her and heard everything Trent said.

His gut was telling him to trust her. If she was working with Max, why would she have put him on the list to be terminated? No, if she was working with Max, then she wouldn't have wanted him gone. Dakota would have wanted him right where he was. Which meant she most likely wasn't working with these guys.

"I think the only way you'd be able to help is if you had access to a special forces group who specialized in kidnapping and retrieval." Trent knew there were plenty of organizations out there who did that sort of thing. But he didn't know anyone who knew anything about it.

Dakota tilted her head and for the first time on this trip, she gave him a shy smile. "I think I might be able to help with that."

He shook his head. "No, you don't understand. My daughter has been kidnapped. And the people who are responsible are here on this train."

"I do understand. And they want you to do something for them, right? And if you do it, they'll release your daughter?" Dakota didn't really need to ask, she seemed to know.

Which begged the question, was she working with them after all? He took in a breath and realized he'd made a huge mistake. He shouldn't have said a word. "How'd you know? Are you working with them?"

"No, not even close. I told you, I overheard part of a conversation right below me. And the rest I just filled in the blanks. What is on this train that they want so badly?" Dakota looked through the portal and nodded before turning back to Trent.

"What? Is someone there?" Trent began to move toward

the door with the window to see if Magnet or Max was coming back. They would, eventually. And he'd have to decide what to do with them at that time.

"No, I was checking to see if all was clear, and it looks to be. Are there more than those two thugs I saw earlier on this train?" Dakota seemed to be saying all the right words, but he wasn't sure.

"There's a third man, Chug. He's short and stocky with ratty brown hair and dull brown eyes. He's pretty quiet and I've only seen him once. I'm not sure where he's hanging out. But I think there are more. Maybe even someone on the crew is part of their team." While Trent didn't know for sure if one of his employees was on the take, he couldn't discount the possibility that others were being forced to help.

The woman narrowed her eyes and nodded. She stayed quiet for a few moments and Trent wondered what was going through her head. "I'd bet there are more involved, one way or another. I wouldn't be surprised if at least two more were being blackmailed or coerced. But I think it all depends on the job. What, exactly, are they after?"

"It's a train robbery, but not the type that we usually see on this route." Trent shook his head and wondered why here and now. Why him. "There is a special car in the back with very valuable cargo. The car is sealed with security like what you'd see at Fort Knox. But somehow Max, that's the leader, has gotten some inside information on the security features." Until Trent was certain she wasn't involved, he would keep to himself the fact that their information was old. That was his only ace up his sleeve and he wouldn't give that juicy bit of information away. Not until he had to.

"I see. So someone back at corporate is in on it." Dakota looked at him and her eyes widened. "Hey, it's not me." She put her hands in the air and shook her head. "If you knew my background, you'd know it couldn't possibly be me."

"Your background?" Trent knew that she was a weekend warrior, but the rumor was she was just a desk jockey for the Army Reserves.

"I'm constantly being vetted for my security clearance." Dakota didn't say more about her job in the Army.

Which only made Trent wonder what she really did. Recently, the Army had allowed women into combat roles. Was she some sort of GI Jane? He knew enough not to push. If someone in the service didn't say more about their role, then it meant they couldn't. Most service members loved talking to others about what they did, or currently did, in the service. But he understood. Even he had some things he couldn't talk about.

But that didn't mean she could be trusted. Although, he really did want to trust her. Especially when her bright green eyes sparkled as she looked directly at him. Which she was doing right at that moment. His heart started to beat irregularly, and he lost all track of time.

At least until she broke the connection.

"So." Dakota coughed. "You need to call in the cavalry to stop a train robbery, but you don't know who you can trust?"

"Yup, that's about it." Trent nodded.

"What about the owner of the cargo? Can you contact them?" she asked.

Trent scratched his chin and thought for a moment. "I don't know if they are involved or not. Max knows a lot of details about the cargo that I didn't even know. Although, I wouldn't know exactly what was in there as the conductor. But, I do know enough that there should be a line marshal on board right now as well as a few armed guards in civilian clothes. They didn't want to bring a lot of attention to this shipment, but they also wanted to make sure they had it protected."

It was Dakota's turn to scratch her chin and then she looked back at the closed lounge. "Is anyone in there?" She pointed to the door.

"Not that I'm aware of. I did check the door and it was closed." Trent moved to the door and checked the lock again. "Yup, it's still locked."

"Is it possible to lock the door from the inside?" she wondered aloud.

Trent had thought of that and wondered the same thing. "Yes, but I haven't heard any sounds from there."

"That doesn't mean no one is back there." Dakota paused for a moment, then asked, "Could there be people inside the car with the cargo?"

He nodded. "Most likely, yes. But I would bet that is where Max's other teammates are hiding. If he has someone on the inside, it would be best to have the guards on the take. And if they're hiding inside the car, then I would bet they are his men."

"Or women." Dakota grinned. "Women can be bad guys, too." She held her hands up in the air. "But I swear, I'm not one of them."

"I hope so. I'm betting on my daughter's life that you aren't part of their crew." Trent knew that if she was part of their team, his daughter was in real danger.

Dakota pursed her lips. "Look, you keep my phone. I don't need it. But I will tell you that I have a sat phone and a few numbers stored on it to people who can help. People who aren't part of our company, or the local police."

"Please, don't do anything that might get my daughter hurt." Trent pleaded with Dakota.

She put a hand on his shoulder. "Trent, I wouldn't dream of doing anything that might hurt her."

He nodded. "Alright. Thanks for the cell phone. But, I have to get going." He looked at his watch and his brows raised in concern. "I'm actually a little behind." With that, he unlocked the door to the lounge and quickly closed and locked it behind him.

Chapter Nine

"HUH. I WONDER WHAT HE'S UP TO NOW?" DAKOTA WATCHED as Trent went through the mysterious door and closed it quickly. So quickly, she didn't have time to follow him. But that was alright. She had her own secret assignment.

One that had her doing something she really didn't like. One of her pet peeves was women on the phone in the public bathrooms. It always creeped her out when she heard other people in the stalls talking. Especially when they had their phones on speaker and a man's voice was on the other end. She shivered just thinking about it.

However, the bathrooms on the train were single use. As long as she didn't use the speaker, and she spoke low enough, no one would be able to hear her. Not even if they had their ear to the door.

It was time she called in the big guns, so to speak.

Fifteen minutes later, she was exiting the bathroom with thoughts of her call on her mind. Tyee Putesoy, one of her reserve buddies, was also a member of the Grand Canyon Search and Rescue team. While he was a member of the Havasupai Tribe, he had decided to join the US Army Reserve and get all the training he needed in order to be part of the search and rescue team in the Grand Canyon. He wasn't the only Native American in Dakota's reserve company. Tyee just happened to have the best job to help her out.

"I keep seeing you all over the train." A deep, menacing voice startled Dakota.

"Oh. Hello." Dakota hadn't looked both ways before exiting the latrine, so she didn't notice that Max had been standing by the door, waiting for her to exit. "It's all yours now."

He practically growled when he told her he wasn't waiting for the restroom.

"I hope you weren't waiting for me." Dakota arched a brow and looked into his eyes for the first time up close. She wished she hadn't when a chill overtook her entire being.

Dakota had to look up to see into his dull blue eyes, which were devoid of any emotion. If questioned, she would have to say they were soulless. Had the man already sold his soul to the devil? Or was that the look of someone who had been living a life of crime for most of their life? In fact, they reminded her of Magnet's eyes. Maybe that was why she thought he had criminal eyes? Or were they psychotic eyes? Either way, she wanted nothing to do with this person.

"What are you up to?" Max leaned in and glared directly into her eyes.

Instinct screamed at her to back up. That man was way too close for her liking. She put a hand up between them and narrowed her eyes in return. "Ever hear of personal space?" He was intimidating, to be sure. But Dakota didn't intimidate easily.

He chuckled without any humor showing on his face. "Think you're tough, huh?"

"No, just don't like it when strange men get too close. Usually, when a man is that close, he's already bought me dinner." Humor, wasn't that what Tyee always used to diffuse intense situations? She'd have to remember to tell him about this, he'd get a kick out of it. She hoped.

"If that is a request for a date, forget about it." Max's

voice had calmed down a bit, and he took a step back, easing the tension that had developed between the two.

"No, it wasn't. It was a nice way to tell you to get the heck out of my personal space." Dakota put her hand on her hip and continued to look him in the eye. Not even giving him one iota of a hint that she was uncomfortable.

"I like your spunk. Which is why I'm only going to say this once. Stay out of my way." This time, the growl was back in his voice.

"Um," she put a finger in the air between them, "I wasn't anywhere near you. You are the one who waited outside the bathroom for me. It sounds more like you're the stalker here, not me."

He blinked three times. She had stumped the man. Dakota figured he'd never been spoken to in that manner before. Most people probably cowered in his shadow. Dakota wasn't going to be like that.

The fact that there were multiple people watching their interaction probably helped her to act tough. But whatever the reason, she was glad she didn't let him see any weakness in her. Men like him thrived on everyone else's weakness. And she wasn't going to feed into his narcissistic behavior.

"I'll make you a deal, Mr. No Name. You stay out of my way, and I'll stay out of yours." Since Max hadn't introduced himself, she figured she needed to pretend as though she didn't know his name.

He blew out a breath that sounded almost like a raspberry. But was probably intended to sound like exasperation. "Excuse me, my lady." That was most definitely exasperation. "Please allow me to introduce myself. My name is Max." He put a hand out.

She took it. "Nice to meet you, Max. I'm Dakota." His shake was stronger than she was expecting, but it wasn't enough to break her, or her hand. However, she knew a power move when she saw it. Or in this case, felt it.

He held on a little longer than necessary, and when he let go of her hand, she stopped herself from shaking it out. That would have let him know she was bothered by his strength. She was, but she'd not let him know it. Instead, she did a tiny curtsy and smirked. The woman's version of a power move.

"Now, if you'll excuse me, I need to find out what happens to Finnick." Dakota turned to leave but slowed when she heard Max's voice.

"He dies. Just like all heroes should." Max chuckled and turned around and went in the opposite direction.

While she knew the ending, Dakota hadn't read the book yet, so she didn't how it all happened. The how was just as good, and important, as the actual end. Instead of responding to his stupid remark, she kept going and trying to get as far away from him as possible, considering she was on a moving train.

She also didn't want him to suspect she was up to anything. While Dakota doubted he could have heard her conversation, she didn't want him to think she was up to anything, or find her sat phone. So, she decided to head back to her seat. There really wasn't anything she could do for the moment anyway.

Then the unthinkable happened, hands reached out and grabbed her. Before she realized what was going on, she was inside a dark, tight room with a man breathing in her face.

Dakota pushed against what felt like a brick wall. "Hey!"

"Shh, I'm not going to hurt you." The whispered words floated across her face and her body relaxed before her mind did.

"It's me, Trent. You're safe."

The word, "oh," released as she exhaled. Then she began to feel a different type of uncomfortable. A feeling of warmth spread throughout her body as she realized she was in a tight and dark space with a very handsome man. "What? Um."

Trent leaned even closer and held her tight to his body. "What did Max want?"

For about two seconds she thought he might kiss her, then when she felt his breath against her ears, the words hit her brain and the sensation running through her body changed. "Max? Oh, yeah. He just wanted to intimidate me, I think."

"Are you alright?" For whatever reason, Trent continued to hold her body close to his and whisper directly in her ear.

It was right about then that Dakota realized she was pushed up against something hard and jagged. Maybe not jagged, as she didn't feel as though whatever was behind her was poking through her clothes. It was just very uncomfortable and not smooth like a wall should be.

Dakota didn't think the closeness was necessary, but as her eyes adjusted to the blackness surrounding them, she realized that the space, or lack thereof, is what necessitated this nearness. She couldn't be sure, but it seemed like a broom closet. When her nose itched from the acrid scent of cleaning products, she realized it was a mop closet. There must have been a wet mop with cleaner still on it somewhere next to her. That was probably what she felt poking against her backside.

"I'm fine. But if any of them catch us in here, I doubt they'll believe we don't know each other." A part of Dakota's brain wanted to keep him near her, and another part wanted to push him away. She wasn't in the market for a renegade conductor. This wasn't the old Wild West where a handsome black hat swept the sweet schoolteacher up and they lived happily ever after.

Dakota didn't have any room in her heart for a man, especially one who would most likely end up in jail if he didn't do something to stop whatever those real bandits were up to. Even if he was only reluctantly working with them, he did seem like he was going it to help them steal whatever was in that last train. She just prayed that no one was injured in the process.

"I know, but I had to see if you were alright." Trent sighed and pulled his head back a smidge.

He was still close enough to her that she felt a tingle run down her arms and the beginnings of butterflies rummaging around her stomach. Well, either that, or her belly was trying to tell her it was time to eat.

Dakota stood there waiting for him to say more, but instead his breathing hitched as he stared into her eyes. Something began tugging at her heart and she felt her own head moving closer to his. For what reason, she couldn't say. At that moment she couldn't even think.

When only a breath separated their lips, she heard an annoying sound that brought her out of the cloud she'd been on.

Trent yanked himself back and hit the back of his head on the wall behind him. "Fiddlesticks."

She arched a brow.

"I have a twelve-year-old. Cusswords are no longer part of my vocabulary." Trent rubbed the back of his head and rolled his eyes.

Dakota nodded, understanding since she had nieces and a nephew. "What was that whistle?" The sound was that of a train signaling something, but Dakota didn't know what it could be.

"That would be my signal to get moving." Trent put his hand on the door to slide it open and then stopped. "You might want to get your things and move forward. There are plenty of open seats in the front of the train."

It sounded to Dakota as though he had made this decision and was going to do something. Whether his action was to help the robbers or stop them, she wasn't sure. "What are you going to do?"

He cleared his throat. "I think it might be best for your own safety if I didn't tell you."

"And what if I told you that I already put a plan into place myself?" Dakota hadn't planned on telling him what she'd just done, but if she could get him to trust her, and hold off on whatever he planned, then she might be able to save him, his daughter, and the entire train full of passengers.

"What did you do? Please tell me you didn't contact the

police? Or even call back to corporate." His hand left the door and fell to his side.

"I didn't call corporate. Like you, I think they must have someone on the inside, besides yourself. And I didn't call the cops. Well, not exactly." She winced. While technically Tyee wasn't a cop, he was with a law enforcement team. But his was federal and she doubted he'd say anything to the local cops.

"You didn't call the marshal, did you? I've looked for him and can't find him. My best guess is he's in on it." Since Trent knew who all the marshals were that worked his route, he would have been able to see which one was onboard when he made his way through the train earlier.

"No, I didn't call anyone associated with the railroad in any way." While that was mostly true, Dakota didn't think that she needed to clarify. The group Tyee worked for was a part of the Department of Interior, they were the ones responsible for patrolling the Grand Canyon, as well as any rescue services that were needed within the national park area. The train let off within the boundaries of the park. So technically, the Grand Canyon Search and Rescue (GCSAR) team were associated with the railroad, but no one ever saw it that way.

As far as Dakota knew, this would be the first time that the GCSAR team had been called on to rescue the train, or its passengers.

"You better tell me what you've done." Trent's voice no longer held a pleasant sound.

Dakota knew that she'd angered him. He didn't growl, at least not like Max had done. But the tone wasn't a welcome one. She couldn't blame him, as far as he knew, she might be messing with his daughter's safety.

She prayed this would help the little girl, not harm her.

"I think that for your own safety, I better not tell you." *There*, she thought. *Let him stew in his own words.*

This time, he did growl. Dakota didn't understand what it was with men and growling. It was almost as though they were still ancient cavemen and hadn't evolved into civilized men yet. She knew that Max and Magnet were definitely still on the caveman path. But Trent? He had seemed more mature, more evolved. Until now.

"This is my daughter's life you're messing with." He stopped himself before saying more. She was sure he knew exactly what was on the line here.

Mentally, it felt as though he had pulled back a gazillion miles from her. In reality, he'd only moved his head slightly since the space was so tight. But Dakota understood. "Look, you need to go and do whatever it is you're planning. I've got your back. That's all you need to know right now."

"How can I know that for sure? You know as well as I do that there is someone on the inside helping them. If it was just me and this train, I'd trust you in a heartbeat. But it's also my daughter. I know that I've said it over and over, but she's all I have going for me in this life."

Dakota's heart melted. He wasn't being a caveman, but a father. And a good one from the sound of it. "Okay. But I doubt you'll like it."

All of the blood drained from his face when she finished telling Trent her plan. Well, hers and Tyee's plan. Tyee really was the mastermind here. And he had plenty of connections to make it happen.

"You do know that this particular train and time was chosen for a reason, right?" Trent wasn't sure how he was going to spin this change in plans. But it would work with what he'd planned, too. He only hoped the distraction would be enough for him to get everything done in time. And that if the line marshal was onboard, he'd just go with it.

"Alright, so you know what to do?" Dakota hoped he wouldn't try to change anything. They needed this timed perfectly if they had any hope of saving the passengers.

"But what about my daughter? If Max suspects anything, he'll make a call and my little girl will die." The anguish in Trent's voice sent another volley of arrows through Dakota's heart.

She put her hand on his shoulder. "Trust me. My friends

will make sure your daughter is safe. In fact, she'll probably be saved before Max even knows what we've done."

Dakota wasn't much for praying and asking God for anything, but in that moment, she prayed for the safety of Trent's daughter.

Chapter Ten

IT WASN'T LONG BEFORE THE TRAIN BEGAN TO SLOW DOWN. Dakota wondered if her plan was already in motion, or if they only slowed for the wide turn the train was about to make. It was this spot where she hoped all would begin.

While she wasn't a train engineer, or even a conductor, she did know enough to understand that the train would take a little while to be able to come to a complete stop. Using the slowdown at Robber's Curve would help to make it all happen so much faster, and easier.

It was this section of the line where the regularly scheduled train robberies took place. Most people won't know anything is amiss. But the crew might question it.

"I'll handle the crew, don't worry. You just make sure you do your part," Trent said just before he exited the broom closet.

Dakota stayed put for a few more minutes, just to make sure no one was watching. And she couldn't have moved even if she wanted to. The time spent with Trent in that tiny space had cracked the case surrounding her heart. Or maybe it was the way he tried to take care of his daughter, even though he couldn't be with her. Whatever it was, she would forever look at him differently.

But for now, she needed to focus on the train robbery. And in order to do that, she needed a moment. A beat really, to get her game face on. As well as to make sure no one noticed that she had shared that teeny-tiny space with Trent.

It was at this point that she was so very glad that she had sent her sister to the front passenger car. That was the car that would have the most passengers in it since it was also a bar car. No kids would be in there, but plenty of adults wanting to escape the crazy kids would hide out there for the majority of the ride. Yes, it was still morning, and they weren't even scheduled to arrive in the Grand Canyon until noon, but it was still an adult-only car. Even if most passengers wouldn't be drinking.

The thought that her sister was safe put a tiny smile on her face. It was all going to work out, she just knew it. The only thing left for her to do was to make sure that everyone from the observation car was elsewhere.

When she made it back to her seat, she noticed that there were only two passengers left up top. "I guess the rest decided to go and check out the entertainment up front?" The entertainment would work its way to her location, but if she could get everyone out of this car now, and keep them out, it would be so much easier.

"Entertainment?" one of the women asked. "No, they went to get some snacks and sodas from the drink car."

"Hmm, I was just in there and didn't see them. They probably heard the singing two cars ahead and went to check it out." Dakota wasn't exactly telling the truth, but there was entertainment happening at that very minute about five cars ahead of them. It would be the best place for everyone to wait this situation out. Sadly, she couldn't say anything about what was really going on or she'd cause a stampede. Or worse, everyone would start calling the cops or posting on social media what was happening.

"Really? What sort of entertainment?" the man sitting with the woman asked.

"I think a country singer is up there belting out some

fantastic tunes. I heard him singing about a train robbery, losing his best girl, and the heartbreak of his horse dying. Or something like that." She hadn't, but thought it might get the couple to head out. And it did.

"Thanks, are you going?" the woman asked.

"Yes, I just wanted to grab my stuff so that I didn't have to come back here when we arrive. I was told that since the train had so many open seats, I could sit up closer if I wanted to." She was about to say something about her missing sister but hoped they had already forgotten about Darla. It would be safer that way. And she did want to move her carry-on baggage closer to the front. If this worked out the way she planned, anything left behind in this car would be held up for a while.

A couple cars up was a snack car. Dakota went there to wait it out. She also left her bag under a chair, hoping she would be able to retrieve it later.

What happened next was quick. Dakota thought it was all going according to plan, until she caught sight of a gun pointed at her sister.

————

TRENT KNEW it wouldn't be as simple as Dakota said it would be. Max and his crew chose this exact train because they knew there wouldn't be any reason for the train to stop along the way. Normally, there would be a fake train robbery where the train stops just past Robber's Curve. He felt the train slow and come to a stop. The passengers he walked past had looks of confusion on their faces as they looked out the windows.

Trent couldn't believe what he was looking at. A band of Indians in full feathers and leathers riding horses were yelling at the train. A couple even brandished firearms. Why would the engineer stop for them? Then it hit him, this was the distraction Dakota had arranged. She said he would recognize it when he saw it.

There was no way a group of Native Americans dressed

up like their ancestors would stop a train of tourists heading to the Grand Canyon to rob them. It wouldn't be worth it. Not only were most of these passengers families, but none of them would have anything valuable enough to rob them of. At least, not in this way. The train was coming to a stop. Would the engineer think that this was part of the entertainment? The company never had Indians robbing the train before.

Just then, a hand grabbed him from behind. "What do you think you're doing?"

Trent turned around to look into the steely gaze of Max. And standing right next to him was his little brother, Magnet. Trent looked but couldn't see Chug anywhere. "What do you mean?" He'd play dumb if it helped keep everyone safe.

"This," Max motioned to the ruckus outside. "Why are Indians attacking the train? There wasn't supposed to be any entertainment that would slow us down or stop the train."

Trent didn't really know what to say. He was surprised by this turn of events. Dakota had said it would be best if he didn't know all the details, and she'd been right. All he knew was that the train would be stopped, and that would give her time to do something. He was supposed to meet her in the back when this happened. "I...uh...I don't know what's going on." He looked around to see if anyone was paying attention to them, but they were all so focused on what was happening outside that they ignored the tense discussion happening right in front of them.

"Somehow, I don't think you're being honest with me. Come on." Max yanked his shoulder and pushed him in front of the little band of criminals. "We're going to check on things in the back of the train."

Everything was going just as Dakota had predicted. And the fact that Trent had been closer to the front of the train than the back was also working in his favor. It took them some time to make it to the back because so many people were in the aisles trying to get a good look at the happenings outside.

Truth be told, Trent wanted to watch the entertainment, too. However, as the conductor he should have been the one to go outside to handle the situation. "Ah, don't you think I should go outside and see what's going on? I am in charge here."

"Wrong. I'm in charge and I say you go with us to the back. We have to check on the cargo first. Then, if all is fine, you can go and see what's happening." Max shoved against his back to get him to move faster.

It didn't take long to get to the observation car and the locked lounge, that was now unlocked and had people standing inside. But when they arrived, Trent was confused. "Who's that woman and why does Chug have a gun to her head?"

"You don't know her?" Magnet asked, then chuckled. "I guess your girlfriend never told you her sister was onboard."

Now Trent was really confused. "What? I don't have a girlfriend."

"Huh, good one. We know all about you and that fancy-pants woman, Dakota." Magnet snorted then looked the other woman up and down. "This here is Darla. Isn't she a pretty one?"

Fear stabbed Trent right through the chest. Dakota had never told him she had family onboard. He also knew from pictures on Dakota's desk that her sister had three kids. Were they here, too? "Like I said, I don't have a girlfriend. I didn't even know Dakota had family, let alone that they were onboard."

"It's just me." Darla looked at him and scowled. She had a backbone and didn't seem the least bit afraid of the gun.

"Where's Dakota?" If Max had Darla, then that meant he must have her, too. And if that was the case, had she spilled the beans and told Max the plan? Or was she hiding in an effort to ensure everything played out as she had planned?

"We thought you might know." Max looked at Trent and pointed a finger at Darla. "She says that she knows nothing of what's going on. But I don't believe her. What did you tell that girlfriend of yours?"

"Nothing." Trent ran a ragged hand through his hair. "Look, I don't know what's going on. It could be that the railway decided to try out a new troupe on this ride. It's possible there's a message on my cell phone, but someone took it and refuses to return it. However, until I go out and speak with those guys, I won't know."

Chug chuckled. It was probably the first sound Trent had heard from the strange man since they got onboard the train.

Magnet bent over and looked out the window. "You don't think they're real Indians trying to rob this train?"

Trent had to stop himself from saying something totally rude. He guessed Magnet never finished high school. Shoot, he may not have even finished middle school. This wasn't the first uninformed comment he'd heard from the idiot. The guy's nickname might have been short for Chick Magnet, but it sure wasn't an indicator of his intelligence, or his ability to attract the opposite sex.

Both Max and Trent ignored the young man.

Darla stayed quiet, but Trent could see her eyes and he could tell she was taking everything in. The woman was probably a lot like her sister. He only hoped that she would keep quiet and stay out of the way.

"Max, we're stopped now. How about I go outside and find out what's really going on here?" Trent needed to get outside if he had any chance of saving his plan.

The crook narrowed his eyes at Trent. "Why are you trying so hard to get outside? Don't you care about your girlfriend's sister?"

Trent shrugged. "Like I said, Dakota isn't my girlfriend and I've never met that woman before. How do I know she isn't working with you guys and you're just trying to use her as more leverage to get me to do your dirty work?" He'd only just thought of that idea. He knew she was Dakota's sister thanks to the picture back on Dakota's desk, but he wouldn't mention any of that. Best not to let Max know that Dakota worked for the railroad if he didn't already know.

After a short pause, Max nodded his head once. "Fine, but don't do anything stupid." He turned to Magnet. "Keep an eye on him. I need to head to the back and check on things there."

Trent headed to the nearest spot where he could exit the train.

Chapter Eleven

DAKOTA HAD SAT IN A CORNER BOOTH, BEHIND A WOMAN WITH a rather large hat. She figured it was the best place on board while trying to hide out. At first, when she saw her sister walk past her, she just about stood up to get her attention. Darla was supposed to stay in the front bar car, not come back looking for her.

But then she noticed a man behind her with his hand on her back. Darla would never allow a stranger to touch her that way. That, coupled with the fact that Darla was heading right to the bad guys' lair, spoke volumes to Dakota.

That man must have been one more of the train robbers.

Once they were far enough in front of her, Dakota began to stand, then immediately sat back down. This time, she did her best to shrink behind the woman with the hat. If Max, or Magnet, saw her, the jig would be up. Not only did they now have Darla, they also had Trent with them. And he didn't look happy. She wondered if he knew they had her sister.

Tyee's tribe was outside the train doing their thing, which meant that Tyee and his SAR team weren't far behind. While they mostly searched for and rescued missing hikers, they had also assisted a few times in some big-time law enforcement operations. Plus, Tyee had trained with Special Forces last summer on his two-week rotation. He knew a thing or two about bringing someone down while saving others. She hoped.

As she sat there, Dakota thought through the plan. She was supposed to make sure the last door was locked and that Max's team couldn't get back inside while Trent was outside uncoupling the last two cars from the train. They had decided that it would be easier to keep Max and his team in the observation car then to try and get them all to open up the vault that was the last car.

Besides, Trent said they couldn't open it. So, sacrificing the observation deck car was the best choice.

Darla being with them muddied the waters.

Could Dakota sacrifice her sister for the safety of the entire train? She wasn't sure she could do that. Maybe they would take her in trade? It would be one thing for Dakota to be held hostage—if she died it wouldn't hurt as many people. Dakota was single with no children. Darla had a husband and three children expecting to meet her for lunch in the Grand Canyon this afternoon.

As she sat there thinking, she realized that Max wouldn't trade. He'd lie. He would say they were doing a trade, but he would keep Darla, or recapture her. No, the best thing she could do for her sister would be to follow the plan. And hope and pray that someone rescued Darla before it was too late.

So it was with a heavy heart that she stood to go and do her job. Something outside caught her eye and she realized that Trent was walking toward the Havasupai band of fake train robbers. At least that part of the plan had been easy. Thankfully, they were all dressed up for a formal demonstration of a Native American ceremony that would have taken place almost two hundred years ago, when the natives still owned the land and had no knowledge of the wars to come.

The tribal lands were only a twenty-minute ride by horseback from that spot along the line and Tyee knew they'd be happy to help stop train robbers. So they put off their demonstration and headed straight over. At least that part of the plan worked as planned.

Now if only Dakota could get Darla to safety.

When Dakota moved to the back in order to block the door, she looked through the window and almost screamed when she saw the gun pointing at her sister. There was no way she was going to let her sister be left with those murdering, child stealing, thugs.

She backed up and thought about the layout of the train, and the surrounding terrain. If need be, she could uncouple the train cars herself. But what was she to do about her sister? Dakota had to find a way to get her sister away from those guys.

As long as they were in the antechamber and didn't go into the lounge, she still had a chance. It was small, but she could find a way to get to her sister. Dakota looked back through the window and watched as Magnet walked up the steps to the observation deck. She was so very glad that she'd cleared the people from that space earlier.

Then her heart fell.

One of the couples had come back to the observation deck and were now walking down the stairs. Right behind them was Magnet. Dakota wasn't sure what they were going to do with the people...keep them as more hostages? Or force them to move to a forward compartment? Either option seemed like a smart move for them.

TRENT LOOKED around at the fierce faces on the Native American warriors sitting astride their horses. He knew it was all an act, but man were they good at intimidation. "Hi, I'm Trent Rollins, the conductor on this train. What's going on?"

The man out front of the group, who also had the largest headdress Trent had ever seen, urged his horse forward. "I'm Chief Thomas Supai, but everyone just calls me Thomas." The man didn't smile, but his eyes sparkled. "I was told that this train needed our help." He narrowed his eyes.

"Did Tyee send you?" While Trent was pretty sure this man was here because of the call Dakota had made, he wasn't one hundred percent sure. Not yet at any rate.

"What if he did? Would it make a difference?" Thomas asked.

Trent rubbed the back of his neck. This was all getting a bit too cloak-and-daggery for him. He blew out a breath and wondered why it was that he had to be in the middle of all of this.

Trent shook his head. "I guess not. So what do we do now?"

Just as Chief Thomas was about to say something, a noise behind Trent interrupted them both.

As Trent was starting to turn around, something hard hit the side of his head, causing him to fall flat on his butt.

"What do you think you're doing?" Max's angry tenor surprised Trent almost as much as what happened next.

Before Trent could do anything to defuse the situation, a group of six angry Indians on horseback surrounded Max and pointed arrows already nocked in bows directly at the man.

"Trent! You better tell your friends to back off now or your daughter is dead." Max glared at Thomas.

"What is going on? Why'd you come out here?" To say Trent was confused would be an understatement. He had no idea why Max hit him or what even upset the crazy crook. But those arrows didn't look fake.

"How did you block the cell signal?" The words barely made it out of Max's mouth before Chief Thomas began calling out in his native tongue.

Or at least, Trent assumed it was the man's native language. It wasn't anything he understood. But what happened next put a huge smile on his face.

One of the Indians who hadn't been surrounding Max walked into the circle and hit Max so hard, he fell to the ground and passed out.

"Did you kill him?" Trent asked, not sure if he would be happy or not over the man's demise.

The giant, tan-skinned man who delivered the heavy blow, was wearing not much more than a pair of shorts covered by leather fringe and a pair of sandals. In a weird way, it reminded Trent of a kilt that was cut in shreds. He looked at Trent. "No, but he'll be out for a few minutes."

"Nice move. Now what?" While Trent did have a plan, he wasn't sure what these warriors wanted him to do now.

"Now, you uncouple the last of the cars and send the train on to the station. We'll take care of the rest." Chief Thomas pointed to the last two cars.

"What if there are more robbers in the other cars?" Trent asked.

"Hurry up, we don't have time." Chief Thomas instructed.

But when Trent made his way back to the train, he saw that the observation deck car had already been uncoupled. The only one who would have done that would have been Dakota. When he looked around for her, he didn't see her. However, he did see through the round window that Magnet was freaking out and Chug was doing his best to calm him down.

This would be his chance to get Darla out of there, except he didn't see the woman. Would she have moved to a forward cabin? Or would she have gotten off on the other side? Now wasn't the time to be indecisive, he had to get this train moving forward before any of the other players interfered.

He reached for his radio and then remembered that Max had taken it from him before he exited the train to deal with the question of the Indians. The only thing he could do was reenter the train and search for a crew member and have them give the order to the engineer to get moving.

Just as he entered the back door of what would now be considered the caboose, he felt the chug of the engine pulling the train. He looked into the confused faces of the people who had been sitting in that car.

"Do you know what's going on?" an elderly woman with a large hat asked him.

"Actually, I don't. I lost my radio in that." Trent pointed behind him. "But I would suggest you all move to a forward car. And do what you can to lock the door. Don't let anyone enter from behind."

"What? Why?" the man with the woman wearing the large hat asked.

"Because they are trying to rob the train." Trent didn't know what else to say. It was better to just tell the truth, wasn't it? Besides, he was getting very tired of lying. He didn't think he had any more tall tales left inside of him.

Those in hearing distance laughed. A person toward the front of the car asked what was going on and Trent heard someone say they were being robbed. The rest of the train's passengers laughed. Trent didn't know if he should be happy they didn't understand the severity of the situation, or mad.

Instead of dealing with them, he turned around and headed back out the back and jumped off before the train moved too far away from the real action. He hoped that Dakota was still onboard the train, but he couldn't be sure. And then he still had Darla to rescue, or at least locate.

One thing was for sure, when Dakota said she had powerful friends, she wasn't joking. The fact that the cell phones had been jammed proved it. He knew from all of his time on this railway that there was cell service here. In fact, he pulled Dakota's cell phone out of his pocket where he had hidden it from Max. Sure enough, zero bars. He quickly tucked it back away and began walking around looking for either of the women. He'd leave the roundup of the bad guys to the Indians.

Trent decided to stick to the side away from where Chief Thomas and his men were, standing guard over Max. Once he was on the other side of the observation car, he heard arguing coming from the front of the passenger car.

"How did they remove us from the train?" Magnet's voice was clear.

A gravelly voice, one that sounded as though it hadn't been used in a long time, answered, "I don't know. But I do know that we need to get that vault open and get what we can before the authorities arrive."

"Who would have ratted us out?" Magnet's voice trailed off as they closed the door.

Trent looked around again, hoping to spy signs that someone had gotten off the train and ran this way to safety. But he couldn't see any indication of anyone walking around here, except for him. Then he spotted a few smaller footprints, what he would expect from a woman who had uncoupled the train on this side. "Dakota." No answer.

At least the distraction worked long enough to get the last two cars unhooked from the train and then somehow, someone ordered the engineer to move it. He was glad for whoever took the initiative.

When he heard some arguing, he made his way toward the sounds. If he wasn't mistaken, it sounded as though the cavalry had arrived. Only, they were twenty-first century cavalry, instead of the sort that might have battled the Native Americans a long time ago.

Sure enough, there were more men on horseback that had arrived. Max had come to and was complaining about Chief Thomas and his men attacking him. Trent's snort wasn't loud enough to grab anyone's attention, so he moved closer to hear them. Then he turned to watch as Magnet and Chug exited the passenger car with their hands above their heads.

Trent had to look all around and then did a double take. He had no idea how this all came about so quickly. It was crazy. How did Tyee and his team do all this? "What just happened?"

Chug spit on the ground in front of Trent. "Like you don't know."

Trent shook his head. "I really don't know. None of this was me."

When a thirtyish man with brown skin walked forward, a satellite phone held to his face, Trent thought this might be the mysterious Tyee he'd heard about but couldn't be sure.

"Trent Rollins?" the man dressed in green Army fatigues asked.

"Yes, who are you?"

"Nice to meet you. I'm Tyee Putesoy, Dakota's friend."

Trent put his hand out and shook the other man's offered hand. "Nice to meet you. How did all of this go down so quickly and easily?"

"Easy? Pft." The voice behind Trent made him smile.

"Dakota? Where have you been?" Trent turned around and took several large steps until he was right in front of the woman. His instincts told him to wrap her in a hug and never let go, but there were too many answers that he needed first.

"I'll explain, but first things first. Tyee, did you get her?" Dakota called out.

Tyee held up his sat phone. "Yes, she's safe and my guy is taking her to her mom right now. We can call her in about thirty minutes. And I'll get the cell service working again."

Trent was so confused, it must have shown on his face.

"When I called Tyee earlier, I explained to him about your daughter. He had another team searching for her. It sounds as though they found her." Dakota grinned from ear to ear and motioned to Tyee.

"What? Are you serious? How is she? Where was she?" A million more questions ran through Trent's head, but when Tyee motioned for him to be quiet, Trent realized that he wasn't giving the man a chance to tell him anything. "Sorry."

"Don't be. You have every right to be upset about your daughter. Dakota said that someone on the inside was in on it. She thought she knew who might be working with those guys." Tyee pointed toward Max, Magnet, and Chug. "She was right. Once we knew who he was, it was easy to get him to talk. He gave up the safe house where Max's girlfriend was watching the little girl. She's fine, other than being upset about the kidnapping."

Trent dropped to his knees and almost sobbed out his gratitude.

"Dakota deserves the gratitude. She knew exactly who to call and who the unsub was." Tyee winked at Dakota. "She's quite the detective."

"What about Darla?" Trent jumped up and looked around, hoping to see Dakota's sister.

Dakota hooked her thumb over her shoulder. "They had her locked up on the top of the observation car. She's fine. She's got my sat phone and is talking to her husband right now."

"YOU! You screwed this all up for me!" A voice no one recognized ran from the last car, the one no one had seen inside of yet. Screaming with his hand in the air holding a rather scary-looking knife. "I would have been set up for the rest of my life if you hadn't butted in."

Dakota turned to see who was coming up behind her.

"Dakota! Watch out!" Trent yelled as he took off running toward the man with the knife.

Something whizzed past Trent's ears and he stopped when the man carrying the knife fell backward, knife still in his hand.

"What? Who did that?" Trent looked down at the arrow protruding from the man's chest, then back at the group of Native Americans. "Those weren't fake arrows?"

Chief Thomas stood tall and proud once he dismounted his horse. "Of course not. None of our weapons are fake. They are all crafted as our forefathers once had."

"Thank you, Chief." Dakota gasped out as she looked from the man on the ground to the elderly man in Native American garb. "He might have killed me if not for you."

"Dakota! Dakota!" Darla screamed from the edge of the train.

———

ANOTHER MAN WAS STANDING THERE HOLDING Darla around the neck.

Fear rippled through Dakota as she realized who held

her sister. "Harvey, let her go! You haven't hurt anyone yet, don't make this worse on yourself."

Harvey was one of the linemen that Dakota had served a pink slip to a little over a week ago. He must have joined the team at the last minute when he realized that he'd have a tough time finding another railway job.

"You ruined my life! I was only a few years away from my pension. Why'd you have to fire me? This is all your fault." Spittle flew out of Harvey's mouth as he railed at Dakota.

She put her hands in the air in a placating gesture. "Harvey, if you would have read your paperwork, you would have realized that we retired you. You have your full pension. There's no reason for you to harm anyone."

He shook his head. "No, that's a lie. Mr. Sumerset told me you lied to me about the pension."

It was all starting to fall into place now. "Mr. Sumerset recruited you, didn't he?"

"Yes, he did. He said that if I helped out, I'd be set for life with my share of the loot," Harvey answered.

"Harvey, he lied to you. Mr. Sumerset kidnapped Trent's little girl." She pointed to Trent. "He did whatever he had to in order to get people to help him out. Do you really think a man who's evil enough to kidnap a twelve-year-old would tell you the truth?"

Harvey looked to Trent with a question in his eyes.

"Yes, she was kidnapped," Trent answered the man's unasked question.

The arm around Darla's neck looked to slacken just a bit as the truth hit Harvey. "Your little Cecilia? I remember when she was only about five or six. She'd come to the depot to visit you with her momma. She told me once that she wanted to be a conductor, just like her daddy."

Dakota was close enough to Trent to see the tears pool in his eyes.

"Yes, she used to tell me the same thing. I even bought her a train set one year and had a uniform made for her that matched mine." Trent wiped the tears away that ran down his face. "But she's safe. Someone rescued her and is taking her to see her momma."

Then Harvey looked down at the body of the dead man on the ground. "If I don't give up, will you do that to me, too?"

"Harvey, I don't want anyone else to get hurt. Please let my sister go and I'll be sure to let the authorities know how you were tricked." Dakota would tell the truth, but she knew she'd never be able to go to bat for anyone who harmed someone she loved.

A few seconds later, Harvey nodded and let Darla go. She ran to her sister and they both hugged something fierce. When Dakota pulled back from Darla, she noticed that Tyee already had Harvey's arms tied up in zip ties behind his back.

Epilogue

To say the week was a nice break would be a lie. Dakota couldn't remember the last time she had felt so drained. They had to wait on the railroad tracks right where they were for another train to come back for them, along with the cops. Because the cargo was worth so much, the FBI had also been called in.

Turned out, the cargo was worth more than several hundred million dollars. It was part of a rare jewelry and gem collection that was scheduled to go on display in the Grand Canyon.

Once Tyee and his team cleared and secured the two railway cars, Dakota asked where Harvey and the dead man came from. It turned out the dead man was the line marshal. He had been brought into the team early on and for some reason, no one had filled him in on the changes to the security protocols.

Both men had been locked in the vault compartment when they broke in shortly after the train left the station. One of the new protocols was that should the vault be opened without the code, it would lock itself until either the proper code was entered, or power was cut to the vault.

When they decoupled the two cars from the rest of the

train, the power was cut. But not before sending out a signal to the museum who owned the gems.

At the end of the week, when Dakota returned home, she and Trent met for lunch. "I still don't understand how a marshal who was so highly regarded could have been talked into joining Max and his crew."

Trent put his fork down and sighed. "I've known Roger for years. When I went to see his wife and give her my condolences, I found out." He paused and looked at Dakota. "Martha, his wife, has cancer. They've tried everything. The only thing left is an experimental drug treatment in the UK. They needed the money to go over there and give it a try."

Dakota sat back in her chair and expelled a long breath. "But how did Max know that he could get Roger to help him?" She held a hand up to stop Trent. "Wait, it was my boss, Andrew, wasn't it? He knew what Roger was going through and told Max. I bet he gave Max a list of everyone and how best to get to them, didn't he?"

Trent didn't need to say a thing, he just nodded.

"You know, I want to hate Roger and think he's such a bad guy. He was a bad man, but he also needed to do something to help his wife." Dakota threw her hands in the air. "Don't people get it? There are so many organizations out there who will help with cancer treatments now."

"I know. And I've decided to donate to an organization that will help Martha get the treatment she needs. I don't know if it will work, but I believe she should be able to try anything she wants to." Trent stood up and put a wad of cash down on the table to cover their check. "Come on, let's go for a walk."

Dakota took Trent's hand in hers and led him outside to the little park next to the café where they had met for lunch. "So, what now?"

"Now? Now, it's time for this." Trent slowly leaned down toward Dakota's face. He gave her time to pull back if she wasn't ready for this. And when she didn't, he let his lips touch her for just a moment before pulling back. He looked into her eyes, and she gave him a tiny nod. Then he took her lips again. But this time, it felt as though it would be forever.

Dakota wrapped her arms around Trent's waist and pulled him closer to her. She returned his kiss with intensity and refused to stop the kiss until they both pulled back after a truck honked its obnoxiously loud horn and someone yelled, "Get a room!"

It took only six months before they did exactly that. It was their wedding night, and they took the train out to the Grand Canyon for their honeymoon, as a gift from the Grand Canyon Express Railway as well as the museum who owned the gems they saved.

Dakota would forever remember the tears of joy that her sister spilled that day and the smile that never left her face. It was her parting comments that made Dakota laugh.

"I'm so glad that our train was robbed. If it hadn't been, you would still be single."

Redeeming the Outlaw

Kit Morgan

Chapter One

Wyoming Territory, 1879

ADDY REEVES DABBED THE SWEAT FROM HER BROW WITH A handkerchief. The train car was stifling. She couldn't wait to get to the next stop.

She watched the landscape go by, her mind on her goal—get enough money to keep the ranch going. It's what John wanted, and Lord knows how hard she'd tried since his death. But the last few years hadn't been kind. She had to find a way to keep the ranch—or let it go and…what?

She wiped the hollow of her throat, the back of her neck. She should think of something to distract herself, or by the time she reached the bank she'd be a nervous wreck.

She noticed a woman with dark blonde hair and blue eyes, much like her own, pass by and go to the front of the car. She joined three other female passengers in conversation. From snippets she overheard, Addy surmised the trio were sisters traveling to Clear Creek, Oregon, as mail-order brides. Would she have to resort to such a thing? If she couldn't keep the ranch going, she might.

The blonde wore a wedding ring, and Addy wondered if she was related to the sisters, but she saw little resemblance. She could easily pass for the woman's sibling, though. Addy wished she was traveling with someone. Maybe Mrs. Blake from home? She was a widow and might like the outing. Once she completed her business at the bank, they could enjoy a meal, spend the night in a hotel, then return home to their dismal little town of Oats.

Addy sighed. No, it was best she was alone. After getting a taste of a *nice* town, poor Mrs. Blake wouldn't want to leave.

The conductor entered their car. "Laramie, coming into Laramie!" He continued down the aisle and through the door at the other end.

Addy retrieved her carpetbag from under the seat in front of her. Parched, she wanted to get off the train and find some water. As soon as the train came to a stop, she headed for the door to disembark. Thankfully she was one of the first ones off and wouldn't have to wade through a crowd to get to the platform's stairs. If she didn't get a drink soon, she might faint.

She wiped the back of her neck again as she reached the steps to the street. After she found some water, should she eat something or go straight to the bank? She licked dry lips. No, water was all she needed for now. If she didn't get the loan, she'd want food and time to think.

She left the station and was crossing the street when she saw a covered wagon speeding her way. She jumped back just in time. "Whoa, there!" she heard the driver call, bringing his team to a stop.

Addy, her hand to her chest, tried to catch her breath. "What in the world?"

A tall man was suddenly at her side. "Are y'all right?" Before she could answer he put an arm around her and headed for the wagon.

"What are you doing?"

"That driver ought to be horsewhipped."

Addy looked at him, noticed he wore a kerchief over his nose and mouth and gasped.

"Quiet." He gripped her arm and kept walking. They'd almost reached the wagon.

She blinked past her shock. "Unhand me—!" He clamped his hand over her mouth.

Two more men were in the back, arms outstretched to... oh, good Lord, they were going to abduct her! Addy tried to scream but it was no use until the man removed his hand and she could get enough air. But as if reading her thoughts, he put his arm around her waist and yanked her hard against him, knocking the air from her before he lifted her to the men in the wagon bed. One shoved a handkerchief into her mouth and secured it with another as the wagon took off, while the other bound her hands behind her back and tied her ankles.

Addy began to weep. Why were they doing this?

One, wearing a blue kerchief, shoved her onto a bag of grain and smiled. "That was easy."

"Yeah," the other said. He wore a red kerchief. "Now all we have to do is wait for instructions."

"How did Spider get this job?" Blue Kerchief asked.

"Some old accomplice of his wired him two days ago. Why d'ya think we hightailed it here?"

"Oh, yeah, the train."

Red Kerchief smiled. "We got here just in time, too." He put his arm around Addy and pulled her close. "And now she's ours." Both men leered at her.

Addy cringed. What would she do now?

———————

JAKE REEVES SAT atop his horse and waited for the others. Once this job was done, he was through with this. A small ranch someplace would do nicely. He could raise a few cattle, maybe breed some horses...

He craned his neck to better see the road below. Eli Randall and his cousin Luke promised this job paid well. They already gave him half his money, and he'd hidden it away as soon as he got it. Now all he had to do was see the job through, collect the other half, and walk away from this business. Being a gun for hire had been exciting in his younger days, but the thought of growing old had more appeal now in his thirties. If he kept going the way he had, he'd never see forty.

He took off his hat, ran a hand through his thick dark hair, and got back to watching the road.

The job seemed simple enough—escort and deliver a woman of means to her relative. Neither Eli nor Luke told him where they were escorting her, and he didn't need to know when he took the job. He only knew it wasn't far from Laramie. He'd help take care of her and act as lookout and scout when needed.

Still, he had to wonder...was someone after the woman? Who was she that she needed an armed escort through the wilderness? He had questions. But he'd learned over the years that some things were better left alone. Besides, it wasn't as if he was riding with some notorious outlaw gang. He'd dipped his toe into that sort of life once and that was enough. He had no desire to decorate a cottonwood. He had his guns, his wits, and a good horse named Bob. He could make do with those.

So here he was doing one last job before retiring his guns for a little ranch somewhere. He knew ranching and could live out his days in peace.

Jake sat straighter in the saddle as he spied dust in the distance. That had to be them. He nudged Bob and headed down to the road below. He knew it cut across open land parallel to the Laramie River before going northeast, then south to Rawlings. There were some ranches and farms along it but not many. It was an old stagecoach route, seldom used now that the train ran through.

Jake pushed the thought aside as he continued downhill. Eli told him they'd have a covered wagon pulled by horses, since they'd be camped out on the road a few nights and wanted the lady to be comfortable. Since the stage didn't run through here anymore, they must be taking her to one of the ranches out this way. He wondered if their destination was the largest one—he wouldn't mind getting a look at such a spread. Maybe it would give him ideas for his own ranch.

He reached the wagon, and the driver stopped it and waved. He didn't look familiar—he was older, unshaven, with gray hair and sported several facial scars and an eye patch. "You must be Jake."

"Howdy. And you are?"

"His name's Spider," Eli called from the back of the wagon.

"Let's get going," Spider said. "We're wasting daylight." He gave the horses a slap of leather and they started off again.

"Ride ahead, Jake," Eli called. "Make sure the road is clear."

Jake steered Bob to the back of the wagon instead. A piece of canvas blocked his view inside. "Eli?"

Eli lifted the canvas and poked his head out. "Ahead, I said."

Jake was about to leave when he heard a muffled cry. "What was that?"

Eli grinned. "Our cargo. Now git!"

Jake looked past him at a pair of bound ankles. "What in tarnation have you got in there?"

Eli grinned again. "Well, I guess it wouldn't hurt to let ya have a look." He pulled back the canvas.

Jake froze. Luke was holding a bound and gagged woman—and he knew who she was!

Chapter Two

ADDY COULDN'T BELIEVE IT! JOHN? BUT HOW COULD IT BE? HER beloved John was dead and had been for eight years!

Before she could get a better look at the man, her captors let the canvas flap fall, blocking her view. "Stop squirming." Red Kerchief shoved her off his lap onto the grain sack. He'd pulled her onto it as soon as the wagon stopped, then put a gun to her cheek. Once he heard a man talking to the driver, he lowered it. She was so scared, she didn't hear what they were talking about. Blue Kerchief obviously knew the newcomer.

Now so did she, given a second to think. Jake Reeves, John's twin brother. She hadn't seen Jake in a decade, didn't even know he was still alive. Last she'd heard, Jake was running with some outlaw gang. John always said he'd amount to no good. Over the years she expected to hear he'd been caught and either locked up or hanged. Now he was abducting her! Did he think John was still alive and that he could ransom her? Tears stung her eyes at the thought.

"I'm hungry," Blue Kerchief complained. Didn't Jake call him Eli?

"Yeah, me, too." Red Kerchief smiled at her. "I wonder if she can cook."

"That's not why we took her, Luke." Eli smacked Red

Kerchief upside the head. "Spider said she's worth a lot of money."

"That don't mean she can't cook for us." Luke looked her over. "There's another use for her besides." He licked his lips and leered.

Addy's eyes widened. She had to find a way out of this! Jake (if indeed it was) might be her chance of escape. Unfortunately, Jake was nothing like John. John was sweet, kind, generous—not perfect, but what man was? He'd been a decent husband and provided for her. He wasn't as decisive as Jake, but once he decided on something he stuck to it. He liked the safety of home and family, while Jake was always chasing adventure...until one day, he didn't come back.

A chill went up her spine. It figured the best chance she had of getting out of this was via the most unreliable person she knew. Jake had abandoned John and their parents years ago and left them with a ranch to run. Once their parents died, there was only John and her, then only her. Now she was on the verge of losing the ranch and maybe her life.

She struggled against her bonds when her captors weren't looking, but it was no use. She was tied tight. Had Jake recognized her? Or what if it wasn't him? She still didn't have a clue why she'd been abducted. If that was Jake, did he know? How far had he managed to sink? Merciful heavens, for all she knew he'd kill her without a second thought.

The tears fell. She mustn't think such things. She had to concentrate on finding a way to convince Jake to free her. But first, she had to discover if it was indeed Jake.

The wagon rolled along for hours, and Addy was growing more uncomfortable. She hoped they stopped soon and untied her long enough to take care of some business. If so, would Jake be around? Hadn't they sent him to scout ahead? Gagged as she was, would she get a chance to speak with him?

When the wagon did stop (thank heaven!) her captors left for a time, then came back and got her out of the wagon. Tied as she was, she couldn't stand and almost fell over. Eli laughed, tossed her over his shoulder, carried her to a large rock, and set her down. "I guess we should give her some water, huh?"

"Let her thirst," the driver said as he approached.

Addy recognized the voice and cringed. He was mean-looking with one side of his face scarred up and wearing an eye patch.

He reached her and got in her face. "If she's thirsty, who knows what she'll do for some water?"

"That don't seem right."

The three men turned. Addy looked at the horse and rider behind them. The sun, still high in the sky, made her squint, but the voice was familiar enough.

Jake dismounted and walked over. "Are you gonna ransom her?"

"No," Eye Patch said. "We're making a delivery."

Eli wiped his brow with the back of his hand. "We ought to give her something. It's hot as Hades out here."

"I know what I'd like to give her," Luke said.

"Back off, Luke." Jake went to his horse, grabbed a canteen hanging from the saddle horn and returned. He looked her over as he unscrewed the cap. "Take that gag off."

Luke complied.

Jake shook his head and shoved Luke out of the way. "Here, drink some of this." He held the canteen to her lips. "Just a little at a time."

"No need to be gentle with her," Eye Patch said.

"Spider, remember the time we abducted that gal and her brother?" Eli asked. "Didn't I tell you that if you want top dollar, deliver your captive in good shape. The worse shape they're in, the less money you get."

"He's right," Luke said. "Slade taught us that."

Spider rolled his eyes. "The man that hired us didn't say what shape he wanted her in."

Addy took another drink, eyes fixed on Jake. *Her* Jake. Did she dare say anything?

"Who is she?" Jake asked.

Spider laughed. "Gentlemen, meet Miss Ivy Pembroke of Omaha." He pushed Jake out of the way and got in her face. "A rich heiress."

"What's she doin' way out here?" Luke asked.

"The man that hired us said she ran away. Now he wants her back." Spider straightened and sneered at Jake. "Since yer the one insisting she have some water, ya can feed her, too. Just make sure she don't try anything funny. Johnson wants her alive."

"Johnson?" Jake said.

"Old associate of mine," Spider said. "He works for the man that wants her back. Now take care of her. We leave in ten minutes." He stomped off.

Addy, her heart in her throat, looked at Jake in horror. What would he do with her now?

———

A TRICKLE of sweat ran down Jake's temple. Some of the questions he had swirling in his head just got answered. One, yes, the woman was his sister-in-law, Addy. Two, they abducted her because they thought she was someone else. Three, they were just the delivery system. Four, they might kill her if they found out who she really was.

Jake bent to her ankles and untied them. "Get up."

She glanced at Eli and Luke who were tending the horses. "Jake?" she whispered.

"Hush if you want to live." He took her arm and pulled her to her feet. She sank, her ankles unable to support her after being tied so long. He picked her up and held her against him. "Addy," he hissed. "Do exactly as I say."

She nodded.

He let Addy get her feet under her, then guided her to some sagebrush. "I'm going to untie your hands. Take care of any business you have, but whatever you do, don't run off."

She stared at him with wide eyes.

"They think you're someone else," he said, voice low. "Best they keep thinking it."

She nodded again.

He pulled his gun and pointed it at her. "Don't do anything stupid," he said loud enough for the others to hear.

That's not all they heard as a rider approached with several horses in tow. "It's Pete!" Eli cried. "About time."

Jake holstered his gun. Great, his one chance of getting Addy out of this easily was gone. Being the only one with a horse, all he had to do was get Addy on Bob, then take off. He knew Eli and Luke were decent shots but Spider and Pete, he didn't know at all, only heard about them. He could conceivably shoot his way out and kill the lot of them, but he was no murderer, and he might get Addy killed in the process. He'd have to come up with something else.

Pete dismounted and went to speak to Spider. After a few moments Addy came out from behind the brush. "Thank you."

He looked at her, saw the red on her wrists and stiffened. "Give me your hands." She did as he asked, and his heart pinched. "I won't tie them as tight." He crossed her wrists in front of her and bound them. "You hungry?"

She glanced at the others. "Yes."

He took her arm and led her back to the rock. "Sit." He went to his saddlebags, pulled out some jerky and gave her a piece. "It's all I have, but it'll do."

She nodded, took it, and ate.

Jake saw her jaw tremble, bent to her, and whispered, "What in tarnation are you doing out here?" He glanced at the horses Pete brought. Spider, Luke, and Eli were checking them over. Were they stolen? He turned back to Addy. "Where's John? Was he there when they took you?"

She shook her head, tears in her eyes. "Jake...John's dead."

Chapter Three

"DEAD?"

Addy saw Jake's shock. How could he not know? But then, how could he? Neither she nor John had heard from him in a decade. There were letters at first, but it wasn't long before they stopped. "Eight years now."

His expression quickly filled with guilt. He straightened. "I'm sorry." Jaw tight, he turned away. His stance was angry, and she wondered what was going through his head. Not that it was hard to guess.

"Well, lookie here." The newcomer, Pete, approached. "Ain't you a pretty thing?" He turned to the others. "I ain't never met no highfalutin' lady before."

Spider joined them and slapped him on the back. "First time for everything, Pete. But hands off. I want what's promised us."

Pete sighed in disappointment. "Dagnabit."

Jake turned around gruffly. "Eat that jerky."

Addy took another bite. Was he broken up about John, or did he even care? She hung her head and chewed. That he hadn't written for years said a lot. If Jake cared so little for John, what hope did she have that he'd help her? It was obvious he was shocked to see her, but after he had time to think, what would he do? Would she have to beg him? Or worse?

She finished the jerky and watched the men, including Jake, return to the horses. Eli and Luke mounted and rode up the road. Pete also mounted, but he didn't go anywhere.

Jake glanced at her, said something to Spider, then came over. "We're leaving." He took her arm and pulled her to her feet.

She stood, legs shaking. There was no concern in his voice like before. He led her to the back of the wagon where Spider waited in the wagon bed. Jake lifted her up like she weighed nothing and handed her to him. Spider none too gently yanked her inside. "Tie her ankles and gag her," Spider ordered, then climbed out. Jake sighed then disappeared. He returned moments later and climbed in, a length of rope in one hand, two kerchiefs in the other.

Addy shook her head. "Please don't."

Spider climbed onto the wagon seat and slapped the horses with the lines. The wagon lurched forward and Addy noticed two horses were now tied to the back of it, one of them Jake's.

He tossed the rope aside and, to her horror, gagged her. So this was how it would be.

Jake bound her ankles, sat on the other sack of grain, and looked out the back. He didn't bother to untie the canvas flap to cover it, as there was no one around.

Addy's heart sank. She was alone with five outlaws and there was nothing she could do.

Her eyes scanned the wagon bed anyway for something she could use to free herself. There was a barrel she assumed carried water, a medium-sized chest holding who knows what, some bedrolls, and a small box of tools. She guessed they'd brought enough food and water to last them a few days. That gave her time to figure out how to get out of this mess. Once they realized she wasn't who they thought she was, she was doomed. And if they didn't, the man that sent them to abduct Ivy Pembroke would.

Addy looked at Jake, still staring out the back. Was he

avoiding eye contact? What had he done with his life since they last heard from him? There were rumors, of course. Outlawry, robbery, even murder, but neither she nor John wanted to believe them. Still, were the rumors true?

Her only solace was that he hadn't told the others who she was. Would he? Her fate was in his hands, and she hadn't a clue what he'd do. If he needed the money, he might keep his mouth shut to protect his own interests. But what would happen when the man that hired them found out she wasn't this Ivy? Would he kill them, too? When were they supposed to receive their pay? Would Jake keep her face covered when they handed her over? She had so many questions she couldn't think straight.

Addy squeezed her eyes shut and silently prayed that Jake's rebel heart hadn't been hardened to the point of no return. If it had, she was a goner.

JAKE STARED out the back of the wagon, Addy behind him bound, gagged, and helpless. His heart went out to her, but if he showed any mercy, it might give him away and they'd both be in trouble. Addy was tough, always had been, but she was still a frightened woman, unpredictable. She might do or say something when he least expected it, like call for his help.

He glanced at her. Her eyes were shut tight, and he wondered if she was trying not to cry. His heart seized at the thought, and he turned away again. He hated gagging her, but he had no choice. She might try to talk to him about John, and Spider would figure out they knew each other.

He sighed. John. How many years had it been since he'd seen his brother? He'd made bad choices, gotten into trouble and out of it over and over again. He couldn't stand the thought of John being disappointed in him, so he never told him about his exploits, and since he didn't want to lie he stopped writing altogether.

Jake glanced at Addy again. Her eyes were still closed,

but she looked relaxed now. With any luck she'd nod off. He hoped she did. She'd need her rest if they were to escape. He just had to figure out how.

He could overpower Spider, shove him off the wagon seat and see how far they could get. But Eli and Luke rode ahead while Pete rode behind. One or all could catch up to them and that would be that. They'd shoot him, then try to figure out why he took their captive when she was such easy money? Then Addy might tell them who she really was. He hated to think about what would happen then.

No, taking the wagon wasn't an option, and he still didn't want to shoot his way out unless he had to. He wasn't sure he could live with blood on his hands, disreputable or not. So what to do?

Addy sat with her back to the wall of the wagon, legs outstretched, head lolled to one side. He remembered when he and John first set eyes on her at a barn dance. She was the most beautiful creature they'd ever seen. Her family had just moved to Oats and started a small ranch, selling horses and beef to Fort Collins. He and John even helped with a few cattle drives to the fort.

But it was John that caught her eye, and Jake stepped back. Though they shared the same looks, John always was the more sensible one. Probably because it took him forever to make up his mind. Jake saw what choices there were and chose one, usually based on what felt good at the time. He'd learned to think since then, which made him wonder how he ended up in this mess.

But if he hadn't chosen to be here, Addy still would be. What chance would she have then? Fate brought them together again, and he should be thanking the Almighty it had. He had a chance to save her, to save a lot of things. But after he did, would she be just as disappointed in him as John would be if he were alive?

He shook his head at the thought. Did it matter? Saving Addy was more important. To heck with his pride or what she thought of him. He'd walked away from her once—he could do it again. Besides, she never knew he loved her back then. She wouldn't now.

The wagon bumped along, and Jake wondered when Spider planned to stop. He was about to ask when he noticed Addy looking at him with those big blue eyes. He saw fear in them and something else—hope? But he didn't dare give her any yet. He was still trying to find some himself.

He hadn't tied her wrists and ankles as tightly as the others had and hoped that brought some comfort. He'd give anything to release her from her bonds but knew Spider wouldn't have it. He'd speak with her when he gave her food and water...if he could figure out what to say. He wanted to trust her but didn't know her anymore. Too many years had passed, during which he'd made some colossal mistakes. How many of those mistakes had she heard about?

Jake decided to worry about that later. He had to save her, that was what mattered.

Chapter Four

ADDY AWOKE WITH A JERK AS THE WAGON STOPPED. SHE blinked sleep from her eyes and rubbed them with her bound hands. Thank heaven Jake didn't tie them behind her back. She wished he hadn't tied them at all.

Still sitting at the back of the wagon, he looked right at her, a coiled rope in one hand. She cringed as he set it on top of the barrel, then approached. "I'm going to untie you now." He unbound her ankles first, then removed the gag.

She coughed as soon as he did, her throat dry. "Water," she rasped.

He grabbed a canteen behind him, pulled the stopper, and held it to her lips. She drank, not caring about what spilled down her front.

"Easy, now." He pulled the canteen away, set it aside, and untied her hands. "We're going outside. Take care of your business, and you can have more water."

She stiffened. He was stoic, almost cold. How could he be a part of this? But this wasn't John, she had to keep telling herself. Who knew what Jake was capable of?

He brought her to the back of the wagon and climbed out. Addy glanced at the front and the team of horses beyond.

"Don't even think about it. I'd reach you before you could so much as take a seat."

She glared at him. "What happened to you?"

"Quiet," he hissed. He held up his hands to her.

Addy frowned but let him help her out. His hands were large, warm, strong. For a moment, she felt safe, then it was gone.

He set her on the ground and bent to her ear. "We don't know each other, understand? They'll kill us both."

She swallowed, her face softening. Was he trying to protect her or save his own skin? Regardless, she nodded.

He did the same, then took her arm and led her away from the wagon. Like before, he found her a spot where she could have some privacy, untied her hands, and left her alone. Should she make a run for it? But with no food or water, how could she survive? She had no idea where they were. There was no more sagebrush—the road here wound its way through grassland spotted with trees and rock outcroppings. From the looks of it, they were heading into the mountains.

Would she die out here? Would Jake? How could she trust him after all these years? But then, telling her to act like they didn't know each other had to count for something.

She stood next to a tree and watched him speak to Pete. Of the five, Jake was the youngest. The others looked to be in their forties, Spider his fifties. How long had they been doing this sort of thing?

Jake headed her way, and a shiver went up her spine. But it wasn't fear...mercy, was it attraction? He did look like John, after all.

"Are you hungry?" he asked when he reached her.

"A little."

He pulled a handkerchief from his pocket, unwrapped it and handed her some jerky. "Eat this. I'll see what else I can find you."

She noticed he didn't make eye contact. He was taking in their surroundings instead. "Thank you."

His head slowly turned, and he locked eyes with her.

Was that regret she saw in them? "You're welcome," he whispered.

She nodded, spied a rock a few feet away, went to it, and sat. No one paid her any mind, and she assumed it was because there was no place for her to go. She nibbled the jerky and watched the men talk, share a canteen, and pass around what looked like jerky and biscuits.

Jake went to the wagon and returned with a biscuit and the canteen. "Eat this and take a drink," he said gruffly, looking around as if expecting a posse to gallop up any second.

She took the biscuit. "Nervous?"

He met her gaze. "Of course," he said quietly. "You should be, too."

She bit her lip to keep it from trembling. "I am."

He nodded and handed her the canteen.

She washed the biscuit down with water, then gave the canteen back. She noticed he hadn't moved. Was he protecting her from the others? She wanted to talk to him, find out where he'd been all these years, but now was not the time. If she wanted to survive, she'd have to do as he said.

"Walk a spell. Your limbs will thank you later."

She looked around to see the others were spaced out, each moving. She strolled to the team of horses and patted one on the neck. "Where are you from?" It was a simple question and hopefully Jake would give her a straight answer. With any luck, she could find out what he'd been up to all these years with the others being none the wiser.

He stood next to the horses' hindquarters. "Texas, originally."

She tried to hide a smile. That much was true. "Originally? What about lately?"

His eyes softened, and he swallowed hard. "I...lived in a nothing of a town called Oats. It's just over the border."

"Colorado?"

"That's right."

Addy bit her lip and smiled. That was also true. "How long were you in Oats?"

Jake stared at the ground. "Not long enough."

———

JAKE, his back to Addy, bent over and picked up a horse's back leg. He pretended to examine it, brushing dirt and debris from the shod hoof. He knew Addy was watching him and probably some of the others.

"How long ago did you leave?"

He let go of the hoof and went to the other horse. "Years ago. I decided I wanted to see the big wide world."

She followed him. "And did you?"

He glanced her way. "I saw more than my fair share." He checked the hooves of the other horse. He owed her answers, and she'd found a way to get some, but he couldn't tell her much without risking her safety. Really, he shouldn't be talking to her at all.

"How long have you been doing this kind of work?"

He stiffened and turned to her. "Longer than I'd like. In fact, this is my last job." He scanned the landscape to see where everyone was. Eli, Luke, and Pete were all out of earshot, and he didn't see any sign of Spider. When he faced Addy again, she was giving him a look that said, *tell me everything*. "Don't ask so many questions. Captives usually don't ask after their abductor's health."

She glanced around, too. "I'm not. I'm asking where you've been all these years." She drew closer. "Why didn't you write us?" she whispered.

"On account I had nothing to say." He fiddled with the harness. "I'm sorry."

"You should be."

He looked at her and his chest tightened. "How did John die?"

"Pneumonia. Eight winters ago."

He caught the sadness in her voice. "I'm sorry I wasn't there." He noticed Spider talking to Pete now and looked over the harness. As soon as Addy joined him, he glanced her way. "I know how you feel about me, but I'm all you've got. Do as I say and if we're lucky, and I do mean *lucky*, we'll get out of this alive, understood?"

She sighed and nodded. "I still want to know what happened to you."

He looked into her eyes. "No, you don't." He looked at the length of rope he'd left on the barrel. He couldn't stand the thought of tying her up again. There was no need at this point, and it was cruel. This far out, where would she go? She couldn't outrun any of them, especially if they were on horseback.

"You still could have written."

Jake jumped. He hadn't heard her come up behind him. "Don't do that."

"I still want to know."

"You won't let this go, will you?"

She crossed her arms in front of her. "Nope."

"Did anything I say get into that brain of yours? Questioning me is dangerous. If you keep doing it…I'll have to gag you again."

She gasped. "You wouldn't dare."

"I dared before."

Her face fell. "You did."

He studied her eyes, filled with fear and disappointment. Who knew what she thought of him? He owed her an explanation and he'd give it, but not now.

Pete was mounting his horse nearby. Jake took her arm and led her to the back of the wagon. "Now behave yourself," he said gruffly. He didn't want any of them to think he was coddling their captive. He took Addy by the waist and lifted her up. "Get in there."

She complied and climbed into the back of the wagon. He climbed in next and grabbed the rope from the barrel as Spider climbed onto the wagon seat. "I'm not going to tie you up. But if you try anything stupid, you won't like what happens to you."

Her eyes widened. "I won't try to run away."

Spider twisted round on the seat. "No, you won't, because you'll be bound and gagged. Do it, Jake."

Jake settled himself on the other bag of grain. "What for? Where can she go?"

Spider growled and faced forward.

Jake sighed and looked at Addy, who managed a relieved smile. He just hoped she didn't do or say anything that would cause suspicion. He should have stuck to his original plan and not spoken to her at all. But now that the horse was out of the barn, he'd have to chase it.

Spider got the wagon moving, and they were off again.

Chapter Five

DARKNESS SURROUNDED ADDY, AND IT TOOK HER A MOMENT TO realize where she was. She moaned and pushed herself up from the sack of grain she'd been using as a pillow. Stiff and sore, she looked around. Jake was gone.

She climbed to her feet and edged toward the other end of the wagon bed. Night had fallen and she wondered how long she'd been asleep. Men's voices drifted to her from the left, and she noticed the orange glow of a campfire. There was another sound, metal on metal, and she realized they must be eating.

Her stomach rumbled at the thought of food, and she licked dry lips as she poked her head out and looked at the ground. How would she climb down? She was about to swing a leg over the tailboard when Jake appeared, a plate in his hand. "Oh, thank goodness."

He held up the plate. "Hungry?"

"Famished."

He set the plate on a rock, then helped her out. "You've been asleep for several hours."

"That long?" She headed for the food.

"Spider says we'll reach our destination by tomorrow night."

Addy, a forkful of beans halfway to her mouth, blanched.

"That soon?"

He nodded. "Afraid so."

She noticed he was speaking quietly and looked around. The others were seated around the fire eating. She looked at Jake and came closer. "What will we do?"

He peeked around the wagon, then looked her in the eyes. "*You* don't do anything."

She almost dropped the plate. "What?" Good grief, maybe he wouldn't help her.

"Except be ready. We'll ride away once everyone's asleep. Got it?"

She swallowed hard then whispered, "Yes."

"We'll borrow Pete's horse. Can you still ride?"

She nodded. He *was* going to help her-hallelujah!

"We'll have to move fast. I'll loose the rest of the horses first. Once the others figure out what's happened, it'll take them a while to catch them. That gives us a head start." He put his hands on her shoulders. "But if they catch us, they'll kill us both."

"Understood."

"Eat up," he said, louder this time. He turned on his heel and strode away.

Addy watched him return to the fire. She saw a coffee pot on a rock and wondered if they'd let her have a cup. She'd need it if they were going to escape tonight. But once they did, where would they go? Back to Laramie, or someplace else? For Heaven's sake, she didn't even know where they were. She hoped Jake did.

She sat down, ate her beans, then inched toward the fire.

"Well, look who decided to wake up?" Pete said.

"Want some coffee?" Eli asked.

Spider tossed his plate on the ground. "What is she, the queen of England? Stop being nice to her."

"What happened to delivering her in good shape for more money?" Luke asked.

"I know what I said," Spider spat. "But that don't mean you gotta treat her like royalty. She can get her own coffee."

Pete and Eli snorted as Jake nodded at the pot. "You heard him. Get it if you want some."

She nodded, set her plate aside, then looked for a rag or something to grab the pot with. There was nothing. The men, she noticed, wore thick gloves. Her lace gloves would offer no protection.

Jake cleared his throat.

She turned around, saw the handkerchief in his hand and took it. "Thank you."

Spider shook his head in annoyance and drained his cup. "Give me some, too, Missy."

Addy's hackles went up. The pot was almost empty. She poured her own cup first, then gave him what was left. She didn't know where her newfound boldness came from but was glad it was there.

Spider growled at his cup and downed the contents. She was surprised he didn't grab hers.

Addy went to the log where Pete and Jake sat and planted herself between them. She still wasn't sure what was in this for Jake. Did he want a reward for helping her escape? If so, she had none to give, save maybe a horse or steer. She'd discuss it with him later. Right now she had other things to think about, like how far they'd get before Spider and his gang started after them. They'd have to ride hard, and she hadn't been on a horse in a while. There was no need—she always drove a buggy or buckboard to town.

Eli and Luke settled in for the night first. Pete stood, stretched, and headed for his bedroll. Spider looked her up and down from across the fire and rubbed his chin a few times. "I think I'll take the night watch and guard our prisoner."

Addy gulped.

Spider stood and walked around the fire. "Yeah, I think spending the night in the back of the wagon with you should be entertaining."

Jake stood and stretched. "I thought you said hands off?"

"Yeah," Pete said from his bedroll. "Besides, you snore so loud she'll never get any sleep."

The others burst into laughter except Jake, who maneuvered between her and Spider. "I've been keeping an eye on her. Why change now?"

"Ya ain't getting sweet on her, are ya?" Spider asked suspiciously.

Jake snorted and rolled his eyes. "She's not my type." He rubbed his thumb against his fingers. "She's money."

Spider looked her over again. "Yeah, she is. Too skinny for me anyway. I like 'em plump." He headed for his bedroll. "Tie her up."

Jake went to the log, pulled her up by her arm and started to drag her toward the wagon. She knew it was all for show but still couldn't help fighting against him.

"And keep your hands off her, Jake!" one called after them.

Back in the wagon Addy sat on a sack of grain. "You're not really going to tie me up, are you?" she asked softly.

"Of course not," Jake whispered. "It would slow us down when the time comes."

"And when will that be?" she whispered back.

"In a few hours. Now get some rest. You'll need it."

————

JAKE WONDERED if he'd lost his mind. One slip and they'd be caught. But he had to take that chance. This was the only way.

He quietly saddled his horse, did the same with Pete's, then untied the rest. Two wandered off, and it wasn't long before the others followed. If they stayed quiet enough, he and Addy could slip away and go unnoticed for hours. Eli and Luke had tied the horses behind some trees, so maybe they wouldn't notice they were gone right away.

He quietly led the two saddled horses to the far side of the wagon, out of sight of the others. He hoped Addy was ready and went to the back of the wagon.

Addy sat up and crawled toward him. Good. "Is it time?" she whispered.

He nodded and reached for her. Once her feet touched the ground, he led her to Pete's horse, helped her mount, then climbed onto his. He put his finger to his lips, then gave Bob a nudge. He wouldn't gallop off and risk waking the others. So far, they were still snoring, unaware of what was going on.

Jake headed down the road. Thank heaven the moon was full and they were able to see. Unfortunately, that meant Spider and the others could see them. He kicked Bob into a canter when they were about fifty yards from camp and prayed Addy followed. She did. They'd stick to the road for now. He didn't want to risk a horse tripping and going lame.

They rode into the night and Jake relaxed a notch. As far as he knew, none of Spider's gang could track well. Still, he wanted a good head start and some high ground when they did stop to rest. He checked on Addy a few times, saw her gripping the saddle horn and wondered how well she could ride. But he couldn't stop to find out. They didn't dare talk over the sound of the hooves. They'd have to whisper once they stopped.

They rode for hours before Jake spotted a trail that led up a hillside into some trees. He brought his horse to stop and waited for Addy to catch up. "Up there," he hissed. "We'll take a little rest, then move on."

She nodded and followed his lead. Up the hill they entered a copse of pine and dismounted. Before Addy could say anything, he held up his hand to keep her quiet and listened. No hoofbeats, no shouts, nothing. "Thank the Lord."

"Jake," Addy whispered. "Do you think they've discovered we're gone?"

He removed his canteen, pulled the stopper, and drank. He wiped his mouth, then offered it to her. "I don't know. Let's hope not."

She stared at him, took the canteen, and drank. "Thank you."

He nodded and looked around. "We can't stay here. We're still too close. For all we know, they're looking for us."

She came closer and looked into his eyes. *"Thank you."*

His breath caught. By heaven, she was beautiful. The moonlight shone in her eyes and wisps of hair framed her face. "Don't thank me yet. Do it once you're home, safe and sound."

"Is that where you're taking me?"

"Unless there's someplace else you'd like to go."

"Home will do." She looked at the ground. "Besides, it would be nice to have you back, even for a little while."

"I won't be staying. Now mount up." He went to Pete's horse and waited for her.

She joined him and once again looked at him with those big blue eyes. "How can I ever repay you?"

"Like I said, don't worry about that now. We have to get out of here."

She took a shuddering breath and nodded.

Jake helped her mount, went to Bob, and did the same. Once in the saddle, he listened again for any sounds of pursuit. There were none. He sighed in relief, then headed back down the hill. With any luck, Spider and the rest wouldn't wake until dawn. Unfortunately, Jake didn't think they'd get that lucky.

Chapter Six

BACK ON THE ROAD THEY KICKED THEIR HORSES INTO A GALLOP and were off. Jake knew their mounts would need to rest soon and that he'd have to find a place they could hide for a few hours. Until then, he kept a sharp eye out and hoped Addy could stay in the saddle.

Had she even slept? He should've asked, but he'd been so mesmerized by her when they stopped, it slipped his mind. Now was not the time for old feelings to resurface. She never knew how he felt about her all those years ago and she wasn't going to. She made the best choice when she married John. His brother didn't have the same wanderlust, nor was he as selfish.

How much *had* he changed over the years, other than wanting to settle down? Would Addy see him as the same old Jake Reeves?

They rode until dawn, then followed a deer trail into some woods, the last before the landscape changed to sage-brush, dirt, and rock. Once they were hidden among the trees, he dismounted and pulled a map from his saddlebags.

Addy climbed off her horse with a grunt, rubbed her backside, then removed the canteen from Pete's saddle horn. She shook it a few times. "There's not much water in here."

"Take a small drink," he said, voice low. "We'll conserve what we can."

"I take it Pete's not one to prepare." She brought the canteen to her lips and drank.

"He's probably the type that takes care of things right before he heads out. I do it the night before. So do the Randalls. I guarantee they'll be ready."

"What about Spider?" she asked nervously.

"They have only two mounts. Unless they use one of the wagon's horses, and they don't have saddles."

"What if they don't need one?"

He shrugged. "Riding bareback isn't easy for some."

She looked at him fearfully in the predawn light.

Without thinking he put his hands on her shoulders. "Addy, I'll get you home."

She took another shuddering breath and nodded. "Of course, you will."

His chest tightened. Was that doubt in her voice? "Trust me."

"I'm trying." She backed away.

Jake let his arms drop and ignored the twist of guilt in his gut. "Stay here. I'm going to look around." He crept to the edge of the trees and tried to see the road in the distance. So far, no sign of pursuit. Good. Unable to help it, he glanced Addy's way. He wanted her to trust him, needed her to. But once he brought her home, what then? He'd told her he wasn't staying but wasn't sure how hard it would be to leave her. Again. This wasn't just attraction flickering back to life. There was a lot more. The sooner he got away from her the better. Besides, he didn't deserve her.

They sat on a fallen tree, ate some jerky, and took a few more sips from their canteens. "There was a small creek a couple hours from here," he said. "We can water the horses and find someplace to hide for a few hours."

"Won't that give them time to catch up?" Addy asked, eyes wide.

Jake fought the urge to take her in his arms and tell her

everything would be okay. "The horses will need to rest and so will we. Besides, if I remember right, the Randalls aren't the best trackers. From listening to them, I don't think Spider and Pete are either."

She sighed. "That's a relief." She left the tree and paced. "Maybe we shouldn't travel in daylight at all."

He pulled the map from his back pocket. "I have a good idea where to go. We'll head west, circle around Laramie, then head for Oats."

"You think they'll look for us in Laramie?"

"It's possible, which is why I want to avoid it." He stepped toward her. "I know it'll make the trip longer and rougher, but if it helps us avoid Spider and his gang, we'll do it."

She began wringing her hands.

Jake stood, put his hands over hers, and she stopped. "I know it's hard, but you have to trust me, Addy."

She closed her eyes. "You're right. It is hard."

His gut twisted again. He'd left a bad taste in her mouth all those years ago and it was still there. "I'm sorry about John. I truly am."

She looked at him in doubt.

"He was my brother. I know I've been gone a long time, but that doesn't mean I didn't love him."

She pulled her hands from his. "I'm sorry, too. You lost him and so did I."

He nodded. There wasn't much else to say.

They mounted and were on their way. Once they reached the creek and watered the horses, he'd keep an eye out for someplace to hole up. If they followed the creek west and didn't run into any trouble, he could have Addy home in a few days. With any luck, Spider would think they stuck to the road and were heading for Laramie. But there were no guarantees.

They rode in silence for the most part, stopping now and then to listen for sounds of pursuit. All they heard were a few birds, the wind, and nothing else. Maybe their luck would hold.

By the time they reached the creek, Addy looked ready to fall out of the saddle. He helped her dismount and filled their canteens while she watered the horses. As soon as they were through, they pressed on and rode alongside the creek for a time.

After another couple of hours, Jake spotted a rise with an outcropping of rock and pointed to it. The road back to Laramie was a couple of miles from there. They should be safe. "We'll hide beneath those rocks. If anyone's coming from the road, they won't see us."

Addy studied their surroundings. "There's not much out here, is there?"

"No, which is why we can't stay long. But the horses are tired and so are you." He kicked Bob into a trot, then a canter. Addy followed and they soon reached the shelter. It wasn't much, but it would do. Unless Spider and the others rode down the creek for as long as they had, they wouldn't see them. For now, they were safe.

———

BENEATH THE ROCK OUTCROPPING, they dismounted, fed the horses some grain from Jake's saddlebags, then sat on the ground. Addy rubbed her arms and flexed her shoulders. Everything hurt.

"Sore?" Jake asked.

"You have no idea how long it's been since I've ridden."

To her surprise, he smiled. "You used to love to ride."

"That was before my accident." She unconsciously rubbed her right leg.

Jake frowned. "What happened?"

She rolled her eyes. "John bought a new horse, and like a fool, I tried to ride it."

His eyebrows shot up. "It bucked you off?"

"Yes, and I landed on a rock. A big one. I broke my leg."

His eyes went to her leg, then her face. "You should have known better."

Addy stared at him. He looked concerned, which was

ridiculous. The accident was years ago. "John bought me a buggy after that. I've been using it ever since. I got used to it, I suppose. Why ride when you can drive?"

"I prefer my horse." He went to the animal and patted him on the neck. "You're a good boy, aren't you?"

"What's his name?"

"Bob."

"Bob?" She laughed. "The Reeves men can't name horses."

He cocked his head. "Why, what was the name of John's horse?"

"The one that bucked me off?" She smiled. "Chet."

His shoulders shook with silent laughter, a reminder that they needed to be quiet.

She decided to smile instead. "Need I say more?"

He shook his head. "Please don't." He stared at the bedroll tied to his saddle and went to it.

Addy got to her feet. "Don't worry about me. The ground is good enough."

He smiled warmly. "Still as practical as ever."

She shrugged. "I try to be. You're still a risk-taker."

He looked her in the eyes. "Sometimes I have to be."

"Such as when you abduct innocent women?"

He sighed. "I did *not* abduct you. I was told I was part of your escort."

Her jaw dropped. "Escort?"

He reached her in two strides and put his finger to her lips. "Quiet."

"Escort?" she whispered as soon as he removed it. "Some escort. You trussed me up like a..."

"I did *not* truss you up."

"You did, too," she spat.

"Only the second time and that was to protect you."

She blinked a few times. "Protect me? Do you have any idea what it's like to be bound, gagged, and carted about in a hot wagon?"

His eyebrows rose and he nodded.

"What?" She looked him over. He was a little over six feet, the same as John, and all muscle and sinew. The Reeves men weren't big and burly, but they were strong. "Do I want to ask?"

He shrugged. "There was a crooked banker that needed something done."

She gaped at him. "Couldn't you have said no?"

"He held Bob as collateral. He said if I didn't do what he wanted he'd shoot him."

Her jaw slackened. "You expect me to believe that?"

He shrugged again. "It's true. Just ask Bob." He looked at his horse.

Addy rolled her eyes. "Still the same old Jake. You take nothing seriously."

He went to Bob and patted him on the neck. "I take Bob seriously. He's all I have. I wasn't about to lose him."

Addy caught that he wasn't teasing. "What happened?"

"I ran some folks out of town who were giving the man trouble. And I got Bob back."

Her hands went to her hips. "That is the most ridiculous thing I've ever heard."

"Believe what you want, Addy. But it's true." He went to the one smooth patch of dirt there was and sat. "You should get some rest."

"What about you?"

"I can last a while longer. I'll wake you, then you can keep an eye out."

"That's fair." She sat next to him, realized how close she was, and scooted away. He watched her with a familiar smirk. "What is it?"

"You can either use that rock behind us as a pillow, or my shoulder. The choice is yours."

She looked up. There was a ceiling of rock above them and a rough wall of it at their backs. She leaned against it, closed her eyes, and folded her hands in her lap. Though she appreciated the offer, she didn't dare get too close to him. She had to remember he was a scoundrel, even if he was family. She'd take what help he could offer, thank him once he delivered her home, then would probably never see him again. But that was Jake for you.

It was a miracle Addy found him the way she did. But sometimes the Almighty worked things out that way. And lucky for her He had.

Chapter Seven

JAKE STUDIED THE LAND SPREAD OUT BEFORE THEM. IT SLOPED down to the creek, then stretched for miles before it changed again. This would be the most dangerous part of their journey. They'd be crossing open country with only sagebrush, a few trees, and the occasional outcropping of rock like this one. If Spider spotted them, he'd try to run them down. But they could also spot Spider. If they did some traveling at night, they could stay well ahead of him. Spider was a lazy so-and-so from what he'd observed. He might cut his losses and run.

He looked at Addy and smiled. She was slowly leaning his way. If he didn't do something, she'd fall over. He scooted next to her and sure enough, her head fell against his shoulder. He smiled again.

It was one thing to have a gang of outlaws after them, another to have his heart after her. He didn't dare listen to it. It was his heart that made him leave all those years ago. Broken, it got him into trouble. Maybe it thought if he was reckless enough, it would make him forget about the woman sitting next to him. It didn't work.

He noted Addy's mussed hair, the rumpled state of her dress. She looked a fright, but he'd never seen her so beautiful.

He shut his eyes. She'd have nothing to do with him. He'd done bad things, got paid to do them. He'd hang up his gun belt once she was safe, walk out of her life, and never look back. It was the wisest thing to do. The safest.

He opened his eyes, scanned their surroundings for signs of danger, and sighed.

Addy sighed, too, and snuggled against him.

Jake froze. Should he move? But she was comfortable, and he hated to disturb her rest. So long as he didn't let his heart talk him into doing something stupid like kiss her, he'd be fine…

Jake studied her mouth. Lord help him, she had the most kissable mouth he'd ever seen. He remembered the time he almost kissed her years ago. It was the night she told him she was sweet on John, maybe even loved him. How could he kiss her after that, or tell her what was in his heart?

Besides, it was his fault she chose John over him. He didn't spend as much time with her as John had. Pa would ask him to do some chore and, rebel that he was, he'd finish it and take off fishing. How come he was the one saddled with all the physical labor while John had his nose stuck in a book? It didn't seem right. He could read and do his numbers as well as John could. One more reason to leave—that's what he told himself, anyway.

Addy moaned softly and snuggled against him. Unable to help himself, Jake put his arm around her. It was more comfortable for them both, and he'd have to remember to tell her so once she woke up. Otherwise, she might slap him.

After about ten minutes, maybe holding her wasn't such a good idea. It only fueled the urge to kiss her. But it also fueled his protective instincts, and he focused on that. He was on high alert now, the thought of having to shoot Spider or the others to protect her not as bothersome. He'd do what he had to. Besides, he could shoot to wound like he always did. But then, what would happen when he and Addy rode away?

Men hired him for protection and to incapacitate others if needed. Whomever he was working for at the time could do what they wanted with them. That was their business. At least *he* hadn't killed anyone. That he knew of.

He hung his head. How could he tell Addy about his past? Rich men hired him not only for protection, but to scare folks off their land so a bank could take it over. He didn't make a living out of it, but he'd done it nonetheless.

He studied the landscape again. He hadn't done that kind of work for a while now. He picked up small jobs here and there across Texas before coming north. He was, he supposed, unconsciously heading home. Now here he was with the only woman he'd ever loved sleeping in his arms. She hadn't a clue he was a gun for hire and what that entailed. He'd worked for as many bad men as he had good ones. So long as he didn't have to kill anyone, he'd take the job. But no more. He should use his skills to protect, not intimidate.

Jake reached up, brushed a loose wisp of hair from Addy's face, then continued to gently hold her. Getting her home with his heart intact would be the hardest job of all.

————

ADDY'S EYELIDS WERE HEAVY. She ached yet was comfortable. Warm. She was also outside. But that wasn't all.

Her eyes opened wide. "What the...?"

Jake looked down at her. "Good afternoon."

"What!?" She scooted away. "Where...oh, yes. Now I remember." She wiped her mouth. Had she been drooling? Mortified, she wiped it again.

Jake smirked. "Sleep well?"

"Oh, you...why didn't you wake me?"

"I wanted you to rest." He got to his feet, stretched, and went to the horses.

"What are you doing?" Addy was flustered but didn't care. She was so disoriented a moment ago she was more worried about drooling on Jake than sleeping on him. How did that happen, anyway?

"Having a look around." He pulled a spyglass out of a

saddlebag then turned to her. "Stay here. When I come back, I'll let you know if it's safe to venture out. I wouldn't mind washing up in the creek." He left.

She watched him head up the slope. What time was it? How long had she been asleep? She pulled some jerky from his saddlebags and took a bite. As she chewed, she tried not to think of how good it felt to wake up in Jake's arms. Too good.

She shook her head at the thought. "No, no, no." It was attraction, that's all. One that had been there for years. Jake was handsome, wild, a rebel, all the things a smart young woman should run from. It was why she chose John all those years ago. After telling her parents about the Reeves boys, they were quick to tell her which would suit. John was dependable, responsible, had good sense. He would make a good match. They also told her that if she chose Jake, they'd disown her. He'd put a stain on the family, just as he had on John's.

Addy never saw Jake that way. He reminded her of a beautiful wild horse that just wanted to be free. But her parents pressured her to court John. After all, he'd asked for permission to court her. Jake hadn't.

She wandered to the edge of their shelter. What would she have done if Jake asked before John did? Would she have courted him? They were friends then. He worked the ranch with his father while John worked the accounts, paid the bills, and everything else that required a working mind. John wasn't physical like Jake and his father. He preferred indoors to out. Not that he couldn't do the work, but he was lackluster about it. Jake once told her his brother wasn't cut out for ranching.

She sighed as she stared at a long, thin line of green in the distance—grass growing along the creek bank. Jake was right; John wasn't cut out for ranching. His idea of hard work was balancing a ledger or reading a book. Did he get the job done? Of course. But afterward, he wasn't interested in much else. Not even children.

She stared at the dusty ground. That was her main regret in marrying him. She was childless and wondered if she was truly barren, or if John couldn't give her any. But did it matter? He didn't want them anyway.

After a few minutes Jake returned. "Okay, I think it's safe. Let's ride to the creek, water the horses, and wash up."

She noted her rumpled appearance. "Good idea." She went to her horse and, with Jake's help, mounted.

As soon as he swung into the saddle, they were off. He led the way, surveying their surroundings like a hawk. Addy knew she didn't stand a chance out here without him and was grateful he'd rescued her. Still, who would rescue her from him?

He still made her head swim with his rugged good looks and easy swagger. He was so different from John. True, she'd grown to love John over the years, and he was the practical choice. But Jake was the one that made her heart pound when she thought of him. He made her feel alive.

Addy watched him ride ahead and noted the width of his shoulders, his dark hair peeking out from beneath his hat. He was born to the saddle and always had a way with horses. His father had him train a few, now that she thought on it.

"We'll have to be quick," he said when they reached the creek. "I'll rest a spell, then we'll leave."

She nodded as she dismounted and led her horse to the water's edge. Jake did the same and as soon as the animals had their fill, she sat on the bank and took off her shoes.

"What are you doing?" he asked.

"I'm going to wash my feet."

He eyed her as one might a naughty child. "And if we have to get out of here pronto?"

She shrugged. "I'll grab my shoes."

He pinched the bridge of his nose.

"What? Don't you want to wash your feet?"

He let his hand drop. "I was thinking face, neck, hand... maybe my chest."

Her eyes locked on said chest and her belly flipped. "I see." She turned to the creek, knelt at the water's edge, and splashed some on her face. It felt good and the thought of water on her neck and chest had merit. Now if she could just keep from watching Jake wash himself, maybe her heart would quit pounding.

Chapter Eight

JAKE STOOD, RETRIEVED HIS SPYGLASS FROM HIS SADDLEBAG AND scanned their surroundings. There was no sign of man or beast. He went to Addy and sighed. "Fine, wash your feet."

She smiled and started to take off her shoes again. He hoped he wouldn't regret this. He sat, pulled off his boots and socks, then stuck his feet in the water. It was wonderful. He watched Addy do the same and smiled at her expression of bliss.

"Thank you," she whispered. "You have no idea how good this feels."

He splashed water her way. "I have some."

She splashed him back.

He tried to keep his expression stoic. "There's no time for play, Addy."

She blushed head to toe. "I'm sorry. For a moment I forgot we're being chased by a bloodthirsty gang of outlaws."

"Until you're safe at home, never forget it," he advised. Jake pulled the kerchief he wore from his neck, dipped it in the creek and proceeded to wash himself. When he was done, Addy was staring at him, her mouth half open, eyes wide. "What?" He looked around. Had she seen something?

She snapped her mouth shut and shook her head. "Nothing. Mind if I borrow that?"

He held up the dripping kerchief. "This?"

"Yes, may I?"

He got up and handed it to her, taking a moment to look for any sign of danger. He saw none. "When was last time you washed up in a creek?"

"If you're referring to the time we had a mud fight, that was the last."

He snorted. "That was fun."

"It was awful."

He looked through the spyglass. "You thought it was fun then."

She dipped the kerchief in the water and wiped the front and back of her neck with it. "We were young and foolish."

"And a year later you married John." He lowered the spyglass. He should change the subject.

She splashed water on her face. "A person can grow up a lot in a year. When I turned eighteen, I had to. My parents wanted me to wed."

"Wed John, you mean." He put the spyglass back in his saddlebag. "Put your shoes and socks on. We're leaving." He went to retrieve his boots.

Addy did as she was told. She wouldn't argue with him. Besides, if they kept talking about John, he might say something he'd regret, like how wrong his brother was for her. But there was nothing to be done about it now. Heck, there was nothing he could do about it back then either.

They mounted their horses and followed the creek. "I thought we were heading south."

Jake shook his head. "Not until nightfall. If we follow this the rest of the day, it will take us well past the road back to Laramie. This isn't the same creek that parallels the road leaving town. I'm hoping Spider will stick to that road."

"And if he doesn't?"

"Then we'll have company at some point. But only if Spider and the others ride hard. My guess is we have over a half day's head start on them. More if they didn't find our tracks when we left the road."

"Won't those tracks be easy to see?"

He shrugged. "Ours aren't the only tracks on that road or the trail we took. Ranchers that live out here use it. We've run across cattle tracks and horse tracks even out here. Not that you noticed."

"Of course not. I wasn't looking for them."

He smiled. He shouldn't tease her. "All I'm saying is that Spider won't want to put himself on some wild-goose chase."

"How long have you known him?"

"A day."

"What?!"

He shrugged. "You can tell a lot about a man by the way he drives a team and how he treats his animals. One thing I noticed about Spider, he doesn't exert himself any more than he has to."

She shuddered. "Well, if you ask me, he's a horrible, mean man."

Jake looked sympathetic. "Sorry I had to tie you up. It was the only way to keep you safe."

She waved a fly off her horse's mane. "So you said. But that doesn't mean I liked it."

"Of course, you didn't." He glanced at her. "If it makes you feel any better, when it happened to me, my captors had me tied up for days."

She gasped. "How awful."

Not as awful as seeing you suffer. He swallowed hard. "It's over. No need to dwell on it."

She nodded and put on a brave face. "You're right. Let's just get home."

His heart warmed at the word. If only he had a home.

———

THEY RODE UNTIL NIGHTFALL, crossed the creek, and headed south. Addy hoped the terrain was as agreeable the rest of the journey. There was nothing but dirt, sagebrush, dead grass, and the occasional tree.

Jake's plan was going well so far, and she began to relax. But trouble could still be following, and she didn't want to let her guard down too much. It was hard enough guarding against her emotions. Every time she looked at Jake the words *what if* popped into her head. What if she'd married Jake all those years ago? Would he have made a wreck of their lives, or taken over the ranch with John as their father planned? Perhaps John would have found someone else, married and continued to balance the accounts while Jake ran everything else.

She shook her head. No, Jake was too...well, Jake. Perhaps leaving was the best thing for him. Speaking of which, "What did you do for work all these years?"

He stiffened then relaxed. "A little of this and that. Whatever I could do to get by."

"Which was?" She steered her horse closer. She wanted to hear everything.

"Cattle drives, ranch work. You know..."

"That's just it, I don't. Because you stopped writing." It was hard to keep the accusation out of her voice.

He looked at her. "I said I was sorry."

She studied his eyes. He was trying to be sincere. "I'm sorry, too. We didn't exactly go looking for you."

"What *did* you do?"

Eyes still locked with his, she swallowed. "Nothing. John said to leave you be. So did your father."

He looked away. "That doesn't surprise me."

"Your mother wanted to look. She wrote letters." She batted at another fly. "I wrote some, too."

His head slowly turned. "To who?"

"To whomever I thought might know where you'd gone. Some of the old ranch hands, one of your father's lawyers. I even asked Doc Barnes."

"You asked the town doctor?" His face softened. "Did you miss me?"

Her breath caught. "Well...of course."

"Did John?"

She caught the flash of anger in his eyes. "We all did."

"Yet no one made an effort to find me," he pointed out. "Except you."

She rolled her eyes. "Well, you didn't make it easy."

He looked ahead. "No, I didn't. And that was the point."

"You didn't want to be found?"

He brought his horse to a stop and turned to her. "Trust me, Addy. You wouldn't have liked what you found." He gave his horse a nudge and continued.

Addy's horse automatically followed, and she pulled on the reins to slow it down. She wanted to ride behind him for a while. She could think better when she knew he couldn't see her expression.

Her curiosity was piqued, and now more than ever, she wanted to know what he'd been up to all these years. Considering the latest company he kept, she had a good idea. But isn't that what everyone thought—that he would come to a bad end, fall in with the wrong company? Gambling, drinking, womanizing—the list John came up with went on and on. Had Jake really done all those things? Was he as bad as John made him out to be?

She kicked her horse into a trot to catch up. "You never wrote John one letter?"

"You know I wrote him plenty, then stopped." He sighed. "If you're trying to fill in the gaps, don't bother. It's best you don't know, Addy."

"You've…done bad things?"

His jaw tightened as he closed his eyes a moment. When he opened them, he looked at her. "Let's not talk about this anymore."

He turned away, and she knew that meant he was through with the conversation. Still, her curiosity kept firing questions at her. What sorts of things had he done? Heaven forbid, he didn't kill anyone, did he? He said he didn't know she'd been abducted, but was he lying? Unless he told her about his past, how could she trust him? For all she knew, he was taking her some roundabout way to their original destination. There he would deliver her, collect his money, and run. She gulped at the thought.

No, no, no. The Jake she knew had his faults, but he wouldn't do such a thing to her. Would he?

Nervous, she looked around. The landscape was the same as far as the eye could see. Thankfully it was all she saw. Maybe he was right, and Spider and his gang thought it too much trouble to chase after them. But that would make it easier for Jake to deliver her and collect the money himself. She wasn't sure how he'd pull that off without letting them see her first.

She shut her eyes against the thought. She had to stop thinking like this, lest she turn herself into a nervous wreck. She should concentrate on the old Jake, the one that used to tease her and tell her jokes. At one time he was hard-working and industrious. Yes, he liked to blow off steam by getting into shooting contests with the ranch hands or even a fistfight or two. But he'd always been there when she needed him. When anyone did, come to think of it.

But they were young and silly. And now too much time had passed. Addy no longer knew Jake Reeves. The sooner she got that through her head, the better.

Chapter Nine

Jake handed Addy a stale biscuit and a piece of jerky. It was all they had for dinner. He didn't want to risk a fire. He eyed the bedrolls tied to their saddles. "It's going to get cold tonight."

Addy wrapped her arms around herself. "I can tell. But last night wasn't so bad."

"That's because we rode through most of it. It's amazing how running for your life makes you forget about things like cold." He didn't want to sound sarcastic, but it was true.

"I suppose." She looked at the bedrolls, too. "Are you sure it's safe to stop?"

"We can't see them, and they can't see us. So long as we leave before sunup, we should be safe."

Her eyebrows rose. "Should be?"

He untied her bedroll and handed it to her. "Let's get some sleep."

She held it against her chest. "Have you slept at all?"

"I admit I'm pretty tired." He untied his own bedroll and joined her. "Spread this out for me. I'll take care of the horses." He strode away before she could say anything. If he thought their time under that outcropping was rough, it wouldn't hold a candle to tonight. If he were smart, he'd stay next to the horses. But he knew Addy might get scared by herself. She always was skittish.

He untacked and hobbled the horses, gave them a little grain, and carried the saddles to their tiny campsite. He set Addy's down next to her on her bedroll. "Use it for a pillow."

"You should sleep." She stood. "I'll keep watch."

Jake's eyebrows rose. He could use some shuteye. "Very well." He looked up. "There'll be a good moon tonight. Look for anything that's moving. If you see something, wake me."

"Do you...think I'll see something?"

"Not likely. But one can never be too careful." He placed his saddle where he wanted it and lay down. "And stay quiet."

She mock-saluted. "Yessir."

He arched an eyebrow at her. She was nervous, he could tell by the way she was acting—silly. "It's going to be okay, Addy."

"Is it?"

He caught the quaver in her voice and didn't dare get to his feet. He might take her in his arms, even kiss her. Instead, he put his hat over his eyes. "We'll be fine. Just wake me if you see anything moving around out there."

"Where's that spyglass?"

"In my saddlebag. But it's hard to see much with it at night."

"I don't care. If it'll help, I'm using it." He listened to her march to their saddlebags and dig through them. "Ha! Here it is. How does it work?"

Jake pushed his hat up and propped himself on his elbows. Addy was holding the spyglass like it was a trophy. "You sure do make it hard for a man to rest."

"Do I just pull it apart?"

He tried not to laugh as he got to his feet. "Here, let me."

"Thank you." She handed it to him.

"Be gentle with it." He showed her how to use it, then handed it to her. "Now you try."

She opened the spyglass and looked through it. "Oh,

you're right. It is kind of hard to see. I can still make things out, though."

He patted her on the back. "Good. Let me sleep a couple hours, then wake me."

"That's not enough time."

"I've gone on less." He headed for his bedroll.

She followed. "Jake...I just wanted to say...thank you. Again."

He stopped. "Addy, I know you. That's not what you really want to say, is it?"

She looked at the night sky and sighed. "I..."

His hands went to his hips. "You don't trust me. I can see it in your eyes."

She looked at the sky again. "But..."

"Addy, like I said, I know you. You're thinking I'm some low-down snake and wondering whether you can trust me."

Her face fell. "How did you know?"

"Common logic. I'd be thinking the same if I were you."

Addy looked away. "Oh."

"But don't worry, honey. As soon as I get you home, you'll never see me again." Jake returned to his bedroll. It had to be said and the sooner the better. Besides, it's not as if he hadn't mentioned it already. But who was he trying to convince, him or her?

ADDY SAT and hugged her knees as Jake softly snored a few feet away. So, he really wasn't planning on sticking around. But hadn't he said as much before?

She rubbed her eyes. With luck, she wouldn't doze off. She hoped he was right and her abductors decided to cut their losses. Still, she had to man her post. She got to her feet and looked through the spyglass. She saw a lot of dark shapes, none of which were moving, thank goodness. She stood very still and listened. There were night birds, the yip of a coyote, and the faint sound of water. There must be a creek nearby. Good, they could water the horses later.

She lowered the spyglass and surveyed their surroundings again. Seeing nothing, she sat, drew her legs up, and hugged her knees again. It was getting colder by the minute. She thought of wrapping her blanket around her but didn't want to disturb Jake. Besides, if she was cold, she'd be less likely to fall asleep.

She thought about what Jake said earlier and sighed. How could he read her so well? Wasn't it simple logic that she didn't trust him like he said? She wondered if he was offended, then pushed the thought aside. Besides, he'd only be offended if none of it… "Was true," she whispered.

Addy face-palmed. *Had* she offended him? Under the circumstances, she hoped so. It would mean he wasn't the scoundrel that part of her made him out to be. *He's taking you home, you fool.* Indeed, if he was desperate for money, he'd have taken her north and delivered her before Spider and the others were any the wiser. But he didn't. They were heading southwest tomorrow. If they stayed the course, he was doing what he said he would.

She didn't know what was more stressful, being hunted by outlaws or being with Jake Reeves. She wanted to trust him. Merciful heavens, she wanted to do a lot more. If she had the money, she'd hire him to help her with the ranch.

Her jaw went slack. Jake wouldn't know that his father wrote him out of his will. Everything went to John, and then her after John died. Is that why he was escorting her, to stake his claim on what he thought was rightfully his? Not that it would do him any good. Legally everything was wrapped up nice and tidy. John and his father figured that if Jake didn't want to be there, he didn't want his half of the ranch either.

She'd have to tell him. Then if he still escorted her home, he was a man of his word.

Addy tried not to think about it and got to her feet, studied their surroundings, and sat again. She repeated the process over and over. Each time she saw nothing and was beginning to wonder how much time had passed. Had it been two hours? Three?

"Addy."

She turned to Jake's voice. "Yes?"

"Come here." He was sitting up now. "You let me sleep too long."

"Did I?" She laughed nervously. "I have no idea what time it is."

He got to his feet. "Lie down."

She didn't argue. She was at the point where it was hard to stay on her feet. "How much time do I have?"

"I'll give you a few hours." He picked up her bedroll, shook it out and covered her with it. "There. I don't want you to get cold." To her surprise, he tucked the blanket around her.

"Thank you."

Even though it was dark, she could see him smile. "Don't mention it." He sat next to her.

"You're not going to sit over there?"

"No. I'm gonna sit here and keep things from crawling under that blanket with you."

She sat up. "What?!"

He chuckled. "Lie down and get some sleep, sweetheart. You're gonna need it."

Her heart melted at the simple endearment. "If you say so." She lay down and hoped the moonlight wasn't illuminating her face. Half of her wanted to talk him into staying with her once they reached the ranch. The other half didn't trust him, but it was coming around fast.

"Addy," he sang. "Close your eyes."

"You can tell they're open?" she asked, mortified. Good grief, had he seen her expression?

"Well enough. Now sleep, honey."

Addy's spine tingled. This was ridiculous! She shouldn't be reacting to him like this. For heaven's sake, he was the bad brother, the rebel, the outlaw! Then why, oh why, did she want him to kiss her?

Chapter Ten

JAKE STARED INTO THE DARKNESS. HE SHOULD WAKE ADDY so they could be on their way. But she was exhausted, he could tell, and trying to be brave. She also didn't trust him—he wanted to do something about it. *Why, you fool? As soon as you have her home safe, you're leaving…*

He pushed the thought aside. There was no sense telling himself otherwise. What would she want with someone like him? He'd sinned too much over the years. How could she forgive him for what he'd done?

He straightened. Would she forgive him for leaving and not coming back? Fate brought them together again, and he shouldn't waste the opportunity to ask for forgiveness. Maybe he could leave with a clear conscience.

Jake went to her and shook her shoulder. "Addy, wake up."

"Five more minutes," she moaned.

He laughed. "No, sweetheart, it's time to go." He didn't know why he kept using little endearments. They just slipped out. He should stop, but…his heart liked them. In truth, he'd like to call her a lot more. But that wouldn't happen.

He swallowed back the lump in his throat and stood. "I'll feed and saddle the horses." He picked up his saddle then headed for Bob. As soon as he saddled and bridled him, he returned for Addy's saddle.

She was tying up their bedrolls. She looked a mess, and he smiled, his heart pounding. "I'll take care of your horse, then we'll eat something and go."

She stared at him with those blue eyes. He'd miss those eyes. Not to mention the rest of her. His heart lurched at the thought. "Okay." She headed for the horses.

Jake grabbed her saddle and followed. She still looked tired, worried, and a little frightened. It tore his heart out. He caught up to her and set the saddle down. "Addy," he said without thinking.

She turned, his bedroll in her trembling hands.

"Addy," he said softly. "What's wrong, honey?"

She closed her eyes. "N-nothing."

His eyes roamed over her. "Are you cold?"

She shook her head, eyes still closed. When she opened them, they were full of...regret?

He took her by the shoulders. "Addy, what's wrong?" His heart leaped as he drew her into his arms. "It's all right, honey. Everything's gonna be all right."

She took a shuddering breath, and Jake held her tighter in response. Having her in his arms was glorious! But did she think so? He drew back. "Are you...all right?"

She looked into his eyes, her mouth moving but nothing coming out. What was going through that head of hers?

Their gazes locked, and Jake stopped breathing. His eyes went to her lips and he was gone. Every pent-up emotion he had for her bubbled to the surface while lowering his mouth to hers. The kiss was gentle, warm, and it was all he could do not to deepen it.

His back stiffened as he broke the kiss. This was the stupidest, most wonderful thing he could have done. He hoped she slapped his face.

She didn't.

"Addy..."

She looked into his eyes, then closed hers. "Jake...we..."

"I know." He let her go. "I'm sorry...I shouldn't have

done that." He stepped back, picked up her saddle, and headed for her horse. "It won't happen again."

The guilt was overwhelming. He'd wanted to kiss her and had. But where would it get him? He needed her forgiveness, not a kiss. But what a kiss! His heart was pounding so hard it was a wonder she couldn't hear it.

He saddled her horse and watched her tie his bedroll to the back of Bob's saddle. He took the other bedroll and tied it to hers. "Addy…"

"It's all right."

He sighed. "Forgive me."

"I said it was all right."

Jake faced her. "I'm not talking about the kiss."

She rubbed her hands over her arms. "What then?"

"A lot of things. Leaving you…" He took off his jacket and put it around her shoulders. "…and John the way I did."

She shrugged. "You've always had itchy feet." She looked away. "Probably still do."

He tucked his finger under her chin and brought her face to his. "My wandering days are over. I took this job for extra money. I don't need it; I just wanted to be on the road one last time."

Her eyes misted. "I'm glad you did."

"So am I." He bit the inside of his cheek to keep from kissing her again. "I hurt you, my brother, my parents. Forgive me."

She shut her eyes and swallowed. When she looked at him, he stopped breathing. He hadn't realized how much he wanted her forgiveness until this moment. But rescuing her from Spider and his gang didn't make up for the years he'd been gone, and they both knew it. "Addy?"

"You were gone so long," she whispered.

"I know."

"We thought you were dead."

He nodded, realized he still had his finger under her chin and lowered his hand. "I'm sorry."

She was trembling again. "Your father…he wrote you out of his will."

His chest tightened. "I can understand that."

"John...he had nothing good to say about you for years." She hung her head.

"That sounds like him." He drew closer. "And you?"

She looked at him, her eyes misting again. "I forgive you."

Jake's heart skipped as his whole chest warmed. "Thank you, Addy." He gave her shoulder a squeeze. "Now let's get you home."

––––––

ADDY STOOD, her heart in her throat, and shuddered. She still didn't know everything Jake's past entailed, only, by his own admission, that he'd done some bad things. But he wasn't asking forgiveness for those. He wanted forgiveness for leaving. Now that she'd given it, he'd do it again. Part of her didn't want him to, part wanted to push him away. And doggone it! When he looked at her the way he did before he kissed her, she thought she might faint.

Did he realize she didn't pull away, didn't slap him, didn't do the things a lady should? At least he apologized. But what would *she* do?

She ate the jerky he offered and washed it down with water. They'd have to refill their canteens at the creek when they got there. She wanted to wash up, and it was as good a reason as any to avoid talking to him. His kiss was unexpected, yet she'd dreamed of him doing so half the night. Now that he had, she didn't know what to think. Other than hoping he'd kiss her again.

She took another drink from her canteen and wiped her mouth with the back of her hand, still sensing his lips on hers.

Addy shoved the stopper into the canteen and hung it off the saddle horn. Jake was fussing with Bob's bridle, a piece of jerky in his mouth. Did he regret kissing her? Would he even speak to her now? She wiped her mouth again. Was he as afraid to talk about it as she was?

She mounted up, waited for Jake to, and they headed for the sound of water in the distance. She scanned their surroundings looking for any signs of trouble. Kiss or no kiss, they had to stay on guard. She hoped this wouldn't distract her throughout the day.

They reached the creek, let the horses drink, refilled their canteens, and washed up. The water cooled her heated skin. Was it wrong she liked his kiss so much? Never mind that when he held her in his arms, she nearly swooned. She was dirty, her hair was mussed, and she'd been wearing the same clothes for days, but all that mattered was Jake and the look in his eyes that said he desired her.

In fact, his eyes held far more than desire. He had *feelings* for her, but she didn't know how strong. They'd been friends, and she'd had strong feelings for him at one time but didn't dare act on them. Her parents wouldn't have stood for it. And letting herself fall for Jake was too big a risk to take. John wasn't wild like Jake. He was practical, steady, reliable. She sighed. *And boring.* But at least he was there.

She studied Jake as he ran wet fingers through his hair. There was nothing dull or boring about him. He was an adventurer and lived life to the fullest the best he knew. From the sound of it he wanted to change his life. Did she dare find out what sort of man he'd become after all these years?

He caught her looking at him and smiled. "Like what you see?"

Addy blushed head to toe. "I wasn't staring."

"Yes, you were."

She licked her lips. If she wasn't careful, she'd start flirting. "We should leave."

He stood, went to mount his horse but stopped. "I'm sorry about earlier, Addy. I truly am."

Her heart sank. *I'm not.* "It's all right."

Without a word he mounted Bob and started across the creek.

She mounted and followed. She noticed he didn't offer to help and wondered if they'd speak much the rest of the trip.

Would he avoid her now? Did he regret their kiss that much? She tried not to think about it as she caught up to him, her throat thick. Jake would take her home and that would be that. She might as well get it through her head. Besides, he was still too much a rebel.

And heaven help her, Addy still had strong feelings for him. Dare she call it love?

Chapter Eleven

THEY RODE UNTIL EARLY AFTERNOON WITHOUT INCIDENT AND took a break in a copse of pines. Jake decided to risk a longer stop and let the horses rest. There'd been no sign of pursuit, which proved he was right. Spider was too lazy to chase them across the plains. Tomorrow they'd bypass Laramie and ride straight to Oats. There were some ranches along the way where they could get food and water and wouldn't have to venture into Laramie at all. Spider wouldn't have a clue where they were.

"What are you smiling at?" Addy asked.

He grinned. "I'm not saying we're safe yet, but it's starting to look that way."

Her shoulders slumped. "Thank goodness. Under different circumstances, this would be fun. Like we're having an adventure."

He chuckled. "Addy, you never cease to surprise me."

She smiled shyly. "You've surprised me."

He hoped she wouldn't start asking questions about his past. How much should he tell her? "Are you surprised I rescued you?"

"Of course not! You wouldn't have let them deliver me to that man...would you?"

Her hesitation said it all. "No. But you thought I would."

"Jake…"

He held up a hand. "It's all right, I understand. You don't know me anymore. No more than I know you."

She took a breath. "I haven't changed that much."

Jake smiled. She was right, she hadn't. "You've done well for yourself. I'm proud of you."

She laughed. "Don't be." She bit her lip and looked straight ahead. "I hired the wrong man to help me with the ranch."

He stiffened. "What?"

When she looked at him, her face was red with shame. "He swindled me out of a lot of money, said the ranch wasn't doing well. Like a fool I believed him."

Now it was his turn to gape. "Addy, what happened?"

"He took the money and ran. I had nothing left to run it with and had to let the other hands go. I've been trying to take care of it on my own ever since. I can't get ahead, Jake." She laughed. "I was on my way to a bank in Laramie to get a loan to keep it afloat."

"So that's why you were all gussied up." He shook his head. "I had no idea."

"How could you?"

She had him there. If only he'd written…

"But it doesn't matter now." She stared ahead. "I'll figure something out."

His gut twisted with guilt. "I'm sure you will." *She's tough. She'll survive.* But how was she going to make it on her own? He supposed he could give her some money to help her out. Maybe all the ranch needed was a push in the right direction. He'd look at things once he got her home, advise her, then leave. She wouldn't want him around anyway. She only thought she did. If she knew some of the things he'd done, she'd think twice.

They rested in the shade of the trees and ate the last of the jerky. "We still have a couple of biscuits," he announced.

Her face screwed up. "Lovely."

"It's food, Addy. Be thankful we have it."

"I'm sorry," she said. "I don't mean to complain."

"We'll save the biscuits for tomorrow. Maybe I can hunt us a rabbit or something for tonight."

"But…won't someone hear the gunshot?"

"I think we're safe. Besides, we're too far from the road for anyone to hear it." He studied their surroundings. If they could find another little grove like this one, they could build a fire, too. "This is almost over."

She sighed in relief and smiled. "That's good to hear."

He nodded and hoped it was true.

"Jake? Do you forgive me?"

"Excuse me?"

"Do you?"

"Addy, you haven't done anything."

"The ranch's ruin is my fault."

"You trusted the wrong person." He scooted toward her. "It happens."

She shrugged. "I guess part of me still thinks it belongs to you."

"I'll do what I can, but the ranch is yours." He stiffened. It was all he could do not to take her in his arms.

"Then you'll leave?"

"Yes."

She looked him in the eyes. "But what if I don't want you to?"

_____

ADDY SHOULDN'T HAVE SAID it. She might as well have told him she loved him. Oh, Lord, did she? She was starting to think so. "Never mind—I…I'm sorry…"

He gave her a tender smile. "I'll be leaving. Trust me, it's better I do."

Her heart sank. "Where will you go?"

Jake shrugged. "Does it matter?" He stood. "We should be going."

She nodded, unable to speak. After a moment she stood, brushed dirt from her skirt and headed for her horse. That was that. He had no plans to stay. And even if he did, what then? It was clear he didn't have the same feelings for her she had for him. He rescued her and was seeing her home. Wasn't that enough?

Her heart plummeted to her toes. Merciful heaven, if she didn't know better, she'd say she *did* love him! Why else would her heart ache so?

Addy glanced at Jake. He stared straight ahead, his jaw set. Life had hardened his heart, and she'd told him that his father wrote him out of his will. She should have left well enough alone. "I want to give you something," she blurted.

He looked at her. "You don't have to."

"You deserve something." She met his gaze as tears stung her eyes. "You deserve so much more than what you got."

He turned away. "I got exactly what I deserved."

She knew he was talking about his past. "Jake, you're a good man, I know you are. I know you've done things, made mistakes. Haven't we all?"

He sighed and turned to her. "The ranch?"

"Exactly. Can you imagine what John and your father would be saying to me if they were still alive?"

"I shudder to think." His shoulders shook in silent laughter. He was trying to make light of her mistake.

She smiled at his efforts. "But our mistakes are behind us. All we can do is carry on and not make them again. We can become better. Both of us."

He smiled. "I know you will."

"And you?"

Jake shoved his hat back. "I try."

"Yes, and part of that was rescuing me. And now here we are. When you think about it, we're all we have left."

He looked at her again, and she couldn't read him at first. Then she caught the sadness in his eyes. Would he still leave once he got her home? Lord help her, she didn't want him to.

They didn't speak much the rest of the day until they found another small patch of pines near a large outcropping. "Stay here," Jake said as she dismounted. "I'll see if I can find water nearby and maybe hunt us some supper."

"I can gather wood for a fire," she offered.

"You do that but stick close. Besides, I think what wood you'll find is right here."

She glanced at their surroundings. He was right—there were small sticks and a few fallen branches. She wouldn't have to venture far. "Okay."

He smiled, tipped his hat, and rode off. She hoped he found water. The horses would need it.

She began gathering wood, but most of the downed branches were too big to use unless they could be sawn or chopped into smaller pieces. She'd have to venture out of their cover to find more.

She tied her horse to a tree and set out. She didn't like being in the open, but there was no help for it. She studied the ground for anything that looked like it would burn. She broke off some dead pieces of sagebrush, found a few more sticks, then started looking for rocks. She found some and used her skirt to carry them back, her stomach rumbling. She hoped Jake was able to catch something—she was starving and the thought of stale biscuits for dinner didn't hold much appeal.

When she returned, she dropped her load, started a circle with the rocks, and realized she'd need more. She barely left the trees when she heard a twig snap behind her. "Jake?" She turned around and gasped. "You!"

"Howdy." Spider smiled.

A loud *thud* behind her spun her around. Pete stood and glared at her. He must have jumped off one of the rocks above.

Before she could draw enough air to scream, Spider clamped his hand over her mouth. "Miss me?" he hissed in her ear.

Addy struggled against him, but he was too strong. In a flash the two had her bound, gagged, and slung over Pete's shoulder. Good grief, they had her again!

And Jake had no idea.

Chapter Twelve

JAKE SEARCHED FOR WATER, DIDN'T FIND ANY, SO TIED BOB TO some sagebrush. With any luck he'd come across a rabbit, but he wasn't hopeful. He reminded himself that some food was better than none, even if it was stale biscuits. He hunted for an hour, gave up, and headed back. He didn't want to leave Addy by herself for long.

Addy. What was he going to do about her? She was right, he was all she had and vice versa. How could he leave her? Yet how could he stay?

He still didn't want to tell her about his past. She'd hate him, tell him to go. Worse, she'd be disappointed he wasn't the man she thought he was. He wasn't sure he could live with that. Better to walk out of her life.

His heart ached at the thought as he returned to their camp. Should he talk to her once more or keep his mouth shut? What if she asked more questions?

"Addy?" He dismounted and led Bob into the trees. Her horse was gone. "Addy?" he shouted this time. Panic struck like lightning. He took a deep breath to calm himself and noted the pile of sticks, wood, and rocks she'd gathered. She might be looking for more rocks to ring the fire and decided it would be easier to stuff them into her saddlebags. He shouldn't fear just yet.

Out of habit, he studied the ground and cursed. "No." He bent down. There were boot tracks, signs of a struggle. Why hadn't he noticed them before?

Jake hurried out of the copse of pines, following the tracks. Addy's tracks had disappeared. They must have tied her up and carried her out. His jaw tightened at the thought as he followed the tracks—including those of Pete's horse—around the trees and up the slope to the top of the outcropping. There he found tracks of two more horses and a note tucked into some sagebrush. "Oh, no." Jake snatched it out.

No one steals from me. Spider

He lowered the note, every muscle tensed. Spider was baiting him, plain and simple. And Addy was the bait. This, of course, meant they'd be easy to find.

He sighed. They must have split up, two taking the wagon to Laramie while Spider and somebody followed his and Addy's trail. He should've thought of the possibility but didn't. He had other things on his mind—namely Addy. His foolish worrying over what she'd think of his past got her abducted all over again, might even get her killed. What a fool he was!

His jaw tight, Jake checked his guns and went to fetch Bob.

————

ADDY LAY against a rock and struggled against her bonds. Pete kept glaring at her, letting her know he still wasn't happy about his horse. He promised to exact payment for that as soon as they shot Jake. Spider wasn't so eloquent—she shuddered at what he said he'd do. The only thing she had in her favor was that they still thought she was Ivy Pembroke. But they didn't care if they delivered her as "spoiled goods" now.

Either way, she'd die. If these two didn't kill her, the man they were delivering her to would. Jake was as good as dead, too, unless she could find a way out of this mess and fast. Being bound and gagged wasn't helping, but she had to try. "Mmmphh!"

"Shut up," Spider snapped at her. "Or are ya getting anxious for our time together?"

She scowled at him.

Spider laughed. "She's so feisty."

"Maybe we better take that gag off," Pete suggested. "Let her scream a few times and get Jake's attention."

"Hmm, good idea." Spider went to her and pulled the gag out of her mouth. "There, now ya can scream all ya want."

Her eyes narrowed further. "I'll pass, thanks."

Spider and Pete exchanged a look. "What?" Spider scratched his head. "Ain't ya scared out of yer wits?"

"Of you?" she said with as much bravado as she could muster. "Ha!"

Spider looked at Pete with a helpless shrug. "Have ya ever seen the like?"

"No. At this point they're usually begging for mercy, crying out not to touch 'em. You know, the usual."

"Yeah," Spider scratched his head again. "Maybe we ought to help her along." He pulled her to her feet and got in her face.

"You wouldn't dare," she said as threateningly as possible.

He smiled and went to kiss her.

Addy had a choice—scream her fool head off like they wanted or bite his nose. She wanted no part of his filthy nose. She screamed.

"There, ya see?" Spider said. "Knew that'd work."

"If I had your ugly face coming at me, I'd scream, too."

Spider let Addy go and shoved Pete. "Hey, I ain't that ugly."

"I didn't say..." Pete turned and froze. "Uh-oh."

Spider spun around, too, and snarled.

"Point a gun at her and you die," Jake said.

Addy looked up. He must be atop the rock behind her, but she couldn't see him.

"Toss your guns," Jake ordered.

Spider and Pete did so, cursing all the while.

Addy jerked in surprise as Jake landed on the ground between her and her captors. "Now put your hands behind your heads and lie on the ground." As soon as they did, Jake looked at her. "Are you okay?"

She nodded and shivered. Now that Spider and Pete were no longer a threat, her bravado disappeared.

"Don't move, you two," Jake said. "You won't like what happens if you do." He bent to Addy and quickly untied her hands.

"How did you find us?"

"It wasn't hard, they wanted me to. But they made it too easy."

"I told you!" Pete groused. "But would you listen?"

"Shut up!" Spider shot back.

Jake untied her ankles then handed her his gun. "One of them makes a move, shoot them."

"Right." She took it with shaky hands. Good thing Spider and Pete were facing the ground.

"She's a good shot, gentlemen. I suggest you stay still." Jake took the rope they'd used to tie her and bound their hands behind their backs.

"How do you know if she can shoot?" Pete asked.

Jake smiled at her. "I've seen her do it."

Addy wanted to laugh. She was a terrible shot unless he helped her, and that was years ago. "You made sure I could."

"I remember."

"What?" Spider cut in.

"Quiet, you." Jake sighed. "Addy…I should have told you things. I'm sorry I didn't."

"Addy?" Pete said. "Who in blazes is Addy?"

Jake ignored him and started to tie their ankles. "I thought about things while following your trail. Things you said."

She stared at him and nodded. "I've thought about things, too."

"What?" Spider spat. "What in tarnation is going on here? Why are ya calling her Addy?"

Jake finished tying them up and got to his feet. "I was wrong about so many things. And I'm sorry."

Tears stung her eyes. All she could do was nod. "I've forgiven you, Jake. For more than you know. Whatever sort of man you think you are is not the man I see before me. You think the bad things you've done define you. They don't."

He swallowed hard. "Addy..."

Her lower lip trembled as she smiled. "Jake, I want you to stay."

He stared at her with the most anguished look she'd ever seen. "No, you don't."

She got to her feet. "I *do*." She handed him the gun. "You're a good man, always have been. Come home." She reached up and cupped his face in her hand. "Rest."

Spider and Pete just looked confused.

Jake holstered his gun and cupped her face in both his hands.

"Land sakes," Pete squeaked. "I think he's gonna kiss her!"

"Yeah," Spider said with an eye roll. "Next thing ya know he'll be telling her he loves her."

Addy looked into Jake's eyes. "Do you?" It was a bold question, but she didn't care. She had to know.

He closed his eyes again, and she could tell he was fighting with himself.

She should just come out with it. "I love you, Jake."

His eyes opened. "You do?"

"She does?" Pete blurted.

"Will you two shut up?!" Addy snapped.

Spider took one look at Jake and snarled, "Oh, disgusting! He *does* love her! Just look at him."

Pete's face screwed up. "Ew."

Addy ignored them. "Jake?"

He didn't answer. Instead, he pulled her into his arms

and kissed her with everything he had. It was as if a dam had broken and everything locked deep inside him was spilling out through that one kiss.

Spider and Pete groaned in disgust.

Addy didn't care. Jake was telling her he loved her! Thank heaven she'd had the guts to tell him even if it risked his rejecting her.

When Jake finally broke the kiss, he rested his forehead against hers and held her tight. "I do love you, Addy. I've always loved you."

"You have?" A tear escaped. "If only I'd known."

"No. I was young, foolish."

"You're not anymore and I know your heart is in a good place now."

He drew back and looked at her. "Because of you. I did something I never thought I could do while following you here. I forgave myself."

Her tears came and she did nothing to stop them. "Oh, Jake. Thank heaven." She laughed, then smiled at him.

"Thank you." He kissed her again and this time, she let it take her where it willed.

Epilogue

The Reeves Ranch, six months later...

"ADDY, HAVE YOU SEEN MY HAMMER?" JAKE ENTERED THE parlor and glanced around. "I can't find it anywhere."

Addy sat in her favorite chair, knitting. "If you'd work on one project at a time, you wouldn't misplace things."

His hands went to his hips. "I know." He went to the fireplace mantel and grabbed the sack of nails he'd put there last night. "I'm gonna need these."

She arched an eyebrow at him. "Only if you find your hammer."

"Oh, stop. You know the sooner I get things fixed around here the sooner we're in business."

"By the way, that mare from the Jones Ranch in Clear Creek is supposed to arrive this afternoon."

"Good. If she turns out to be as good a broodmare as Ryder Jones promised, then I'll buy another from them."

"But their ranch is so far away." She checked her stitches. "Couldn't you find stock here in Colorado?"

"There's a ranch outside of Creede that has some good horseflesh. I might take a trip down there."

"You didn't take a trip to Clear Creek," she pointed out.

"I didn't need to. The Jones' reputation is good enough." He looked around the room again.

Addy got to her feet. "Does my husband need a little help?"

He sighed and smiled at her. "The last time you helped me find a missing tool, we wound up..." He glanced at the ceiling.

"Ah, yes." She put her arms around him. "Your saw. It took all afternoon to find it."

He smiled and kissed her on the nose. "Well, I suppose things could've been worse."

She thought of the day he re-rescued her and professed his love. "Isn't it amazing how bad things can turn into good ones?"

He kissed her forehead this time. "I know. I should thank Spider and his gang for all the trouble they caused."

"That's just what I was thinking, but that's not who I'd thank." Her eyes moved skyward. "Though they did play their part."

"And so dramatically, too."

She laughed. "They did whine a lot on the way to the sheriff's office."

"I'm sure they're enjoying a nice rest in prison. I still can't believe they told the judge they wanted to attend our wedding just so they could stall going to jail."

Addy burst out laughing. "The judge thought they'd gone 'round the bend."

"Too bad the Randalls got away."

She nodded. "Thankfully, they're long gone by now."

"Good riddance." He kissed her and she melted against him. "Now, Mrs. Reeves, I need to get back to work and so do you." He glanced at something behind her. "What are you knitting?"

Addy smiled and put her hands over her belly. "Just a little something for a little someone."

His jaw dropped. "What?"

She smiled and nodded.

"Addy!" He pulled her into his arms and swung her

around. When he set her on her feet, he kissed her again. "I love you."

"I love you, too." She smiled and ran her hand through his hair. "Now wasn't all this worth a second chance?"

"I can't tell you how much. Thank you for giving it to me."

"Thank you for listening to your heart and taking it."

They smiled at each other, then kissed again.

No Quarter

Kathleen O'Neal Gear

March 6, 1836. Before dawn

A COOL BREEZE FILTERS THROUGH CRACKS IN THE ADOBE WALL and chills my face where I stand beside the bullhide door, listening to the silence. I've been straining to hear voices for so long, it's hard to breathe. Last evening, when the cannon bombardment stopped, I tried to sleep, but my frayed nerves wouldn't allow it. I jerked awake at every tiny sound, and now I'm so afraid of the eerie quiet, sleep is impossible.

Resting my forehead against the wall, I just try to get air into my lungs.

"Bettie?"

"I'm right here, Charlie. I'm not leaving you."

In the back of the room, Charlie lies curled on the floor at the Colonel's bedside with his rifle clutched in his hand. He was wounded eight days ago, and I can smell his leg from four paces away. He's a big, strong man, but I don't know how much longer he can last without a hospital.

"What's happening out there?" He sits up with a groan and leans back against the wall.

"Don't know, but it's too quiet."

"Can you look outside for me? Are the sentries awake?"

I pull open the door and peer out through the slit. As clouds pass overhead, moonlight pierces the swirling mist in bars and streaks of dusty silver. The plaza is over 450 feet long and 160 feet wide, with walls up to twelve feet high and three feet thick. To the east a long row of barracks borders the courtyard. My eyes strain to see anyone moving out there, but everything alive seems to have vanished. Then, on top of the north wall, I make out two men standing like black silhouettes. "I see two sentries. One man is pointing out into the darkness, like he sees something."

"How long 'til dawn?"

"Half hour. Maybe a bit longer. Moon is still bright, but it's hard to tell with the fog. How are you? How's your leg?"

He doesn't answer for a long moment. "Awright. Don't worry 'bout me."

I stare blindly out at the plaza. Every building and cannon shines wetly. I'm pretty sure Charlie's dying. The gangrene has gone too far. "You just hold on. I'm going to get you out of here, Charlie."

I can hear the smile in his voice. "Truly? How you going to do that?"

"Once those gates open, I'm packing you right out through the middle of Santa Anna's army."

"Don't think they'll try to stop you, eh?"

"Not if they know what's good for them, they won't."

He laughs. "Awright. Just tell me when to get up."

"I will," I answer, even though I know there's no way he can stand up by himself, and I'm not sure I can hold him up if I manage to get him on his feet. He's a big man, and I'm barely five feet tall.

"Bettie, I—I've lost track of days. How long has it been since the siege started?"

I have to think about it. One day has run into the next like water rushing down a creek. Eleven days? No. Twelve? "Thirteen, maybe."

"Thirteen? That long?"

"I guess so."

Hard to believe we've been holed up in this crumbling fortress that long, while a purgatory of noise thundered just beyond the walls. I ain't never been this awake in my whole life. Every crack in the adobe stands out like a chasm dropping straight into the fiery abyss. I swear I can see bottom rising up to meet me.

"Ursula?" a weak voice whispers.

Sucking in a deep breath, I find the strength to answer, "She'll be right back, Colonel. Won't be long now."

For days I've been soothing Colonel Bowie's fevered cries for his dead wife by telling him Ursula stepped out to tend the children or to fetch food...laudanum...speak with Travis about some matter that concerned the Colonel. It's been enough that he could fall back into tormented sleep.

"Our voices must have woke him," Charlie says softly.

"Check his pulse for me, will you?"

Charlie shifts. After a few moments, his voice is reverent. "I reckon the Colonel's 'bout done."

When tears rise, I blink them back. The news brings a strange mixture of sadness and relief. The Colonel bought me nigh onto six years ago. If he's dead, and I can escape, I'll run to Monterrey with Charlie. There's supposed to be a beautiful cathedral there. We could get married.

"Charlie?" My voice sounds faint even to me. "What's going to happen to us if Colonel Bowie's dead? Think we'll go to his wife's relatives, the Veramendis? I heard he owes them money."

"Don't know, Bettie. Can't think on it now."

"But they could sell us off to different folks." *No, no, Lord, not that.*

"...Ursula?" Bowie whispers.

I find the strength to answer, "She's coming, Colonel. Went out to fetch water from the well. Be right back."

Charlie exhales hard. "Everything depends on who wins this fight. If the Texians win, then we ain't got no choice. They'll haul us off and give us to whoever they figure is our new owner, less we can escape in the bedlam. But if the Meskins win..." His voice fades.

"You think Santa Anna might let us go?"

There's a pause, and I hear Charlie's bootheels rake across the floor as he shifts his wounded leg. "I've thought on that. It's possible. If *El Presidente* did, free us, we might could go up north to the Indian nations."

"No, Charlie, let's head to Monterrey. Please? It's deeper into Mexico. Slavery ain't legal there. It's safer."

"Well," he says gently, "we ain't gotta decide now. Everything, everything depends on this fight."

My traitorous knees tremble. If the Texians lose, freedom might be a few hours away. Need to start planning out what we'll do. First off, run, run hard, before anyone can take it back. Can't help but worry, 'cause another slave told me the Colonel didn't call us slaves. Called us indentured servants, and indentured servants are legal in Mexico. But the Meskins know the truth, don't they?

Hope is tearing me apart. Every slave in Bexar has been whispering about it, speculating on what will happen to them. "Texians will make slavery the law of the land. We won't have no chance..."

A shout splits the darkness outside, then I hear a Mexican voice call: "*Viva Santa Anna!*" followed by, "*Viva la República!*"

"Bettie?" Charlie cries in panic. "Tell me—"

"Colonel Travis," one of the sentries yells, "the Mexicans are coming!"

I open the door wider and stare out at the misty plaza. "Defenders are throwing off their blankets, running for their posts."

Travis' powerful voice carries as he charges for ramparts. "Come on, boys, the Mexicans are upon us, and we'll give them hell!"

The heart-numbing melody of a bugle wavers. It's called *El Deguello*. Meskins have been playing it off and on for days. Awful and beautiful, the notes seem timed to the blasts of cannons, shotguns, and rifles. Somewhere to the north a long chorus carries through the unholy music—eternal, undying, torn from the muzzles and throats of desperate men.

Dear God, please make it stop.

All I can do is stand suspended like a feather, unable to move or think while the roar shakes me apart.

Propping my head against the cold bullhide door, I close my eyes, but it doesn't help. I can still see them out there, half-transparent in the mist, their mouths wide open as they race across the plaza of this broke-down old mission.

"How bad? Bettie...?"

"Bad as can be. I hear axes banging. I think they're smashing through the wooden doors along the west wall."

When I open my eyes, liquid silver moonlight twines through the shifting smoke, outlining the huge plaza. In the volleys of gunfire, the faces of the Mexican soldiers are lit by unearthly flares of gold as they pour over the north wall and into the fort.

Men scream in Spanish and English. Shotguns blast, then a long volley from the enemy. Hoarse screams. There's a flurry of activity as men everywhere abandon their posts and rush to the north wall to try to hold back the tide of enemy soldiers.

Finally, I manage to say, "*Soldados* swarming over the north wall."

"How'd they get inside?" Charlie cries.

"Must have sneaked through the mist and thrown up dozens of ladders. Texians are falling back, running for the low barracks on the east side."

Gunsmoke drifts across the plaza in pale blue streamers. The crackle of muskets is constant. In the midst of the haze men stagger or run, coughing, trying to reach a safe place that no longer exists. A defender trips over someone lying on the ground, and when a scream erupts, he says, "Oh, Lord, I'm sorry. Didn't see you."

When I close the door, the soft thud resembles the last clod of dirt hitting a grave. There's a ring of eternity to it.

Charlie exhales the words, "Well, ain't nobody ordering me to fight now."

His rifle clatters as he lets it fall to the floor.

I ease down to sit beside the door. It's a strange feeling. I have to look, as though these final moments are my entire life—all I've ever known, or ever will know. Survivors leap about in a darkness punctured by flashes and screams. Somewhere a man pants like a woman in the throes of childbirth, but I can't see him. Could be coming from the kitchen next door. Claws at my heart. Part of me wishes I'd run off at first opportunity. Left the sick Colonel to die on his own, but I could no more abandon a sick man than I could abandon Charlie just 'cause his leg is wounded.

"Santa Anna might free us, Charlie," I repeat.

"You know what that music means, Bettie? 'To cut the throat'. And you seen that blood-red flag they hoisted from the Cathedral of San Fernando. Means no quarter. No mercy. Even if we surrender, the general ain't likely to spare the life of anyone inside these walls. Meskins want every one of us dead."

Gunfire penetrates the bullet holes in the walls and strobes the room with flares of dirty rose. It's a wrenching, otherworldly color, a color found only on a battlefield, I expect. I turn around when the details of the long room spring into existence: The Colonel's cot shoved against the wall in the back, Charlie sitting on the floor beside it, his long musket close by and his shot-up leg extended. I used a strip of my yellow skirt to bandage it, but the color got soaked up by blood long ago. A few other items appear—a water bucket with a ladle, Colonel's red shirt tossed on the floor, an extra pair of boots resting in the corner. My eyes fix on Colonel Bowie. He's bundled in blankets like a dying skeleton. Looks dead, but I can't be sure. His last act was to prop himself up, lean back against the wall, then draw out his pistols and knife and place them on the blanket beside him. Sometime during the night, his head lolled to the side. Greasy locks of hair hide most of his face, but for a moment our eyes seem to meet through the darkness, and I am filled with fear.

Underneath the cracking gunfire, a low guttural moan rises and wavers over the plaza. Haunts me, for there's a terrible hope to it. A relief. As though each man is grateful to see Judgment Day arrive at last. One thousand years from now in my dreams, I'll hear that moan filtering down through the cold earth that covers me, and I'll be right back here in this goddamn godforsaken crypt, desperate to run off to Monterrey with Charlie.

Look outside. Watch. *Remember*.

I force my gaze back to the door.

Dozens of soldados race across the courtyard, leaping the dead, bayoneting the wounded, heading for their compatriots in the southwest corner who've captured the eighteen-pounder, a big cannon. Are they going to blast the defenders out room by room? Officers wave swords, and the steel glitters, sprinkled with the bizarre diamond fire of pistol shots.

A tall man shouts orders in Spanish. I learned some over the years, but my heart's thumping so loud, I can't understand anything he's saying. When the soldiers swab the cannon and load it up with iron scraps and chopped up horseshoes, my stomach twists.

It's going to tear people to pieces.

My gaze moves over the rushing soldados and fleeing defenders and fixes on the unearthly blue moonlight that coats the low buildings on the east side where the Texians hide. The pearly gates must shine like that when the moon rises in heaven. If me and Charlie can escape in the confusion, we'll run as far as we can go. We'll find a place to pass the summers rocking on our porch, and watch our babies playing in the yard. I can see their little faces clear as day, smiling at us, loving us. God above, the longing feels like slivers of flint in my veins.

"It's almost over, Charlie."

As I stumble to my feet, my legs shake so hard I grab onto the wall to make my way to where I can ease down between Charlie and the Colonel's cot.

Charlie wraps his powerful arms around me and kisses my hair. "Least we're together. That's all I ever wanted. To grow old holding you in my arms. Lord, I had sweet dreams for us. Always thought the Colonel would finally give us permission to marry."

I gaze up into his dark eyes. Brightness passes across his

face, like spring sunlight off the river—breathtaking, fragile, and swiftly gone. Lifting a hand, I feel his forehead. It's like fire.

"We might not need permission now. Not if Bowie's dead. Not if Santa Anna frees us, and we can run off south or north, or anywhere else that nobody can ever find us again."

"If…"

Reaching out, I place my fingertips on Colonel Bowie's wrist. His eyes are wide open, wider than I have ever seen them, and staring blindly at the door. As though even in death, he's keeping watch, prepared for one last battle when it bursts inward.

"Anything?"

"Can't feel nothing."

As though utterly exhausted Charlie slides sideways, soft as silk, and rests his head in my lap. The heat from his face penetrates my skirt. "Everything's awright," I tell him and stroke his hair. Should I sing to him? He loves it when I sing. His hand moves instinctively toward mine, and I take it in a tight grip. Songs seem to have slipped out of my heart, leaving it unable to remember any of the words to his favorite tunes. "I'm right here," I whisper. "I'm not leaving you. Not ever."

"You have to, Bettie." He nuzzles his cheek against my leg. "If you get the chance, don't you wait on me. You skedaddle. Fast as you can. It will soothe me to know you're out there running free for Monterrey."

I let my fingers tenderly trace the line of his dark cheek, then I desperately reach out to check the Colonel's wrist again. I wait a long time, trying to feel anything, no matter how faint. It's hard. The air itself beats with gunshots, shouts, and long ululating screams.

"I'm pretty sure he's gone," I softly say. "Thank you, Lord. Been too long in coming. Too much suffering."

For days, Bowie crawled out of bed around noon and staggered into the courtyard where people could see him and be encouraged by the knowledge that he was still alive. The defenders needed to see Bowie, and he knew it. His appearance always brought a wave of cheers and hoots. But as the siege wore on, the Colonel grew weaker, delirious, and unable to breathe.

Drawing my hand back, I rest it on Charlie's hot throat. His heartbeat is rapid, fluttering like a dying bird's. "I reckon the Colonel would be mad about this. He ain't never quit in the middle of a fight in his whole life."

"Well, least they can't humiliate him now," Charlie says. "That's something."

"It is."

Charlie shifts to look up at me. He has the kindest face I've ever seen, though he looks much older than his thirty-two years. Silver glitters through his hair. "If I die, I want you to—"

"You're not dying. We're going to make it, Charlie. Both of us. I know we are."

He just sighs and nuzzles his cheek against my leg. "Maybe. Hope so."

While I tenderly pet his hair, my mind is racing. *Strange, the things you think about at the end. There's a war raging right outside this room, and I'm thinking about my name.* "Charlie, I— I can't recall my name."

He seems puzzled. The deep lines that cut across his forehead crinkle. "What do you mean? It's Bettie."

"No, I mean my true name. The name I was born to. I think it was Khady, though I could be recalling somebody else's name, my sister or mama, maybe."

Dirt and grit—torn loose from the adobe walls—shower us when another cannon blast explodes. Gently, I brush it away from Charlie's eyes and cheeks.

"Never knew mine," he says. "Wish I did. I'd keep it locked up inside me. Nobody'd ever know it, 'cept you."

First thing the slave traders did is take away our born names and give us names from their people: Sam, Joe, Ben, Sarah, Bettie, Charlie. What would it feel like to stand guard over the other's true name, to keep it wholly inside where no one could ever take it away? Maybe we wouldn't even speak our names aloud. Even when we were alone.

"I know the name of my people, though," Charlie says. "The Wolof. I was only three or four when they chained me with the other babes down in the belly of that ship. Don't recall much except the journey. Only 'bout half of us survived. But before he died, there was a—a *griot*, an old storyteller. He kept repeating that we were the Wolof. The great warriors of the Wolof." A faint smile turns his lips. "I'll never forget that. From West Africa, I think."

"Wolof." I taste the word as it moves upon my tongue. It's sweet, like deep well water. Takes a while, before I can get the strength to say, "I had dreams for us, too, Charlie."

"Oh," he replies barely audible and tenderly runs his calloused fingers over my hand. "I know you did."

The next cannon explosion deafens the world, and the walls crack and shudder as though about to topple over us. Every breath now tastes like gunpowder.

Charlie grabs me around the waist. "Hold onto me! Don't let go!"

I cling to him with my eyes squeezed closed, and my heart hammering like the hooves of a white horse galloping out of the sky, cutting through the smoke and cries for help as it thunders down toward us.

Across the plaza, men and women cry out in terror, then all goes quiet, except for sporadic *goddamns* and *sonsofbitches* that lace the early morning air.

When I open my eyes, the room shimmers with falling dust.

"Bettie, listen to me, you have to get out of here," Charlie whispers. "I want you to sneak down to the kitchen and hide there."

"What for? They'll just root me out of there, same as—"

"Pretty soon now, somebody's going to ask where the Colonel is. Soldados will come and hit this room hard, maybe with a cannon. You gotta go."

"Awright. Let's go."

Rising, I reach for Charlie's hand.

"No, Bettie, I can't—"

"Get up, right now."

I reach down, grasp his hand, and haul him to his feet while he chokes back pain. His wound must have broken open. The strong odor of rot fills the air. Don't want to think too much on it. On what will happen to that leg. On what will happen to the man I'd die to protect.

Slipping his arm over my shoulders, I stagger forward. He's gritting his teeth and limping badly. The four paces to the door seem to take forever.

We walk out into the cold night, and I can't force my feet to take another step. *God almighty…*

Ashes fall from a pale azure sky, white as snow and as pearlescent as moonlight. Their radiance bathes the smoke rising from the cannon and the solemn faces of the soldados who surge, with bayonets fixed, into the devastated barracks. Somewhere, a man bellows, "Meskin bastards, take this!" and a rifle booms. More booms.

Cries lance the smoke as the defenders fight it out hand-to-hand.

"Gotta…hurry, Bettie. Can't stand up much longer."

I stagger forward again with Charlie limping beside me.

From the eastern barracks, soldados drag dead defenders from blasted rooms—by feet or arms—haul them out into the plaza and pile atop one another, then return for more.

Not dead. Not all of them, for I see a hand sneak out of the pile and weakly grab hold of earth as though it steadies him for the journey ahead. Feet kick. These moments go beyond horror. As I watch, men die like falling stars torn loose from the heavens, flying away into a distant darkness I can't conjure. What are they thinking? Are they wondering if they squandered time? Wishing for the ability to say a few last words to a loved one, maybe to beg forgiveness for a long forgotten hurt?

When we reach the kitchen door, I shove it open with my boot, and we step into the soft red glow coming from the fireplace. A dead man slumps against the wall to my right. He's curled up on the floor like an infant waiting to be born. The fireplace where I've spent long, hot hours cooking for the garrison stands to my left. Pots and pans hang on the back wall in front of me.

"Awright, let me down now, Bettie. Gotta sit down."

Bracing my feet, I lower him to the floor, where he sags against the wall breathing hard. His face is a mask of agony. "Oh, Lord," he says as he reaches down to rub his wounded leg. "Sit down, Bettie. Ain't nothing you want to see out there now."

"I gotta look, Charlie."

Dropping to my knees before the ajar door, I place my body between Charlie and what's to come. I know they'll cut through me like a hot knife through butter, but if Charlie only lives for another five heartbeats, the world will be a better place for that long.

The scene outside is wrenching. I stare wide-eyed when the undead erupt from the margins of the dust and smoke, the graveyards of destroyed rooms, and throw themselves at the victors. Who are these men? ...Crumbling...crumbling apparitions, heads, hands, gusting away like old leaves blown loose from skeletal trees. Knives flash, swords cleave the smoke, and men screaming in rage and pain grapple with one another. The nightmare...the nightmare...never ends. It's the tips of the bayonets I can't take my eyes from—they shimmer with moonglow where they stab through spines and skulls. This holy ground runs black with blood, and all I can think about is freedom. We might be headed south before noon. Me and Charlie, and Sarah and Joe, and the other slaves locked up in this fortress. We could all head south together, maybe make our own town along some creek in the backcountry.

An odd hush descends over the plaza.

"What's happening, Bettie?"

"The end, I expect."

My gaze lets go of the dead and climbs into the sky, where clouds drift in wispy flames like horsetails that have caught fire. What day is it? Sunday? I—think it must be. Are you up there, God? *Come, behold the works of the Lord, what desolations he hath made in the earth...*

Be still. Be still.

Shapes in blue jackets, sabers flashing, march across the plaza through the unnatural gleam of approaching dawn. They're either our murderers or our liberators.

I ease the door closed.

"Soldados coming, Charlie."

"Then get away from that door, Bettie!"

I slide back and lean against the wall with my shoulder pressed against his. All I can think of is the buzzards that used to roost in the trees at dusk. Tomorrow, they'll be back by the hundreds to wait for the soldiers to leave.

"Everything's fine," Charlie says. "Just look at me. Don't stop looking."

He takes my hand, and I turn to him. Everything I ever wanted is right there in those dark eyes. "We'll go live in peace together somewhere on the frontier," I tell him.

"We will," he whispers. "Won't bother nobody, less they bother us first."

The bullet holes in the walls wink, going dark, then light, as men march in front of them.

In accented English, a man shouts, "I am told this is Colonel Bowie's room. Are you in there, Colonel? For the sake of God, if you are in there, come out!"

Sabers and spurs jingle, but there's something beneath it, another sound, faint and haunting, like the far-off crackling of a thousand impatient black wings.

Leaning my head against Charlie's arm, I dream of the beautiful little girls we'll have and the brave boys who will look like him...of harvesting our crops while the children chase each other through the tall golden cornstalks, laughing, happy...

When the soldados kick down the bullhide door and rush into the Colonel's room, Charlie clutches my hand harder. Bowie's alone in there, already dead, but a pistol blast shakes the walls, then I hear the Meskins shout, "*Cobarde!*" and "*Marica!*" Over and over they call him a coward, a sissy, a chicken. Each curse is followed by a muffled thud.

I frown up at Charlie, and mouth the words, "What are they doing?"

"Bayonets."

My throat goes tight. *Where's the sense in bayonetting a dead man?*

"Bettie?" Charlie whispers. "Help me stand up."

"Why?"

"Just help me, please."

He slides his arm around my shoulders, and I heft him up while he suppresses groans. "Leave me leaned up against the wall now, and go hide yourself in the back."

"I am not leaving you—"

"Just do it."

I have trouble letting go of his hand. Our fingertips touch until the last moment when they slip apart, and I walk back to duck down beside the old fireplace where red coals flicker. The dirty pots stacked in the corner smell of grease, corn, and fried beef from the last meal I fixed.

Just outside, five paces away, boots pound the ground as the soldados leave the Colonel's room. They hesitate outside the kitchen. My gaze is locked with Charlie's. A square of moonlight filters around the door and I can see him clearly. There's enough love in his eyes to last me a lifetime. Charlie's leg gives out suddenly, and he staggers back against the wall panting.

"Come out!" a man calls. "Is someone in there?"

Charlie closes his eyes, but says, "Yes, sir, there's two of us. We ain't got no guns."

"Put your hands up and come out, then."

Charlie licks his lips, doesn't budge, as though he's trying to decide if it's better to fight or die right now, or take a chance that we'll be slaves forever. After a while the door is pulled open and a Mexican head appears and disappears. Soldados burst into the room with bayonets. When a young officer, half Charlie's height, enters, Charlie grabs him to use as a shield.

"Stop this!" the officer cries. "I mean you no harm!"

"I'll kill you if you don't let Bettie go! I mean it!"

The soldados leap forward, trying to stab Charlie with their bayonets. He has no choice but to swing the officer this way and that, using him to block the cold steel that still drips the Colonel's blood.

"Wait! Back away!" the officer shouts to his men in Spanish. "Stop this!"

Grumbling, the soldados step back, but each stands poised to lunge forward and tear Charlie to pieces.

The officer lifts his hands. "Tell me what you want?"

"I want you to promise you'll let Bettie go!" Charlie shouts. "Let her go! She ain't done nothing. She's just a cook! And we didn't have no choice being in here. They made us come!"

"Are you slaves?" the officer asks.

"Yes, sir, Cap'n."

"Then you have nothing to fear! Slaves will not be harmed. You are non-combatants, yes?"

Charlie fought like a bear, 'til he was wounded. Colonel ordered him to. I'm scared to death he's going to tell the truth, but he says, "We didn't do no fighting. Bettie fried beef, and I hauled wood."

"Release me, and I give you my solemn oath you will not be harmed."

Hope is strangling me so that I can barely breathe. Is he telling the truth? Or lying so Charlie will let him go? Does this officer have the authority to keep such an oath?

Charlie glances at me, and I can tell he's thinking the same thing I am.

"Let him go, Charlie," I plead.

Charlie's arms shake as he releases the officer and sags back against the wall with his chest heaving.

The officer gives me a curious look, then says, "We are gathering survivors outside. Can you walk?"

"I can," I say and leap to my feet. "Charlie can walk, too, if I help him."

The officer gestures to his men. "Let them join the others in the plaza. His Excellency will wish to question the man."

Charlie leans on me as we stagger through the kitchen door into the faint gleam.

The sight stuns my senses. Hundreds of bodies lie in heaps. Odd, odd glints...everywhere... The silver buttons on the soldados' blue coats flash as they bayonet corpses or shoot into dead faces. What are they feeling? Does their vengeance taste sweet or bitter?

As I watch them, a sickening mix of longing and terror burns through my body. These men hate us. They hate all Texians. They see us as Texians, too, don't they? How could they ever free us?

A fierce gun battle is going on inside the church. I hear women and children shrieking while men blast away at one another.

Finally, from the smoking church, a half dozen defenders are marched out with their hands over their heads. An officer herds them toward another officer who's just entered the captured fort, an elaborately dressed man with a big official-looking hat. They speak briefly, then soldados draw their swords and wade into the defenseless prisoners, chopping them to pieces.

The air in my lungs goes cold and still.

Barely audible, I hear Charlie pray, "Take care of them, Lord."

Sobbing women and children appear. Soldados with muskets push out of the church and into the center of the courtyard. They huddle together. One woman keeps screaming, "You murdered my little boy! You murdered him!"

Sporadic gunfire erupts here and there, inside and outside the walls.

Charlie winces as he takes another step, and murmurs, "Must be hunting down survivors who managed to run."

I barely hear him. Dear God, the dark luminosity of the sky fills me up so full that every whisper of spring scent, greening up grass and blooming flowers, penetrates the heavy smoke as clearly as those perfect bugle notes. Above the old church a pale pink halo pulses through thin clouds. Dawn's coming. I'm going to see it. One last dawn.

The officer turns to Charlie and orders, "March over to where the women and children stand."

"Yes, sir, Cap'n," Charlie answers.

As I support Charlie, headed toward the women, we pass two cannons, and I see Sarah...I think it's Sarah...sprawled dead between them. It's her blue dress. My friend. She was my friend. A few more paces and I frown at Mrs. Melton, who stands drawing circles on the ground with an umbrella. The soldados veer wide around her, and I wonder if they think she's lost her mind. I wonder the same thing. What does she see in those strange circles? Souls spinning 'round? Spiraling up toward heaven?

Charlie stumbles and almost takes me down with him. Wrapping my arms around his middle, I manage to brace my feet until he steadies his shaking legs. My arms are all he has now. I have to help him, to shield him from fearful dreams of no tomorrows, no sons or daughters, no smiling at each other when we're old and gray. Dark and holy dreams that whisper, *it was never gonna be.*

Three men run to hoist the Mexican tri-color over the fort.

In English, a man calls, "Are there any Negroes present?"

Slaves start edging from hiding places. Joe—Colonel Travis's slave—yells, "Yes, here's one." When he steps out of a room on the west wall, two soldiers immediately attack him, one shooting him in the side and the other striking him with a bayonet.

A ragged cry of, "No!" escapes my throat. "You liars!"

Charlie hisses, "Bettie, be quiet! Quiet!"

The officer bounds toward Joe, shouting, "Halt! Leave him alone!"

"But, Colonel," a soldado yells, "I saw this one shooting down at us!"

"Lower your weapons!" the officer orders. "He's a slave. *El Presidente* has given strict orders to free all slaves."

For an instant I can't move. Blood drains from my head, leaving me floating so high above the ground I can't feel my body. "Charlie?"

"Don't believe it, Bettie. Not yet."

The man in the big hat walks forward with a lordly bearing to speak with Joe.

Charlie's eyes narrow. "Never seen him up close, but I reckon that's Santa Anna."

Can't hear what they're saying. Joe points a lot. Little while later, Joe limps past us without a second look, leading General Santa Anna across the plaza.

When I glance back, I know they're headed to Colonel Bowie's room. Santa Anna and Joe enter. Does the general want to gloat over his defeated enemy? Perhaps to add one final sword thrust to a man already mutilated by his troops?

My whole body starts to tremble. Eventually, one sees too much, knows too much about the way the world works, and every shred of hope cuts like glass. I wish...I wish so hard that I'd...

"Bettie?" Charlie's voice is soft. "Don't think on it. Don't do no good now."

I fix my eyes on the ground at my feet where shotgun pellets litter the dirt like chicken scratch thrown out.

My God, my God, when I lift my gaze the dawn is so beautiful I half expect winged angels to swoop out of the heavens with blazing swords and avenge the dead scattered across this sacred ground.

"Listen to me now," Charlie murmurs. "I reckon they're going to haul off the men to question them, but if they see fit to set us loose, and we're separated, we need to figure a place to meet up. I was thinking—"

"Monterrey, Charlie. I'll be waiting for you at the cathedral in Monterrey. We'll get married. We'll have a family."

Tears silver his dark eyes.

"I'll be there," he answers in a loving voice. "If I can."

October 2, 1836. Nightfall

GATHERING UP THE HEM OF MY FADED GREEN DRESS, I SIT DOWN on the bottom step of the magnificent *Catedral Metropolitana de Nuestra Señora de Monterrey* and watch twilight settle over the pueblo in a soft blue veil. It's been a hot, hot summer. Heat waves shimmer on the sand and make the road seem to dance. I've been sitting on this step every evening for seven months, studying the carts and wagons that rattle up the rutted road that leads north through the white oaks toward Texas.

In the far distance, a coyote howls. It's a mournful sound, filled with sad longing, as though she's begging someone to answer her, to tell her she won't be alone in the coming darkness. The lilting call moves through me. I, too, wait to hear a voice I know, a voice I remember.

The scents of frying tortillas and hot stones slaked with water carry on the breeze. Fragrances always seem stronger at dusk. There's even the faint perfume of flowers wafting from the garden around the side of the cathedral.

People lift hands to me as they walk by. Most are peasants dressed in loose-fitting clothing and wearing floppy hats. I wave back and wonder what they're thinking. Are they loving their children in their minds, eager to get home and hold them? Perhaps they're listening to the boys' latest adventures of catching lizards or field mice. The little girls may have crawled into their laps to inform them they've decided the color yellow is better than blue, or they've grown another inch taller in the past two days.

My children have turned to stones in my heart. Three boys and two girls, all dead infants, beautiful babies that never grew up. They no longer move, or laugh, or love me. It's as though their faces have frozen into the fabric of eternity like dead animals in ice. Each night, their opaque eyes stare up at me through a blue haze.

My gut wants to believe that when Charlie was taken after the siege, the Veramendis came, claimed him, and his wounded leg was tended to. Isn't that what would have happened? Of course, they might have sold him off to someone who hauled him way up north. That's why he hasn't come. He's a slave again.

The only other possible explanation is that Charlie died from his wound.

Even after all these months, the uncertainty is a living thing coiled in my chest. Keep telling myself, I shouldn't have run off. I should have stayed with Charlie until he got well or died, even if it meant I was a slave for the rest of my life. But I suspect that would have broken Charlie's heart. If he's alive, he's dreaming of me walking free, surrounded by open spaces. He's holding tight to those images in his dreams at night. Just as I hold tight to visions of Charlie walking down that northern road toward me, coming to sit with me on this step, and wrapping his arms around me.

Bowing my head, I let my thoughts drift for another hour or so, until darkness has turned the sky sapphire, and the vault of heaven, full of soft, shining stars, stretches vast and fathomless above me, then tears tighten my throat.

This lonely vigil gets harder every night.

When I rise to leave, I hear Padre Ramirez step out of the cathedral's doors. He closes them and trots down the stairs toward me, as he does every night on his way to water the flowers in the garden. "Bettie, how are you tonight?"

"Muy bueno, padre."

He smiles. The priest is a tall man with black hair and blue eyes.

When he reaches the bottom step, he stands looking down at me with a sad smile. "You are finished cooking for the day?"

"'Til first light comes. Then I'll head back out to the Madrigon hacienda and start baking."

"They tell me they love your breads."

"Good to hear."

In the lull, starlight powders his face. He takes a deep breath, and holds it for an instant before he says, "Anything could have happened to Charlie, you know? Seven months is not so long a time. Don't give up on him."

"I haven't." But I wonder if that's true? Maybe I just come here out of habit now, not hope.

As shadows drown the plaza, the breeze turns cooler.

"Peaceful tonight," Padre Ramirez says and hesitates. "Bettie, I know you do not wish me to preach at you." He pauses to judge my tight expression. "But loneliness is God's way of asking you to turn to Him, to allow Him to help. Would you like me to pray with you?"

"No, padre. I'm prayed out, but I appreciate the offer."

"Very well. Then perhaps you'd like to take a walk with me? We can talk while I water the flowers. It's been so hot."

"'Course. Let me help you."

As I rise from the bottom step, evening deepens, laying everywhere like an indigo blanket. The walk around the cathedral is silent and pleasant. When I see the *peon* wandering among the flowers with a water bucket, I smile. The garden is surrounded by towering cottonwoods and oaks, and bordered with huge cactus.

"José, it's late," Padre Ramirez calls. "Thank you, but please go home to your family. Carmen must have dinner ready."

José waves, finishes emptying his bucket on a clump of lilies, and wipes his perspiring brow with his sleeve. "Si, padre! Buenas noches."

"Vaya con dios, José."

While José places his bucket beside the well, I study the bright colors of the flowers. The garden is a patchwork of white, red, and yellow.

As though worried, Padre Ramirez says, "Do you know that man? He's watching you very carefully."

I frown in the direction he points and notice a man leaning against a huge cottonwood. He's tall and so thin I can see his ribs sticking out through his white shirt. The dark skin of his face has shrunken tight over his bones, so that I'm sure he's starving to death. He stares hard at me.

There is something familiar...

Pain lances through me as my gaze goes over him in detail, noting the way he leans against the tree. Takes me a while to see through the mosaic of shadows and finally understand that he has a wooden leg and can't hurry to me.

A small cry escapes my throat. "Charlie!"

I run as though my life depends upon reaching him. When I throw my arms around him, tears are streaming down his face.

He wildly kisses my face and hair. "Came as quick as I could, Bettie. Sorry it took so long."

If you like this, you may also enjoy:

Tin Angel

By Kat Martin

AVAILABLE ON AMAZON

Ault's Heir

By C.K. Crigger

AVAILABLE ON AMAZON

The Whippoorwill Trilogy

By Sharon Sala

AVAILABLE ON AMAZON

Thin Moon and Cold Mist

By Kathleen O'Neal Gear

AVAILABLE ON AMAZON

About Kat Martin

New York Times best-selling author Kat Martin is a graduate of the University of California at Santa Barbara where she majored in Anthropology and also studied History. She is married to L.J. Martin, author of western, non-fiction, and suspense novels.

Kat has written more than sixty-five novels. Sixteen million copies of her books are in print, and she has been published in twenty foreign countries—including Japan, France, Germany, Argentina, Greece, China, Russia, and Spain.

Born in Bakersfield, California, Kat currently resides in Missoula, Montana, on a small ranch in the beautiful Sapphire mountains.

Her last twelve books have hit the prestigious *New York Times* bestseller list—her most recent in the top ten spots.

About C.K. Crigger

Born and raised in North Idaho on the Coeur d'Alene Indian Reservation, C.K. Crigger lives in Spokane Valley, Washington. Imbued with an abiding love of western traditions and wide-open spaces, she writes of free-spirited people who break from their standard roles.

In Crigger's books—whether western, mystery, or even the science fiction/fantasy—the locales are real places. A fan of local history, all of her westerns or mysteries are set the Inland Northwest and make use of a historical background.

She reviews western books for WWA's Roundup magazine, mysteries, and science fiction/fantasy for CnC Books. You'll find many of her reviews on Goodreads, Amazon, and Barnes & Noble.

Crigger is a member of Western Writers of America and holds multiple Spur awards.

About Sharon Sala

Sharon Sala has over 135 books and novellas in print, published in six different genres—romance, young adult, western, fiction, and women's fiction and non-fiction.

First published in 1991, she's an eight-time RITA finalist, winner of the Janet Dailey Award, five-time Career Achievement winner from RT Magazine, five-time winner of the National Reader's Choice Award, five-time winner of the Colorado Romance Writer's Award of Excellence, and winner of the Heart of Excellence Award—as well as winner of the Booksellers Best Award. In 2011, she was named RWA's recipient of the Nora Roberts Lifetime Achievement Award. In 2017, the Romance Writers of America presented her with the Centennial Award for recognition of her 100th published novel.

Her books are *New York Times*, *USA Today*, and *Publisher's Weekly* best-sellers. Writing changed her life, her world, and her fate.

About Jenna Hendricks

Jenna Hendricks writes clean and wholesome contemporary romance with Christian values. She loves to write about the cowboys she wishes she would one day meet but is happy to wait on God's timing.

Until then, she enjoys listening to audiobooks, eating chocolate, traveling the world, and spending time with her extended family. You can get a free eBook, discover her recipes, and see pictures of the places she visits by joining her newsletter or reading her books.

About Kit Morgan

Kit Morgan has been writing for fun all her life. Her whimsical stories are fun, inspirational, sweet, clean, and depict a strong sense of family and community. Raised by a homicide detective, one would think she'd write suspense—and she plans on getting around to those. In the meantime, she likes fun and romantic westerns!

Kit resides in the beautiful Pacific Northwest in a little log cabin on Clear Creek, from which her fictional town from her Prairie Brides and Prairie Grooms series is named after.

If you'd like to join her newsletter to keep up on new releases and get free and discounted books, just text 'Cooke' to 22828. You can also check out her website at www.authorkitmorgan.com.

About Kathleen O'Neal Gear

Kathleen O'Neal Gear is a nationally award-winning archaeologist, historian, and *New York Times* best-selling author and co-author of 53 novels. There are 18 million copies of her work in print in 29 languages. She's been inducted into three halls of fame: the Women Who Write the West Hall of Fame, the Western Writers Hall of Fame, and the California State University Hall of Fame.

In 2007, along with her husband W. Michael Gear, she received the Literary Contribution Award from the Mountain Plains Library Association. In 2015, she was honored by the United States Congress with a Certificate of Special Congressional Recognition.

In 2021, Kathleen and Michael jointly received the Owen Wister Award for lifetime achievement in western literature.

9 781639 773046